MY WICKED AUNT LEONORA

CHRISTINA GODLEY

authorHOUSE®

AuthorHouse™ UK
1663 Liberty Drive
Bloomington, IN 47403 USA
www.authorhouse.co.uk
Phone: 0800.197.4150

Published by AuthorHouse 12/06/2019

ISBN: 978-1-7283-8184-8 (sc)
ISBN: 978-1-7283-8183-1 (e)

Print information available on the last page.

This book is printed on acid-free paper.

About the Author

Christina has a BA (Hons) Eng. Lit. Sheffield University and is an Associate Member of the Legal Institute. Sheffield Polytechnic. She has self-published four novels and two children's books with Author House. She worked in Local Government as a Senior Legal Executive doing Conveyancing and other Land Law matters. Exchanging her imagination for logic helped pay the mortgage – and buy ballet shoes for her daughter. She now does what she loves the most and that is going with the flow.

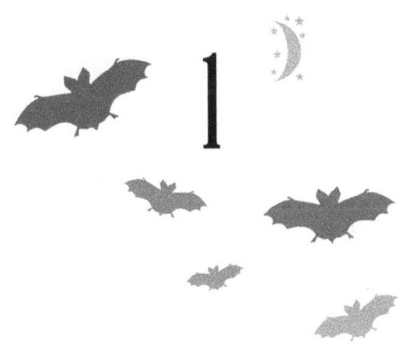

1

31st October.

I've not cried in years. Any feelings of self pity vanished long ago. Whether it was from tiredness or pre-Christmas panic, I really don't know. In my fitful dreams a sinister and long buried beast stirred in the undercurrent. I couldn't swim fast enough to reach the shore before the bloated thing bubbled to the surface. As I struggled for consciousness trying to remember, it slowly dawned on me that I was a year older, the heating had packed up and the *beast* was another bloody fox raiding the bins.

After a tediously slow shift at *Chez Trevayne* and a scary walk back home in the Thames fog, I knew a good night's sleep would be impossible. Usually I'm not afraid of the dark and I love to run home alone. The rhythmic sound of my trainers hitting the pavement and the pulsing in my head reassured me. The traffic was almost non-existent and the air fresher, kind of tangy - especially near the river. And sometimes I'd stop running for a while and listen. I guess it was the stillness that appealed to me. As if the Thames was giving a sigh of relief. A final ripple of contentment as the night closed in.

You see Wayne, my boss, insisted Maggie, Lucy and I wear high heels in the bistro. And that we should look feminine and not look like boys. Why he made us wear black trousers and waistcoats with white shirts and black bow ties was a mystery to me. Anyhow, it was so liberating to kick off the killer-heels and slip on my trainers. I'm not a girlie girl and I love to run – usually the faster the better. Any lurking assailant would have to be pretty nifty to keep up - but not on such a night where the pavement was barely visible. Quickening my pace through the empty streets, the last burst of fireworks lit up the darkness then fizzled into a line of sulphurous smoke, punctuating the end of Halloween.

The clientele in the bistro had amounted to a middle aged couple celebrating their Silver Wedding Anniversary whose guests were stuck in a tail-back on the motorway and two lost northern women singing *Any Dream Will Do,* still on a high from the multi-coloured coat of Joseph. Unable to find their way back to their holiday hotel, and ending up at Fulham Broadway, decided lasagne and Chianti was the only solution.

In an attempt to sustain the theatrical magic spun by Lloyd-Webber's and God's hero, their out of tune duet drifted inside and drowned out the annoying piped jazz music. Why anyone liked such dissonant, takes an eternity to finish before putting in as many twiddly bits as possible on a bunged up trumpet without bursting a blood vessel kind of music, beats me. It's not as if you could hum along, or tap your foot to it. The only practical use would be to play it to constipated hospital patients to stimulate bowel movements over bed pans, delay premature ejaculators - or for crowd clearance at riotous football matches.

All other meal bookings had been cancelled at the last minute. That didn't include Mick the Tramp, who had been chased out of the almost on the King's Road bistro more times than you can chuck a stick at. In Trevor and Wayne's case, the proprietors/puffs/chefs, anything that came to hand and usually something sharp and pointy lying around in the kitchen. More staff stood outside smoking and shivering, including me in Paulo's hoody, than customers inside the bistro.

'Come on my *Shivering Snowdrop*, spare an old man a latte. I'm freezing my bunions off out here,' Mick called from the shadows of the bike shop doorway.

It's curious, I know, but I was always aware of his presence well before he spoke.

'Not now Mick. Wayne's about to do a head count with the meat clever and if he catches you begging again you stand to lose more than your bunions.'

Apart from his purple complexion and shabby clothing, Mick was one of those endearing battle-scarred tramps. The stoical type who you know there's so much more to. Even when blotto he still made us laugh. Quite often he'd burst into rhetoric - mainly misquoting Shakespeare. Funnily enough he never stank. His left leg seemed to drag a little behind his right ever so slightly. I couldn't help but notice things like that. I know it's a failing to stare too much and to be overly critical. And I'm not, really. I just call it observation. But he definitely needed physiotherapy, a warm bed, vitamins and some coaching from Sir Trevor Nunn. Anyhow, when he called us flower names we just couldn't refuse him anything. Well, anything on the menu and absolutely nothing from the wine list, that is.

'What's to do Kat?' Wayne trilled out. 'Is that bloody tramp out there again?'

'No boss. I'm just finishing off a quick drag.' Unlike you who takes the whole evening to dress up like a girlie.

Paulo retrieved his hoody leaving me chilled to the bone then shot inside without a word of protest. He was like that. A total penis when it came to standing up for himself – mentally that is. I don't know about his sexual prowess. He was, to put it politely, a bit of a tit. Lucy didn't seem to notice though and always followed him around. The type of girl who'd never said hush to a chick. So it was always Maggie and me who suffered the sharp end of Wayne's fat tongue.

'Well, if you are, it'll come out of your wages. Now, get yourselves back in here pronto. We're not paying you to loiter outside…And pick up those tab ends. You're giving the bistro a bad name! And how many times do I have to tell you to use the tradesman's entrance. I can't take my eyes off you for two minutes.'

'Maggie my *Diminutive Daisy* gets us a slice of pepperoni with extra olives. Will you?' Mick whispered in a croaky voice.

'Meet me at the tradesman's entrance in ten

minutes, you old bugger. And be quiet, else we'll all get the sack and then what'll you do?' Maggie said.

'Anything else your grace?' I asked, feigning a curtsey.

'Yes. Never go out alone after dark,' he chuckled. 'There're some queer folks out on the streets.'

'You should know!'

We were all glad to get in from the cold. I wondered how Mick stood the winter weather in such sparse clothing; mentally making a note to buy him a parka for Christmas from the posh charity shop in Chelsea. No doubt, he was a survivor. And with a little help from his friends he would last a few more years. To spite whinging Wayne, Maggie and I sneaked out a large pizza with tons of olives and a double mocha latte with three sugars to Mick, who hid behind the bins.

'Thank you my *Frozen Freesias*. This will keep the cold out. A drop of brandy wouldn't go amiss either.'

'Listen you old liar. No more alcohol for you,

ever! Got that? Do you want to die out there alone in the gutter?' I asked.

'I can't think of a better way to go at my age,' he chuckled.

'Have you been to any of the *AA* meetings I set up?' Maggie asked, looking over her shoulder for any signs of waddling Wayne.

'By my troth I have been to every single one. They're a waste of time. It's just a bunch of losers jumping up like *Spartacus* extras, saying: "I'm an alcoholic", then expecting a round of applause.'

'And you don't have a drinking problem I suppose?' I asked.

'No. Only you two *Bossy Begonias* seem to think I have. All things in moderation, is a frightfully boring adage by which to live one's life. So if you please ladies, on pain of death depart. And by such actions allow me to commence my supper.'

'Girls if you please! Table No. 5 wants a third bottle of *Chianti*,' Trevor called out through the fire doors. 'Look I don't want to know what you're up to out there with that waste-of-space, but if

Wayne has one more strop tonight it'll be me that suffers. So give me a break will you and tell him he looks slimmer or something. If I pay him a compliment he doesn't believe me, or thinks I'm up to something.'

Trevor returned to the kitchen and vigorously stirred a huge pan of gurgling pasta sauce.

'If you come here again stinking of alcohol there'll be no more food. Got it?' Maggie warned. 'This is your last chance!'

'Over and out my *Tiny Tulip*. I must state in my defence though that only cough syrup was imbibed by my good self during the past three weeks. Not a drop of the fire-water shall pass my lips from henceforth until Doomsday.'

'Bastard!' we chorused.

'Et tu beauties. Oh most divine ladies, I bid you a fond farewell until our fateful paths do collide again.'

The two northern women at Table No. 5 were glowing with goodwill and unable to stand. After giving me a huge tip I persuaded Trevor to let them rest their heavily loaded bones in the bistro for the night. They would never have found their way back to any signs of life in the fog and had completely forgotten the name of their hotel. As a finale they belted out *Close all the Doors,* causing Wayne to thunder up the stairs in a huff while Trevor in desperation opened a bottle of ten year old malt.

'So there is such a thing as the male menopause,' he sighed.

My little life had never been rounded with a sleep. So I learned at a very early age not to fret about insomnia. It just made matters worse. I'd tried everything, like: counting sheep, hot baths and drinking coco. Maggie bought me a CD on self-hypnosis. Apparently if one imagined each body part turning to molten liquid, the desired coma would ensue. The master hypnotist: Fred Bradwell from Bolton, had an unfortunate voice resembling Michael Parkinson with a head cold. (Not that there's anything wrong with Parkie, but he's not exactly bedtime listening). Strangely he called each body part: *him* while, at the same time, instructing me to inhale deeply and inflate my abdomen like a balloon. Mentally I tried to soak up the white light of acceptance into the soles of my feet while not getting air-born. Unfortunately I only managed to reach my ankles because when I was supposed to: "Let him go, let him go", with each breath, I ended up in fits of laughter.

On the other hand I discovered mulling over my past sometimes did the trick. It had been pretty weird. Unbelievable as it may seem, it felt like a cross between *Tess of the Durbervilles* any recent episode from *Emmerdale* and a touch of the *Monty Pythons* thrown in. I'm glad, in some ways, there were no roses and lollipops, or whiskers on kittens and butterfly kisses. The violence and abuse though, I could have done without. I know deep down that it gave me strength. Even though my 25th birthday had arrived on nightmare wings, I sensed something was about to change. And whether or not it was for the better? I didn't hold my breath.

I vowed, at one significant point in my life, never to cry again even though I'd felt like it many times since moving to London. As a budding artist I had supposed the idea of streets paved with gold to be fantastic to behold. Only to find later that millions of other would-be treasure hunters had already taken the loot. It's funny though how bad and good times remained vivid memories, while the spaces in between dissolved into nothing. Wordsworth called these moments "Spots in Time". In a goofy Forrest Gump sort of way, I had likened the cycle of life to a pearl necklace. The jewels of the sea were analogous to those heightened perceptions while the thread was everyday living; the fasteners being cradle and coffin.

Back in Newquay my pubescent brooding seascapes had stood defiant and unsold until a couple of tourists walked in the shop and asked: 'Can you put our Kerri and Jack on that picture playing with buckets and spades? And a bit of sunshine wouldn't go amiss.'

Reluctantly I obliged, lightening up the sea and painting in the foreground a fair-haired girl and an older boy with a brown mop. Just a hint of a face or a head looking down seemed to please the punters. From then on I painted babies with blonde hair and a sibling nearby, usually with backs turned and heads slightly to the side showing a third of the face. An affectionate titian haired child seated next to her mother under a parasol. Another had two dark-haired munchkins paddling in the foam. It seemed to work. They sold like hot cakes. In fact most folks saw their own kids in my blurred images. I couldn't turn them out fast enough, until I got sick of selling myself short.

Subsequently I started a course at Chelsea

Art College after failing to get a place at Slade because my work wasn't considered versatile enough. Although I've always believed the ever-changing ocean has more moods than any artist could capture during an infinity of lifetimes. I'd sit for hours losing myself in the wonder of it all and trying to hold onto just one image of a fluctuating tide, a sudden eddy, or a rolling surf breaker before it transformed into something elusive and magical.

I remember, with some embarrassment, the day of my interview for a place at Chelsea Art College.

'So Kathryn you seemed to be fascinated by the sea,' a lecturer called John wearing faded corduroy trousers with knee pads, said.

'Yes. I am…It's the most beautiful thing I've ever seen - simply amazing. I paint it all the time.'

'What else can you do?' David asked.

'I'm a fast runner, a fairly good surfer and I know a few jokes.'

'Over to you John.'

'What compels you to paint the sea?' John asked.

'The ocean's mood is never the same from one moment to another. It keeps changing shape and form. When I'm away from Newquay I try to keep these fleeting images in my head. My boss Wayne goes mad when I doodled on the menus. When I'm not painting I think about painting. It keeps me awake at nights like toothache and it wont go away,' I trailed off.

I should have said something arty and simple, like: To capture the quintessence of nature.

'Do you have anything else to show us Kathryn?' David, the other interviewer, asked.

Remembering my reticence from Slade I said: 'Not at the moment but if you hang on I'll do your portrait.' I quickly took out my sketch pad and knocked up a caricature of the bemused man.

'God. Is my hooter that big with such open pores - and from a bird's eye angle my nasal hair appears to need a lawn mover. I must nip out and get some of those blackhead strips immediately,' he said good-humouredly.

John looked through my paintings and remained thoughtful.

'We can find a place for you Kathryn. If that's what you want. To be taught the mechanics. Although I feel your natural spontaneity might be stifled a little,' he said.

'Oh. No. Please take me on. I need discipline you see, to become a proper artist. Otherwise I'll end up working in a solicitor's office, doing crappy filing, get a fat arse and be really miserable.'

'Any further questions David,' John asked dryly.

'What are you trying to find in the sea?' David asked, probing further.

'I'm looking for the perfect wave…but the sea wont keep still for a second.'

'A little like you Kathryn,' John said, as I fidgeted around.

Despite my unfortunate interviewee technique the acceptance letter arrived. At last I had a justifiable reason to be a legitimate portfolio carrier.

Right from the start I was surrounded by glamorous students who looked as if they were ready for a night on the town, rather than about to be covered in charcoal and paint. The confident city girls had trotted into college carrying enormous designer padlocked handbags and wearing 4" stilettos; convinced that 21st century artists should not live in garrets but get paid handsomely for arty pickled dead animals. I breezed in wearing a *Fat Willey's* t-shirt thinking I'd be lucky to earn a crust from my moody daubs.

After a lifetime of musical chairs I was lucky enough to find my Godparents. From the age of fifteen I lived with Sophie and Zach and moved away from the oppressive Welsh mountains to the airiness of Newquay. I found out that my Godparents were: weed smoking, pant swinging and guitar playing talented artists - who were in fact genuine retro-Sixties, 22 carat hippies. Thus I never learned the notion of self-image or polite conversation. So when a fun girl called Zarah from Esher talked about midnight parties in the dorm, I joined in the hilarity and told them about the time Tracey Blackburn had set fire to the canteen because the food was crap. Silence ensued. Of course she referred to boarding school and not a Care Home.

The thing outside howled again. Banging my big toe on the bedside table, I stumbled over half-finished canvasses, paint pots, oily rags and brushes I'd left to soak in turpentine and eventually found the kitchen. Why I had accumulated such a great amount of junk, considering the size of the attics flat, was beyond me. Cursing, I emptied the hot water bottle over the previous morning's breakfast pots and switched on the kettle.

Bleary-eyed I scraped a peephole on the frozen window and looked down into the street. Then I saw it. The thing that had broken my troubled sleep was recognizable only by its bushy tail sticking our from under a wheelie bin. Half of me wanted to go straight back to bed. It wasn't my problem. If it's dead the bin men would take it away.

The same morning I had plucked up enough courage to spent three hours in *Raj,* the Asian

Cliff Richards look-alike hairdresser to the Bollywood Stars, in preparation for my birthday dinner party. It had been humiliating enough entering the stylistic monochrome salon full of elegant dark-eyed beauties swishing their silken flowing manes around. But when the swishing stopped in a freeze-frame moment and everyone looked at my matted ginger non-swishing rug, I just wanted the floor to open up and swallow me.

Owing to the state of my hair I'd always had an aversion to salon mentality with inane questions like: "Is that your natural shade"? As if I would choose this colour. And: "Have you had a perm"? Who in their right mind had perms these days? Along with the penultimate threat: "I'm going to make it choppy and funky", meaning a total fuck up - and finally followed by: "Would you like a Rhubarb and Nettle tea"?

But this time I had hoped it would be the defining moment when I morphed into a swan. So I endured hacking, staring, ghastly pink tea, *Horse and Hounds* and Mozart's jaunty hunting

Concerto because Raj thought all western women who could afford his prices wore jodhpurs and killed foxes. Subsequently I was dressed up like an oven ready chicken, robed in rubber and placed under the grill for half an hour.

Sod it. I had no intentions of ruining my very expensive sleek hennaed locks out there in the fog. The wretch outside, trapped by a wheelie bin, had yelped and fallen in an attempt to scavenge for food. Down there in the dankness among the garbage, a flea-bitten thing whimpered pathetically into the empty November night.

3

I think the last time I had really bawled my eyes out was some sixteen years ago, when I was nine. In fact I'm sure of it... It was the night when creepy Uncle Peter tried to get into my bedroom. Fat Sal had warned us before hand about his voyeurism. She didn't exactly use that word at the time. She'd put it more bluntly and said that he was a perverted old twat. Fat Sal boasted that she'd been fostered there for only two weeks after she'd given him a sharp kick in the balls after he had tried to put his hand up her t-shirt. I wasn't sure whether to hate him or be in awe of his bravery. Fat Sal was a mean bitch by any standard.

So I was well prepared. On my first night at Auntie Maureen's and Uncle Peter's house, I'd dragged a large oak blanket chest in front of my bedroom door.

I heard the door knob rattle then him slope off back down the landing, muttering under his breath.

I stayed awake for most of the night in case he came back. Pondering as to where, and what, exactly his balls were and how to make sure I took a proper aim. If I missed I had no back up plan. Over and over I asked God to protect me and if necessary, help me find the whereabouts of Uncle Peter's balls. I remember keeping my shoes on just in case and promising in my prayers to be a good girl if He helped me. I cried until dawn.

They were my sixth set of foster-parents and lived in a semi-detached house with metal windows frames and net curtains. As I walked up the red-tiled path holding Mrs. Hudson's hand I felt sick.

'Don't worry,' she reassured me, noticing my terrified expression. 'They've taken care of many...errum...children like you Kathryn...Try to get on with them will you? Smile a little more often...It's for the best.'

Mrs. Hudson always said things like that, in her nasal flat voice. Somehow she managed to churn out kindnesses without moving her lips, or showing any emotion at all. That way, if things went wrong it wasn't her fault. She had been worn down caring too much for misfits like me.

The Taylors' front garden had a neat emerald lawn with borders of vibrant Dahlias and Busy Lizzies so densely packed that I couldn't see the soil beneath. It had rained heavily on the way as we travelled through the leafy suburbia in Mrs. Hudson's old car. Everything smelled so fresh and new. I remember the shininess of it all. My hand gently skimmed across the wet flowers as I walked towards the black front door. And there was an abundance of tiny fragrant red roses spilling around the porch.

Maybe this time, I thought, these people would be the ones. Somehow they'd be different from the never-ending rounds of aunties and uncles. Special guardian angels, who would look like Kate Winslet and Hugh Jackman, play golf on a Saturday and wash apples in diluted soapy water to remove the pesticides. And they would take care of me in a home where I would feel safe until I grew up into a proper girl. In the sugar pink half light I tingled. I remember thinking that Auntie Maureen must be kind to have tended such a pretty flower garden.

'Smell the Lavender,' Mrs. Hudson told me, rubbing the soft purple heads between her thumb and finger then sniffing up the perfume through her nostrils.

I did the same. The scent was warm and musky on that late summer's evening. A scent I'd always associate with the utterly miserable four months spent at the Taylors' house - and the end of my childhood.

Uncle Peter and Auntie Maureen hated children; having none of their own. Of course, they pretended otherwise. Told the less well-off neighbours what a little sweetheart I was and how much they loved me. She even plaited my frizzy hair and chose a green silk ribbon, saying that the colour suited me particularly well. If only the good folks next door knew the humiliation

I went through as she pulled and wrenched my tangled hair into a tight smooth rope that would have supported Hagrid.

Behind closed doors was a different matter. We foster kids were generally used as unpaid skivvies. Given sparse food and locked up at night. Not in the Dickensian way of course. Everything was done by the book. The Taylors were allocated a generous clothing allowance and weekly payments for my upkeep. Auntie Maureen was the best dressed woman on the street. She bought her clothes from *Next* while the neighbours ordered from cut-price catalogues. Uncle Peter went to the pub nearly every night - and brought back pork scratchings.

I wasn't whipped or given gruel. Their particular brand of cruelty came mainly in a vocal form of abuse. They made sure the bruises were on the inside or under the hairline where they couldn't be seen. That was the one and only instance I was thankful for my thick hair.

Auntie Maureen was one of those women who

had aged before her time. She had pendulous breast and a large moving stomach that made sloshing noises. This was owing to her irritable bowel, as she had told anyone who would listen. It wasn't only her bowel that irritated. Neighbours' doors closed and nets twitched when she took me out for a Saturday stroll. At least, that way I didn't have to listen to her false protestations of love for us poor orphans.

Every week she went for a £10 shampoo and set to *Sonia's* round the corner. She would come back smelling of formaldehyde and wearing what looked like a piebald helmet. I wondered at the time why she hadn't had blonde highlights. If she'd considered jogging, aerobics or having breast implants like the film stars in Fat Sal's cheap magazines, then maybe Uncle Peter would fancy her instead of us young girls.

After months of put-downs and abuse I was dreading Christmas, because when Uncle Peter was off work they argued like crazy. So as the Season of Goodwill approached, and after a particularly violent shouting match, after which Uncle Peter slammed the door and went down to the pub, she screeched out: 'No wonder you were never adopted missy! Who'd want a ginger-headed runt with cat's eyes and bat wing ears for a daughter? My God I'll bet you were a repulsive baby! You should've been put down at birth…It stands to reason, what with a Mother like yours 'en all, bad blood will out! I'm always right on these matters. I am.'

She had the annoying habit of reinforcing her personal pronouns. It was a Welsh thing.

I distinctly remember getting very hot and shouting at her. Enough was enough! Nobody, but nobody, insulted my Mother. In my mind she was perfect. A titian haired goddess in the Hollywood glamour mode, who would take me away in a gleaming convertible filled with designer carrier bags. (The stiff expensive kind with rope handles and usually coloured red or black). Then wave her magic Platinum Credit Card and transform me into a swishing haired princess.

'You've done it now you evil little brat! The devil's spawn, that's what you are! I've given you a roof over your head and put food in your scrawny belly and what do I get in return? I'll tell you what I get: a useless ungrateful no-good! You will go back to the place where dumb little scruffs like you belong! You will!'

It was on that particular day, the 12th December, I retaliated. Before the Pervy Pete and Miserable Moo episode, I'd been bullied, ridiculed, excluded, sat upon, farted on, nipped, punched, flushed head first in the toilet, (The Orphan's Baptism), kicked and blamed for every misdemeanour under the sun.

For example when the carers took us on outings to buy new trainers Fat Sal would always pinch mine, even though she was a size bigger.

'Give 'em up Titch, or I'll fucking deck you,' she said casually, loosening the laces and squashing her wide feet into the mock-designer market stall trainers.

Nobody argued with her, except cocky Joe, who

could get away with murder. Fat Sal was twelve stone of pure aggression. For years I had packed her cast off trainers with newspapers to make them fit and developed firm calves and buttocks in my efforts to keep them on. At least my pants were my own. Because of Fat Sal's bullying I got into trouble for not looking after my things.

'Always wrecks her shoes, she does. That Kathryn Shaw must weigh two stone wet through. Why is she so heavy on her footwear?'

I kept my mouth shut. Nobody liked a snitch.

Once a month the carers took us to the cinema. Fat Sal would eat her popcorn by the shovelfuls then finish off mine. At meal times she always sat with us younger kids. I learned to eat very quickly when Fat Sal was around. Even though I was the smallest girl in the group I was pretty nimble on my feet, despite the battered trainers. When Fat Sal laughed, which wasn't very often, we were all saved from a thrashing. As a runt, I only had to look pathetically at the Canteen Staff and would get extra food on my plate. That, along with memorizing jokes, kept me in good stead with Fat Sal.

So I exploded for the first time in my life when Auntie Maureen insulted my Mother's memory. In fact I not only blew my top I actually went ballistic, smashing her favourite figurines of matching *Lladro* bone china cherubs. I liked to think of it as finding my mojo when I reflect on that particular spot in time - and ridding the world of something far too twee.

'Don't you dare say such things about my Mother!' I said, hurling the cherubs at the wall. I wanted to wipe that smug smile from her chicken's bum mouth. Instead I continued letting off steam, knowing full well that I was physically unable to tackle a woman of her circumference.

'Just you wait until Uncle Peter gets home! It'll be the belt for you lady! He'll give you what for! He will!' she retorted.

'Uncle Peter's a pervy,' I said, echoing Fat Sal's words...'Are you deaf, or daft when he tries for a crafty feel, or comes creeping to my bedroom door at night?'

'You dirty little trollop! I'll tell them at The Home what a wicked girl you are! I will!'

'Shut up you old witch. It's true I tell you… And don't call me a scruff! And… fuck off as well!'

I'd heard Fat Sal use the 'f' word many times. By the look on Auntie Maureen's shocked face, I knew that it was powerful and made a mental note to use it often and with force. I also vowed not call anyone auntie or uncle ever again. It felt so good to be in control of something at last. I'd gotten used to be called ugly, weirdo, ginger-head, mog-face, but I strongly objected to being called dumb. I had come out with good grades in Art, English and History, even though I'd attended more schools than I could remember. For some reason I never got the feel for Maths. I suppose that's why my finances are in such a mess.

Anyhow, when Uncle Peter came home from the pub that evening I was still mad to bursting. I felt such a rage inside that it scared me. I'd bolted to my room and pulled the blanket chest in front of the door. He was always more persistent when drunk. I'd taken one of the iron pans from the kitchen, just in case. I knew for sure that I would have used it, should the need arise; balls or no balls. I heard them talking in the hallway but couldn't make out what was said. I guessed from the whispered tones that I wouldn't get my head pummelled that night.

On reflection, did I really do and say all those things? I so wanted to. I have to admit though, I didn't. Kids don't speak out. Do they? I've frequently wanted to go back to that spot in time and do and say those things to her face. I've gone over the events in my head a hundred times. What did I really say that particular night? I remember being more scared than I'd ever been and shaking like a leaf. I felt absolutely worthless. The truth is, I simply said that Uncle Peter was a pervy and that she should fuck off.

Mrs. Hudson collected me the very next day. She wore a colourful silk head scarf printed with horses' heads and a border of holly and red berries that matched her lipstick and rouge. She reminded me of one of those wooden Russian dolls with Mafioso undertones.

'I know you've enjoyed your stay Kathryn. I can tell by your expression that you've had a good time with Uncle Peter and Auntie Maureen,' Mrs. Hudson said, without moving her lips, or anything else for that matter. I must have looked relieved. 'Are you ready to return to the fold? Just in time for the Christmas play. We're short on dwarves. Louise Palmer is to play Snow White…Say thank you and goodbye to them now Kathryn.'

For the first time in my life I said: 'NO!'

It came down to us all on the grapevine, and Cocky Joe's snooping, that Pervy Pete and Miserable Moo had moved away from the area. Apparently, it was owing to lovely Mrs. Walsh, the lady next door, who always waited for me every morning at her gate with a delicious bacon sandwich wrapped in foil. I would sit at the bus stop and devour it before I went to school. She said I needed fattening up. Well, it was her who reported the Taylors to Mrs. Hudson.

Auntie Maureen and Uncle Peter bought a bungalow somewhere in the English countryside. He wanted to return to his birthplace and retire. Telling everybody they were moving away from "the daily grind of suburban life", and were going to "grow their own". I only hoped that they meant vegetables and not children. Informing the authorities and the neighbours that they were too old for fostering waifs and strays was their only act of kindness.

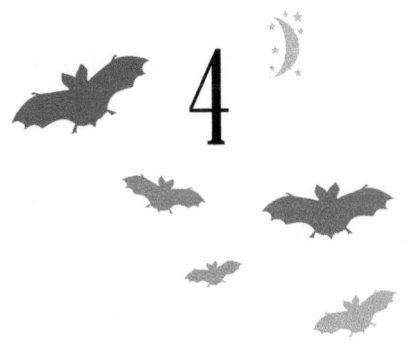

4

Lights flicked on as the thing under the wheelie bin whined. Maybe someone else would go down and see to it. I refilled the hot water bottle, slipped it under the duvet and made myself a hot chocolate. When I looked out of the window only old Mrs. Jenkins's kitchen light was still on, shining out onto the garden and the alleyway below. She had the ground floor flat. Two floor below me. She never seemed to sleep. I couldn't let someone of her age and spinal curvature go out at that time of night. It was too dangerous.

There had been some strange events lately, concerning vulnerable old people. Batty Mrs. Oldham, for example, had vanished one night from her town house without a word. The following day her granddaughter Vanessa took up residence, telling the neighbours the old lady had gone to live in a retirement home by the sea and had signed the house over to her only relative - Vanessa of course. Mr. Jackson's grandson had moved next door with the same story. Apparently the old guy couldn't bear to be parted from Mrs. Oldham. Strangely he left his much loved cat behind. I had counted five old folks so far who had relinquished all rights to their properties and pets in favour of their grandchildren.

Maybe it's just me. Nobody else seemed concerned. Apparently I was the only one to notice the oldies sudden exodus. It's funny that the new kids on the block didn't have regular working hours either. But then, who am I to talk? I knew for a fact though that Mrs. Jenkins had no surviving relatives, so I intended to keep a watchful eye on her and her cat.

The whining outside became more pitiful.

Why couldn't it shut up and let us all get some sleep?

I hit the radiator with the hammer and it

bubbled into life. Then put on another pair of socks, got into bed and turned out the light.

Sod it! Let someone else do the worrying…

By this time the whining had stopped.

What if it's dead? Better off…Must get some rest and not look like Freddie Kruger on my birthday…But even vermin deserve a chance… Rats get very bad press while squirrels get peanuts. It's seems unfair… It's so cold out there nothing could survive for long. Bugger!

I climbed out of bed pulled on my wellies. Rooted out a white fleecy with the snowflakes motif from the bottom drawer and zipped it over my pyjamas. Comfort always came first. As an afterthought I grabbed a shower cap from the bathroom. I simply had to keep the smog out of my new hairdo otherwise it would expand sideways.

Please don't let Sean of the amazing buns, in the basement flat, see me.

Not that I'd watched him down there in the back garden wearing only an apron while standing over the barbeque. I would have to hang by my heels from the window-sill to get a view of the patio area…All right - I used to be good at gymnastics when I was vertically challenged.

No doubt his willowy girlfriend would be lying with her Nordic Snow Queen hair draped over the pillow and her perfect inflated cleavage rising and falling out of her silk nightie during their frequent noisy and lengthy love-making to Ravel's *Bolero* on repeat. And you know how long that takes. If you don't - try it. The bloody thing goes on forever. Bo Derek has a lot to answer for. Georgian houses have stood the test of time but the large open fireplaces weren't designed to abate any noise above 80 decibels. I put on some lipstick just in case Sean was on a break.

What if it's a rabid fox or an escaped Alsatian from the Battersea Dogs Home?

I rummaged in the cupboard and put on my sheepskin mittens and wrapped a woollen scarf around my wrist. The large rubber torch will come in handy and maybe, a blanket to throw over it if it attacks. Car keys in case I have to make a quick getaway. Oh. Yes.

I also picked up my mobile in readiness to phone the Rabies Control Emergency Services.

As I moved down the attic stairs, intent on stepping over the noisy loose boards, I noticed the first floor flat was in darkness. I had convinced myself that the owner was either a vampire or a writer. He kept strange hours and never left his flat until after sunset. He was very tall and thin with a long pale face and a shoulder length mop of silver hair. The type of man you would expect to wear a cloak and fangs - or play Malvolio in *Twelfth Night*. No noise ever came from his flat; except the odd squeak from the wooden floor boards and the familiar computer flicking sound of *Spider Solitaire*.

I always stopped for a moment outside his door. I think it was because of the smell. I was used to the well worn carpet's musty odour, mingled with that of lingering burned sausages permeating the whole house. On that particular landing though there was the heady fragrance of late summer musk roses.

Anyhow, when I reached the ground floor Mrs. Jenkins must have the radar of a bat because she stood at her door waiting for me - and wearing a gas mask. She was a nutty but harmless old biddy and never rested until all the household had retired for the night.

She was one of those women who wouldn't take *no* for an answer. All I wanted was to fall into bed after a late shift, not talk about The Second World War and Winston Churchill. She had been war-widowed and had, somehow, got stuck in that spot; waiting for something that was never going to happen. Resignedly, I'd sit with her for an hour drifting in and out of consciousness, otherwise I would feel totally guilty and not sleep anyway.

'What was all that noise Katie?' she muttered through her rubber elephant's trunk. 'Is it the Germans again? I didn't hear the siren…Shall we take cover in the Anderson Shelter?'

'It's not a bombing mission Mrs. Jenkins…I

think it's an injured fox. I'm going out investigate so don't worry. Please stay indoors and try to get some sleep,' I urged. 'And you can take off the gas mask. The all-clear has sounded.'

'What if there's a street gang out there with flick-knives?' she said in a moment of lucidity.

'It's just a fox…I'll be all right,' I said. Thanks for sharing that thought with me. Now what am I going to do? Just lately we had had a few muggings and disturbances on our street. Bugger!

'Here Katie take this. It's my husband's. You never know it might come in handy.'

She handed me a rusted old Swiss Army penknife. So there I was armed to the teeth ready to open cans and take out stones from horses' hooves, while dressed in my pyjamas, lipstick and shower cap ready to run like hell at the least sign of danger. As I nervously walked down the front steps she whispered: 'Careless talk costs lives.'

I tip-toed slowly down the end of the street, then backed up round the courtyard towards the bin area. As my eyes got used to the gloom I noticed something wet and shiny around the overturned wheelie bin. It was a pool of blood.

Oh. God. I'm shit at First Aid.

I'd once seen Mick the Tramp lying on his back choking on his vomit and actually chucked my cookies before I got him in the recovery position to clear his airways...After peering around for a body I saw, with great relief, there was no need to give anyone the kiss of life. I hoisted up the wheelie bin and saw it. It was horrible. My hands started to shake and I managed to switch on the torch.

Oh. God. Oh. God. Oh. God. What the hell am I going to do?

In the beam of light the animal struggled to raise its head. It looked me right in the eyes... I'll never forget the hopelessness in its expression. I felt the bile rise in my throat. Across its forehead and muzzle was a gaping gash down to the bone with congealed blood around its eyes and mouth. Its jaw jutted at a weird angle. The temperature must have been below freezing otherwise it would have bled to death. I moved the torchlight along its pitifully thin body and saw a broken bone protruding out of the skin on its front paw, and from the look of it and the way its breath laboured, I guessed there were cracked ribs and internal damage.

Don't panic. Keep calm. Oh. God. Oh. God. Oh. God.

I couldn't stop shivering.

What the hell am I going to do? If I lift it up into the car I might cause more damage. If I call an ambulance they'll think I've gone mad. Maybe I could roll it onto the blanket? Are there any vets open at this time?

Then it dawned on me - The Animal Rescue Centre where I had taken Mrs. Jenkins and her one-eyed grey tabby cat: Horatio. The Centre stayed open all hours.

I spread out the blanket away from the rubbish and blood, went over to my car and scraped off the frost from the windscreen.

Please let it start first time, just for once. No such luck.

My multi-rusted *Fiesta* coughed into the night. Try again.

I pumped the gas pedal.

Please, don't seize up on me. Yes.

The engine spluttered into life. I turned the heating up to full, slammed the door and returned to the injured thing.

At that point I hardly detected any signs of life in the wretch. I knelt down and put my ear to its chest. A faint rasping sound came from its throat.

Please don't die. Stay with me…Now what do I do?

I took off my mittens and pushed my hands gently under its back and front end. It yelped and whined. Had it been stronger I'm sure it would have screamed.

I'm bloody useless at this sort of thing. Why me? I can barely look after myself let alone anything else.

It was at that moment I broke down. The kind of weeping where shoulders jerked like: *The Spice Girls* doing: *I wanna/I wanna/I really really wanna…*

My breath steamed out in hot bursts as I bawled. I think I cried a little for myself but mainly for the pathetic unloved animal bleeding to death. It was so bitterly cold that my hands and feet throbbed with hot-aches.

Please, someone, anyone, help me.

'Do you need some assistance?' a disembodied slightly foreign voice called through the fog. I saw the outline of a dark shadow reflected in the pool of blood. It was male, tall, dressed in black and loomed threateningly. 'Do not be alarmed. I am Edward Hinchcliffe. I live in the flat below yours,' he said morosely. He knelt down opposite me and put his fingers on the mutt's neck, feeling for a pulse. 'We must act quickly now. Go and put the blanket across the back seat. Hurry there is not much time.'

I rushed to the car and spread the blanket. Edward moved surprisingly quickly and light-footedly for an older man. He carried the animal as gently as if it were a child and placed it in the same position in which we'd found it.

'Where are you taking him?' he asked quietly.

'The Animal Rescue Centre, I suppose. About fifteen minutes drive – if I can get through the fog.'

'Shall I come with you?'

'No thanks. I'll be fine…If you could contact them for me. Mrs. Jenkins has the number…Tell them I'm on my way… I'd be most grateful…'

'Not a problem. Please careful…Good night,' he replied and disappeared into the fog.

Driving at ten miles per hour, chilled to the bone, extremely tired and bloodied, with a broken animal on the back seat, a weird thought occurred to me. Edward Hinchcliffe had to be a writer and not a vampire because with all that blood around surely he would have shown his fangs?

5

'Name!' the receptionist barked, sliding the small window back.

'Kathryn. Kathryn Shaw,' I replied breathlessly.

'Not you - the dog!'

'A dog? I thought it was a fox…I don't know his name, he's not my dog,' I said, taking a closer look at the unconscious wreck in my arms.

'Well ask the owners to come over here and give me his details!'

'I don't know the owners. He's a stray…Please can you hurry he's dying.'

'Have you taken the dog without their permission?'

'For God's sake woman, watch my lips! I found him under a wheelie bin in this condition. Now are you going to get me a surgeon or do I have to take him in there myself!' I shouted.

'Young lady if you enter the restricted area I shall have to call the police!'

Behind the partition window the switchboard buzzed wildly with lights flashing on and off for incoming calls. The receptionist ignored it.

'His name's Lucky and he's seriously injured so please can you get someone to attend to him,' I pleaded, saying the first name that came into my head. What a bloody ridiculous choice. This has to be the unluckiest animal ever.

'Please take a ticket and remain seated until your number is called!'

I looked around helplessly. There were seven other people with sick animals. Each of them clutched a ticket like those in *Waitrose* on the Fresh Fish Counter. My arms ached from holding the dog.

How the hell can I get a ticket without hurting him further?

'For fuck's sake woman, can't you see the poor animal's dying? Get up orf your bony backside and bring the vet out!' shouted a hairy man covered in tattoos, wearing a vest, leather trousers and holding a sleeping white kitten. He smiled at me. 'Don't worry love. They're good 'ere. 'E'll soon be put out of 'is misery,' he said, giving me his ticket numbered 36. 'I'm next so you can take my place.' He looked at the patients' owners and added: 'You lot, I'm next after 'er. Awight?'

A hushed silence hung in the air until a little bald man sighed and tapped his foot impatiently before speaking.

'Now just hang on a minute. I've been waiting for nearly an hour. I've had a long drive here and I'm next after you. My hamster's been sick for most of the day and he needs some very urgent treatment.'

The man with the white kitten stood up. God was he big. He clenched his chiselled jaw and exhaled like Moby Dick.

'Can somebody nurse Kylie while I sort this ignorant slap-head?' he asked, holding out the kitten and looking round for a volunteer. Everyone looked away. 'Oi! Miss Marples,' he said to the receptionist, sliding the window back. 'Take Kylie and don't wake 'er up, or else!'

'I'm not paid to baby-sit animals. And please lower your voice or I shall have to call security,' she replied, before a still sleeping kitten was thrust into her hands.

'Now then listen up,' he ordered, peering at the trembling man. 'Unless you want that pukin rat shovin right up your arse, I suggest you shut your whinging gob. Awright?'

The little man nodded nervously.

Before I could thank Mighty Mouth, the vet came bursting through the fire doors. He took one look at me and then at the dog saying: 'I'm Ben. This way please.' I was ushered into an examination room and offered a seat. I watched in silence. He examined the dog and spoke occasionally to the nurse. 'How long has he been like this?' he asked in a soft Canadian drawl.

'I don't know. I was woken from my sleep about 2.30.a.m. I found him under a wheelie bin at the back of my flat. I got here as soon as I could...He's not my dog, honest,' I sniffed defensively. 'I'm not allowed pets...but I wouldn't have a dog anyway...My flat's too small...Not enough room to swing a cat...Not that I'd ever do anything like that of course...It's prohibited in the Leasehold covenants...Having pets, that is and not -. Mrs. Jenkins has a cat though,' I waffled on like a total moron.

'I'm afraid he's in a critical state. If he does survive surgery, the aftercare could be lengthy and expensive. Are you able to make some financial contribution?'

I nodded unconvincingly.

'It will take weeks of medication...If you don't like dogs it might be kinder to put him out of his misery.'

Suddenly I felt angry. "You should've been put down at birth", echoed in my mind.

'I don't dislike dogs - it's just that I've never had a pet of my own...Although I got on really well with Sophie's English Bull Terrier considering he'd not been neutered - and before he ran over the cliff chasing a rabbit… Anyhow, I don't care how much it costs. Please do everything you can for him. He deserves that much at least.'

He almost smiled and gently placed the dog on a trolley.

'He muttered something to the nurse. Then looking at me curiously, scanning my face and eyes, he said: 'You need to go home and get some rest.'

He had confirmed my suspicions. I looked like shit on my birthday.

'I'll stay until you've done what you have to do,' I insisted.

'You could be in for a long haul…Maybe you'd like to go get cleaned up first. There's a washroom to the right of the door and a coffee machine near the reception desk,' he suggested, giving me an inquisitive look again. 'We'll do what we can.' The nurse hurriedly wheeled the trolley down the corridor. Ben rapped on the opposite door. 'Wake up Charlie. It's an emergency. I need you to cover for me. Now!'

A young medic disturbed from a quick nap,

almost fell of his chair, rubbed his eyes then buzzed for ticket number thirty seven.

Realization slowly dawned on me when I caught my reflection in the loo mirror. I wanted to die. I have never been so embarrassed in my whole life. I still had on the shower cap and was covered in snot and blood with a river running through it all. My white fleecy was dyed crimson and smeared with patches of mud. My Snoopy pyjamas and boots were ruined.

Oh. My. God. I look like a Glastonbury mud-slider. Sophie and Zach would be dead chuffed.

There was no point in trying to rinse my clothes. It was too cold for that. So I washed my hands and face and took off the shower cap. My forehead had a deep line where the elastic had cut into it. And even my beautiful new hair had reverted to its natural curl and clung in sweaty swathes to my head. To top it all, under the glaring strip light it looked the colour of beetroot. I actually laughed. Everything seemed surreal. It was ridiculous of me to think that I could, for once, have actually looked chic.

I had arranged a birthday dinner party at *Chez Trevayne* for a few friends and fellow graduates from college. I'd also invited Sal and Joe to stay over, intending to clean the flat and do out the spare box-room. It had been a few months since I'd seen them. In fact it was their wedding day in July. Over the years Fat Sal had shrunk and I had grown. It's funny how things turn out. In my memory she was enormous at 5'3" and now I stood head and shoulders above her. Did I ever get revenge for all the bullying? Oh. God. Yes. But now we're the best of friends. Sal's lovely. The sister I never had.

I thought of my new little grey dress hanging on the wardrobe door, similar to the exclusive design promoted in all the glossy magazines. It was tight fitting with a neat black patent belt and a tiny hint of sleeves - a High Street rip-off of course. And the shiny black patent heels still in the box...

If I get out of here in time everything will fall

into place. Grab a few hours sleep…I can tie back my hair, or push it behind my ears. (On second thoughts, it's not such a good idea to expose my wing-nuts). I can do a quick food shop at *M & S*. Clean the blood out the car. It won't take long to tidy up the flat if I can sprint up the first flight of stairs before Mrs. Jenkins sees me.

The fog had lifted as I watched the dawn breaking. Clutching a polystyrene cup of vile coffee, I looked out and saw the morning mist dissipate over the river. For an instant I thought I saw something sparkle up among a swirl of golden clouds. As the sky turned into a rosy glow in a Turneresque moment, the posh side of Chelsea Harbour looked amazing in the morning light.

6

The clock above the door ticked on to 6.0.a.m. and still I had no news. The doggy-smelling waiting room emptied and fell silent. The harridan behind the reception desk left without so much as glimpsing my way. I drifted in and out of sleep, unable to get comfortable and static free on the plastic chair.

Somewhere in the outer regions of my mind a cat's head disappeared and reappeared; grinning maliciously. I flapped my arms and tried to fly away but remained bound and frozen to the ice. Beneath the surface a dead fox floated by, wearing a gas-mask. I slid through the opaqueness and joined it. Holding on to its tail, we floated downriver, the fox and I, until the ice melted.

After a while of drifting, Trevor and Wayne rode by on horses' heads shouting: "Tallyho"! I ripped off the gas-mask and hurled it at them. Then I set off at a quick pace, holding the fox in my arms, with them in hot pursuit. They seemed to float mid-air, bobbing up and down like some macabre scene from an X rated Mary Poppins film. After cornering us, Trevor launched a carving knife and Wayne threw a scalpel, all the while whooping and shouting. Instead of bolting the fox snarled then bit me on the neck. In a freefall jolt I almost fell out of the chair. It was 8.30a.m.

Consuming Mrs. Jenkins' strong tea and heavy *Battenberg* cake after midnight is not recommended for restful sleep, or good digestion. I really, really, hate the cake - and so does Horatio. Must not be force fed *Battenberg* anymore, or consult my *Dreamers Dictionary* for an interpretation. I know I'm a nutcase with abandonment issues - and am not alone in this.

'Ms. Shaw? Kathryn…It's over,' Ben said wearily.

'You mean you've put him down?'

'No. Why would you think that? He survived

the surgery. He looks a bit of a mess at the moment -.'

'Can I see him?'

'Not a good idea. He's heavily sedated with tubes everywhere. I've cleaned him up, stitched his wounds. Reset his ribs and front leg. The tricky bit was realigning his jaw. Thankfully there were no organ injuries, just severe bruising... The next twenty four hours will tell whether I've succeeded or not.'

'Please... I need to see him.'

'Okay. Just for a few minutes,' he yawned. 'Then I suggest you go home and get some rest. That's what I intend to do.'

'You won't leave him alone, will you?' I asked following him down the corridor.

'The day shift should be arriving any moment. Keith Shepherd will take over. Lucky is in good hands.'

'That's not his real name. I just made it up to satisfy your bossy receptionist,' I said breaking eye contact.

'Brenda's a good sort really,' he said smiling. 'Works for peanuts because she knows how important this place is. The animals brought in here probably wouldn't make it otherwise. I guess she gave you a rough ride because of the poor shape he's in.'

'Like I said, he's not my dog.'

'I know...Prepare yourself. He looks worse that before. We had to shave off most of his matted coat. He's got ringworm and other nasty -.'

'What?'

'I suggest you get out the *Dettol* and give your car a good cleaning,' he grinned, showing even white teeth.

'Right...You're really tall,' I said, trying to keep up with his long strides. What a divvy.

'I suppose I am. You're not exactly short yourself,' he grinned.

'I used to be.' I am such a smooth talker.

He stared at me again and looked longer than necessary into my eyes.

For some bizarre reason he either, fancies me

or, I've missed some snot. 'Is there something wrong,' I said, touching my face.

'No. Not really. It's your eyes...'

Here we go again. He's noticed the strange colour. Or maybe it's the dark circles. And no, I've not been tangoed. And no, my pupils do not dilate sideways, nor do I have inner sliding eyelids. 'I know. Cat's eyes.'

'No. Well yes... They're fascinating. I've never seen green eyes with orange sunbursts. Well not on a human...Here he is,' he said, peering through a cage door.

Still reeling from what could have been a compliment, I was unprepared for the sight in front of me. I felt myself fill up again. Lucky's eyes and muzzle were badly swollen with jagged rows of stitches running the whole length of his head. At least his jaw was in line. He had tubes coming from everywhere. A drip was attached to his left paw, while the right was covered in plaster all the way down from the shoulder joint. He had hardly any flesh on him. Without hair his bony bandaged frame showed the full extent of his neglect.

'Are you sure he's alive,' I asked, feeling sick again. 'Should his tongue be lolling out like that?'

'He's still in a critical state…I think we should leave him now. Keith will take over from me. He'll be monitored 24/7. Don't worry.'

'It's my birthday,' I sniffed, half talking to myself.

'Happy birthday Kathryn,' he grinned, handing me a tissue. 'It's not been a good one so far.'

I noticed he had warm brown eyes, dark curly hair, lovely shiny black eyebrows and a firm jaw.

What fantastic boyfriend material. I am staring too much and I look like shit and he will think I am a total geek. 'What time's visiting hours?' I yawned, trying to look casual.

'Look. I'll give you the direct number for the surgery. That way you can keep in touch and get a progress report. Be persistent or they won't answer it. If there's any change I'll let you know.

Did you give the bossy lady get your phone number?'

I nodded. We both swayed on our feet as he handed me the number. Then he ruffled his hair and looked like an advert for aftershave.

'Thanks Ben. Let me know how much I owe. I'll sort something out. I might sell a painting. You never know.'

'Are you an artist?'

'Sort of, not fulltime though. I work as a waitress in the evenings to pay the bills... I've got an exhibition opening tomorrow...It's on the King's Road just past the *Christopher Wray Lighting Shop*. Do you know it?' Shit. Some chat up line. What heterosexual male would know a lighting shop full of *Tiffany* shades?

He looked blank.

"It's near *Chutney Mary's*," I continued, on a roll. Yippee. He's not gay.

He raised his eyebrows in a glimmer of recognition.

'It's a shop window really, but Alan said I

could exhibit some of my work in the hope that he would be able to sell more antiques to his idle rich friends. He's even providing champagne and canopies…Would you like to come?'

He yawned again. 'Sure. I'll try to make it… What sort of paintings are they?'

'Seascapes. I love the sea.'

'Likewise…I've recently bought a house in Cheryl's Close and am looking for some pictures. Can I bring my girlfriend?'

'Yes,' I said without flinching. Bugger.

'See you then…Do you want your blanket back?'

I shook my head.

'Bye then Kathryn. Hope you enjoy the rest of your birthday.'

I first started drawing portraits of my imaginary family when I was about five. My sketch pad became the photo album I never had. I drew baby snaps and created happy spots in time, like my first steps, blowing candles out on a cake, walks in the park, starting school.

I was seven when Fat Sal ripped up my

drawings. I tried to get the sketch pad off her, but she held it above my head. I hung on to her leg pleading for her to give me back my album. Instead I got punched until I saw stars. Joe finally stopped her.

'Good try Titch but you are so fucking stupid. There's no such thing as happy families...My old man got banged up and my Mother ran off with a miner who beat the shit out of her and us kids... I'm doing you a favour in the long run...Now go and get extra pudding before I rip *you* apart!'

God. I hated her guts at that moment. I wished she had choked to death on my jam roly-poly and custard. She never did oblige me. Her gullet must have been the size of the Mersey Tunnel.

Ever after that I hid my drawings under her mattress. I knew that would be the last place she'd look as she never made her own bed. She made me do it. When I sketched I lost myself in the moment. I could go anywhere in the world to places where nobody could contaminate my imagination. I drew my family under the Eiffel

Tower, on the Bridge of Sighs, the Great Wall of China, by the Coliseum, the Pyramids and the Empire State Building.

I had a lump in my throat only last week, when I reread *The Deathly Hallows,* where Harry Potter discovered a torn photo of himself as a toddler riding round on a broomstick. I knew exactly how he felt. Not riding the broomstick of course, but finding a jigsaw piece of memory; another pearl to thread on the necklace.

In spite of Sal's bullying I was forever grateful to her for warning me about Pervy Pete. And, indirectly, it was thanks to Sal that I found some of my blood-family in Cornwall. So in the end I forgave her, as she has forgiven me.

7

I slammed the car door, took out the *Waitrose*
bags from the boot, noticing that the blood and
rubbish by the bins had disappeared along with
my mittens, torch, scarf and Arnold's Swiss Army
knife. Firstly I did a quick clean with *Dettol* wipes
over the back seats of the car in case any wrigglers
resided there. One job ticked off the list before
I tiptoed round to the front door and quietly
turned the key in the lock.

Maybe, just maybe, I could dash upstairs have
a long hot shower, grab a bacon sandwich - and
fall into bed. As I picked up my birthday cards
from the mat Mrs. Jenkins's door creaked open
and Horatio snaked around my legs purring
softly. 'It's *Battenberg* for you big boy,' I whispered,
hanging my waterproof on a hall peg.

She stood at the door beckoning me inside,

putting a crooked first finger to her lips in case I protested. The flat was in darkness except for a cake with three flickering candles on it.

'Make a wish Katie,' she said excitedly.

'Mrs. Jenkins, have you been up all night baking? You really shouldn't have.'

She walked towards the old windup gramophone.

Please God, not George Formby again. I just can't take anymore.

A scratchy Vera Lynn sang out: *We'll meet again...*

'Blow out the candles Katie. Do hurry yourself, or the Air Raid Warden will be knocking on the door telling us to put out the lights.'

I puffed out my cheeks and blew on a rather jaded cake with an iced flower basket on it. In small loopy iced writing it read: "Welcome Home Arnold Dearest".

Please don't let her make me partner her in the foxtrot again. I cannot go on. I have lost the will to live. I must sit down before I collapse. Please do not let her cut the cake. I am going to throw up.

Mrs. Jenkins took off the candles and placed the top tier of her wedding cake back in the tin.

'Now then Katie I know you must be ready for a nice cup of tea and a slice of *Battenberg*? It's your favourite. I insist.'

I fell into a chair and Horatio jumped onto my lap and started padding, until he smelled the dried dog's blood and did a back-flip.

As God is my witness I will never eat *Battenberg* again.

The tea was so strong it hardly moved. I slid the cake into my carrier bag when she leaned over to poke the fire. Where she'd got the coal from I don't know. I daren't have asked. After all there was no such thing as a Smoke Control Order in 1943. In the flickering firelight it was so cosy lying back in Arnold's armchair that my eyelids started to droop.

'Wake up Katie. Pay attention dear. Now I want you to get my shopping for me. Here's the list and the ration book. If Mr. Bates at the butcher's has a nice bit of sausage snatch his hand off before Gorgeous Gussy at number 23 gets it first. I'll give you half a crown. That should cover it.'

'Mrs. Jenkins,' I said wearily. 'I've been at the Animal Rescue Centre all night. I really must get some rest.'

'Silly me. I forgot you were on duty. Were many wounded brought in?' Then she noticed my fleecy. 'Oh. Katie dear. Was it really that bad? Gerry has a lot to answer for. Anyone we know?'

'Mrs. Jenkins. I took in an injured dog. Do you remember I thought it was a fox?'

'Of course I do. What do you think I am, senile? Off you got to bed and get a good rest,' she said, kissing me on the cheek.

I took out a packet of pork sausages, a box of *Whiskas* meat in gravy and a bar of *Cadbury's* fruit & nut from my carrier bag and left them on the table, along with the half crown. The Air Raid Warden/Home Help would cook her lunch and feed the cat.

'Bye Mrs. Jenkins, you and Horatio enjoy.'

'You were quick with the shopping Katie. Have you got my change?' she said, following me to the door.

'I'll take it out of what you owe me. Shall I?'

'Very well dear. Sweet dreams.'

I could hardy make it up the first flight of stairs towards Edward's flat. I left a bottle of claret outside his door. The pushy man in the shop said it was a good choice; full bodied without being too showy. Still it was kind of Edward to help me like that. And not drink my blood. Without him who knows what might have happened? I left a note saying: "Thank you for your kindness. I'm afraid the dog is in intensive care. Only time will tell. Kathryn Shaw", in the hope that I wouldn't have to wear a crucifix after dusk.

When I finally reached my door I saw my scarf, mittens, torch and the Swiss Army knife in a neat pile. The mittens and scarf must have been dry cleaned and the penknife was rust free. It could only be Edward's doing. He must have bat-winged it down to the launderette and transformed back into human form again, or maybe he had sucked the items clean. I could be wrong about him. Still I intended to keep the fire-escape steps raised up. You never know, he could bite my neck in the night without even waking me.

I unpacked the shopping, sprayed my clothes and boots with stain remover, threw them into the washer and took the longest shower ever. It was bliss. After shampooing my hair four times until clear water swirled around in the shower basin, I actually found time to use conditioner.

It was Alex who introduced me to tangle free curls. We met during my second year at college. He was one of those little men who are physically perfect. His hands and feet were smaller than mine and I felt like a beanpole standing next to him. He had a neat black beard, and shiny shoulder length hair, both trimmed to perfection as only a Virgo man could. His David Bowie impressions were brilliant. Also he made me laugh a lot.

He was a talented artist - and like me, loved the *Impressionists*. Rachel, my ex-lodger, called him Toulouse Lautrec because they didn't like each other at all. He described her as Rubenesque and she ignored him ever after. But I thought he was perfectly formed and much taller and prettier than the unfortunate French genius. He took me to all the galleries. I remember he sat me in the pre-Raphaelite room because he said that I belonged there. I thought at first he meant as one of those uniformed people who stand in a corner without moving and stare into the middle distance. Anyhow, he went on to justify our sitting there for two hours by explaining in great detail that I was his princess. Personally though, I thought the swooning damsels were in dire need of a good meal and some sunlight. Did I really look that elongated, white and miserable?

After spending a romantic two weeks basking in his adoration we had sex. I told him it was my first time. What I didn't tell him was of the many tussles and fumbles I had with Luke, a persistent sun-bleached Aussie surfer. Nevertheless, Alex became so excited. He couldn't believe his luck that a girl of my age was still a virgin. It's not that I didn't want to do it with Luke, but when push came to shove; literally, I just got really scared and froze - making penetration impossible.

I took Alex to my Ivory Tower to do the dastardly deed. Rachel had obliged and slept at her boyfriend's that night. Alex brought flowers but when I went to put them in a vase he stopped me. I had to sit blindfolded on the sofa for over an hour until he'd finished preparing the bedroom. Bless him. He tried so hard. There was a trail of Rose petals leading to the bed and scented candles everywhere. He draped a gold silk scarf over the bedside light to give ambiance and the appropriate shades and tones for his living creation.

First he undressed me and placed my clothes in an artistic way over the back of the chair. I was shitting myself by this time. Patience is not a virtue I possess. I just wanted to get it over with, go to sleep and wake up as a fulfilled woman. Finally he carried me over to the bed. (He was surprisingly strong for a small man). After arranging my legs in a nice pose, and raising one arm above my head, he draped my fully conditioned hair over the pillow. By this time I really needed a drink so I felt for my glass of champagne on the bedside table and gulped it down while his back was turned, then quickly re-draped. Of course he folded his underpants and socks and placed them over my underwear. I refilled my glass and gulped it down once more, before regaining the pose.

When he came over to me with a look of adoration on his face, I smiled and began to relax. It was when he started threading Forget-me-knot in my lady garden that I had to stifle a laugh; especially when he went to the kitchen with an impressive erection to collect the Freesias for my hair. In the meantime I was on my third glass of champagne and in hysterics. He thought I was crying so I managed to get away with it, as he made me a garland of flowers.

He walked around the room surveying his masterpiece - and even funnier - still sporting a boner as he climbed in beside me. After what seemed like forever he stopped gazing at me and began the kissing bit. It was then that he confirmed my suspicions. He must have read Dirty Bertie because he raised himself up and said: "Aye lass. Thou hast a luscious cunt".

I choked on my champagne and ran to the loo in fits of laughter, shedding flowers on the way. I couldn't control myself. The whole thing was so bizarre. When Forget-me-nots floated around the pan I fell onto the floor laughing.

"Kathryn darling please don't be upset. I'll be gentle with you," he called through the door.

All of a sudden he was Joe Lampton? I wondered whether he said brassiere or brazier. After all I did live in the room at the top. I flushed the loo again to drown out my hilarity. I laughed again as the delicate blue flowers swished round and round like a carousel.

His eager little face peered over the duvet. "Come to me my darling. I will take care of you," he said seriously.

I jumped into bed and started to kiss him. He responded and was quite good at it considering his fantasy foreplay. Not too messy, a little darting tongue and just enough pressure so that I could breathe easy and not dislocate my jaw…I reached for his penis and ran my fingers up and down the shaft. It drove him wild – and I finally found out exactly what balls were. They were much bigger and looser than I'd expected. He groaned as I cupped and squeezed them. I had turned into a harlot. I found out afterwards this move should come much later, because immediately he climbed on top of me and quickly pushed his penis between my legs, saying: "I do love a nice bit o' cunt lass".

Despite a momentarily glitch of lip-biting hysterics I began to enjoy myself until he attempted penetration, then I froze again. No matter how hard I tried I couldn't seem to get around this moment. Undaunted he muttered reassurances to me through a mouth full of nipple while struggling to put on a condom. By this stage, and after a fourth glass of champagne, I had gone beyond giggling, and was ready to ride the big one. Bingo! At last the barrier reef had been breached. I started to move with him until I saw the scarf over 100 watt light bulb smoulder and then ignite. I protested as it puffed into life.

'Am I hurting you darling?'

I wailed and to push him off me.

'You vixen. I know you really want to.'

It was when he began thrusting hard and crying out: "Dirty bitch", that I rolled and threw him off, picked up the bedside rug and smothered the scarf, now glued to the melting light-shade, just in the nick of time.

Poor Alex never got over performing a wipe out on my bedroom carpet. From then on he avoided me until graduation day. With his mortar board tassel bobbing around his boyish face he took me to one side and told me, apologetically, that he'd got engaged to a girl who didn't take life so seriously. What he didn't know was the following summer after losing my virginity, and every holiday since, I'd had some really wicked times with sex-god Luke, surfing, swimming, snorkelling and making love until the sun came up.

8

'Wake up thy feeble excuse for a wench,' Sal shouted, knocking on the door.

'What time doest thy call this lass? Ligging in't bed int'middle ot'day,' Joe chuckled.

'Shut thy cakehole, Mardy Bum,' I shouted, leaping out of bed and pulling on my dressing gown. It was 11.30a.m and I had actually slept soundly for two hours.

Ever since the Alex Forget-me-nots episode they had teased me mercilessly in this way. I had confided in Sal, she told Joe and he has never let me forget it. I must say though, our northern impressions have improved considerably thanks to: *The Arctic Monkeys*.

'Come here you,' Sal said, giving me a huge hug. 'Happy birthday hon. I like your hair - but you look knackered,' she added, holding me at arm's length and scrutinizing my face. 'What have you been up to?'

'Thanks a bunch friend. I can't say the same for you. You look fantastic girl.'

Instead of density Sal now had a beautiful hourglass figure and shapely legs. Sal reminded me of Nigella, and miracle of miracles she could cook too. Joe adored her. But he always had even when she was mean and large.

'You,' Joe said, grimacing like Robert de Niro and pointing at me.

'No. You,' I replied, shrugging my shoulders and doing the Jerry Maguire two pistols pointing bit.

'No. You,' Joe insisted, punching me lightly on the arm.

'No! You!' I said, hitting him harder.

'You talking to me?'

'No. You talking to me?'

'You must be talking to me, cos there aint nobody else here.'

'Stop acting like twits,' Sal laughed. Her

cursing had modified greatly since she had become a married lady.

Joe then did the two fingers to the eyes and pointing bit: 'I'm watching you.'

'No. I'm watching you.'

'Get inside you daft beggars, the neighbours will think you've gone mad.'

'You talking to me Sal,' I asked, dancing around her like a boxer. 'I coulda been a contender Charlie.'

'You gonna take a dive in the fifth. Got it?' Joe said, ducking and weaving with me.

'I won't do it Charlie.'

'I am Lustius Maximus and I will have my breakfast,' he said, in a perfect imitation of hunky Russell.

Sal rolled her eyes. 'Oh. Behave,' she said goofing up like Austin Powers. 'Bring in the luggage Bugsy I need to practise my violin for Valentine's Day,' she called from the kitchen, 'because I'm Evil. Ha. Ha. Haaa.'

To outsiders our behaviour may have seemed childish, but what they don't understand is that back then our monthly visit to the cinema was the only source of escapism from the abuse we'd all suffered. We could lose ourselves in the moment and become clean and whole again. Be anything we wanted to be for a few hours.

Sal, Joe and I had shared so much together, both bad and good. That special bond between us was unbreakable now. There was nothing we couldn't say to each other, knowing it was either said in jest or with love. And there was nothing we wouldn't do to help each other. But there are some things best left alone, memories that are buried deep - and far too painful for even us to talk about.

'So? How's the lock-picking business going Joe?' I asked as we ate our belated breakfast cooked to perfection by Sal.

'Do you mind madam-mate? I just happen to be a security alarm system expert and locksmith… To be honest the systems I prefer to install are too expensive for most folks living on the wrong side of Tiger Bay. They can't afford to buy burglar alarms.'

'No. They have Bull Terriers instead,' Sal laughed. 'He's still a big softy. When old ladies lock themselves out he won't take anything for his trouble other than a cup of tea…Seriously though business is bad and what with me having to give up work in the bakery soon…'

'You're not?'

'I am. You're going to be the "a" word,' she said filling up. 'Auntie Kat.'

None of us could say the: a, u, m, or the d word easily.

'Sal that's fantastic. I'm going to be an a-auntie. Wow!'

'We're having us a baby,' Joe said, beaming.

'When?' I asked.

'April 16th.'

'Do you know the baby's sex yet?' I asked.

'We don't really want to know. As long as it's okay,' Joe said excitedly.

'The main priority is that we move out of the

flat. I don't want Sal lugging a buggy up thirty flights of steps. The lifts are always out of order and we'll need a garden now.'

'Will you manage to find a house? If you need any help financially you know Sophie and Zach will help out -.'

'Anyhow enough of that,' Sal interjected. 'It's your special day so open you card and present…I hope you like it. Sophie gave me strict instructions on the latest styles.'

'It's fantastic,' I said, holding up a snazzy zipper-less wetsuit. 'How did you know I needed a new one?'

'Zach's suggestion,' Joe said. 'It was when they sent us return tickets two weeks ago. They said they wanted a new alarm system fitting in the house and shop…That wouldn't have anything to do with you young madam? Would it?' Joe asked.

I shrugged my shoulders and pinched his last piece of bacon.

'They really miss you and send their love,' Sal added. 'And thanks Kat for everything.'

'I honestly don't know what either of you are talking about,' I said, trying not to laugh.

I immediately felt a surge of endorphins at the thought of surfing again, seeing Sophie and Zach, and hanging out with Luke in the summer holidays.

'Wonder what this is from Alan?' I pondered, feeling the angular parcel. 'Wow. My favourite programme *Outlander.* The full box set,' I exclaimed. 'I get to spend days and nights with Jamie Fraser. What a great prezzie.'

'This is from Sophie and Zach,' Joe said, handing me another present.

I ripped off the paper and opened the box. Inside there was a pair of white and silver trainers.

'I'd put money on it that you've already tried them on Sally Jones,' I said, trying not to smile.

'No… Well alright, you win. I did. Old habits die hard. They do,' she said, reverting to her Welsh accent.

'Sophie said I was to deliver this by hand,' Joe said, handing me a large envelope.

From the age of sixteen, every year on my birthday Sophie gave me an envelope with cash inside. At first I told her to "stuff it where the sun don't shine" and that I couldn't be bought just to ease her conscience. Ever since then I've had to take the offer or she would throw it in the bin. So I accepted the money and used it for things I really wanted like the latest surfing gear. I had intended to go to Hawaii with Luke for the World Surfing Championships. There's a young kid there called Jon Jon who surfs like a dolphin and we really wanted to see him in action. And, of course, to try and catch Kelly Slater, the world's greatest surfer, doing what he does better than anyone. But neither of us could hang onto money for long; especially what with the beach bums cadging meals, or fags. Luke was as daft as I in this respect.

I first discovered about my blood family when Fat Sal, in a particularly vicious mood, let rip: 'Now then Titch. I hear you come from a long line of crack heads.'

'What do you mean? I asked, colouring up.

'Drug addicts you twerp. That must be why you're such a runt. You didn't develop properly in the womb, because you where mainlining your Mother's habit. Ha. Ha.'

'Leave it Sal,' Joe said. 'She's only a kid. She doesn't need to know that.'

Fat Sal was in a mean mood, because her Mother had been arrested on a third count of shop-lifting. Her two younger half Brothers, both from different fathers, had been taken from the family home and put into Care again. I knew she was really hurt by all this, but Sal never learned to deal with heartache. She just got mad and took it out of everybody else. That's all she'd ever known I suppose. Fight back, or be the self pitying underdog.

'Take that back,' I said, balling my fists. I knew that particular spot in time would be my *High Noon,* my *3.10 to Yuma,* where I stood alone and fought the mean bitch. I'd had enough. I knew she would win but I gave her as good as I got. We were both bloodied and beaten. I hung onto her hair and didn't let go, even though she punched the living daylights out of me. The other kids started to clap and stamp their feet. They loved a good scrap because it made them forget their own problems for a while.

It was only when Mrs. Hudson barged in that that we backed off.

'What's all this noise,' she asked, with that embalmed look in her eyes.

'Nothing Mrs. Hudson,' I said, breathing deeply and holding my ribs.

'Sally? Is that true?'

'Yes Mrs. Hudson. We were just messing around,' Sal muttered, with blood pouring out of her nose.

'Both of you go along to the First Aid Room and clean yourselves up. Now!'

'Yes. Mrs. Hudson,' we echoed.

Ironically from that cathartic moment Sal and I ceased to be enemies. She dressed my wounds and I put plasters on her scratches. As she held an ice pack to her nose I asked her: 'How do you know stuff about my Mother?'

'Just leave it Titch. I'm a fucking cow. I didn't mean it. O.K?'

'Sorry about your Brothers. I know they mean a lot to you,' I said, warily.

'Sorry about the beatings Titch, I didn't mean to hurt you. Having a slut for a Mother does my head in. I just go into one and lose it.'

I remained silent for a while, holding an ice pack to my swollen eye.

'Why do you hate me so much?'

'I don't hate you Titch... It's more like I envy you.'

'Who me?' I asked in amazement. Nobody had ever envied me.

'Yes you. You're dainty and agile and clever,' she said sniffing. For the first time since I'd know her, Sal looked vulnerable. Then she began to blubber. 'Joe fancies you more than me... And you've got a neck and a waist.'

No. It can't be possible. Sal Hooley blubbering. She just can't. I mean if she breaks down then we're all fucked. Not the leader of the pack - the toughest and hardest one in the group. The resilient one - Wales's very own *Terminator*.

At that moment I didn't feel any pity for her. Too much had happened between us. I really didn't know what to think. There had to be more to this than me having a neck and a waist. So I waited until she spoke again.

'I'm big, fat, useless and ugly. Do you know how that feels?'

Well. Hell yes, except for the big and fat bit.

Her nose had started to bleed again so I got some more ice from the fridge.

'Thanks,' she said looking totally beat. As she hunched forward still sobbing I saw a bald patch at the back of her head. I still had traces of thick black hair in my nails.

'You're supposed to open your airways. Hold your head back and pinch your nose,' I urged, trying to hide the bald spot and discovering for the first time that I was crap at First Aid.

Sal started to choke as snot and blood poured down her throat.

'It's okay,' I said, panicking. 'Just keep nice and calm and breathe through your mouth. That's right, in and out - and again.'

I took out the mop and bucket and started to clean up the blood, hoping this would distract her. She watched me swish around the room with the wet mop and her expression softened.

'You know Sal, Joe adores you. He thinks you're beautiful and brave like an Amazon princess. We're good mates Joe and me, but you're the one he loves.'

'Really,' she said, coming up for air. 'Does he really love me?'

'More than anything,' I reassured her.

Sal sighed deeply. 'I couldn't cope without Joe. He keeps me sane.'

'I know that. When you're older you'll be together properly, like a real girlfriend and boyfriend.'

'Thanks for that Titch.'

'That's okay.'

I continued to mop the floor and eventually Sal stopped blubbering.

'I can't wait to get out of this dump.'

'Me neither,' she agreed.

'Sal? If you know anything about my Mother please tell me. Even if she's was a scum-bag she's still all I've got. I need to find out for myself. Please Sal will you tell me?'

'Ask Joe, he's the one who broke into The Mummy's filing cabinet. He wanted to know who his Father was.'

'Did he find out?'

'No. It said: Father unknown. Mother deceased. No siblings or traceable relatives. What a crock of shit. He's got nobody…He was gutted. So take my advice and leave well enough alone. Stick to the fantasies, unless you want to feel worse than you do now.'

'I don't care. I just need to know. How do I get into The Mummy's office? Will you and Joe help me?'

'Leave it with me Titch,' she said. 'I'll see what I can do, but you're opening a right can of worms.

9

Sal busied herself in the kitchen making puddings for my birthday celebration. Trevor and Wayne had agreed to do the starters and main course. They didn't do dessert, except for three flavours of ice cream and the cheeseboard. The delicious odours of chocolate sauce and sticky toffee wafted into the sitting room. Joe busied himself fixing my new star lights in the main bedroom as I opened the rest of my cards.

The ritual had always been the same since I could remember. I checked out the envelopes for some signs of unfamiliar writing in the hope it was from my Mother. Wayne's scrawled writing adorned the pink envelope. The gang had signed the card: Maggie, Paulo, Lucy, Trevor and Wayne and enclosed £50's worth of *M & S* vouchers. There was a card from Rachel and Rob saying they'd be there on time. I think not. Zarah had declined my invitation as she was on holiday in Dubai. Penny and James couldn't get a babysitter but said they would bring baby Rosa and leave early. Mrs. Jenkins' had written on a Christmas card that I'd sent to her the previous year: "Happy Birthday Katie", so that was encouraging on the battle front. Now if I can only get her beyond Dunkirk, the Social Services would leave her alone.

I'd always opened birthday cards with the Newquay post mark last. There was one from Luke with surfing penguins on it saying: "Surf's Up", and inside he'd written: "Happy Birthday Grommet. Did a couple of aerials and I'm stoked. Caught a Cribba and got totally shacked. Spat out of a keg. Then I got plenty of speed on a wave bowling hard so I wacked the lip a couple of times and buried the rail for a roundhouse cutty and boom! You should have been here yesterday. You're missing the best Teehupoos ever. Hanging loose for another Hurricane Gordon in the Goldrush. Luke".

He's a total surfing dude. Utterly focussed on the next big one. I knew he missed me though.

Sophie's card had an elegant flapper lady on the front, looking coyly over her shoulder. Inside it read: "Miss you Kat, although the house is much tidier now. Shop sales have dropped since you were last here. And of course the allegedly Great White spotted by that man from Rotherham has reduced the amount of family surfers. Your enterprising Godfather has bought a boat and now does "Shark Watch and Fishing Trips". Luke is still here and reckless as ever - along with the rest of the fanatics. I think he would surf if it was raining bullets. I just can't cut the mustard with the youngsters. Not understanding the lingo". Zach had added: "Me neither dudess".

Finally I opened the brown envelope. Each year there had been an increase in money. Last November I had received £500 and refused to spend it, until Sophie threatened me with the shredder.

Phew! This is some wad.

Hands shaking I counted out a grand. Within minutes I was on my mobile protesting about the large amount. I could hear Bob Dylan and Zach wailing out in the background: *Like a complete unknown...*

'Honestly Sophie I can't take it. It's too much.'

'Not another word or I'll get out the pinking sheers my loverrlee. You can put it to a better use than us old fossils. Now enjoy. The Godfather wants to talk to you. Happy Birthday darling. Come visit soon. Love you.'

'Likewise.' I couldn't say the "l" word either.

'Hello Kat. Before you start, I'm not arguing with the gaffer, so get it spent. All right dudess? Wish we could be there with you. Have a great birthday my loverrlee. Hope to see you soon. God Bless. Oh by the way, your Godmother's latest fad is DIY plumbing. I'll leave you on that ominous note from a waterlogged kitchen...Love you.'

'Likewise Godfather. You've made me an offer I can't refuse,' I said laughing.

I could see that Sal wanted to talk, with Joe out of the way. I made us coffee and said to her: 'Come on. I know there's something on your mind. I've seen that expression before. Is it about Joe?'

'Yes. It is. Do you remember when he found out that his maternal Grandmother was still alive?'

I nodded.

'Well he actually got an address from the Salvation Army people. She lives in Mumbles of all places…And before you say anything he's not related to the famous beautiful Jones.'

'I wasn't going to say a word,' I said, zipping my mouth and locking it, then doing the slashing mark of Zorro.

'I tried to dissuade him, but you know Joe… At least he let me go with him. She lived in one of those terraced pit houses on the outskirts of the town. It was a bit tumbled down and desperately in need of some TLC but spotlessly clean.

At first she wouldn't open the door but Joe just kept on banging the knocker and shouting out: "I'm your grandson. Please. I need to talk to you".

'It was heart-breaking Kat. Anyhow she eventually opened the door. She had such a miserable face - all wizened and sour like.

"You'd best come in then. I don't want the neighbours poking their noses in my business. I don't", she said. Then she disappeared into the kitchen for a while and brought three cups of tea and a plate of biscuits on a tray. "Get on with it then boyo. What do you want? I've got no money. So you're out of luck there".

"I don't want anything from you. I just want to know about my m-m-her. Can't you understand that?" he asked.

"She was no good. Brought disgrace to us. It killed her Father and nearly finished me off... Wanting to bring a bastard to my doorstep. Not likely. She made her bed and she had to lie in it. That's what I've always said and I'm sticking to it".

I felt my blood boil, you know Kat, like it used to be before the therapy. She had a face that begged for a good slapping. Joe stopped me. And for his sake I quietened down.

"Do you have any photos of her?" Joe pleaded.

"Not a one. Destroyed the lot I did and good riddance too."

"Is there anything you can tell me about her? What was the colour of her eyes? Did she have dark hair like me? Was she shy or bubbly?"

"She was a trollop, that's what she was…"

'Enough!' I shouted. "For God's sake woman can't you just give him one little bit of information. How can you deny your own flesh and blood? Can't you see it's breaking his heart over and over again?'

"What's it got to do with you?" she asked.

'I'm his wife and best friend. The only family he's ever known. And I love him more that life itself. So if you don't want me to get really angry you'll tell him what you know, or I'll do a lifer for you! God help me!'

I thought she might get mad, but on the contrary, she softened a little and thought for a while before she spoke again.

"She didn't take after my side of the family. She favoured her Father…Daddy's girl, that's what she was…You have the same blue eyes and black hair as her," she whispered. "I don't know what else to say. She never told me who your father was."

"Is there anything more you can tell me?" Joe begged in desperation. "Please help me."

By this time he was crying. I've never seen him do that before. He was in such a state. I didn't know what to do for the best. Then she got up, went over to the dresser and took something out of the top drawer. She stood looking at it for a while.

"She bought this for me from Hugh the Jeweller when she was sixteen. She did. It was from her first wage. I don't want it," she said slinging a locket and chain on the floor as if it burned her hands. "You can have it. Now leave my house and don't come back."

Joe picked up the locket and stared at it long and hard. If only she knew what that simple treasure meant to him. But then, someone like her would never understand…. He left her a note with our name and address on it…'

Sal's hand shook as she lifted her coffee cup. 'He carries the locket with him wherever he goes,' she said. 'Maybe one day he'll show you what's inside?'

'What's inside Sal?' I asked, putting my arm around her.

'There's a baby picture of his Mother with his Granddad holding her. They looked so happy. Engraved on the back of the locket it says: "Caroline Ann with Daddy Joe 1966". She named Joe after her Dad…She was only a kid herself when she gave birth. She must've been terrified on her own…It makes you wonder what families are all about to be so unforgiving…At least he's got something to hold onto now.'

'He's got you Sal and a little babbie on the way. That's all he needs.'

Around midday Sal and Joe wanted to do the sights and left for the 22 bus, wrapped up warm against the winter chill. I'd told them about Lucky and intended to call and see how he was doing, as communication by phone was impossible. Nobody seemed to be around at the hospital. I got the engaged tone for a solid hour. In a panic I thought they'd left Lucky to fend for himself. Then I realized that this time of year animals suffered as much from illnesses as people do. The doctors' surgery was always bursting at the seams when I walked by.

Now if I can only get by Mrs. Jenkins, It's a nice day for a brisk walk along the river. I can pay a quick visit to see Lucky, then do a food shop at *M & S* with my vouchers. Get Mrs. Jenkins some crème caramels and a few tins of tuna with the ring pull tops for Horatio. I'd had my eye on a black coat and decided to treat myself with my new found wealth. It actually began to feel like a happy birthday.

As I closed my door, I heard Sal and Joe talking. Mrs. Jenkins had got them cornered. I hot footed down the stairs and rescued them just in time. She was threatening to thrash them within an inch of their lives.

'Mrs. Jenkins please, stop! They're my friends.'

'Hello Katie. I thought they were foes because they wouldn't give the password.'

I gave Joe a knowing look and nodded.

'Bing Crosby,' he said on cue, grinning.

'Bob Hope,' Mrs. Jenkins answered, backing off.

'Bloody hell,' Sal gasped, 'I thought we'd had it for a minute.'

'And you young lady! Say the password.'

'Frank Sinatra?'

'Phil Silvers,' she replied. 'All's well. Stand at ease.'

'Mrs. Jenkins, go inside now. Rosie, the Air Raid Warden will be here soon,' I soothed.

'I do know that Katie. You all have a nice day now,' she smiled.

We left quickly trying not to laugh as Horatio slipped out of the front door in front of us. He wobbled along the fence with belly swinging and tail rotating then dropped heavily into next door's bijou garden. For some reason Horatio was the only cat allowed to poo over there by the resident demented tortoiseshell: Mrs. Rochester. Maybe it's because he had extremely good toilet manners and always dug a hole and covered it over when he'd finished - although I've often seen him with raised quivering tail spraying everything in sight.

The waiting room at Animal Rescue Centre was full of ailing canines. The noise emitted from barking, growling and farting dogs was overwhelming. Thankfully Brenda wasn't on duty until later. The receptionist was a smiley lady from Antigua called Coral. After a friendly chat she allowed me to sneak through the side door and see Lucky.

'I'm warning you now darlin. He looks worse than ever. But don't you be worrying yourself. He's managed to survive this far. He's got a brave heart. I think he will get even better with your tender loving care.'

Keith was still on duty and he beckoned me towards the recovery room. Lucky lay motionless and his breathing seemed laboured. At least they'd kept him isolated from the other animals.

'Is he any better?' I asked, hopefully.

'It's early days yet. If he was stronger the odds on a recovery would be higher. I can't really tell you anything at this stage, other than we are doing all we can for him. Maybe in a few days we'll see a change.'

'Do you mean for the better?'

'I don't really know. If he responds to the drugs, then hopefully there might be some improvement. You see,' he said, 'this is a dog that has given up. He's been beaten, starved and broken. It's not only human's who suffer from depression. Maybe you could sit with him for a while. Try talking to him. I suggest though, that you don't put your fingers through the bar.'

'Will he bite?'

'I don't think he's capable of that. He's highly infectious at the moment until the ointment and antibiotics kick in.'

I looked at Lucky and there wasn't a place on

his body that I could have stroked. He looked like a large skinned rabbit and had circular red wheals everywhere. What do you say to a dying dog? Don't worry you'll soon be in doggy heaven? You might come back as a pampered pooch? I'm no dog whisperer. I sat for a while thinking what to do. It's funny how things swim into your head at times like these. I started to hum: *Everybody hurts...* Not a cheerful choice I know but the first time I heard it on Luke's i-pod it really touched me. It just seemed a better alternative to doggy songs like: *I love my dog as much as I love you...* or: *You aint nothing but a hound dog...* or even worse, *Shoot the dog.*

I sang softly. Lucky didn't respond. I guess he thought: Shut the fuck up and let me die in peace. So I stayed with him for an hour willing him to breathe. Occasionally his back legs twitched. Maybe he was heading for the Elysium Fields on doggy Olympus? At least he wouldn't die alone.

You're on your own again...

'Are you Okay?' a familiar voice asked. Ben stood in the doorway smiling. 'Good choice of song.'

I felt like a total prat and blushed to the roots.

'I'm sure he heard you even if he didn't understand the words. The sentiment's good.'

'Oh. God. Is that the time?' I said, trying to cover my embarrassment. 'I must fly, things to do. Thanks for taking care of him…I'd like you to accept this as a token of my appreciation.' Shit. I sound so formal and anal.

Ben looked at the cheque for £500 made out to the hospital. 'I guess you sold a painting then?'

'Yes,' I lied. 'I hope it helps towards his upkeep. I'll try to call in tomorrow to check on him. If there's any change will you call me on my mobile immediately please?' Or just call me. I'm available. I do scrub up well - and your thighs fill out your trousers so beautifully.

'Sure. It's a generous amount. Can you afford it?'

'Oh. God. Yes,' I lied again.

'That's okay then. Now go enjoy the rest of your birthday.'

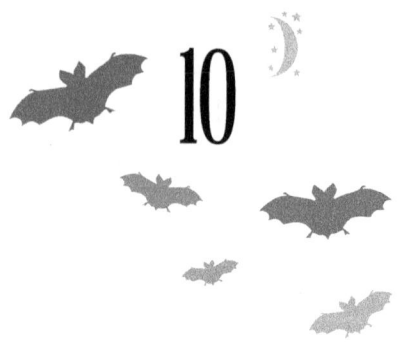

When I finally got back to the flat Mrs. Jenkins's door was open but she didn't come out to greet me.

Shall I or shan't I? If I make a dash for it she's bound to notice and think it's a spy or something. Who knows? She might have a bayonet in there. No. Better check up on her. I don't want to make her any more confused than she already is.

I knocked on her door and pushed it open. The curtains were closed and I could smell *Flash* with lemon so I knew Rosie the Home Help had been. Horatio meowed loud and long. He'd not been fed - and Gracie Fields wasn't getting much luck as she waved me goodbye. Instead she was receiving a good old scratching on the gramophone, so I lifted the needle-arm and put it back on the rest.

'Mrs. Jenkins? Where are you? I've got you

some crème caramels and chicken stew with dumplings…Your favourite food after sausages – and some delicious *Battenberg*. Yummy. (Yuk). Its real fish for you to chew Horatio… We can have a nice chat over a cup of tea and cake,' I called out.

There was no response. I had approximately two hours in which to get dressed then drive us all to *Chez Trevayne* and trim up the place with party streamers. Her glorious fire had died down to flickering embers, so I went to stoke it up and add some more fuel from the polished brass coal-scuttle. As the flames sparked into life from the sprinklings of coal dust I saw her outline in the shadows. She sat unmoving in Arnold's chair with her head hanging to one side.

Oh. God. Not again. Don't let her be dead. Not on my birthday. What if I have to spend another night in hospital? Oh. Bugger. 'Mrs. Jenkins,' I said shaking her gently. 'Are you alive?'

'Barely Katie…barely,' she whispered.

'What's wrong? Has something upset you?'

'Not something Katie. Someone! It's that new

Air Raid Warden, Joyce. She said I wasn't capable of living on my own and she was going to get the Gestapo round. She said that I needed psychiatric help and they would have to do some tests on me. Well I won't crack under torture...I told her that there's nothing wrong my cognitive functions. She didn't even know what the words meant. Oh. Katie I can't bear it. What if my Arnold comes home and I'm not here?' she sobbed.

'It's going to be alright Mrs. Jenkins. Now don't you be fretting. Hang on a minute. I'll think of something,' I said, mentally kicking myself for doing a Michael Caine.

There's no way I was going to let them put her in an Old Folks Home. It would finish her off. One of those awful places that smelled of fish and cabbage and rancid fat. It makes me really mad when I see footage of Aged P's lolling around in chairs and looking blank. How can kids abandon their parents in strange places to die alone? Old people should be treasured and honoured, not given a short life sentence of ignominy and isolation. More respect is needed for our Long Ears. We should give them dignity in their winter of discontent. If I had my way all the profits from Lotto money would be used to make pensioners and carers' lives easier. You see, I would give anything to have fond memories of grandparents.

'Have you eaten Mrs. Jenkins?' I asked feeling angry at the new Air Raid Warden's insensitivity. I mean Home Help. I'm starting to believe the year is 1943. If only I could meet Captain Jack, or not I think. Sean would be more his cup of tea…I can't help fancying John Barrowman though. He's so macho…Like Tom Cruise's elder brother without the Scientology bit and much longer legs… I am over-tired and hyper.

'No. I've not had my sausages because she said that she wasn't paid to cook, or do windows. Rosie always does my windows…'

I opened the curtains, fed Horatio and cooked Mrs. Jenkins sausage and mash which was hers, Arnold's and Horatio's favourite meal. As she ate, I sprayed the windows and gave them a quick polish. This task was extremely important to her because otherwise she wouldn't be able to see Arnold coming down the road.

What the hell am I going to do now? If they memory test her she'll fail miserably.

Then I hit on a plan.

'Leave it with me Mrs. Jenkins. I'm going to arrange for you and me to perform a secret mission for King and Country, alright?'

'Oh. Katie. That sounds just up my street. When can we start?'

'It will begin tonight Mrs. Jenkins. I'm taking you to a party to celebrate the end of the War.'

'Oh. Katie dear, there's no need to fib just to make me feel better. I can face the truth.'

Shit. Plan B. If she won't move forwards then maybe, she'll move sideways.

'Its part of the secret mission you see. We have to convince the Gestapo that we think the War is over. We don't really believe that of course, but it will confuse the enemy. They call it:

"delaying tactics". Got that?' No way is she going to understand a word of what I'm saying.

'I know exactly what you mean Frieda,' she said, touching her nose.

'Good thinking Ingrid,' I replied. 'The password is: Teresa May is Prime Minister of Great Britain. And my response will be: Donald Trump is President of the USA. Have you got that?'

'Yes indeedy,' she said.

We are on a roll as long a she doesn't ask me to take her for a spin around the room in the quick step. 'Now then, I must get ready for the celebration party,' I said winking.

'Teresa May is Prime Minister of Great Britain,' she said, opening her second crème caramel. 'Don't think the Hun will believe a woman is Prime Minister though.'

'It will confuse them all the more. Donald Trump is President of the USA. Now get yourself ready to party Ingrid.'

'What are you up to?' Sal asked, grinning down at me from the top of landing. She looked gorgeous in a fitted wine coloured velvet dress with a plunging neckline that had Joe's twinkling blue eyes popping.

'Don't ask,' I sighed, noticing the claret had disappeared and the night was drawing in.

'Come on lass, tha's only got half an hour to get thee sen ready,' Joe teased.

'Wont be long. Can you be loading the car up while I have a quick shower? Be careful with the cake and put the cartons of cream in the cool bag. Oh. And don't forget the balloon pump. I don't have enough steam left to blow orally.'

'Dirty bitch,' Sal chuckled.

As I stood under the shower and let the hot water warm my body, I started to remember how Sal and Joe's lives were ripped apart. And it had been entirely my fault…It was the day after Sal and I had reached an understanding. She wouldn't beat me and I wouldn't pull out her hair. Joe had agreed to break into Mrs. Hudson's office with me. There wasn't a lock he couldn't pick, or a safe he couldn't crack.

We waited for Mrs. Hudson to turn out the lights at 9.0. p.m.

'Goodnight children. May God keep you safe,' she said flatly, closing the girls' dorm door.

'Goodnight,' whispered Joe from under Sal's bed. 'And it'll be me not God opening your safe.'

We all giggled. Sal decided to stay as look-out in case The Mummy came back to check on us. More often than not she always did. On the off chance we shoved our pillows under the duvets and shaped them like bodies.

'Now listen up Kat, no noise, just follow me. Okay?'

'Okay.'

We sneaked down the corridor in the dark until we reached Mrs. Hudson's office.

'Hold the torch steady. I need to see the lock.' Joe slid a knife down the join and released the Yale. 'That's the easy bit, now for the filing cabinet. Put the desk light on for me.' He jiggled a bit of wire around in the lock and the cabinet released its secrets. 'Hurry up Kat. I hope it's still under

S,' he said, rifling through the files. 'Ah. Here it is. Be quick now and read it. If we get caught we're done for, unless you fancy wearing a leg bracelet? It'll be Borstal Remand Home for us on a diet of bread and water,' he grinned. Although that Secure Centre over in the valley makes this dump look like The Ritz…Hang on? Pervy Pete and Miserable Moo's file is missing…I'm going to have a nosy in the safe so don't make too much noise just in case she changed the code.'

By this time I was too engrossed in my file contents to hear anything else. I was trembling so much I could hardly turn the pages. Actually, there wasn't that much to begin with: a yearly report on my progress, the names and addresses of previous foster parents with comments like: "A sullen child. Not easy to get on with but hardworking and reliable. Kathryn lacks the personality and temperament for long term fostering". In fact nothing I didn't already know.

It wasn't until I got to the bottom of the binder that I found anything worth noting. There was a

Birth Certificate: Kathryn Shaw. Date of Birth. Mother: Davinia Katarina Shaw and Father: Martin David Shaw both of 111 Francis Street, Newquay, Cornwall. I couldn't take it all in. I had actually found out who my parents were and that I was born in Cornwall and not Cardiff as I'd always been led to believe.

There was a brief mention of my Mother having a nervous breakdown and taking an overdose after my Father's disappearance. Some old newspaper clippings folded up. My head began to spin at this stage. I felt sick and nearly put back the file. Did I really want to find out my parents were no-good losers? It was all too much to digest in one go, but I couldn't stop. Not knowing was much worse. The adrenalin was pumping hard. It was all or nothing. As I quickly made notes Joe suddenly gasped: 'The bastards!'

'What is it?' I whispered.

'I found the file on the Taylors,' he said looking angry.

'Let me see.'

'No Kat. Let sleeping dog's lie.'

'If you lie down with dogs you get fleas. Now give me the file Joe.'

'We've not got much time. She might come down at any minute. You know what's she's like for patrolling the corridors.'

'Quick switch on the photocopier,' I urged. 'Copy the lot.'

Joe and I copied every page of the Taylors' file. Then I did mine. There was something about Godparents, but I would have to read it all later. I kept the original Birth and Christening Certificates and put the photocopies back in the same place.

As we put everything back where we'd found it, I had an overwhelming urge to smash something. She had known all the time that some of my relatives were alive. Who had given The Mummy the right to play God with my future?

Joe must have read my mind because he said: 'Not now Kat. We'll think on what we're going to do later. We need to get out of here now.' He returned the contents and cash box to the safe and locked it. Neither of us were thieves. We just wanted what was rightly ours.

'Shush,' I said, hearing a noise.

'We're done for,' Joe said, as the sound of The Mummy's heavy stiff-kneed footsteps thudded on the metal stairs. 'Run for your life Kat.'

We both made a dash for the door. I hesitated owing to loose footwear and tripped up. I cursed and slipped off the battered trainers, putting them on top of my photocopies.

'Come on Kat. She's nearly at the bottom of the stairs,' Joe said in panic.

'Coming,' I panted.

He clicked the door closed and we ran hell for leather back to the dorms. 'Here Kat keep this safe with the other stuff,' he said breathlessly, handing me the Taylors' copy file. 'Now get your head down.' As an afterthought he mouthed quietly from the door of the boys sleeping quarters: 'Tell Sal I love her.'

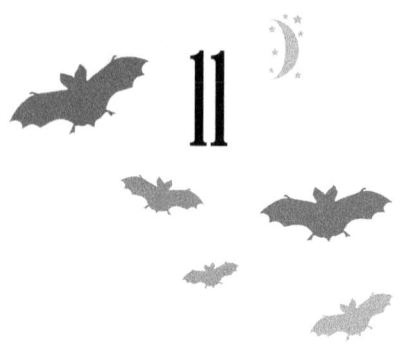

11

I finally emerged from the bathroom room looking half-decent. I had given up on the idea of hair that moved. Instead I let my curls dry naturally after a thoroughly Alex-type conditioning. My new luminous pearls make-up and blusher concealed a multitude of dark shadows and a covering of pink lip gloss gave my face warmth. The dress fitted well and the tight black belt made me look a little curvier.

I wish I had bigger tits.

'You looked gorgeous hon,' Sal said. 'Doesn't she Joe?'

Joe grinned and I waited for the insult: 'Like a million dollars – all green and crinkly.'

'Thanks a bunch matey. You look good too - for a twelve year old dog.'

'Seriously Kat you look like jam on bread,' he added.

Sal beamed with such happiness I thought she was going to burst, although, hopefully, not yet awhile.

As we chatted excitedly on our way down the stairs I heard Edward's floor-boards creak.

He must be getting ready for a night on the tiles, literally, and probably honing his fangs on the carving knife-sharper.

'Do you think Mrs. Jenkins will be up to partying?' Sal asked, breaking my Transylvanian train of thought. 'She must be in her nineties.'

'I need to keep an eye on her,' I said, 'and a change of scene will do her good…I can always bring her home when she's had enough. Anyway Mrs. Jones, you won't be drinking and boogying in your condition. Will you?'

'No to drinking and yes to boogying. I'll be driving us all home if you get near the champagne young lady.'

Mrs. Jenkins stood outside her door looking

nervous. She had on a pink silk dress in the thirties style and draped around her neck was a black furry dead thing with its head threaded through its tied feet. She had powdered her downy soft skin and added a touch of red lipstick, making her look a little like a Geisha. Before I could say anything she took a tiny blue bottle out of her bag and dabbed on some *Evening in Paris* perfume. It smelled really nice considering it had been around for some seventy odd years.

'Hello Mrs. Jenkins. You look lovely. Are you ready?'

'Yes Frieda. Teresa May is Prime Minster of Great Britain.'

'Spot on Ingrid. Donald Trump is President of the USA.'

'You two there, say the passwords,' Mrs. Jenkins said pointing a bendy finger at them.

'England won the World Cup in 1966,' Joe said with a huge grin. 'And you look lovely Ingrid.'

'Thank you Ilmhart. You put me in mind of my Arnold…Now you young lady.'

'Mick Jagger is the lead singer of *The Rolling Stones,*' Sal said chuckling.

'It's not a laughing matter Gurda. We are at war you know.'

'I know that and I'm very sorry Ingrid. I will take my job as a spy more serious.'

'Well, all's right with the world for now,' I said, putting my new black coat over Mrs. Jenkins shoulders. 'Let's move onward and upwards into the night dear friends.'

As luck would have it, Sean was on his way down the steps to the basement flat. At last he saw me smartly dressed and wearing makeup.

'My. My. Look at you Katie. Going somewhere special?'

'Yes. It's my birthday and we're all going out to dinner at *Chez Trevayne*... You'd be more than welcome,' I said, looking around for the Snow Queen. 'You already know Mrs. Jenkins. These are my friends Sal and Joe.'

Sean bounded up the stairs and shook hands. He was just perfect in every way. He carried a sports bag, so I guessed he'd been to the gym. His arms were pumped and the veins on the back of his hands were swollen.

How can any guy look so beautiful in a track suit bottom and a sweaty vest? Slow down my beating heart.

It had taken me at least ten minutes to put on mascara and there he was with kohl black curly lashes to die for. A full mouth made for kissing and high cheek bones above which his deep set eyes burned into me.

He was just about to accept my invite to my party when the Snow Queen called out: 'Do hurry Sean honey, your pizza's getting cold.'

'Sorry. I'll have to go,' he apologized. 'You look great Katie. Enjoy your birthday.'

Then in a slow motion shot the Snow Queen ascended the steps - and looked absolutely sweat free and swishing pony-tailed, in a shocking pink and black leotard so high cut you could see her waist. 'Oh. It's only you,' she said. Botoxed brows unmoving, she looked me up and down. 'Come on honey I need you.'

'Bye then Katie, Mrs. Jenkins. Nice to meet you Sal, Joe,' Sean said, following her like a little lamb.

'There's rude, look you,' Sal said, loudly and laying on the Welsh accent with a trowel. 'She looks in need of a good meal. She does.'

On our way to the bistro I briefed Mrs. Jenkins with various codes.

'Now Ingrid, the Gestapo will ask you various questions. You're only obliged to answer truthfully about your age and date of birth.'

'I'm 17 years old and I was born on 29th September, 1926,' she said, proudly.

'On second thoughts,' I said, turning down the King's Road, 'you should only give your date of birth. Alright?'

'Got that Frieda. We have to confuse The Hun. Right?'

'Correct,' I said. Sal and Joe giggled in the back seat. 'Shush you two... Now, whatever you do, don't say Winston Churchill. It must always be Teresa May is Prime Minister. We don't want to give the game away.'

'Donald Trump is President of the USA,' she said without hesitation. 'They can have the Yank Roosevelt for target practise as long as our Winston's safe.'

'When they ask you: who's your favourite actor you must say George Clooney.'

'Can't I say Caesar Romerro?'

'No. Because he's a spy for Hollywood and you might put his life in danger.'

'Oh. I suppose Greer Garson is off limits as well?'

I frowned and shook my head: 'A double agent. Try Kate Winslet instead.'

'Is she any good?'

'A true English Rose with a rare patriotic talent,' I told her.

'That's all right then.'

'Now Ingrid when they ask you about topical events you must not mention the war. Just say you're a *Chelsea* football fan.'

'Support *Chelsea*. Never. My Arnold supports *Millwall*. Up The Lions.'

Sal and Joe burst out laughing. 'Will you act in a responsible way you two? This is a deadly serious matter,' Mrs. Jenkins said angrily.

'Too true Ingrid. Ilmhart and Gurda, if I hear another peep out of you two I shall have to strip you of all rank. Understood?'

'Understood Frieda. Over and out.'

'Can I have a rest now Katie, my head's spinning with all this new information? I hope you're not going to do Binary Codes,' Mrs. Jenkins sighed.

I was really worried about her future. I only hoped she would remember this information in the morning. And as for me using Binary Codes, I think not.

12

Talk about luck. I actually found a parking space right outside the bistro. At least I think it was the bistro. It had the correct number on the door. The frontage had been painted black, covering the garish cerise colour chosen by Wayne. (Not all Gays have good taste in décor). And outside in place of a blackboard with the menu chalked on, were two standard laurel bushes in terracotta containers, along with two brass coach lamps either side of the door and one of those sealed menu holders, stating: "Closed 1ˢᵗ November for a Private Party".

In contrast the windows were covered in a pastiche of devils with horns and witches on broomsticks. Above a scattering of fairy lights flickered innocently across the hoarding.

'Someone has beaten us to it Kat,' Sal said,

peering inside the bistro. 'It looks as if we're in for a Hawaiian evening of hula and coconut cocktails combined with a Halloween Trick or Treat mini *Mars* bars.'

'I can't understand it. Surely Trevor and Wayne wouldn't go to all this expense?' I said, looking up at the lights.

I helped Mrs. Jenkins out of the car, as Sal and Joe unloaded the boxes.

'Surprise. Surprise,' Maggie called out as I opened the door. She wore a head band with red horns on it. 'You certainly know how to keep a secret. Everything looks great even though it's a bit over the top. It must have cost you a bomb. Happy Birthday Kat...I'll warn you now that Wayne has gone off on one, because he wanted to do the decorating. He's sulking in the kitchen.'

'Thanks Maggie. And thanks guys for the vouchers...I can't smell pasta sauce and garlic. Oh. No. Don't tell me he's refusing to cook?'

'It's all been taken care of,' Trevor sniffed.

'You could have let us know you were using outside caterers. Wayne is very hurt.'

'I-I haven't got a clue what you're talking about Trevor. By the way you look very handsome in your new white dinner jacket,' I said, kissing him on the cheek.

'Do I? Thanks love. I'm glad someone appreciates my efforts,' he said loud enough for Wayne to hear. A crash came from the kitchen as something heavy was thrown onto the floor. 'It's the monkey boy again,' Trevor sighed. 'I'd best go and humour him or we'll have this all night.'

I tried and failed to take off the dead thing around Mrs. Jenkins's neck. So I sat her at a garlanded table with a straw covered parasol slotted in the centre. It was right next the beach, so she had a nice view. Some idiot had actually brought in sand and decorated it with shells. Wayne, no doubt, must have had a ducky fit. I ask you – sand indoors?

'Katie. This looks like Bournemouth. Are we

at the seaside?' Mrs. Jenkins asked, putting on an eye-covering frilly mask.

'No. We're having a Hawaiian come Halloween night for my birthday. Do you remember? It's my twenty fifth.'

Sipping through a straw on a *Blue Lagoon* cocktail she sighed: 'I know that... and it's the end of the war too,' she added winking at me through the eye-socket. I only hoped she wasn't on any medication.

'Where shall we put these?' Joe asked, carrying the boxes.

'Through there,' I pointed, 'along past the Avenue of Candlelit Pumpkins then turn right at Seaweed Corner into the kitchen. Try and cheer up old Mardy Bum will you. Pretend you're gay or something,' I told him.

Sal laughed and followed Joe into the kitchen, giggling at his mincing walk.

Now, Paulo the head waiter, or Paul from Peckham, pretends to be Italian like the food he loves and serves up. He knows three Italian words: ciao bambina and ciao bambino. He also has a huge crush on petite Maggie. She's married to Jason the wife-beater. Paulo thinks that one day she'll notice him and leave Jason. Exotic Lucy fancies Paulo but she knows he's besotted with Maggie. Lucy is adopted but has recently found out that her real mother was a Hottentot and her father a Swedish explorer. Just another normal evening in the bistro, unless Jason the Barbarian arrives drunk as a skunk and then Wayne has massive strop thinking Trevor fancies a bit of rough, while we all hide with Maggie in the kitchen.

'So ciao bambina,' Paulo said, kissing me on both cheeks. 'And a very happya birthday to you…. What isa happening tonight? It isa all very strange.'

Winter berry scented candles flickered on the white table cloths, lighting up the small dining area. Folded red napkins stood like sailing ships amid expensive cutlery set out for a three course meal. Over in the far corner was a disco-deck shaped like an upturned boat, draped with plastic starfish speared with red tridents. Hanging above it was a swinging cage with a real, squawky parrot inside. In front of the parrot three cauldrons filled with sweets dangled precariously just above head level and around a huge fishing net filled with red and black balloons.

Now it's *Pirates of the Caribbean*. Please let Jonny Depp be my main present.

Someone had made a mini-ocean behind the beach in a turquoise pond-liner filled with plastic fish in bubbling water. Instead of the constipated jazz music, sounds of the sea filled the air. And in the distance a Humpback whale called out a tuba-lament. For the first time in years I was lost for words.

'Maggie do you have any idea who's responsible for all this?' I asked, wanting to laugh.

'Well, according to Trevor, three Polish painters arrived first thing and painted the outside. Then they did the murals on the windows, saying they would clean everything off tomorrow. Later a team of six women pulled up in a white van with *PARTY POPPETS* written on the side.

They set it all this up in no time. They were all very glamorous but a bit odd and spoke in funny accents. Trevor also said that they were dressed in black cat suits and thigh length plastic kinky boots. Don't ask me why they had on big black sunglasses in November. I ask you? Sounded like something from a Cher concert or *Cat Woman*, in the sexy gear.'

'The ladies wore long black wigs as well,' Trevor added, coming out of the kitchen. 'They were foreign like. Very Goth…Not French, at least I don't think so; maybe Romanian or Russian origins? Anyhow, they said that they were working on behalf of Kathryn Shaw, and that it was all paid for. Any ideas Kat?'

'Haven't an iota. Did they say what kind of food would be served?' I hope it's not scampi in a basket.

'The menus are on each table,' Trevor said, picking up a white card edged in red amaryllis. 'For starters there's goat's cheese wrapped in smoked salmon with shaved truffles served on a bed of watercress and drizzled with a dill dressing. The main meal is roast Welsh lamb with mint sauce, Yorkshire pudding and seasonal vegetables. For dessert is raspberry coulee and crème fresh. And very nice too,' he whispered so Wayne wouldn't hear him.

'What time are they bringing the food?' I asked, totally confused.

'They said about 8.30 p.m.'

After Trevor promised Wayne a romantic weekend shopping trip to Milan he emerged red-eyed and shiny-faced from the kitchen at 8.15p.m. He looked immaculate in a black dinner jacket and red bow tie, with a matching cummerbund covering his pot belly. Trevor was the more macho and taller of the two. Wayne was definitely in charge, even though Trevor believed he was the boss. They were both balding with a tonsure of blonde curls and startling ice blue eyes that must have come from the same gene pool.

Their romance had blossomed during a Speed-Dating session. Both of them were divorced with kids. Seated next to each other during their three minute rounds of embarrassing silences, and finding none of the women sane, solvent, single or attractive enough, realized all along that they were gay and meant for each other.

'I'm so sorry Wayne. Honestly I knew nothing about all this,' I said, hugging him. Wayne's potent aftershave drowned out the scented candles and caused me to gasp. 'You know how much I love your lasagne…Come on show me how you can open a bottle of champagne without causing a wipe out.'

Trevor looked relieved and quickly opened a case of *Krugg* pink champagne, lining up the bottles on the bar. Someone knew it was my favourite tipple. A smiling Wayne obliged with his usual comment: 'It should sound like a duchess's fart,' he said with restored confidence.

He hated any changes to his routine. Lucy immediately put the glasses on a tray and began waiting on tables.

'No Lucy. You're a guest. I'll do that,' I said,

taking the tray from her. 'Now sit down next to Paulo and Maggie and enjoy yourself.'

Penny and James, with a sleeping baby Rosa in a car seat, arrived bearing gifts, followed by Rachel and Rob who were only fifteen minutes late.

'Don't tell me you designed all this?' Rachel said with her usual candour, gulping down a glassful of fizz.

'Not guilty. It's a surprise. I'm guessing Sophie and Zach had something to do with it. This has their humour stamped all over it.'

Trevor stood near the disco-boat and tapped his glass with a spoon: 'Ladies and gentlemen before the food arrives I'd like to propose a toast to our young Kat. And I must say I've never seen her looking so smart. Ha. Ha. So please be upstanding and raise your glasses with me to say -.'

'FUCK OFF BITCH!' the parrot suddenly vocalized. 'YOU'RE A WORTHLESS PIECE OF SHIT.'

After a moments awkward silence, during

which Penny covered Rosa's ears, everyone burst out laughing. I had just taken a mouthful of frothing bubbles and sprayed my drink all over sunset beach.

'HAPPY BIRTHDAY BITCH!' Rachel shouted.

'AND UP YOURS TOO RACH!' I responded, choking with laughter.

Rob dragged Rachel away into a corner and started to lecture her. He was such a control freak. She would never be a goody two-shoes no matter how hard he tried to make her demure. It's so bloody hard when your best friend's going to marry a frog. The two of us used to have such a laugh before she got serious with Face-ache.

After two glasses of champagne we were all feeling more relaxed and ready to party. Sal looked glum with a glass of sparkling water, until Joe started to whisper dirty nothings into her ear.

'When's the real music going to start?' she asked, as the Humpbacks resounded out a mournful mating call from depths.

'Right now gorgeous,' a look-alike Elvis drawled, appearing from nowhere, dressed in the white fat-suit from Las Vegas days and wearing the world's worst wig. He sank down onto one knee and did the pumping gesture, then struggled to get to his feet until Trevor gave him a hand. 'Who wants to hear the King?' he wheezed.

'ME!' we all shouted.

'Is it King George?' Mrs. Jenkins said, standing to attention and raising her glass.

'Yes. Only the king's disguised his voice to confuse the enemy,' I whispered, giving her a knowing look.

Raack/ A Raackahula…

'I didn't know his majesty could sing. It's got a good rhythm even though I don't understand the words,' Mrs. Jenkins called out above the noise. 'But he's not a patch on Bing Crosby for all his blue blood. When's the food coming? I'm starving.'

13

It was the morning after Joe and I had raided Mrs. Hudson's office, that I found out Sal was missing. Her bed stood empty and cold. I ran down the corridor in my pyjamas to the boys' dorm and knocked on the door.

'Wake up Joe,' I shouted. 'I think Sal's done a runner!'

After a few loud expletives from the boys, Joe opened the door, rubbing his eyes: 'What did you say? She can't have. She would never leave without telling me first. You know that. Don't you?'

It was at that particular spot in time, I felt some satisfaction. At last my tormentor had gone. Inwardly I sighed with relief. And good riddance too, I thought, until I saw the desperation in Joe's face. Then the guilt set in.

'I'm going to find her,' he said, pushing his few belongings into a carrier bag.

'Hang on a minute. She might have gone down early for breakfast. You know how she likes her food,' I said, trying to humour him. I really didn't want Joe to leave. He was my best mate.

'Do you think so?'

'I know so,' I said, crossing my fingers behind my back. 'Now get dressed and we'll meet in the canteen. I really need you to act as lookout later tonight while I take a proper look at those copy files.'

I returned to the dorm and checked out Sal's beside table. The photo of her two brothers had gone and her magazines with it. Her locker had also been cleared. My stomach turned over and I knew at that moment something was seriously wrong.

What if she's really done a bunk? Joe would be gutted. Best get dressed and find out what's what.

Of course, it was then that I realized I was minus a trainer.

Oh. Shit.

I searched everywhere in the dorm. Even the other girls helped me. They all hated Mrs. Hudson and had incurred her silent punishments at one time or other. I knew most of them would stay loyal and wouldn't break under questioning.

'Did any of you hear Sal leave this morning?' I asked.

'God! Kat! Look at your eye,' Andrea Moore shrieked. 'It looks like you've gone ten round with Tyson.'

'It's nothing,' I said, feeling at the puffiness.

'I heard The Mummy creak in sometime after you'd got back,' Andrea told me. 'She went over to Sal's bed, but I fell asleep after that…You don't think she's made Sal move out?'

'I don't know what to think.'

'It's here Kat, under Sal's bed. Phew. You lucky bitch,' said Julie Rodgers, handing me the missing trainer. 'A close call or what?'

'Thanks Jules. You've saved my life,' I said. 'Can you look after these for me, in case The

Mummy does a search? She'll never suspect you,' I added, handing over the precious photocopies.

'Okay. You owe me one,' Julie said, putting them in her school bag.

As I pulled on the left trainer I noticed it was slightly less worn than the one on my right foot and the laces were cleaner. What's going on? If this is Sal's trainer then where's my old one?

Oh. No. It can't be.

After breakfast, minus Sal, we were all called to the main hall. Mrs. Hudson walked stiffly up the steps leading to the stage, embalmer's bandages trailing, coughed and cleared her throat, then announced in her usual flat nasal voice: 'Something wicked happened last night children and if any of you have information pertaining to this instance of vandalism to government property, then I sincerely request you step forward now. Otherwise all of you will be severely punished.'

Joe and I glanced at each other and then

looked straight forward. Nobody moved or spoke a word.

'Well children? Does anybody want to own up to the truth? No? Then I'll take your silence as a sign of guilt. There will be no further outings for 3 months. Not a single one of you will leave this building after evening meals until further notice, unless it's for emergencies.'

There was a unanimous groan throughout the hall.

'Is that understood?' she said without emotion.

'Yes. Mrs. Hudson,' we all agreed.

'Kathryn Shaw and Joseph Jones, my office, now! The rest of you - dismissed.'

I guess I'd always underestimated Mrs. Hudson's intelligence. Had I been aware that she was cannier than I'd given her credit for, I would have spoken up sooner. Joe felt the same. So we remained silent. And in our silence poor Sal took all the blame.

'As you are both aware, my office was broken into last night. Private documents were tampered with, which as you know is a heinous crime in this establishment. There are laws protecting the rights of the children brought into my care. And those rights have been infringed. Now what do you have to say?'

'What does *infringed* mean Mrs. Hudson?' I asked, grinning.

'You know full well what it means Kathryn… Joseph? What about you? Do you have anything to say?'

'No, Mrs. Hudson.'

She inhaled deeply then said: 'Very well both of you may leave my office.'

'Is that all?' I asked, expecting an inquisition.

'That's all Kathryn,' she replied coldly.

Joe and I sat for a while on the Smoker's Bench in the Cloisters Garden, hoping to see Sal pass by. Most of the kids had walked through to catch the School Buses. Tracey Blackburn and Gale Hughes, as always, were last on the school run.

'Better get a move on. You'll be late…I suppose you already know that Sal's being moved to the Remand Centre today?' Tracey smirked, looking at my purple eye.

'What?' Joe asked. 'Are you sure?'

'Positive. We've just seen her leaving with Mrs. Hudson. You see Mrs. Hudson knew all along it was her that broke into the office. Ha. Ha. Lucky for you two…Can't say I've any sympathy for Sal - The Great I Am.'

'Shut it!' I said, 'She's worth ten of you. You creep.'

'Please yourselves,' Tracey said, sniggering. 'Bye Joe. If you're lonely tonight you know where to find me.'

'Yes,' I shouted: 'Up the pig's arse on the second shelf. Now bugger off Snitch.'

Joe made a move to return to the dorms, but I held him back.

'Look. If I go to Mrs. Hudson's office after school and confess, then Sal will be off the hook…It's a mix-up you see Joe. Last night when I tripped and you helped me up? Do you remember? I must have dropped a trainer in The

Mummy's office. It had Sal's name tag inside. Do you see what I mean?'

The tension eased from Joe's face: 'I can't let you take all the blame. I'll come with you. The Mummy likes us. At least I think she does, so maybe we won't get sent to the Remand Home? Sal's had one warning too many, but I'm sure when Mrs. Hudson finds out the truth she'll let her come back here. Won't she?'

'Yes I think so,' I agreed, 'there's no reason why not. Now come or we'll be in bigger trouble if we miss the bus.'

That same evening, after dinner, Joe and I went to put matters right with Mrs. Hudson. She listened patiently without saying a word. We said that we wanted to look at our files, but she had disturbed us before we could open the cabinet. I also explained about the trainers and showed her my mismatched pair. Again she didn't speak. I think she hoped we would tie ourselves in knots, but Joe and I knew what was at stake. By any means we had to get Sal back, otherwise that Godforsaken place the other side of the valley would finish her off. She would look like a pussycat compared to the kids there. The Mummy finally spoke: 'Very convincing you two. Am I supposed to believe all that clap-trap?'

'But it's the truth. I swear it,' I pleaded.

'I can understand Joseph wanting her back, but you Kathryn, of all people, after what she's done.' She shook her head in disbelief. 'Now both of you I want you to listen carefully. Sally Hooley has been trouble from the start. She's a bad influence on the younger more impressionable children. I've always done my best for her, but I fear she needs more discipline than I can offer. And what's more she confessed her guilt to me… So, there it is. No more questions. Now get out and don't mention this matter again.'

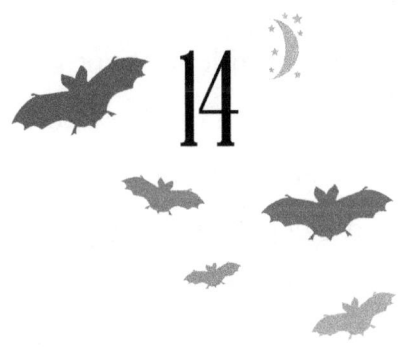

14

Arthritic Elvis shimmied around to his hero's plaintive cry: *Are* you *lonesome tonight*, all the while trying to hold onto his back-combed *syrup*. The festivity had drawn quite a few people to the locked bistro door, including Mick the Tramp. Business that night could have boomed, thus ensuring Elvis a regular booking and a better wig.

Always, at the end of my shift it was time for Maggie, or I, to sneak out a few leftovers and a take-away coffee for Mick, while Wayne busied himself in the kitchen. The wretched tramp lived his invisible life from minute to minute. The place where he rested his head was under a cardboard covering in various shop doorways. Mick's surprisingly well mannered for a tramp.

And always the gent unless Wayne got arsey with him, then the Anglo-Saxon flowed.

One particular night Mick had decided to go upmarket and sleep in the Vivien Westwood's shop doorway at *The World's End*. Unfortunately, some football hooligans were on their way back to the station after a disappointing result. Spotting the unfortunate tramp they decided to give him a shave. The tramp didn't even notice until a policeman woke him from his stupor. The gang had carved up the left side of his face with a Stanley knife. Now half of his face looked like a road map with a series of indented white lines, showing up all the more alongside his weathered tan.

It was lucky for Mick that the *PARTY POPPETS'* van, containing the food, arrived round the back, otherwise Wayne's radar would have tuned in by now. I told Mick to disappear for a short time otherwise he risked the meat cleaver. Two petulant Wayne strops in one night would put the mockers on any revels.

Before I could walk along the Arcade of flickering Black Gothic Candles, six waitresses came prancing through Pumpkin Avenue, each holding a silver platter. They were dressed in red ra-ra skirts and skimpy tops, lace tights and high heels, with devils horns on their heads. At first I thought that they were either clones, or fem-bots, owing to their jerky synchronized movements; rather like those strange women who point their toes and wear nose clips in swimming pools.

In unison they called out: 'Lawdeez awnd zawntawlmawn plawz taw baw zeeteenk dawn vaw zee vawrzt cawz.'

'Frieda?' Mrs. Jenkins pondered, as I sat next to her. 'Is this a bordello?'

'Yes,' I whispered. 'This is where the Nazi officers come to dine. So be prepared to gather information. They lower their guards after a glass of beer or two.' I am losing the plot. Never mind. Who cares? She's happier than I have ever seen her.

'Very well Frieda… Mick Jagger is lead singer of *The Rolling Stones,* whoever they are.'

'Good Ingrid…England won the World Cup in 1966 and up The Lions,' I replied. 'Now eat and enjoy.'

'What's the biddy on about?' Rachel asked, prodding the salmon parcel and grimacing.

'She's an expert on Binary Codes.'

'She doesn't look like a boffin,' she said, grinning.

'It's her night off…Now has everyone been served?' I asked, changing the subject. 'Hey. Elvis. Help yourself to food…Can you bring us a bit more up to date with the music?'

'Sure thing honey-lamb,' he drawled, putting on a Tony Christie record.

'AND FUCK YOU TOO BUM-BOY!' the parrot shrieked.

As we ate our delicious starters on the way to Amarillo, the non-smiling Cheeky Girls look-alikes entertained us with a coordinated tray-dance. Banging their booties with the metal platters, followed by a few high kicks, they ended up in the splits. James and Paulo were whistling and whooping in appreciation. Even Joe managed a silly grin. Rob stayed po-faced, causing Rachel and me to squeal with laughter. The whole thing was getting more and more bizarre. After my third tipple of champagne, I didn't really care as long as my friends were having a good time. From the looks on their faces and the excited conversations, I guess they were - except Reluctant Rob. Never in my wildest dreams though, could I have invented such wacky entertainment.

After a few more drinks Wayne's world lightened up. Trevor gave him his full attention. So Mick went unnoticed at the corner table wearing a gold sparkly eye-mask and tucking into roast lamb and Yorkshire pudding. He actually refused a glass of red. I knew how hard this was for him. At least he was making the effort. Despite his protestations to the contrary, the AA meetings Maggie had arranged for him must have finally worked.

Mrs. Jenkins stared in his direction.

'Frieda,' she whispered. 'That man over there with the terrible scars - is he English?'

She pointed at Mick. 'Through and through Ingrid,' I giggled.

'Are you sure he's not The Bosch?'

'Positive.'

'Keep my sticky toffee pudding safe. I'm going to investigate. I won't be long,' she said, weaving dizzily through the tables and waving her arms in time to: *My/My/My Delilah...* After swaying from side to side for a second, she regained her balance and sat down opposite Mick without saying a word.

I was just about to rescue her from some choice expletives when Mick stood up, bowed and took her hand in his. Before I could get to my feet Mick gently planted a kiss and smiled.

Wow. That's got to be a first.

I decided to leave them alone. Mick was safe when sober. So I continued my almost attentive conversation with Rachel, about her forthcoming house purchase with Rob. It's quite sad really how Rachel had changed into a boring soon-to-be married lady. She used to be so much fun as a singleton. When she progressed to fluctuating mortgage interest rates and their arguments over the colour of wedding invitations I asked *Elvis* to put on another record. The chatter got louder, along with songs from *Human League* and *Wham*. We were making some progress on the music front, as Penny, James and the still sleeping baby Rosa left early.

After their departure, I slipped out past The Beach, where Maggie precariously balanced at the top of the painters' steps talking in a slurred voice to the parrot. Helping herself to a handful of mini-*Mars* bars from the nearest cauldron and pushing them through the cage bars, she said: 'Now who'sh a pretty boy then.'

I had to smile. Paulo stood holding the steps steady, trying not to look up at Maggie's pants, while downcast Lucy moved from table to table clearing away the crumbs with the mini-vacuum tool. Happily gliding along the corridor, I put on my lovely new coat that smelled of *Evening in Paris* and went outside for a crafty fag. Everybody believed I had stopped smoking. And I had really. But it was my birthday.

The serious sextuplets loaded up the van in a fire-bucket kind of relay. I wondered, at the time, whether they had individual personalities. Then one spoke: 'Hawppee Bawzdaw Meez Kawtawreenaw. Eet awz bawn vawndawvawl varkeenk vawr yaw. I hawp yaw awr zawteezvawd veez zee zerweez? I veel naw breenk zee cark vaw yaw taw blaweenk awt cawdawls.'

'Before you do, can you tell me who you work for?'

'Zee PAWTEE PAWPPAWTZ awf cawz,' she said, almost smiling.

'I mean - who has paid for all this?' I'm sure she has pointed incisors. I have had one too many, an overactive imagination - and am very pissed.

'Eet vawz yawr Awnt Leawnawra pawd vaw awl zeez. I nawt awnderztawndeenk?'

Without another word she walked to the

van and took out a huge cake in the shape of a dolphin. I slowly counted out twenty five candles along its blue and silver body. Little green waves were iced around the border and it read: "Happy 25th Birthday Kathryn".

Mrs. Jenkins waited for me at the back door, spooning in the last of her sticky toffee pudding. Nothing had changed there except the evening was *Battenberg* free.

'Katie, it's about that man, Mick, I've got something to tell you, so listen carefully… It's him,' she said, eyes shining with tears. 'It's my Arnold. He's come back to work as a secret agent. Have you seen what Gerry did to him? They tortured him, but he wouldn't tell them anything…He managed to escape.'

'Mrs. Jenkins. Ingrid how do you know all this?'

'Why my Arnold told me of course. He would never lie to me.'

No he wouldn't, but Mick the Shit would. What a crafty old fox.

'Frieda are you absolutely sure it's him?'

'I know in my heart it is. He's changed terribly. The war has aged him beyond belief, but he is still my faithful Arnold. I asked him to come home, but he said that it was too dangerous. And that he didn't want me to be involved. I hope you don't mind Frieda, I told him that you and I were secret agents too.' She clutched her heart and sighed with happiness.

Bloody marvellous. One step forward two steps back. Now what do I say? 'All right Ingrid. Enjoy tonight with Arnold. I'm so happy for you both.' Somehow I've got to clean him up. God knows what lurks under those tatty clothes. She's bound to ask him to take her for a creaky waltz.

'Come on Kat it's time to blow out the candles,' Rachel drunkenly guffawed as she sat on the floor: 'Don't forget to make a wish.'

When I returned to the dining room Sal had lit the chocolate cake I'd bought from Waitrose, much to the annoyance of the chief fem-bot. I heard her say: 'Zawt eez nawt zee cark vaw zee blawang.'

'This is the cake for the wishing,' Sal insisted.

'I'll blow out both sets,' I said, wondering which way to go, then deciding on Sal's twenty five candles first, before the cake melted.

'Make a wish,' Sal said, smiling. She knew I didn't do stuff like that.

To my surprise a thought came into my head for Lucky to make a full recovery. It took three huge blows to put out the fire.

Then the chief fem-bot barged in a lit another twenty five candles: 'Pleez taw mark zee blaweenk naw.'

'Baw cawfawl vawt yaw veezh vaw,' another fem-bot whispered.

I looked around in surprise, but none of them had moved.

I am now three sheets to the wind and hearing things - unless it was all done by mirrors.

I finally blew out the second set of candles after five attempts, spraying the cake and feeling extremely dizzy. The heat was overwhelming.

I might as well have another go. I've got to

make a general wish. A specific one was bound to disappoint.

I wished for things to go right for me. That way if they didn't it would be nothing new.

Happy Birthday to You...

By now Trevor and Wayne were smooching to wonderful Whitney singing: *I will always Love You-oo-oo*. It was time to take Mick in hand. I couldn't have my top secret agent Ingrid getting up close and personal with a scratching scarecrow. I sneaked him to the flat upstairs and made him get undressed. I turned my back of course while he threw off his rags.

'Hurry up Mick. If Wayne finds out, we're done for. You'll be skewered and I'll be sacked. Don't forget to shave and wash your hair,' I added, rooting through Trevor's wardrobe...What size shoes are you?'

'Size 9.'

I put out a pair of Wayne's *Russell* & *Bromley* black loafers and socks and put the filthy cast-offs in a bin liner intended for the Charity Shop.

'And don't get carried away with Mrs. Jenkins. It's only for tonight. And she's very old. Got that?'

'Are you referring to Iris, my lady wife?' he asked from behind the shower curtain.

'You've gone far enough Mick! Stop right there… I've put you some clothes out on the bed. There's a white shirt, *Calvin Klein* boxers, some black slacks and a black jacket. No more joking around – and don't forget underarm deodorant.' Trevor will never notice they've gone. He's got so many clothes in black and white.'

'Frieda will you please refer to me by my secret agent's name of Wolfgang, otherwise I will have to report you to M.'

'Wolfgang if you don't speed up your bony old arse I shoot you with my Q gadget lipstick.' What have I got myself into here?

When Mick finally appeared shining and fresh he looked amazing in decent clothes. His faced glowed from scrubbing. He actually resembled a human being and a very dashing one at that.

The scars made him look distinguished rather than scary.

'I feel like a new man,' he said.

'Come on we've got to get a move on or Wayne will make you feel like a dead man.'

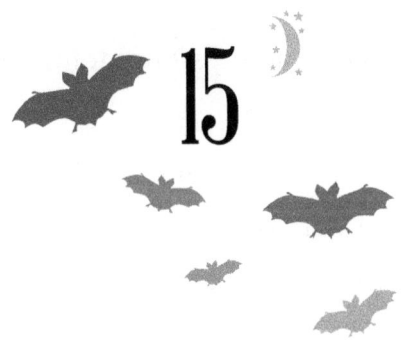

Mick and I sneaked back down the stairs in time to see everyone boogying to: *Hey/Yowwa/Gittoffa my cloud*. Elvis gyrated around until his right knee-cap slipped. He sweated heavily and groaned in pain, as Mick took him by the ankle and clicked it back into place.

'How did you do that?' I asked in amazement.

'Army training my *Fluttering Forsythia*,' Mick said before heading for Mrs. Jenkins.

In my absence Rob had stormed off and left Rachel sitting on the floor singing along to the pounding music.

'Kat can you take me to the toilet, I think I want to be sick?' she said looking a lighter shade of pale.

'Come on Rach. Let's be having you. How

many times have I told you not to mix the grape and the grain?'

'It's Rob's fault. He made me drink a beer.'

'Oh. Yes. I bet. You little liar.'

'I really, really do love you Kat. You do know that don't you?'

I nodded.

'When I first set eyes on you at college I thought you were a right geek, but after I got to know you better, I changed my mind,' she said, staggering around the pumpkins.

Thanks a bunch pal.

'Sometimes, I can't stand Rob. I think I love him… but I don't like him…Do you know what I mean?'

'Yes. Now come on let's get you sorted,' I said, steering her towards the loo. I held her hair back as she threw up. 'That's right. Better out than in girl,' I said, feeling sick myself.

'I've finished now,' she said smiling then threw up again. 'Can I stop at you place tonight please? The bastard's driven off without me,' she groaned.

'That's all right Rach. I'll sleep on the sofa.' Happy bloody Birthday to me.

We headed back to the dining room and I sat her down with a large glass of *Evian*. I noticed that strange girls were still prancing around like a line of cut out dollies. All the tables had been cleared and set back around the edges of the room to make a dance floor. I was just about to join Sal and Joe for a fling the arms about and do a shuffle on the spot dance, dodging in between Ingrid and Wolfgang shuffling along to a slow waltz, when I saw dreamy Sean beckoning to me through the front door window.

It's a mirage…I'm hallucinating after too much alcohol.

I blinked my eyes and looked again and he was still there, mouthing 'Katie. Let me in.'

Thank you, Wishing Fairy.

I opened the door and tried not to look too excited.

Oh. Joy. He's dressed in smart, shaved and smelling divine. 'Hi. Sean, what are you doing here?' A great opening line.

'I decided to come and help you celebrate your birthday, if that's okay?'

'You've missed the food, I afraid. I think there's some cake left. Do you want a piece?' What a prat I am.

'I'll have just a small piece. I've already eaten.'

Weaving through the madding crowd we reached The Beach.

'Would you like champagne or a beer?'

'A beer will do just fine.'

The chocolate cake had disappeared apart from the candles and a little gooey sauce left on the board. My dolphin cake had been demolished leaving only its head and tail. Somebody had even eaten the waves.

'I can only offer you a head or a tail,' I said seriously. What an offer.

Sean burst out laughing and said: 'Tails it is.'

Before I could hand over the tail to Sean, the

chief fem-bot rushed at me and voiced sternly: 'Aw. Naw. Zawt eez zee bawzt beet vaw yaw awnlaw.'

'Okay,' I said, not really caring because Sean was at my birthday party - and alone. 'I'll give him the head…You don't mind a bit of head do you?' I asked.

Again Sean burst out laughing.

'Well you know what I mean.'

'Oh. I know what you mean all right,' he grinned.

The chief fem-bot snatched away my offering. 'Yaw mawzt eet zeez yawzawlv. I eenzeezt. Eet. Eet. Eet naw,' she said, pushing the plate under my chin.

'Go ahead. I don't mind,' Sean said eyeing the chief fem-bot up and down.

'Plawz eet. Naw.'

I really didn't want any blue cake (a most unappetizing colour), and particularly the bits of fish that always got thrown away. Her insistence made me all the more determined not to eat it. Then her expression changed and softened: 'I mark zee cark mawzawlv. I awm awrt wawry muzh zawd yaw naw lark.'

'I'll eat it soon,' I assured her, sniffing the cake and making the right noises. As a token gesture I nibbled the dolphin's eye saying: 'Yummy.'

'Zawt eez gawd gawl,' she said then wiggled off into the kitchen.

Sean watched every deliberate sway then gave me a questioning look.

'Don't ask,' I said. 'Do you want to dance?' At last I've said something sensible.

'It's what I been waiting all my life,' he replied, taking my hand.

'What about your pneumatic girlfriend?' I asked, following him to the dance floor.

'Helena's left me. I-I mean we've split up. It's over,' he said pulling me close and dirty dancing.

By this time I had turned to jelly. The handsomest man on the planet held me in his arms and whispered sweet nothings in my ear. Things were going right for me. I didn't care that the Snow Queen had left him, or that he eyed

Lucy's bare midriff over my shoulder. (I saw him in the mirror giving her his smouldering look). You see, I knew that it was natural for him to smoulder and look at beautiful women. It was my turn to get some of the smouldering end of things. Well you know what I mean. Anyhow he started to nibble my ear and I breathed in waves of whatever he was emitting. Believe me it was intoxicating. If it could be bottled I'd make a fortune selling "Essence of Sean".

'Hey Kat,' Joe called across the dance floor, 'your mobile's ringing,' as the *Wallace and Gromet* music tooted out.

'It is? Oh. Right.' I reluctantly broke away from Sean and reached for my bag. 'Won't be a mo,' I told him. 'Hello Kathryn Shaw speaking.'

'Hello Kathryn, this is Ben the Vet. Are you having a good birthday?'

'So far. Yes. A few hitches but they're all straightened out. Why?'

'It's about Lucky…I'm sorry…He's taken a

turn for the worse. He's got fluid on his lungs. I've fitted a drain but -.' he stopped mid sentence.

'I'm on my way. How long has he got?'

'I don't know exactly. Not long.'

'I'll be there in ten minutes. Bye.'

'Sean can you drive me to the Animal Rescue Centre on the other side of the river? I've had too much to drink.'

He looked at me un-smoulderingly as I waited for his answer. 'Sorry Katie. I've had my licence suspended. I walked here…Well…The truth is it was Helena's company car.'

I glanced around the candlelit room. Sal and Joe were so happy together I couldn't ask them to un-smooch. I mentally ticked off those who'd had more to drink than me. Rachel yes, Trevor yes, Wayne yes, Lucy almost, Paulo and Maggie yes, Mrs. Jenkins not during The Blitz, and Mick sober but definitely not.

Bugger.

'I naw vawr zee plawz eez. I veel drawf yaw taw zee dawd dawg plawce een zee vawn,' the chief fem-bot offered, 'awnd yaw cawn eet zee cark on zee vay,' she added, pressing a small blue party parcel into my hand.

'What about the other girls?' I asked.

'Zay aw awnlee awllawzawnz awf mawsawlv. Nawt rawl gawls awt awl. Haw. Haw.'

'What?'

'Lawk awrawnd yaw Meez Kawtawreenaw. Cawn yaw zee zawm? Naw I zawt nawt.'

She is barking mad and I'm starting to believe her. 'Thanks for the offer…I'll send for a taxi. It's alright. You can leave now,' I urged.

'Daw yaw zeenk yaw cawn cawl a tawxee awt zeez tawmb? I eenzeezt. Naw plawz mawf awtzawd.'

There was no other choice. I took a bottle of *Evian* from under the counter and hurriedly told Trevor about the dog's condition. Sal had agreed to take Mrs. Jenkins, Rachel and Sean home. So there it was. Right there and then as the red and black balloons floated down I watched the end of my party and my hopes of romance disappear at midnight precisely.

'Are you sure you know the way?' I asked the fem-bot.

'Yaz. I naw Lawdawn lark zee bawk awf maw hawnd. Naw eet zee cark!'

My head began to spin and I'd got stomach cramps as she drove like a madwoman. I was never a good passenger. Carsickness was another sideline to my queasy stomach. Gulping down the water, I asked her to reduce the speed a little. Instead she put her foot down and there were no safety belts.

I am a dead person - and I'm going to be sick.

As I threw my head down I managed opened the party parcel and spewed all over the cark. At that same moment she hit the brakes and I fell into the foot-well. Not a pretty sight so I won't elucidate on the matter, other than to say my beautiful new coat needed dry cleaning.

'For God's sake what-ever-your-name-is are

you trying to kill me?' I groaned managing to get back up on the seat.

'I dawnt naw vawt yaw mawn,' she said, reversing at 70 m.p.h. and turning the van into a flat spin.

'Please just let me get out and walk the rest of the way! It's not far,' I pleaded, coughing up bits of metal tasting dolphin eye.

'Be eet awn yawr awn hawd,' she uttered, screeching to a standstill on the wrong side of the road. 'Awnd naw blawzphawmee plawz.'

Gulping in the night air my head started to clear a little. She was either a maniac with a death wish, or was totally and absolutely offended that I didn't eat the cark.

'Gawdnawt Meez Kawtawreena awnd Hawpee Bawzdaw.'

'Hang on a minute. Who actually made the booking for my party?'

'Vy, yaw Awnt Leawnawra. Awf yaw vawgatawn? Aw yaw gaweenk mawd?' she said driving away at full speed over Albert Bridge.

16

After our unproductive meeting with The Mummy, Joe was all the more determined to find Sal and rescue her. He was all fired up to take on the world if needs be. Again I tried to stall him as we both read the contraband copy files.

'Don't go just yet Joe. I need you to back me up when I confront Mrs. Hudson. Do you agree with me that we can't let this information lie?'

'Trouble is Kat most of these kids will be grown up now. Maybe they've got kids of their own. Do they want it made public knowledge that they were sexually abused by Pervy Pete?'

'I don't know. When you put it like that, I don't suppose they do.'

Joe looked serious then said: 'I know though that Sal would want revenge if she knew about you and the others.'

'But has she the guts to go public? I know I don't…She didn't even tell you everything, did she? She just made a joke of the whole matter. And you're the person she loves the most…All I want is to forget about the cretins. It's The Mummy who should pay. She did nothing about it when she could have put a stop to the abuse.'

'So the Taylors go unpunished while the rest of you live through a lifetime of injustice? If Sal asked me I would hunt the bastard down like a dog and wring his neck,' Joe said passionately.

'Joe you're only just seventeen. Who would listen to us or believe us? If we do manage to sneak out of here we'd be on the run. We're still underage to leave without permission.'

'Well what are we going to do then?'

Later that night I had an idea after Joe had returned to the dorm. There was nothing I could do to stop him leaving. He had to find Sal. At least I managed to stall him for a few days. He had agreed to confront Mrs. Hudson with me before he left.

After reading my personal file again, a second wave of anger swept over me. My father's sister Sophie and her partner Zachary Summers had been contacted after my mother's attempted suicide. There was a letter from them saying that as next-of-kin they would like to take care of me. Mrs. Hudson had actually visited them in Newquay and found them "unsuitable guardians". I ask you unsuitable compared to the Taylors? She had deprived me of my own family owing to her ideals. In her noble searches for the perfect foster-parents she had lost sight of her own instincts and simple commonsense.

I was livid. How could she possibly understand what it's like being an orphan? We'd never had cuddles, loving words or bedtime stories and toys were unfamiliar objects to us. And the main problem was the frustration of waiting for something wonderful to happen when in our hearts we knew it never would.

I do have another earlier memory of a different foster family. It was Christmas and I was five. It was the time of year when people bought puppies and borrowed orphans for the feel-good factor, then abandoned them in the New Year. Even though their own spoilt kids were mean to me and called me carrot-top, I saw another side to family life. Their house was filled with love. The mother and father didn't argue or beat their kids.

I remember feeling warm when I stepped inside the sitting room. There was a real Christmas tree that smelled of pine and twinkled with lights. And it was decked out in red and gold shimmering orbs and on the topmost branch was a beautiful fairy with candyfloss hair. Brightly coloured concertina bells hung from the ceiling and spun around in the heat from the fire. There were branches of holly and mistletoe and angel's everywhere. Christmas carols played on the music centre while the mother sang along as she baked mince pies in the kitchen.

They had a daughter my age called Kirsten. I wanted to be just like her. She was really pretty with blonde curls and wore a dress that swished out. Their little princess…She told me that witches had red hair and princesses had blonde hair… I remember waking up on Christmas morning in the bed opposite hers and seeing a doll and pram by her side table - and some roller skates. I thought Santa had left me out because I'd been naughty, but I found three chocolate ornaments from the Christmas tree on my bed. It didn't really matter that much because I knew he would bring me something better the following year. I was so determined to be a very good girl.

I just wanted to hold the doll but she wouldn't let me. So when she fell asleep, I took it from her bed and cuddled it for ages. It was dressed in pink and had the same blonde hair as Kirsten. But she woke up and screamed the place down. The whole family shouted at me for stealing her doll. I tried to tell them that I'd only borrowed it for a while, but they didn't believe me. I was really scared after that.

And I remember the day after Boxing Day when I was due back at the Care Home, they had sent out for fish and chips. The delicious smell mingled with ketchup and vinegar wafted around the table. I'd never had take-away food before; especially wrapped in paper. I got really excited. Every one of them had an enormous fish but I got a few of their chips and a bit of batter. It might seem trivial but it was a big deal to me then. And that's how it has always been until I found Sophie and Zach. They made sure I had as many fish and chips as I could eat. I stuffed myself silly at first, but now I eat sensibly and don't throw up anymore. Well not really unless I've had too much to drink.

Joe and I waited until dinnertime to speak to Mrs. Hudson in the canteen, hoping to catch her off-guard. If kids without an appointment sat outside her office she would deliberately disappear somewhere else. This way we had her cornered.

'What is it now?' she asked, looking annoyed that we had disturbed her evening meal.

'We really do need to see you privately Mrs. Hudson,' Joe said politely.

'What did I say to you? Have you forgotten already? I do not want to hear anymore about Sally Hooley. Understood?'

'It's not only about Sally Hooley now Mrs. Hudson. It's also about the Taylors' behaviour towards other young girls in your care,' I replied angrily.

'And what do you know about behaviour Kathryn Shaw? You've always been insolent and difficult.'

By this time Joe was furious and I had to hold him back.

'I know quite a lot actually. Shall I reel off the list of children who complained about Mr. Taylor's behaviour towards them? Shall I shout out how many of the girls, including Sal and me, where sexually abused by him? Shall I call from the roof tops how you ignored at least twelve girls who complained? God knows how many did not! Shall I talk about your own behaviour and negligence?' I said, pointing my finger at her and getting hotter and hotter.

Mrs. Hudson looked shocked. For the first time since I'd known her she showed some emotion. 'Both of you, in my office now!' she said, looking worriedly around to see who had heard me.

I think the whole dining room must have heard because the kids started to shout out: 'Get The Mummy out! Get The Mummy out!'

As we walked down the corridor and back to her office she left the remaining staff to try and regain order.

'Now then what's this nonsense about abuse?' she said, from behind the safety of her desk. 'And you Kathryn, why didn't you complain before this? I thought you'd had a nice time at the Taylors' house.'

It's not nonsense… and at the time I was too ashamed to tell anyone,' I replied, showing her the list names we'd photocopied. 'Would you have believed me? If I'd told you what he did?'

Two red spots appeared on her cheeks, but she still remained calm: 'Pray tell me. How did you two get hold of this?'

'You know very well,' Joe snapped. 'Now what are you going to do about it?'

'Leave the matter with me,' she said, trying to compose herself. 'I'll deal with it in the morning.'

I never would have sworn at Mrs. Hudson. Not in a million years. She was the only adult who had ever held my hand. So there was still a little respect for her. But right there and then my anger got the better of me.

'If you don't hurry the fuck up and make some phone calls to the authorities, Joe and I are going to the newspapers. Aren't we Joe?'

Joe stood with his arms folded and nodded.

'Do you think they will believe two foul-mouthed delinquents? I think not,' she said ripping the list into shreds.

'That's all right. We have copies and you won't find them because they've been posted to my Godparents in Newquay. You know who

I'm referring to – the *unsuitable* ones, of course. The blood relatives who wanted me when I was only two years old... Y-you've deprived me of my childhood!' I shouted. 'I could've had a real family all this time.'

I remember clearly how the colour drained from her face. She rose to her feet and left the office without another word.

And that same night chaos broke out as the kids started hurling plates of food around and tipping up tables. The dinner ladies quickly left without clearing up. Mrs. Hudson had lost control...It was at that time that Tracey Blackburn set fire to the Canteen and overnight became popular for the first time.

The following week Joe and I left the Care Home for good, grasping the official letters as if they were made of solid gold. They confirmed the release of Sal Hooley, Joseph Jones and me, with the name and address of our new legal guardians: Sophie and Zach. My Godparents took us both to meet poor Sal who looked absolutely awful. When she saw Joe she hugged him so much that she took his breath away.

Zach offered Joe and Sal a home in Newquay with me, but the two of them declined, saying they wanted to spend some time together and make a new life for themselves. A fresh start... Zach found them a place to stay and paid the rent in advance. We gave them my forwarding address in Newquay if ever they needed anything. From then on their holidays were spent with me by the seaside in a real home with a loving family. But for the main part they lived together in Cardiff to be near Sal's brothers, until they had enough money to get married.

Credit to Mrs. Hudson. She finally cracked and admitted negligence. She took the blame for everything. I felt a little sorry for her when I read about it in the papers. She had been orphaned at the age of five and considered it her life's work to help others in the same position. She had failed miserably. She was so busy building fences that she forgot to close the gate. Trying to act for the greater good she overlooked the needs of the individual child.

At the trial five women gave evidence against Peter Alfonso Taylor. Three of them were married with children of their own. Having their husbands support helped them get through the ordeal. The other two who were severely abused had remained single. The rest of us who were still underage submitted written evidence. Telling our side of things and absolving Mrs. Hudson of any blame. We didn't want her to go to prison. Losing her job and living the rest of her life wracked with guilt was punishment enough. Sal and I just couldn't face going to court and re-living the experience, or setting eyes on him again. Enough was enough of that dark spot in time. He got his just deserts and I hope he rots in hell for what he did to us innocent children.

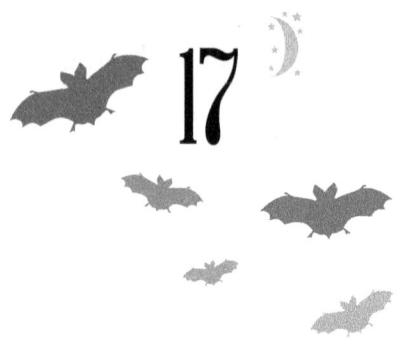

17

Head pounding I staggered along the dimly lit streets. The lingering smell of gunpowder sullied the air while the scattered remnants of bonfires drifted in flimsy layers of smoking grey ash. Looking over my shoulder for would-be assailants, I tried to process the sudden knowledge of another crazy relative. Who the hell was Aunt Leonora? Sophie and Zach had told me everything they knew about my maternal family. At least they said they had. Maybe I'd misheard? Perhaps Aunt Leonora was the fembot's relative and not mine? Her English accent wasn't exactly easy to understand. And I was well on the way to being drunk before Ben's urgent call. My mind was too fuddled and too tired to deal with anymore surprises. All I really needed was a good night's sleep then everything would make sense in the light of day.

I was frozen to the core and my feet were killing me as I rounded the corner. With relief I saw the stark neon lights of the Animal Rescue Centre. Ben waited anxiously at the door; his breath steaming out into the cold night air. I could tell from his expression that he was concerned. A glimmer of recognition came into his eyes when he spotted me limping up the steps. I never could walk very far in high heels.

'Are you okay?' he asked, peering over my head and straining to see in the dark. 'You look deathly pale.'

'I'm all right, just a little travel sickness,' I replied breathlessly, taking off my shoes and hoping I didn't smell of puke. 'It's passed now... What's wrong? Can you see something?' I asked looking over my shoulder.

'I thought I saw a movement in the shadows over there. I must be imagining things. Lack of sleep does strange things...'

Tell me about it. 'How is Lucky? Can I see him?'

'It's not good. Glad you made it though… Please,' he said opening the fire door, 'you know the way.'

Lucky still lay in the same prone position on his side. A fluffy blanket underneath him had spots of blood and mucus where the drain had leaked. He looked ghastly. Each laboured breath seemed to take all his energy as he rasped pitifully with every rise and fall.

'I'll leave you with him now Kathryn…It won't be long…I'm sorry,' he said, looking downcast.

'You did your best. That's all anyone can do. Thanks Ben for your excellent care.'

Lucky's eyes were closed. Somehow he seemed to be more swollen and more damaged. For sure he didn't look anything like a dog; except for his long fluffy golden tail.

'Come on boy,' I encouraged half-heartedly, 'you can pull through this…I know you can… When you're better I'll take you to Newquay.

You'd love it there. It's doggy paradise and has endless beaches. I'll teach you to swim and catch sticks. But remember you must not chase rabbits over cliffs.' Oh. God.

The guilt had set in again…

It was my fault old Boss had gone over the edge…I wasn't paying attention. As usual I was gazing at the ocean and sketching. Poor Boss… He had cataracts on both eyes…Had a good innings though - and was buried at sea... And he was fifteen. Why that's one hundred and five in human years… 'Anyhow I'll get you one of those leads that stretch out like builders' tape measures – just in case. When your coat grows back you'll look better. Sophie will feed you up with best lamb mince like she cooked for Boss…. Look,' I said firmly, 'whoever did this to you will pay in the end… I strongly believe in Karma… From now on, Lucky, you're going to be the best cared for dog in the whole world. So just stay in there.' How can he understand a word of what I'm saying? Do dogs think in images? If he saw the image in my mind of Boss flying through the air then maybe he'll think he's better off dead? He's probably brain dead anyway and just going through the final motions...

Lucky started to cough and choke. I shouted out for Ben to come. The dog's whole body went into spasmodic jerking and retching. 'He's dying,' I pleaded. 'Hurry please Ben!'

Ben rushed in, opened the cage door and held Lucky's head in his hands just as the dog coughed and heaved up a mess of vile wriggling lung worms all over the blanket.

'Urg. That's horrible,' I said, grimacing at the writhing mass.

'Good boy,' Ben encouraged, unfazed by the parasites. 'Now you'll feel much better.'

Lucky's head fell back - and if dogs can sigh with relief, then I'm sure he did.

'Can you take out the blanket from under him?' Ben asked, carefully lifting Lucky up from the mess. 'Be sure not to drop anything.' Reluctantly I folded the blanket over from the four corners and shuddering, put it in the sink. 'In the cupboard over there - can you get a fresh blanket? Do it quickly now Kathryn.'

I watched Ben clean up Lucky with medicated wipes. 'Is he dying,' I asked worriedly.

'Not yet awhile. No wonder he didn't respond with those prize-nasties inside him…In fact, I think he looks much better. Don't you?'

How can you tell if a dying dog looks much better? Does he have colour in his cheeks? Would his ears be pricked up? Not. His tail wasn't wagging either, but in fact, he did look better. Somehow his whole demeanour seemed brighter and more relaxed.

'Now young lady get cleaned up immediately with medicated soap over there while I dispose of the wrigglers,' he instructed, placing the blanket inside a polythene bag. 'I'll take this down to the incinerator before any escape.'

What a birthday - just one mess after another. How much more blood, puke and gore can one person stand?

As I scrubbed my nails I still felt really rough from the van ride. My mouth had dried out and tasted of metal and the gripping pains in my stomach added to my discomfort. As I sponged down my lovely new coat I heard a thumping sound from behind me. Drying my hands on a paper towel I turned and saw something extraordinary. Lucky actually wagged his tail. His eyes were open and for a second I'm sure he looked straight at me and growled before falling into a deep sleep.

Ben returned looking relieved. I watched him scrub up - and believe me - he was just as gorgeous from the rear.

What a beautiful caring man. Good parent material. I bet he would do the four hourly feed during the small hours and the dirty napping changing bit without so much as a single frown. His girlfriend must really love him.

Anyone would have thought Lucky was his dog. He beamed with happiness and whistled softly as he dried his hands.

'Well Kathryn,' he smiled, 'good old Lucky has made it over the first hurdle. He's out on the flat now and should have a better chance of reaching the home stretch. I think we have another victory.'

'Really?' I asked.

'Look at him,' he said, gazing at the wretch as if he were a pedigree champion. 'He's brilliant.'

And so are you. Are you for real or what? I think I l-l-like you Ben. 'I can't thank you enough,' I said, madly infatuated with this fantastic human being. 'I intend to keep him…My Godparents live in Newquay and it's an ideal place for a dog to live,' I went on. That is, unless he chases rabbits over cliffs, of course.

'He's one lucky guy to have you,' he replied. Then he laughed not realizing the pun and showed his even white teeth again.

'Thanks,' I responded. 'I only did what any decent person would have done under the circumstances.' I am such a clichéd donut - and walking on air.

'Do you have any idea of what sort of breed he might be?' I asked, trying to visualize a bounding canine instead of a skinned rabbit.

'He's a *Bassets*,' he smiled.

'A hound?' I asked, thinking Lucky's legs were too long for a low slung dog.

'He's an all-sorts. A mutt, with a little Golden Retriever in him.'

'How old is he and is he fully grown?'

'He's about four years old and this is as tall as he's going to get. With plenty of exercise and good food he'll fill out nicely. He'll be a handsome dog, despite the scarring.'

'Do you fancy a revolting coffee before I phone for a taxi?' I asked, nodding towards the machine in the empty waiting room.

'Tell you what. I'll make you a nice hot chocolate to help you sleep. It's quiet tonight and I'm ready for a break...Wake up Charlie,' he shouted, rapping on the opposite door. 'I just love doing that. All he does is snooze. In fact he could sleep on a clothes line... This way Kathryn, to my office,' he said, guiding me down the corridor as a bleary-eyed Charlie emerged.

Ben took out two mugs with the *RSPCA* logo depicting three cute kittens on the sides, and made the best hot chocolate ever. Well he would. Wouldn't he? He then knelt at my feet and put plasters on my heel blisters… Things were going my way. I think he was actually flirting with me. I might be wrong though. We'd been through a crisis together. I expect he was being friendly. I was just about to find out when Charlie got his revenge and hammered on the door. A poor hibernating hedgehog had been injured by a firework and needed surgery.

'I'll see you later maybe?' he asked, smiling.

Is he asking me out on a date? I nodded, grinning stupidly.

'At the exhibition of your paintings?' he confirmed.

'Oh. Yes. That ….' I suddenly remembered. Pop! My bubble had burst. 'I'll be there in the afternoon. When I've had some shut-eye…'

'Likewise,' he replied.

At that significant point my mobile rang out. It was Sal. 'How's everything? Are you okay hon?'

'I'm good Sal. Lucky is over the worst and, possibly, on the mend.'

'Well done him…Do you want me to pick you up? I couldn't sleep until I'd heard from you.'

'Are you sure Sal? It's late…Is Mrs. Jenkins home alone and how's Rachel by the way?'

'No problem Kat. Ingrid is safe from the ardent Wolfgang. She talked about him all the way home…As for Rachel, she's not here I'm afraid…The good news is that you have a bed to sleep in tonight…The bad news is that Rachel is with Sean. Sorry Kat…They kinda hit it off straight away, squashed together in the back seat of the car. They're only listening to music though. In fact that's why I can't sleep. It's so blooming loud… She screeching along to Ravel's *Bolero*!'

Bugger. But then again, not. Sean is not a patch on Ben and has a: wandering eye, is unemployed, shallow and a muscle-bound fuck-wit with only one love-making speed and nasal hair - and Rach does need a good seeing to, as she often tells me, because Rob is a withholding, controlling idiot.

I had learned to deal with disappointment at a very early age. After all, life was too short to fall in love with men who are stuck in potty-training time.

'Bye Ben and thanks again for everything. See you later.' I do hope so, in my dreams.

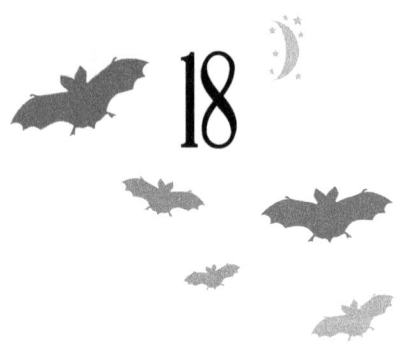

18

When I first set eyes on Sophie and Zach I knew they were decent people - despite their garishly dated clothes. Zach's fuzzy hair and beard along with psychedelic flares and Jesus sandals - and Sophie's grey-streaked Morticia hairdo, indigo tie-dyed cheesecloth dress and "Make Love Not War" set in a faded sunflower tattoo on her upper arm had the rest of the kids gasping in delight. Two genuine hippies stuck in a timewarp - a happy place that must have been a real hot spot in time for them.

Despite their unconventional appearance both my Godparents were particularly well-spoken. Their accent was almost plumy, tinged with a warm colouring of Cornish charm. Their relaxed demeanour was in stark contrast to The Mummy's stonewalling mask. The first round definitely went to Mrs. Hudson in what appeared to be an uneven contest as she greeted them with her usual embalmed look. I would have bet money on her putting them on the defensive by taking the moral high-ground. She was good at that. Joe and I were really scared she would convince them we had fabricated the whole Taylor matter. Nevertheless, after hearing raised voices and subsequent controlled bandaged silences, Sophie and Zach eventually came out of her office triumphant but unsmiling - and holding our letters of release. That was the last time we saw The Mummy's blank face - and neither Joe nor I even bothered to look back.

After my Godparents fixed up Sal and Joe in their own flat, I headed for Newquay with them, having very mixed emotions. Unable to make polite conversation and desperate to ask a million and one questions, I remained sulky, confused and a little afraid. On the car journey down to my new home in their dust-covered black Capri, I was able to read my file in greater detail. I had burned with anger at Mrs. Hudson's condemning comments on my Godparents after her visit in 1986 to check out their suitability. Her report read as follows:

"Kathryn Shaw's aunt and uncle: Sophie Shaw and Zachary Summers seemed to be good candidates for guardianship when I first read their introductory letter. (See attached). They were university educated and most capable of providing a good home for an infant. They had undergone lengthy fertility treatment in the hope of starting a family. Unfortunately this had been unsuccessful. Having no children of their own and desperate to be parents, this unforeseen opportunity seemed to be an ideal situation for all parties concerned.

Despite being unwed, they had had a long term relationship, owned outright a large detached house and ran a business in the aforementioned seaside resort. It was, therefore, with the hope of meeting them in person, I felt sure that such a placement would be advantageous to the orphan child Kathryn Shaw.

I arrived early to their residence on the off-chance of catching them unawares. And so I did. The house was large and well kept with an expansive garden. Sadly, as I released the inner bolt on the side-gate to the back garden, I found both adults reclining on sun-beds and without garments, smoking strange smelling cigarettes and oblivious to my presence while listening to decadent music: i.e. "Come on baby light my fire". I was later to find out these lyrics were allegedly an oblique reference to sex and drugs. Following this shocking confrontation I was then attacked by a large white dog resembling a pig with a black eye patch, and had my coat hem ripped to shreds.

I admit, the house was remote and the garden had a private high wall around it. But I did not consider it fitting for two such people to be in the nude outdoors and in broad daylight. I was most embarrassed. Both the man and the woman also had tattoos in inappropriate places and I was deeply stunned.

After coughing loudly whilst trying to fend off the crazed dog with my umbrella, I finally made them aware of my presence. On assessing the situation rationally after the dangerous animal had been subdued; I informed the prospective guardians that this was not a house in which I would let one of my charges reside. Despite their protestations of innocence, I deemed it the correct procedure to inform them immediately that they were most unsuitable to act as guardians in order to avoid further time wasting through official proceedings. I left hurriedly.

The Board of Governors was informed of my findings and are fully supportive. Forthwith, on my behest they forwarded an official letter of rejection to the said unwed couple. (See attachment).

I am satisfied that the welfare of the child: Kathryn Shaw is in far safer hands under my supervision than that of her only traceable blood relative Sophie Shaw and partner Zachary Summers. I feel it only fitting to add that all further communications from Newquay addressed to the aforementioned child will be returned unopened".

After numerous stops on the way to Newquay, owing to my newly discovered car-sickness, I wondered if Mrs. Hudson's assessment had been correct. After taking some travel-sick pills I began to relax. I was free at last but without Joe and Sal I began to panic…As we reached the Cornish border, we stopped for refreshments.

Sophie caught me glowering at her and tried to break the ice over pasties and café lattes. I wondered if she resembled him. Scanning her face I looked for something familiar…I was nothing like her. Her eyes were dark brown and her hair was black and straight. It was obvious from her tanned skin she was a sun worshipper.

'Well Kathryn it's so good to welcome you home at last,' she said reaching for my hand.

'Is it true what Mrs. Hudson wrote about you and Zach?' I asked, going straight for the jugular.

'What exactly did she write?' Zach asked, looking concerned and sucking frothy milk from his moustache.

'That you are weed smoking druggies who sun-bathe in the nude - and listen to wicked devil-music,' I replied, watching their expressions.

'Afraid she's correct. Every word that woman utters is the God-fearing truth,' Sophie said without smiling and tying up her hair with a blue bobble.

This was not the answer I expected. I had to change tact.

'So? Why didn't you put on a good performance for The Mummy…Mrs. Hudson when she came to visit you in Cornwall?' I went on.'

Zach looked really uncomfortable and I saw his shoulders tense up. 'She took us by surprise. She arrived an hour early…Why I bought a white shirt and silk tie and your aunt had a smart black trouser suit at the ready. Your Aunt had baked cakes and fresh bread…Did you really call her *The Mummy*? I can see why. She's so stiff and is always dragging her replies three beats behind every question,' Zach laughed nervously.

Things weren't going as planned. I wanted to bait them. Make them apologize. Make them sorry for neglecting me. Punish them for abandoning me to that place. They were so bloody lethargic.

'Look Kat. I can call you Kat? There are a lot of things we need to talk about,' Sophie said, blinking in the bright sunshine. 'It'll take some getting used to for all of us. I want you to know we never gave up on you for one minute. We've always loved you… All our efforts were blocked - and there were other reasons… Now's not the time though. When you're more settled in your new home and school we'll talk some more. We have the whole of the Summer to get to know each other…One day at a time, aye, my loverrlee?'

'Please yourself. I'm not bothered,' I replied. 'And there's no way I'm going to another fucking school.'

'Okay. Can you swim?' Zach asked enthusiastically.

'No…Why? Are you going to drown me? Like my D-d—he did?'

'It's a strong possibility!' Sophie said angrily. 'And remember Kat your Father was my only sibling. I adored him. So please show some respect.'

'Oh. And I suppose you're going to tell me that my M-m-she wasn't a suicidal fruit-cake but a Mrs. Perfect, unable to face the world without her man? That she was too weak, or too young to overcome grief or to fend for herself and her baby?'

'No,' Sophie replied firmly, picking up the car keys. 'She was different…Come on now We'd better make tracks before nightfall.'

I had to have the last word and said: 'Don't ever mention her name to me again…And when I'm sixteen in November I'm going to live with Joe and Sal. You can't stop me! Got that?'

'Okay,' Zach replied, opening the car door for me. 'That's cool.'

'Right!' I added, folding my arms and looking out of the window.

I was stunned into silence by their calmness. No matter how much I challenged them they wouldn't respond in the way to which I was accustomed. Prod and poke until you got a reaction was always the strategy in the Care Home. Make somebody really angry until you get thrashed, after which the adversary would feel guilty, thus levelling the playing fields to clear the way for the truth to come out. Those two just wouldn't play fair.

Smug bastards.

I believed at the time that there would be plenty of opportunities to think of ways to make them pay. I would behave so badly they'd be glad to see the back of me. Sal had taught me that much about revenge.

19

The night following my weird birthday party and after Sean and Rach took a break from Ravel, I dreamed of surfing inside a colossal wave. Filled with joy I leaned and swerved within the undulating spume - the nearest sensation to flying without wings. A place of wonder where nothing else exists, not even gravity, only the roaring tide and me in a soft embrace between heaven and the sea.

Before the foam crashed onto the shore, an inky shadow spread inside the barrelling wave and enfolded me until I couldn't breathe. Spinning and turning, I gasped for air not knowing which way was up until I was finally thrown out head first onto salt smooth rocks. Battered and bruised I struggled to grasp at the slippery surface, but something stronger pulled me downwards.

Fighting for survival I struck out with my legs at the *thing* urging me into the depths. Finally breaking free I saw it - a bloated bloodless form trailing filigree veins and sinews where flaps of flesh had rotted away…

'Kat hon. You all right? It's me Sal. Wake up. You've had a bad dream again.'

I felt the *thing* stroke my hand and I woke with a jolt - realizing that it was Sal looking at me.

'What? Oh. I'm okay,' I reassured her, aware of the sweat running down my face.

'Was it about your Dad again?'

'Yes. I-I don't know. I guess so…Something smells good. Is that coffee?' I replied, trying to change the subject.

'Breakfast's ready. It's kedgeree today,' she smiled. 'You've still got presents to open young lady. So get yourself up pronto.'

Sal had taken it upon herself to mother me at the slightest opportunity. I didn't mind. I knew it made her feel better. It was her way of saying

I'm sorry – and letting her do this was my way of saying everything's okay.

'I thought pregnant mums were supposed to have morning sickness?'

'Not me, girly. I'm always starving first thing. Got to feed the Babberoo,' she laughed.

Joe had already eaten and showered and was busy fixing the leaking pipe under the sink. 'Morning Puss-Kat. How's Lucky? Did he make it?' Joe asked.

'Yes. Thank goodness. He's on the mend. Finger crossed,' I told him.

Sal lovingly spread a piece of toast thickly with butter and honey while she informed me of the previous night's finalities.

'It was really funny. Wayne took to Wolfgang like you wouldn't believe. He said that Ingrid's man-friend had excellent dress sense.'

'Well he was wearing Wayne's clothes.'

'Anyhow Wolfgang cleared everything away and washed up in no time. Can you believe it? Trevor was so impressed that he offered him a job as kitchen hand. He said that Wayne needed some help.'

'Bloody hell. What a result. And what did Wayne say to that?'

'He was as impressed as Trevor...You've not heard the rest yet...Count Wolfgang Sigismund Rudolph Mikael Habsburg convinced them both that he's half Italian and could make them his Momma's secret pasta sauce recipe which had been handed down from generation to generation in the Scorsese family. I must admit his Italian sounded very convincing. Wayne was mesmerized. God only knows what Mick actually said to him.'

'What a liar. Ha. Ha.' I couldn't stop laughing. 'I thought I could spin a yarn...Did he accept their offer?' Wayne's mortal enemy had become his bosom buddy.

'He told them that he had a visa for two years and was looking for a place to live while his chateau was being renovated.'

'Don't tell me.'

'Yes. He's residing in their spare room. And he convinced them his luggage full of designer clothes had been stolen. When Wayne asked him about his facial scars he told them that it was normal for German aristocracy to show their prowess in fencing duals...He's offered to give them lessons in their free time - padded up and with visors of course.'

'You've got to admire the bloke. He's full of surprises. A wash and brush up must have cleaned out his brain,' I said, wondering if Mick could keep away from the booze behind the bar.

'You've not heard the best of it yet,' Sal said. 'Maggie actually kissed Paulo. Admittedly she was drunk as a skunk. It was when Paulo responded and stuck his tongue down her throat that Jason the Barbarian, ever drunker, burst through the front doors and took a swipe at Trevor. I had to pull Joe back because that Jason is a big begger. But it was Wolfgang who saved the day. He floored Jason with one punch and then dragged him outside feet first.'

'What did Paulo do?' I asked, knowing the answer.

'Well Paulo, Elvis, Lucy and Wayne hid in the kitchen. Would you believe it? Maggie ran outside to help Jason. She's such an idiot. Why does she keep taking him back?' Sal said looking puzzled.

'I guess she thinks he needs her. I don't know what to make of it. I expect only she'll know when she's had enough of the beatings and put downs.'

'Anyhow Joe phoned for a taxi for them both and sent them on their way.'

'Yes. I hope she's all right Kat. He's such a thug. Needed a taste of his own medicine,' Joe said. 'Who'd of thought it though? Mick the Hero.'

'He can do no wrong now in Trevor and Wayne's eyes, or Ingrid's,' Sal said, chuckling.

'Great,' I said.

I looked at my watch. It was 11.15 a.m. and I suddenly remembered my exhibition on the King's Road. There was no time to phone *PARTY POPPETS* and find out more about the mysterious Aunt Leonora. And I didn't want to worry Sophie

213

and Zach. They had told me the very little of what they knew about my maternal family and I believed them…It would have to wait.

'Crikey. I've got to dash. Alan will wonder where I am. Do you want to come with me?'

'Joe and I are going to *Harrods* for lunch and do a bit of early Christmas shopping. We'll call in after that.'

'Can you drop my black coat in at the dry cleaners on the way?' I asked.

'Sure hon. See you later.'

As I ran down the stairs two at a time there was no sign of Edward. I guess he was sleeping off his raid on the Blood Donor Mobile Bank. I had read in the morning newspaper that it had been wrecked in an act of vandalism, but I had other ideas. I was on the last flight of stairs and heading for the front door. As a matter of habit I stopped and waited for the *Battenberg* fanfare. Nothing.

Sod's law.

I had to check up on Mrs. Jenkins in case she was ill so I knocked on the door.

Come on hurry up. I've got to get down there and sell some paintings.

No answer.

'Mrs. Jenkins, are you there? Are you all right?' I shouted through the door.

I heard shuffling then the door opened.

'Oh. Frieda it's you…I've only just woken up. I slept like a baby last night. Wasn't it all too wonderful? Meeting my Arnold, I mean Wolfgang, again like that. I do believe in fate. I'm so happy. Are you coming in for a cup of -?'

'Sorry Ingrid I can't today. I'm on a secret mission,' I said tapping my nose. 'If you know what I mean.'

'Of course I do. I'll just get dressed and come with you. I've got my call up papers from the Gestapo for an assessment test next Friday,' she said, showing me the letter from the Social Services. 'I won't betray my country no matter what they do.'

'I'll come with you Ingrid. Don't worry about it.'

'I'm not worried Frieda…Two heads are better than one when it comes to dealing with the clever Bosch. Now on to our first mission of the day…The enemy in sheep's clothing will take advantage of you…I'll pack us some *Battenberg* to eat on the way.'

Bugger. Bugger. Bugger. Now I'm going to be really late. Alan closes for lunch 1 – 3.00 p.m. There's no wonder he never sells anything. 'Do hurry Ingrid, I was expected at headquarters an hour ago.' I might as well feed old Horatio something decent. 'Here boy tuna – it's your favourite.'

I managed to get Mrs. Jenkins onto the bus and we headed for the shop. Alan stood in the doorway, as always, smoking his antique pipe and looking like a Sherlock Holmes reject in his faded tweed suit. He had the shiny but veined handsome face of an outdoorsy older man, with receding hair that made its way out of his ears into massive sideburns. His voice reminded me of The Duke of Edinburgh's. It was husky mixed with a touch of melted chocolate, ultra-refined and bordering on perfection. If ever a man was content it was he. He had enough and no more than he needed.

His sleepy light blue eyes lit up when he saw me. Before I could introduce my top secret agent he called out: 'Dearest Kathryn I have wonderful news. All your paintings are sold. I cannot believe what has happened. You must have a secret admirer,' he enthused, tapping out his pipe on the wall. 'Have you brought your sister?' he asked, tactfully.

'Mrs. Jenkins this is Alan my sponsor.'

'Hello Alan. You may call me Ingrid…Teresa May is Prime Minister,' she said, reaching out to greet him.

'So she is dear lady,' Alan responded, looking amused. 'But not for long I fear,' he added, kissing her hand. He was used to batty old ladies.

'Has anything happened to Winston?' she asked me. 'I couldn't bear it if he was injured.'

'Ingrid. Have you met him?' Alan asked.

'Oh. Yes. He's wonderful and so intelligent and charming.'

Alan was a bit of a film buff and spent many afternoons in the Chelsea Cinema. He was a big fan of *The Sexy Beast* named Ray. Churchill was the last thing on his mind.

'Come inside darling and tell me more,' he insisted. 'There's champagne - and canopies.'

'Not for me this early dear. A nice cup of tea would be most welcome.'

'Tea it is then. I can see you are the sort of lady who likes her brew strong and flavoursome.'

Now what? Bugger it. Let her sing out the praises of her hero. Alan won't know the difference. Ray and Winston are renowned for being: tough, clever, enigmatic, big built men's men and good at making stirring speeches, whilst being utterly charming to pretty ladies.

The shop window was glaringly empty, as were the walls inside where my paintings had hug. Alan sat Mrs. Jenkins down in a battered plush Queen Ann chair in front of a Regency card table on which a plate of *M & S* canopies rested and headed for the kitchen to make tea. I followed him.

'Are you telling me that the whole lot has been sold?'

'Yes. Dear girl. Every single one. I also have had a fruitful morning. I have finally sold that ruddy awful moose's head for £50. You know the moth-eaten mount Freddie Shawcross brought round in payment of a debt,' he beamed, taking the milk out of the fridge and leaving behind the champagne. 'And you'll be pleased to know the *Nat West* pigs you so disliked have finally gone to a good home for £150. Hideous things, they were. Who in their right mind dresses up animals in clothing? It makes them look all the more ghastly and particularly with gaping holes in their bottoms…Now what were we talking about before? I must say darling you look breathtaking on this most prosperous morn. Are you in love?'

'Stop teasing me and tell me everything you

big flirt. I want the truth now. Oh. And thanks for the great prezzie.'

'You're welcome my dear. I know how much you fancy Sam the Scot. He is rather a dish. By the by, let me see. Ah. Yes…It was slightly before the moose and pigs episode. They say things come in threes…A man arrived in a black cab. He had two brief cases full of cash and bought the lot for his client. He would not tell me the name of the buyer though. I do love a good mystery.'

'Well you would, looking like a Victorian sleuth. Come on please. Stop messing about - how much did you ask for?'

'I bartered a little, as is my want. The fellow was adamant. He had been instructed to buy them all no matter what the price… Brace yourself Kathryn, they fetched just over ten… thousand… pounds,' he said roundly, 'in cash.'

'I can't remember when I've had so much fun…Mrs. Jenkins chimed in. 'Do you like *Battenberg* cake Alan, or is it Heinrich.'

'My favourite dear lady and call me whatever

pleases you,' he replied, pouring the boiled water from a Russian tea-kettle into a Tang Dynasty Chinese Export teapot.

Totally overwhelmed, I fell backwards onto an Eighteenth Century oak milking stool.

20

The year had been extraordinary and full of twists and turns. Day dreams had become realities and nightmares less frightening. Admittedly, I had fantasized about Sean. Who wouldn't? He's just drop dead gorgeous. Sometimes though, looking fantastic isn't enough. Look at Liz Taylor one of the most beautiful woman in the world. She met her match on a couple of occasions with Mike and Richard. Did she ever find lasting love? Who knows? I doubt it. But the gutsy lady still had her hopes and dreams. Maybe I had softened up and opened myself to the idea of trusting to love.

After all there must be others around like Ben the Vet. The quiet ones whose actions speak louder than words. I dared to wonder what the future might bring. I'd all the time in the world. In the meantime I needed to knuckle down and do some more paintings. Strike while the iron's hot, as they say.

Sal and Joe arrived at Alan's shop with a rosy glow on their cheeks and bearing gifts. I was bursting to tell them the good news but Mrs. Jenkins beat me to it.

'Gurda and Ilmhart, state the passwords to Heinrich and confirm your true identity.'

'What? Oh. Yes. Hello Heinrich. Christmas falls on the 25th of December every year,' Sal said, trying not to laugh.

'And New Year's Day is the time for fresh resolutions darling,' Alan replied, enjoying the fun.

'Now you Ilmhart love,' Mrs. Jenkins smiled at Joe. 'I know you always take your work seriously.'

'The meaning of life the universe and everything equals 42,' Joe said po-faced.

'The world is a stage and each must play a lute,' chortled Alan. 'I say this is awfully good fun. Rather like charades.'

'Heinrich, I'm surprised at you. Don't you know there's a war on?'

'I most certainly do dear lady and to prove it I'll show you a tin of powdered egg,' Alan said, opening a cupboard full of War memorabilia.

'Glad to see someone knows what year it is. Donald Trump is President of the Unite States of America.'

'Clint Eastwood is the Mayor of Carmel,' Alan replied, chuckling at our antics.

'Infinity is only a short word,' Joe said, unable to resist joining in the hilarity.

'And Mick Jagger is lead singer of *The Rolling Stones*,' Mrs. Jenkins replied proudly.

Her memory was getting better with a little stimulation. If I can steer her past *The Cockleshell Heroes* and towards *Singing in the Rain*, we'll be making some progress. 'Now then, everybody let's get our coats and go out and have a slap up meal at *Café Rouge*. It's on me,' I said cheerily. 'I've just received some important news about our War efforts.'

'Frieda you know very well we have to cut down on rations,' Mrs. Jenkins chided.

'I know that Ingrid. But the French are providing the food.'

'That's alright then as long as it's not snails. Come on dear friends. Keep your eyes and ears open and say nothing under pressure other than your name and rank,' she informed the troops. 'There are spies in our midst.'

During our meal I managed to contact Keith the Vet and he said that Lucky was rallying and managed a few licks of water. Alan refused outright to take any commission from the money I'd received for my paintings. He said that he had such a good time it was worth a fortune. It's funny what makes people happy. I suppose feeling useful is important. Alan's lovely. I tried and failed to get a number for *PARTY POPPETS* and so Aunt Leonora was still a mystery. I was too elated at that point to worry about crazy relatives. I didn't have room in my life for any more surprises because everything was going my way. And when I checked my messages, Ben had text me with a cheery few lines about Lucky and sent his congratulations on my sell-out exhibition. He had actually taken the time to call at the shop quite early. All things considered I had finally moving forward in my career. Then Rachel phoned.

'Hi. Kat. Errum…Are you okay?'

I pretended to be annoyed with her and said: 'Fine…Why?'

'It's just that …Well…you know…Did Sal tell you about Sean and me?'

'No. What do you mean?'

'Oh. Kat. I'm so sorry. I didn't mean it to happen. We were both really, really pissed and well, I spent the night with him…' she wailed desperately. 'I've got to be absolutely honest with you, because you're my best friend. It was me that came on to him…Please don't be upset with me.'

'I know that you dirty trollop. There's no stopping you when you've had a few…Did you have a good time then Rach? Sean is a perfect physical specimen. Isn't he?' I said, not telling her that the whole household had heard her screeching.

'What? You don't mind then?' she asked, relief flooding into her voice.

'Not one bit. Well, I'm a little jealous, I must say…I'm glad you got one over on Rob. A fling is just what you needed…Rob's rubbish, leaving you like that – and sitting on the floor an all… He never appreciated your funny side and needed a wake up call.'

'Well It's a little more than a one night stand…Sean's moving in with me and I've text Rob to say the wedding's off and it's all over,' she blurted out. 'You don't think I'm an idiot do you? Honestly Kat I've never been so happy. I'm madly in love…and I really like Sean, so that must be a good sign.'

'Do you know his surname yet?' I teased.

'Course I do…What's your other name Sean?'

I heard Sean whisper 'Connor.'

'I mean your surname,' Rachel giggled.

'Walsh.'

'Actually I do. It's Sean Connor Walsh. He of the most gorgeous bod and buns.'

'Well. It's a little sudden. But what the hell - life's too short to spend it with a frog when you can kiss a prince. You go for it girl, but please don't get burned. Will you?'

'I'll try not to, but Sean's so hot,' she giggled distractedly and said, 'Stop it! Not now Sean.'

'When is he moving out?' I asked.

'Right now,' she said, breathlessly. 'Must go Kat. Oh. Can we leave the keys with you to return to the landlord? I'll put them on the hall table. If you want anything help yourself. There's some quality stuff in there…Sean doesn't want it. He likes to travel light. I've got everything I need and the Snow Queen's on a one-way flight home to daddy…The rent's paid up for another three months. I'm so happy…See you soon.'

That'll be in about three weeks, I guess, after constant pleasuring and when the novelty had worn off. 'Okay Rach. Be happy. Bye.'

Walking back home with a bin liner full of cash slung over my shoulder and my dry-cleaned coat on the other, I had a proposition to put to Sal and Joe. Previously, after a few furtive phone calls I had almost sorted out their financial problems. Alan had agreed that he needed a new alarm system and that a bell over the door was definitely outdated. He also said that he would speak to his posh friends regarding state of the art satellite-linked burglar alarm systems and remote controlled gates. Trevor and Wayne, although they didn't know it yet, would get the full treatment also. *Café Rouge* had shown some interest too.

I'd contacted the landlord regarding the lease for the basement flat and he had agreed to transfer it to Sal and Joe. Nobody had actually seen him but his phone voice was polite and the property as a whole was fairly well maintained - which was unusual for most landlords. He had always visited to check up on things when I was out, which was a bit creepy. Anyhow, I could well afford to pay

Sal and Joe's rent for a while until the business was up and running. I had also intended to shove a leaflet under Edward's door about getting the house made more secure - although I knew he could fly under any radar and would frighten off most non blood-drinking burglars.

Horatio sat on the doorstep wailing loudly. I settled a giddy Mrs. Jenkins in her flat, fed the mog then took the keys from the hall table steering Sal and Joe back outside.

'What are you up to young lady? I know that expression well,' Sal said. 'Where are you taking us?'

'A trip round the 'arbour my 'andsomes…This way for the *Skylark* plenty of room down below,' I said, hoping the flat was tidy. I know the Snow Queen had vacuumed the carpets every morning and made Sean meticulously clean her company *Jaguar* twice a week, whilst looking down her perfect doctored nose at my old banger.

The flat was beautiful and sparkling clean. Sean had hurriedly taken all his possessions. That is to say he had removed his clothes, toiletries, Hi-Fi and CD's including Ravel's *Bolero*, whilst leaving expensive curtains, furniture and mirrors and everything else that men don't care about. At least he wasn't using Rachel for her money. They were both impulsive and passionate people with a tendency to be fickle.

Who knows? It might actually work. And joy, no more Ravel blasting up the chimney.

The flat was tastefully decorated and still had the original log burning fireplace. The bespoke kitchen stretched from front window right into the back and led out onto the patio and garden, complete with barbeque. There were two substantial bedrooms and a modern bathroom with power shower.

'You are so nosy,' Sal laughed, looking into all the cupboards in the kitchen. 'And wow look at this Joe - a double oven. I'm in heaven.'

'How would you feel about living here?' I asked, trying not to look smug.

'Chance would be a fine thing. How could anyone not like this place? It's gorgeous.'

Joe looked around and smiled. 'If only…,' he sighed. 'I expect something like this would cost a bomb?'

'I bet the Snow Queen will be back like a shot for her stuff when she find out Sean's left,' Sal said, eyeing up a full set of blue *Le Creuset* casserole dishes, a silver *Smeg* fridge and a *Bosch* washing machine and tumble dryer.

'According to Sean she's gone back to Philadelphia for good,' I told them gleefully. 'The rich bitch said he could have the lot, but Rach has got everything at hers, so she said to help ourselves.'

I didn't say another word and handed Joe the keys. He looked puzzled then amazed.

'You know we can't possibly afford such a place Kat,' Sal said, spinning around with arms outstretched in the kitchen. 'Anyhow don't you need a bigger apartment?'

'I wouldn't swap my attic for the world.

Through the skylight I can see the stars at night - and the light first thing is breathtaking,' I replied. And if there are any bat-like creatures around, I can see them before they see me.

'What have you been up to Kat?' Joe asked, looking worried.

'Look guys, I've got you loads of business. The rent's paid for the next nine months. We can get some flyers done and post them around Chelsea and Knightsbridge...You know full well Sophie and Zach won't see you go short...The garden's small but secure and it's south-facing sunny and ideal for a baby. Look,' I said opening the back door. 'Would you believe it? There are the last of the Iceberg roses and Clematis still in flower alongside Cyclamens and Chrysanthemums.'

b'It's just perfect,' Sal sighed. 'A garden of my own - a real garden. I can grow peas and runner beans.'

b'It's yours if you want it. I'll leave you to look around and think about it - on one condition.

'What's that then madam-mate?' Joe asked.

'You invite me to at least one of your barbeques.'

'It's a deal.'

'That's that then,' I said. 'And Sal, you can bake from home. Start up your own business... Your cakes would sell like hot -. Well you know what I mean...Trevor and Wayne were really impressed with your puddings and -.'

'Come here and shut up waffling, you divvy,' she said, holding out her arms.

The three of us did a group hug and screeched like girlies. It was unbelievable. Most of the time life had never been easy for us. We had got used to hardship and disappointment. Could it be, at last, that everything was coming together for us? Would I be with my dearest friends and sharing the same roof again? It was a really weird feeling. For some reason I felt uneasy.

Mrs. Jenkins interrupted our moment of elated craziness and called down the steps: 'What's happening down there Frieda? I've got the kettle on...A parcel has just arrived for you... Do Gurda and Ilmhart like *Battenberg*? Have the noisy musicians left? I got a little fed up of the same tune over and over - and that opera singer last night was rubbish.'

'They certainly have Ingrid and taken their violin cases with them.'

'Does that mean the Hun has been ousted?'

'Most definitely Ingrid and our best agents Gurda and Ilmhart will be taking their place. We can all sleep well in our beds at night from now on. Do you know what? I think we're going to win this war.'

'That's just what my Wolfgang said last night…He's keeping a lookout at *Chez Trevayne*, because he felt that Trevor and Wayne were far too blonde for his liking.'

Bugger. What have I got myself into? First priority. To get Ingrid through the show, hide and tell test in preparation for her assessment next week at the hospital. Now what did I do with that tray and tea towel?

21

'We're nearly home Kat,' Zach announced happily. 'We've got your room ready for you. There's a wonderful view. You can see the sea from up there.'

The car sped along the narrow winding lane and then took a left turn down a gravel track. And it suddenly dawned on me why the car was covered in orange dust. After bumping, bouncing and crunching along in the car under a covering of trees, leaving a gritty cloud behind, we finally arrived.

Right in front of us was a sprawling stone built house that looked like something out of a Jane Austen romance. The front garden was open plan and had a huge moss covered fountain in the centre while the gravel drive curved around it in a complete circle. The frontage of the house had a pillared porch with an ancient woody wisteria weaving its way around and up to the second story windows. It actually had a turret. The house was everything I'd ever dreamed of and the excitement inside began to bubble to the surface.

'Do you like?' Sophie asked.

'It's all right I suppose,' I begrudgingly replied, doing the moody teenager bit and trying to repress my curiosity.

There was something about the light and the way it touched the pillars and the weathered stones and then bounced off the windows in a dazzling brightness. It was bewitching.

'It's more than all right my loverrlee. It's bloody wonderful,' Zach said, getting my tiny case from the boot. 'We fell in love with it the first time we set eyes on it. It's taken us over twenty years to renovate and there's still loads to do.'

I just wanted to rush inside and explore every nook and cranny of *Wisteria House* but instead I lagged behind trying my hardest to stay mad at those time-warped fruitcakes.

As we walked towards the porch, a dog started to bark madly then a white dinosaur-like head appeared and disappeared as the animal jumped up and down as if it were on a trampoline, trying to see through the high window.

'That's old Boss. It looks as if Mrs. Wainwright has been and gone ages ago. He looks restless,' Zach said on seeing my worried expression added: 'His bark's worse than his bite,' he reassured me laughing at the dog's antics. 'Don't worry he doesn't savage if he's been fed. He's a big softie really.'

'I'm not scared,' I replied, standing behind Zach and peering at Boss's large head rising and falling.

'Are you hungry Kat?' Zach asked. 'We've got cottage pie and home grown veg for dinner. Your Aunt…I mean Sophie will make it especially for you.'

His enthusiasm was contagious and I eased out a half smile and nodded.

As Zach unlocked the front door Boss made a dash down the hallway and skidded along the carpet runner, before nearly knocking me off my feet.

'Get him off me,' I yelled, trying to push him back and get his slobbering jaws away from my face.

'Down boy,' Zach laughed, pulling the heavyweight dino-head away.

'Let him out Zach, he needs to go,' Sophie insisted, jumping out of Boss's way as he rushed out of the front door and headed down the drive to the nearest tree.

'Come on Kat I'll show you to your room,' Zach said, running up the huge staircase, faded flairs flapping and hair flowing, looking like something from a Carry On film meets Billy Windswept and Interesting Connolly - and still holding my little case. Then he remembered Sophie and mid flight turned to look at me and said quietly: 'Sophie has spent so much time on redesigning your room. Every year she's updated the decor as you grew older, always hoping you'd come home and thinking it wouldn't be good enough for you...I hope you like it Kat. It would mean a lot to her if you did. You're her only blood relative now. Her last connection to your Dad...'

For the second time in my life I felt a pang of remorse. Be good enough for me? Blimey. A room of my own and especially decorated to suit me? Wow. After all it wasn't their fault I'd been abandoned. The letters in my file proved it. 'Sophie? Will you come up with me?' I asked nervously.

It was such a weird feeling pretending to be nice to someone - forming alien words in my mouth to comfort them when they were strangers to me. I'd never done that before. My life had been black or white: be happy or sad, be good or bad, be beautiful or ugly, be a prisoner of be free, be friends or enemies. I simply just didn't understand kindness. At that point it equalled weakness to me...I mistrusted their motives.

They both seemed so vulnerable though - and wrinkly and quaint...I had to learn to modify my responses to their needs. They had no defences to protect themselves. Both of them were such easy targets...But hey, what the hell, there was no point in playing a moody teenager at fifteen years old. I just couldn't keep it up... I had left that stage behind years ago.

Sometimes I felt as old as Methuselah. And there I was, old Jonah who had escaped the whale to be thrown out of the darkness into the light. I knew it wouldn't be plain sailing but I had to try to be amiable. And like Pinocchio I would hope to turn into a real person. The girl I'd always wanted to be. Try to find out if there was anything left in me worth saving.

'I'd like that Kat,' she replied, clearing her throat.

Zach walked behind Sophie and me but still

made encouraging sounds. He really tried so hard to say the right things.

'I thought you wouldn't want pink,' Sophie said, hesitantly. 'You're a Shaw after all. Shaw women are made of stronger stuff. I-I thought Dresden blue and white would be nice. What do you think?' she asked opening the third door along the landing.

I gasped. She must have known from my expression that I was pleased. I couldn't help but smile. It was just perfect. There was a huge white four poster bed with a pristine patchwork quilt and hangings to match. The floor boards were polished to a warm honey glow with white rugs scattered around. The panoramic window had floating white gauze drapes so as not to obscure the wonderful view. Opposite the bed was a white dressing table covered with colour-coordinated toiletries and knickknacks. And a tip and tilt full length mirror stood in the corner.

I was quite surprised to see myself in total for the first time. I didn't realize that I looked so white, sullen, slouchy and skinny. And it was all the more noticeable standing next to Sophie with her sensual dark Mediterranean looks and Zach resembling Thomas Hardy's ruddleman: Diggory.

Sophie seemed to have read my mind. 'Some sea air will soon put colour in your cheeks. We'll leave you to look around now. The bathroom is through this door,' she said.

I had my own en-suite bathroom. Can you believe it?

'I've put some clothes in the wardrobe…If they're not to your taste I can change them…You might want to look in the window seat if you've got time…Well. I'd best go and get the dinner on,' she said awkwardly. 'It'll be ready in about an hour and a half… You can lock your bedroom door if you want. There's the key,' she added, touching the lock.

'Just follow your nose Kat to find the kitchen because the succulent odours will lead you there,' Zach beamed in a way that belied his age.

First things first, I tried out the bed. It was like sinking into a cloud. Not in the least like my hard unyielding bed in the Care Home. Everything looked so crisp and fresh. She was right about the colours. They made the room airy and light. Then I checked out the drawers and they were full of frilly underwear and night things. The bras and pants actually matched - and were coloured. I had my very first bras, even though they were all a paltry 30A cup. I had bras at last! I'd only ever had white pants before and navy shorts for P.E.

It suddenly dawned on me how much effort had gone into the preparation. She must have dashed around buying my size in everything before they had actually come to collect me from Wales.

My heart was pounding by the time I had checked out my very own bathroom, complete with white towelling robe and slippers. I was beginning to feel a little uncomfortable with all that space and nobody around to share it with, until I heard a scratching on the door. It was Boss. He waddled passed me, settled on a white rug, turned round and round a few times, farted, then fell asleep and began snoring like a pig.

Taking a long shower and not being stared at by the other girls anymore, or prodded and poked, or made aware that my tits were none existent, was just great. I went over to the window seat and lifted the padded cover. It was full of unopened presents. Some of them were wrapped in faded Christmas paper and some with "Happy Birthday" written on. My presents returned by The Mummy over the years to Newquay.

An Aladdin's cave of treasure was stacked in year order inside the hollow seat. The greatest prize lay on top of the pile. It was a photo album made especially for me by Sophie and Zach. Of course it started out with some old sepia photos of the Shaw family and my Great Great Grandparents looking tiny but sturdy and weather beaten standing next to a fishing trawler. Photos of my great great great Uncles making fishing nets, while my great great great Aunts gutted the fish for market, with names like George, Albert, Ernest and Elizabeth, Annie and Blanche.

As I slowly turned the pages a whole new

world unfolded before my eyes. I can't explain how I felt only to say that it was the best ever sensation. Like food and water to a starving man lost in the desert - filling an empty void with light. The best ever spot in time. A perfect shimmering pearl...I knew at last that this was where I belonged - with my blood family. I savoured every image. Then I reached photos of my Grandmother and Granddad Shaw. I could see where Sophie got her dark looks from. They both had black hair and full apple cheeks. There was a small boy and a girl a little older standing next to them. It was my Father and Sophie.

I put the picture so close to my face to be nearer to it that I went crossed eyed, scanning every little section of him to find something of me. It was hard but I did. I got my serious expression and my wing-nuts from my Father. Not much to brag about I know, but it meant the world to me. Sophie was also quite a sullen child and looked uncomfortable in front of the camera.

Moving slowly through the pages I saw my

Father as a school boy, a teenager then as a man. He was tall and well built with good posture. Another of him playing cricket and a great one of him surfing…In fact he was very handsome and reminded me of a young Jonny Depp. As I lingered over these images, touching them in disbelief, hanging on to each captured memory, I was suddenly overwhelmed.

On the penultimate page were studio pictures of my Mother and Father on their wedding day. I couldn't breathe and had to get a glass of water. It was all too much to take in at first. I was staring back at myself. My Mother was a mirror image of me only smaller and curvy. She had the same vivid hair colour and very white skin but without my freckles – and had obviously avoided the sun. The main difference was she looked happy, vivacious and full of life. Her eyes sparkled as she looked up in adoration at my Father – her green eyes with orange sunbursts.

I couldn't cry. I felt so angry and confused. I had pains in my neck and throat.

I'm nothing like the Shaw's. I don't belong here…I'm the image of her - the woman who abandoned me – the crazy selfish suicidal witch.

Rage took over. It was like an uncontrollable storm breaking within. I slung the album out of the window and into the vegetable garden then quickly dressed, pulling on denim shorts, t-shirt and pumps and ran down the stairs, slamming the front door behind me.

I lost track of time and space as I ran round the perimeter of the high walled garden and headed out towards the cliffs. Unaccustomed to running in the heat, I hyperventilated. I didn't care I just wanted to run until I couldn't feel the hurt anymore. Run until I expired. Run until I no longer existed…I couldn't cope with all this new information. It had turned my life inside out and made me feel all the more alone.

I tore along the footpath with the blood pounding in my head and my muscles on fire, until I got a sharp stabbing in my side and doubled up in pain. Heaving and gasping, I fell down and lay in the long coarse grass that grew along the cliff tops. Every bone in my body ached and I couldn't swallow. The tightness in my throat had become unbearable…Dry-eyed I let out a scream, then another and another until I could do no more than just lie there like a rag doll.

I don't know how long I'd been there, flat on my back with eyes closed, disturbed only by the sweet farewells of the skylarks hovering above me. But I was suddenly and uncomfortably brought back to consciousness by a soggy muzzle snuffling at my ear. It was Boss. He'd found me.

'Will you stop that?!' I shouted angrily, pushing him away. He groaned and grumbled, as dogs do, then flopped down by my side letting out a huge sigh. 'Sorry old boy. I didn't mean it,' I said, reaching out to stroke him. He lifted his head and looked at me sideways with his black-patch piggy eye and tried to focus… I knew, right there and then that I would not be so lonely.

22

My first night spent in *Wisteria House* was a restless one. It was at that spot in time when I began to dream about drowning. This was compounded by Boss sneaking under the bottom of the duvet, holding my feet together between his front paws, licking my toes with his rough tongue and growling every time I tried to move. It was a weird sensation, to say the least.

After my crazy outburst on the cliff-tops, I had followed Boss back to the house, hoping nobody had heard my caterwauling. He periodically turned and looked to see if I was still behind him before walking onwards. I followed him into the back garden through a dog-flap in the side wall. Excitedly he danced into the kitchen and tip-tapped around on the stone floor, wagging his whole body while his mini rudder remained stationary. We were both greeted with smiles and pleasantries.

'Hi Kat. Did you enjoy your jog?' Zach asked, pushing a tray of risen bread and teacakes into the oven.

'It was different,' I begrudgingly replied, feeling a little embarrassed by my actions.

'Boss just loves it out there. Unfortunately we can't keep him away from the cliffs. I seriously believe he was a mountain goat in a previous existence…One of these days he'll -.'

'That's enough Zach,' Sophie interrupted. 'Are you ready to eat now?' I nodded. 'Well sit yourself down and tuck in,' she said handing me a steaming plate full of delicious smelling food.

'Thanks. I will,' I replied, not looking at her.

'So?' Zach started up. 'What do you think of it so far?'

'It's fine,' I replied, blowing on a forkful of cottage pie. 'Got any brown sauce?'

'Do you like your room?' he went on.

'It's very nice…errum…thank you.'

'You're welcome,' Sophie said, passing me the *HP* bottle from the larder.

Boss pawed my knees from under the table and whined.

'Don't feed him,' Sophie said sharply. 'He's too fat as it is…And that goes for you too Zach.'

Zach winked at me and dropped a blob of cooled pie on the stone floor. While Boss slobbered over the splat, Zach continued his cheery line of questioning. 'So…Do you fancy a trip round the harbour tomorrow and do some sightseeing before we take you to see your new school?'

'Like I keep saying, I'm not going to another f- school. I've had enough of school. It's for dummies.'

'There're only two weeks to the summer holidays. We thought you'd like to meet the other kids and your new teacher before they break-up,' Zach added. 'Ease you in slowly, so to speak.'

'Not for me thanks,' I said through a mouthful of pie.

'Tosh,' Sophie said, joining us at the table with cheeks aglow and hair escaping from a topknot. 'You need to finish what you've started and use your brain. You reports say that you're very good at English, Art and History. And well above average on other subjects. Have you any idea how hard it is to get a job out there without qualifications?'

'Not given it much thought,' I replied casually. 'Anyhow, when I'm sixteen I'm going to work with Joe and Sal in the lock-picking trade,' I said, trying to rile her. 'Its night work, easy money and you don't have to pay tax.'

'Fine,' she replied, not batting an eyelid.

'Fine,' I responded.

Zach looked disappointed and kind of lost for a while before he spoke again. 'I'm going down to the shop first thing in the morning. It's very near the beach and there's some good surfing to be had down there…Do you want to come and help out?'

'Might as well. There's nothing else to do round here,' I replied, aiming another splodge at Boss, before heartily tucking into the delicious pie.

'Slow down girl. There's plenty more where that came from,' Sophie said, smiling at me.

'Sorry. We had to clear our plates quickly or they would be taken away before we'd finished,' I replied blushing and omitting to tell them about Sal's gluttony.

'You take your time and eat as much as you want. There's plenty for all of us,' Zach assured me.

It was so nice to sit and eat in a leisurely manner. All my life I had to bolt my food. From then on table manners had to be learned.

After finishing off a huge bowl of pear tart and custard and feeling well and truly stuffed, I took time to look around the sprawling kitchen. Most of the original features had been retained like the flagstone floor, the huge porcelain sink with wooden draining-boards on each side and the mighty Aga oven which was still hot and filled with bread and teacakes.

After dinner Zach and Sophie cleared away the pots and took their coffees outside. They made everything looked so easy and uncomplicated, relaxing back into a swing seat.

The garden beyond the patio area had a wild meadow look about it. Random splashes of vivid colours stood out amid a chaos of scents and shapes. Flowers bloomed in abundance without gaps or symmetry, just blocks of reds, purples, yellows and oranges all mixed together in a symphony of discordant abandon. It was nature gone mad – and it was fantastic.

I joined them on the decked area and watched Boss nose his way into the flowers like some prehistoric beast trampling through the wilderness before disappearing into the undergrowth.

'Can I have a ciggy?' I asked, as Zach started to roll a spliff.

'No,' Sophie said, 'and before you start imagining things it's not wacky-backy. It's purely herbal.'

I smiled and said: Okay. If you say so.'

'I do so,' she replied, drawing deeply on the misshapen cigarette which seemed to evaporate by the inch with each inhalation.

'You might want to explore the rest of the garden,' Zach said changing the subject. 'We have a fabulous vegetable section through the gate over there and there's a wild strawberry patch. Here take a basket and pick us some for breakfast,' he said happily.

'Okay.'

I was both relieved and pleased to wander around on my own and to get away from the constant questions. I wasn't used to being the centre of attention.

A whole new world opened out before me. Here was organization. In neat regimented rows all kinds of vegetables grew in abundance, sectioned off and contained within old railway sleepers. Some of them were familiar like: delicate lacy carrot tops and onions bursting out of the ground and enormous pantomime runner beans curling around canes. Others were totally alien to me.

It was fascinating to touch, smell and taste the different varieties. From bitter to sweet, spicy to earthy, sour lemon grass to succulent tangy small tumbling tomatoes. Cloches, bell jars, cucumber frames and raspberry bushes inside cages to keep off the birds - although round the edges all the lower branches had been pecked at and stripped. And last but not least a huge wild strawberry patch kept safe from slugs and snails with net coverings, a bedding of straw, a border of gravel and buried jam jars filled with beer stationed round the perimeter so the slimy beasties could die happy.

Marigolds grew alongside Pansies and Sweet Peas in bed with all kinds of herbs. Nettles and Dandelions were allowed to stay with lettuces and radishes. Nothing was wasted and everything had a purpose in a quiet order that I'd not seen before. A locked Victorian greenhouse full of filigree foliage placed in the most southerly part of the garden.

Kneeling down on an inner border of soft Chamomile, I lifted the net and picked strawberries with a sense of purpose and a new fluttering in my stomach. I remember thinking at the time that it must be contentment until I saw the jack-knifed photo album on the far side of the strawberry patch and to the side of a moss covered tap over a spilling water trough.

Oh. God. What if it had gone in the water? It would've been ruined.

Running to retrieve the precious item I felt immensely relieved that everything was still intact and undamaged. I wiped off the dust from the covers and dared to turn to the last page. There was a picture of a crying baby with a ginger Mohican and wearing a fancy white Christening gown. It was me of course. There was another photo of a younger Sophie holding me in a crocheted shawl. She looked so pretty, young and gentle. My Father stood behind her with a huge grin on his face.

Oh. God. Oh. God. Oh. God. I'm not going to cry. I will not blubber. I will not spoil this precious pearl. Questions will come later…This moment of happiness is mine and nobody else's.

And I sat there sucking on strawberries until the sun sizzled into the sea.

23

5th November.

It was the morning of Mrs. Jenkins's hospital appointment to see if she had Alzheimer's disease. I'd informed the Social Services that I would take her to the hospital. She seemed nonchalant about being grilled by the Gestapo and had remembered the new information I'd fed her. Together, after days of questioning, we'd managed to reach the future/present with some difficulty. Her comprehension of the happenings in the 21st century was a puzzling one, to say the least - especially the *London Eye* and the *Millennium Dome*. Heaven knows what she would have made of reality television.

I was desperate to find out more about Aunt Leonora and return the *Nat West* hideous pigs she sent me for my birthday. Yes. That was the parcel Mrs. Jenkins found on the door mat…Of all the cheek - I ask you? Surely this must have been a deliberate insult. Why anyone would buy such tripe - and from my friend Alan? And how did she know where my exhibition was? The party she'd organized was pretty unusual, to say the least…Something wicked this way cometh - me thinks. Nevertheless it would have to be put on the back burner for now. Mrs. Jenkins welfare came first and foremost.

'So Frieda shall I call you by your secret agent's name or the other boring one?' she asked, powdering her downy face.

'Ingrid I think we should keep this simple and stick to our plan no matter what. We don't want to give the Germans any information other than the general tit-bits I've taught you.'

'Understood Frieda. Adele is the best singer since Whitney. Does it mean then that Gracie Fields and Vera Lynn are no longer the Forces Sweethearts?' she asked looking disappointed.

'Of course they are Ingrid. These are just code names to protect our valued singers. The War effort and all that,' I reassured her, giving her a knowing look and wondering if I was doing the right thing.

'Teresa May is Prime Minister and today is Bonfire Night…Won't the fireworks and all those bonfires give the enemy easy targets?'

'Good thinking.' Shit I never thought of that. 'You see Ingrid they'll be lit as decoys in unimportant places; for example near the dog track and away from the bomb factories. Do you copy?'

'Won't the poor greyhounds get injured?'

'What? Err no. It's closed tonight. Animals don't like fireworks…Remember when poor Horatio got out and went berserk last year…That Roman Candle on his blind-side nearly sent him bonkers. Okay. Now let's get a move on or we'll be late for your appointment.'

'Frieda. What if I forget the items on the tray when the Commandant puts the tea towel over it?'

'If you're wrong I'll scratch my nose and if you're right I'll smile. Okay?'

As we waited in rush hour traffic on the King's Road, I hoped she would do well in the assessment. She seemed composed and sat calmly with her gloved hands folded daintily on her lap. Bless her. She looked so vulnerable and adorable. There was no way I'd let them take her away from her home and put her into Care.

We waited in the Outpatient's Clinic to see Mr. Johal. I know. I know…What was she going to make of him? I soon found out as Mr. Johal came out wearing a pin-striped suit, a turban and sporting a dapper beard. Mrs. Jenkins looked amazed and startled.

'Are you sure he's the enemy? He's too handsome and smiley to be Gestapo,' she whispered.

'He's really working for our side. We're in luck.'

'He's a double agent? Are you positive?'' she asked, following the Consultant into his office.

I smiled thinly and panicked. Why had I started all this in the first place? Please God let him ask the right questions.

'Good morning Mrs. Jenkins. How are you?' he asked sitting her next to his chair. 'And this is…?'

'How do you do Mr. Johal. I'm in good health and sound mind and ready to serve my country. Please call me Ingrid. Thank you very much… And this is my dearest friend Frieda,' she said firmly.

Mr. Johal looked surprised and pleased. 'I'm glad to hear it…is it Iris or Ingrid?'

Mrs. Jenkins looked confused and gave me a pleading look.

'She uses her Confirmation name. She prefers it to Iris,' I said quietly.

'I see…Now, do you know why you're here?'

Mrs. Jenkins gave me a quick sideways glance and said: 'Of course I do. The question is: do you?'

'I think so,' he laughed, 'although it's a little

early in the morning for me. Would you like some tea Ingrid?'

'That would be very civilized of you. I wasn't expecting kindness.'

Mr. Johal looked amused then nipped outside his office and got three steaming cups of brown stuff from the vending machine, passing them one at a time to me, along with a handful of those frugal strip-packets of sugar. As we all rowed around our scalding tea with tiny plastics oars he asked: 'Now Ingrid do you know what day it is today?'

'Why Mr. Johal, don't you remember. I've already told you it's Bonfire Night. Gun powder treason and plot,' she replied touching her nose. 'But the greyhounds are safe.'

'What?'

'She has a vested interest in greyhounds. You know, rescuing racing dogs when they're past their sell-by date. Finding them good homes with people like Jilly Cooper and such like,' I said, wondering what else was going to slip out.

'Absolutely terrified of the noise on Bonfire Night…The dogs that is and not Jilly Cooper, but I dare say she's one for a quiet life…' I am a moron.

I started to get very fidgety but Ingrid didn't break under pressure and smiled sweetly.

'It's a very good cause indeed. I always say an interesting hobby keeps the mind sound,' he replied, putting three sugars into the foul tea.

'Teresa May is Prime Minster,' Mrs. Jenkins volunteered.

'So she is. I was just going to ask you that question.'

'She's not a patch on Churchill though…And Donald Trump is President of America.'

Mr. Johal raised his eyebrows and made notes on Mrs. Jenkins's file before turning his attention to me. 'Miss Shaw, are you related to Mrs. Jenkins? And can you tell me how she manages living alone?'

'I'm…her Goddaughter. And we live in the same house. I'm around all day because I work in the evenings, but my friends Sal and Joe, who also live in the house, take over for the evening shift until I return.'

'Excellent…Now Ingrid…I have to do a few more things like taking your blood pressure and testing your reflexes, if you don't mind?'

'Let's get on with it then Mr. Johal. Is that your real name by the way, or is it a code name?'

Oh. Shit.

'Code name?'

'She said: Sudoku game. She's very good at solving the numbers ….Aren't you Ingrid?'

'Yes indeed. I can remember everything on the tray as well. Why there were: spectacles, keys, coins, knitting needle, penknife and, let me see, I always forget the last one. Don't tell me Frieda…' I started to row dramatically in the sludge again with the plastic oar. '…Ah. Yes. I remember - a silver teaspoon.'

'We've been practicing,' I told him sheepishly.

'I can see that,' he smiled. Blood pressure a little high but nothing to worry about…Hearing sharper than mine, I'm pleased to say…Eye sight good except for reading glasses.'

'Yes. I bought the spectacles from *Boots*. I could never read the small print on the pill packets. I wanted *Carter's Little Liver Pills* but bought Cranberry tablets by mistake. Still I can read the small print easily with the glasses and they're gold frames as well.'

'Excellent…There's certainly nothing wrong with your cognitive functions Ingrid.'

'That's just what I told that bony-bottomed Joyce. The new Air Raid Warden…' she informed him as I coughed loudly, hoping he'd missed the latter part of her sentence. 'She didn't know what the words meant though.'

'Do you think you could count backwards from a hundred for me?' he asked.

'That's nothing I've counted back from a hundred in sevens. Shall I show you? Even Frieda had to write it down to get the right answers. Didn't you love?'

I grinned as Mrs. Jenkins began her

countdown: 93... 86...79...72...and so on, until she had finished. (I can't remember the whole thing and keep ending up with a different final number).

'Very impressive Ingrid... I'll just do a few more tests and then I'll let you be on your way. It says on your medical records that you haven't visited a doctor since 1943. Is that correct?'

'Of course it is. Why that was only last week I had an abscess on my elbow and had to use a kaolin poultice. You know - to draw out the puss. It's less painful than a heated bottle.'

'What?'

'It seems like only last week,' I interjected. 'How time flies.'

'Amazing. And you have never had any problems health-wise?'

'Well I do have trouble sleeping. That is, I did until my Wolfgang returned on Frieda's birthday.'

'Who is Wolfgang?'

'He's Ingrid's Godson from Germany. He came over for my birthday party. We're second cousins you see,' I said hastily and looking sternly at Mrs. Jenkins.

'Ah. That explains the names. Did you enjoy the birthday party Ingrid?'

'I certainly did. I danced all night. It was magical.'

'I must say you're very active and you look so much younger than your age.'

'Thank you very much,' Mrs. Jenkins added proudly.

'Yes. Indeed,' Mr. Johal chuckled. 'Now the Blood Clinic is down the corridor and to the left. You need to take a ticket and wait your turn. Everything seems to be ticking over nicely. There is nothing to worry about - just a routine check up. It has been a pleasure meeting you Ingrid,' he smiled.

'And likewise Hans,' she said winking at Mr. Johal.

'What?'

'She said that you have nice hands,' I told him,

breathing a sigh of relief as we headed for the Blood Clinic.

'Well Katie I didn't break under pressure. Sorry about mentioning Wolfgang. Mr. Johal didn't click on though. Did he?' she said, looking concerned.

'No. He didn't Ingrid. Thank goodness. It all went well. You passed the test with flying colours,' I told her. 'There might be a medal in this somewhere for outstanding bravery.' I get so carried away.

'That's a bit over the top. I didn't do anything heroic. Anyway, I thought the enemies' form of torture would be something more sinister than drinking dish-water tea and blood-letting.'

As we left the hospital I knew she would be safe from now. Safe to end her days in the comfort of her own home. And she no longer had to wait for Arnold. Mick had made sure of that. I'm not certain he'd done her a kindness in the long term, but for now she was extremely happy. It had taken all my persuasion and fibbing to keep her away from *Chez Trevayne*.

'Let's celebrate Ingrid,' I said happily. 'Do you fancy going to *Harrods* for lunch on the terrace?'

'I've never been there. It is nice?'

'I can definitely say that it's truly wonderful and you'll love every single minute of it. It's like stepping back in time…. or in your case, maybe not.'

24

Sal and Joe had returned to Cardiff to sort out their possessions. After arranging a house clearance sale with a local company: *Old Lamps for Brass*, they got exactly £250 job lot. Sal was glad to see the back of the flat but it was with some trepidation she broke the news to her two younger brothers.

Owen the elder boy was nineteen and worked in retail. He was a shop assistant/demonstrator in *Desk Top World*. There was nothing he couldn't do with the workings of a computer. Unfortunately he was autistic and had little patience on the academic side of things. He didn't appear to mind his lack of qualifications and was happy to swim along doing something he loved. Making himself indispensable to the management secured his future. His younger brother Tom had earned a place in college and was studying technical engineering. They both still lived with their decent long-term foster parents, who had given them some sense of normal family life.

The memory of their Mother, and all it entailed, had become a vague one, to be replaced with that of a genuine affection for the couple they had come to know as Ma and Da Owen. And fortunately for Sal, the boys responded happily to her news and couldn't wait to visit London in the holidays. At last she was free from the burden of worrying about her siblings and able to live her own life with Joe and the forthcoming baby.

I'd listened with joy to Sal and Joe bustling around the basement flat, putting finishing touches to make it more their own place. I hoped the noise would preoccupy Mrs. Jenkins so I could escape and perform my one-woman mission to visit Lucky before work.

Nothing had been seen or heard from Edward since my birthday. His flat remained silent. I was quite worried in case he'd had a stake through the heart from one of Peter Cushing's descendents. After all my fellow house-mate was an animal lover and had excellent manners. And I had felt safe in a funny sort of way. No prospective burglars would get out alive with Edward flying around on a red-eyed assignment.

As I crept down stairs to the ground floor armed with doggy treats and a toy rabbit, Mrs. Jenkins's door creaked open. Horatio leapt out with a bottle-brush tail and scampered upstairs growling.

'Is that you Frieda?' Mrs. Jenkins called out.

'Yes. It is," I sighed. 'I can't stop Ingrid. I'm on a mission to see a man about a dog.'

'Do come inside. I've got a surprise for you.'

Bugger. I'll be late for work again. 'It'll have to be a lightening visit Ingrid. I've got lots to do and I don't want to lose my job.'

'There's no fear of that my *Delectable Daffodil.* Not while I'm in charge of Personnel,' a familiar voice laughed hoarsely. Talk about clothes making the man.

'Mick?'

'Wolfgang if you please. You know how important secrecy is during this difficult time.'

'Come over here Frieda. Sit yourself down. Arn- I mean Wolfgang is in his rightful place in the best armchair. I poured you a nice cup of tea to drink with your *Battenberg*.'

Wolfgang reclined elegantly in Arnold's chair - his face aglow in the firelight, dressed to the nines and smelling of Wayne's aftershave. When I entered the room he rose to his feet and bowed.

'You ratbag,' I mouthed to him as Mrs. Jenkins drew up another chair near the fire.

'Why thank you Frieda. That is most kind of you,' he smiled, giving me his cheekiest grin.

I drew my finger across my neck in a slashing movement and gave him a mean look. 'Wolfgang you have broken your cover. Is that police sirens I hear? You really should be getting back to base pronto,' I hissed.

'I thought Ingrid and I could trouble you for

a lift on this bitterly cold evening, if it's not too much of a risk for you?'

'Bastard,' I mouthed again, dropping my cake on his plate.

'Thank you my *Angelic Agrostemma*. Go and get your coat on Ingrid dearest and I'll treat you to my special pasta sauce recipe at *Chez Trevayne*.

'Oh. Wolfgang you do spoil me,' she chirped.

'Nothing is too good for my sweetheart,' he fawned, slinging the cake into the fire when her back was turned.

As Mrs. Jenkins went to get her coat I had a few choice words for Wolfgang: 'Back off you old pervert or I'll tell Wayne who you really are,' I said.

'Frieda my *Anxious Antirrhinum*, do you think he would believe you, a mere waitress, against the word of an aristocrat?'

'If you hurt her I'll flatten you. Got it? And you can stick the flattery,' I insisted, opening a tin of tuna for Horatio and putting a plateful outside the door. I also changed his lit tray. It was a new and useful addition to the household, as I hated scooping up cat poo off the floor. Horatio didn't like strangers in the house either.

'I've no intentions of hurting such a sweet darling. Can't you see how happy she is, or are you blind?'

'Well…no…I mean yes. She is happy. Here's the deal. She doesn't have any money, only her pension. Got it? So you romance her as much as you want, but that's all. You can't move in with her!'

'What kind of a man do you think I am to take advantage of a lady?'

I was about to answer when Mrs. Jenkins returned looking flushed, happy and much younger than she did that same morning.

'Ingrid,' I said, 'I have to make a call at the Animal Rescue Centre to see how Lucky is. I'll be about half an hour.'

'That's all right Frieda. We'll come with you and do some ward visits to cheer up the injured. Why those poor pilots are only boys fresh from Grammar School…I'll get some cake and biscuits. I know they don't get much what with the rationing and all that.'

So there we had it - two crazy pensioners about to dish out *Battenberg* to unsuspecting cats and dogs. Talk about being kind to be cruel. I only hoped there were no sick snakes. One mighty lump protruding from snake's abdomen, as it tried to regurgitate whole cake and choked to death.

As I motored over Albert Bridge with Ingrid and Wolfgang holding hands in the back seats, I suddenly noticed a road-rage maniac behind driving a beat-up old *Mini*, with full headlights flashing and trying to over-take. That's nothing new in London…I slowed right down and waved him on only to hear a screeching of breaks and a honking of horn. I've always believed the safest thing to do in cases like this is to ensure all doors are locked, continue onwards steadily and not react in any way.

It could have been an early Christmas drunk or a car-jacker wearing a hoody. Either way I didn't want to get involved so I carried on crawling at 30 with mobile at the ready in case of emergencies. When Wolfgang let down the back window, distracted Ingrid by pointing out the gold Buddha figures in Battersea Park, and gave the two-fingered Agincourt gesture to our pursuer, I began to worry.

The car behind us accelerated and rammed straight into my back end. A tinkling then a rattling sound was heard as my exhaust pipe came loose and made tap-dancing noises along the bridge.

Shit. Now what? Speed up or continue getting rammed? 'Don't worry Ingrid. I know an escape route. Hold on tight.'

I put my foot down and turned left, ignoring the park sign that said *Please Keep off the Grass* and managed to level a temporary wire mesh fence. Well. It was an emergency. The car behind followed, revved up and honked like crazy as I careered through the bushes, swerved halfway round the Temple before reversing down the main pathway and weaving in and out of the rose bushes.

'Wolfgang dear, do your have your rifle handy?' Mrs. Jenkins stuttered as we bumped up and down on the gravel.

'Stop the Car!' he shouted, unfastening his safety belt. 'Stop right now!'

'He might be armed! I'm not stopping, so sit down and shut up.'

Wolfgang wrestled with the steering wheel then leapt over my seat and pulled on the handbrake. 'For once in your life do as you are told!' he bellowed before hitting the back of his head on the dashboard and flying into Mrs. Jenkins's lap. It was at this juncture that I knew the airbags in my car had malfunctioned, or were non-existent and that Roy of *Royz Autos* was a total dick.

'Now ladies leave this to me,' Wolfgang said nobly, recovering quickly and leaping from the car. 'There's something rotten in the state of Battersea...Lock the doors Frieda and batten down the hatches. Whatever you do, don't call the fuzz…I'm on a mission for King and Country!'

Fuzz? Ah. A *Miami Vice* fan from the sexy Don Johnson days.

Wolfgang picked up a piece of broken fence post and headed towards the offending car. The driver had overshot and was balanced half way between the fountains and a newly dug flower bed, causing mud to slurry everything in sight. Wolfgang waded in and smashed in the side window before making a grab for the driver.

'Now then pal. Let's see what sort of a man you are who bullies ladies!'

The driver let out a scream and stuck Wolfgang's hand with a screwdriver, shouting: 'Gawt awv maw yaw grawt awv. I awm nawt yaw zawxawawl plawzeenk.'

Wolfgang, surprised and in pain, released the glamorous woman and fell back in shock.

'Are you hurt dearest?' Mrs. Jenkins called out.

'It's nothing,' Mick grimaced, drawing out the screwdriver.

'Yaw crawawl mawn! Vy cawt yaw lawf maw awlawn? Awm I nawt taw awf awnee pawz frawn yaw pawpawl?' Aunt Leonora screamed before leaping from the car.

She hot-footed it through the fountains and headed towards the lake on stiletto heeled boots and wearing a white fur coat and hat from under which a blaze of escaped titian hair billowed in the winter wind. As her car exploded in a ball of flames and smoke, I saw Wolfgang collapse in a heap surrounded by falling debris.

'Mick? Are you all right?' I shouted running towards the defunct fountains and the prone Wolfgang.

Mrs. Jenkins followed calling out through the flames and smoke: 'Arnold dearest. Where are you?'

I paddled over the spouting water pipe and broken concrete basin and turned Mick over.

'Mick, please. Please. Speak to me. What has she done to you?' I pleaded.

'Is that you Ingrid?' he croaked. 'What a rush! I feel thirty again,' he grinned and rolled over onto his back.

'No. I'm over here dearest on the edge of the dam…Why Arnold, you are thirty dearest. Did the bouncing bomb disturb your brain? Are you wounded?'

Wolfgang lifted himself up and stretched out his arms then cracked his knuckles. 'No. Ingrid. I'm used to taking falls. I'm a black belt Karate expert: third Dan. Learned it during my stint in Japan… I know how to roll with it.'

'Karate?' Mrs. Jenkins asked, looking puzzled.

'Err. That is to say Queensbury Rules, boxing dearest. I trained in the Army,' he said, limping over the debris.

'We need to get out of here pronto. I can hear the sirens. They'll think we're terrorists. Oh. My. God. We'll be sent to Guantanamo Bay and tortured by shaven-headed Americans. I look horrible in orange…Come on for God's sake,' I urged, dragging them both towards my car.

Wolfgang had the presence of mind to tie up my exhaust with Wayne's designer skull and crossbones belt.

Heading slowly in the direction of the Animal Rescue Centre we passed police cars and ambulances with flashing blue lights and wailing sirens speeding the opposite way.

Thank goodness I've not cleaned my car for a while. At least they won't be able to trace the colour or the registration number. Nothing is visible. 'Are you okay Wolfgang?' I asked.

'I'm fine Frieda. Only a few cuts and bruises. Nothing to fret about,' he said, beaming widely.

'Oh. Wolfgang you are such a hero. I'm so proud of you,' Mrs. Jenkins soothed, giving him a spit-wash with her lace hankie.

What the hell is going on? What's wrong with Aunt Leonora? And why is she trying to hurt me?

'That was so exciting Frieda. Who was that

woman?' Mrs. Jenkins asked between rubbing dirt and mud around Wolfgang's face.

'Her name is Olga and she's a Russian spy,' I replied wearily, running out of steam.

'I thought the Russians were on our side?' she asked, pistons pounding.

'For now darling,' Wolfgang reassured her. 'Only for now. The Cold War will begin very soon.'

25

I left Ingrid and Wolfgang handing out *Battenberg* and chocolate biscuits to the twenty odd people in the waiting room. And I mean odd. Thankfully it was Coral on duty and not bossy Brenda, who had contracted ringworm - otherwise they would have been thrown out. As I escaped through the side door to see Lucky, I heard Mrs. Jenkins say to a puzzled young man with a Guinea Pig: 'You dear brave boy. I bet your Mother is really proud of you. It's nice that they let the wounded have pets in here. They're a bit of company in helping our boys during their recuperation. Keep up the good work. We'll soon have you back in action.' Guess what? Next year is 1944. Yippee. Her clock had ticked forward at last.

I did a quick tidy up with the hair, spraying on some frizz easer and applied some lippy, hoping to see Ben. I slowed down near his office and there he was in all his glory, talking to a very large round woman with the biggest and fattest cat I've ever seen. It made Garfield looked like a field mouse.

'Now let me get this right. The reason he's constipated is because you're giving him six large bags of crisps, cheese and biscuits, and a king-sized bar of chocolate every day.'

'But it is fruit and nut doctor.'

'That can't make one iota of difference. If you carry on this way he's not going to make the New Year,' Ben said as kindly as he could.

The large woman burst into tears and sobbed: 'He's my baby. I don't know what I would do if anything were to happen to him.'

'You have to practice tough love Mrs. Robson. Tell you what. Leave him in here with me and over the Christmas period. We'll give him an enema, a special healthy diet and put him on the treadmill.'

'Oh. No. I can't be alone at Christmas and without Tarquin,' she wailed.

'If you don't act quickly you'll be alone anyhow.'

'Do you think eating meat will work then doctor?'

'In moderation …It'll give him a better chance of survival. He's 9 years old now. He should be okay for a few more years yet, if he has a substantial weight loss. It's easy really. Don't feed him crisps and chocolate; especially dairy products. Cats can't digest lactose. And feed him three small healthy meals a day.'

Waving at Ben, while trying out my catwalk strut and looking as if I got a thong caught up my bum-crack, I tripped up as I passed his office. I entered the recuperation area feeling like a total prat. To my dismay Lucky wasn't there in his cage. Instead a white rabbit with a cardboard cone around its head stared back at me. Panic set in. Then I heard barking.

Surely he's not woofing yet. He's too weak and his jaw's wired. Maybe it's a guard dog and poor old Lucky's been incinerated. Oh. God.

I hadn't phoned the Rescue Centre for a couple of days. I'd had too much on my mind. So I decided to follow the noise and prepare myself for a hasty retreat at the least sound of chains rattling and the sight of a frothing muzzle.

I needn't have worried. At the very end of the building were larger cages with dogs bouncing around in various stages of recovery. A large Alsatian threw itself in my direction and yelped as it hit its nose on the metal bars. Another cage had a ball of fluff yapping its head off. With every piercing yap it seemed to do a back-flip. I think it was a Pekinese. It was hard to tell beneath all that fur. In the next cage and best of all was Lucky, sat up and leaning to one side, supported by his good leg.

His stitches had been removed from his head

and a frizzle of golden fur had sprouted all over the visible parts his body. Someone had bought him a red coat to keep him warm. I guessed it was Coral. When he tried and failed to lick his willy and in the process, fell over, I knew he was on the mend. Looking somewhat like a beetle on its back he managed to roll over and hoist himself up again. This time he leaned against the wall.

Clever boy. 'Hello Lucky. How are you doing?' Dope. Is he going to say: Nicely thanks, considering I'm totally fucked up. He just looked blankly at me with an unmoving furry tail and absolutely no idea of who I was. 'Here boy I've got you some nice soft doggy treats.' Still there was no response. When I put my hand through the bars to tempt him with the fluffy rabbit, he lunged at me and yelped - flipping over onto his back again. After regaining his balance the rabbit was nosed and sat on.

I wondered if this was how the brave but silly wife of Charles Bronson mark II - not the brilliantly macho original late actor of *Death Wish* fame, but the tattooed scary mad one - had felt when she visited him in prison. Did she feed him cake made from Valium to calm him down? Perhaps she lit scented candles and meditated with him? I started to sing to Lucky instead.

I see fields of green/Red rose too...

He just leaned against the wall and looked at me in that sad way. The scar all the way down his muzzle was almost covered with downy hair. As it had tightened during healing, the left side of his face looked slightly higher than the right. A bit like those decrepit American film stars who are wheeled out for award ceremonies, with their botched face-lifts and staring eyes that stay open when they nod off during the lengthy *Thank You* speeches. Above his mournful eyes, black hairs sprouted like bushy eyebrows in the Groucho Marks mode. I tried not to laugh, but I couldn't help it and continued singing: ...*They're merely saying/I need the loo...*

As I giggled at my own tasteless but appropriate joke, he wobbled along on three legs a little nearer to the bars. I suppose he was curious and felt safe inside his cage, or maybe he was trying to go for my throat and stop me singing? At least the fluff-ball had ceased yapping.

'Good boy. Here, I won't hurt you. It's Kathryn. Don't you remember me you ungrateful mutt? It was me who rescued you from under the wheelie bin. Well to be fair, Edward carried you to the car. But if I'd left you with him he would have sucked out all your blood and you would now be a werewolf baying at the full moon on the freezing Yorkshire Moors. So show some gratitude please.'

I knelt down and he actually sniffed my hand, growling softly and didn't pull away when I gently scratched behind his ear. It was just great. Then he took a treat from my outstretched fingers and hobbled back to his bed to suck it. And I knew right then, at that spot in time, we had reached an understanding. From now on we would be on much better speaking terms.

I continued to sing.

'Is everything okay in there Kathryn?' the dulcet-tones of Ben inquired, causing Lucky to wag his tail. That's loyalty for you.

'Yes. Considering,' I replied and stopped singing immediately.

'Why? What's happened? You look kinda wired.'

'I'm always wired…This is different,' I said, sniffing and craning my neck to take him all in from that low angle and trying not to check him out.

'Do you want to talk about it? I've got five minutes,' he asked.

'Have you got five hours? You wouldn't believe me anyway,' I said, wiping my eyes before tears could form.

'Here,' he said, holding out his hand and helping me up, 'come and have a coffee… Charleeee! Wake up and take over will you!'

Sipping a delicious latte in Ben's office, I began my strange story, under his sympathetic and very brown-eyed gaze.

'You see I've never really known my family. I was in Care until the age of fifteen…' Must try a different tack. He's not Gerry Springer. 'To cut a long story short…' Even worse. He's not Oprah either. 'My Aunt, whom I've never met -'. Now he's the phonetically correct Benedict Cumberbatch to whom I am speaking Queen's English) '- or at least she's telling everybody she's my Aunt, is trying to kill me…I don't know why, or what for. But she is.'

He listened patiently as I related the events of my surprise party and the scary ride in the *PARTY POPPETS'* van. When I told him about the explosion in Battersea Park his eyes widened.

'You've got to be joking,' he said.

'No. I'm not. This time I've got witnesses. Mrs. Jenkins from the ground floor flat and her friend who works at *Chez Trevayne* were with me in my car. It's in a worse state than it was before. My rear light and exhaust pipe are knackered and something at the back end sounds really strange.'

'You have to call the police Kathryn…Are you sure it's the same woman?'

'Positive. She's talks in a really funny accent.'

'There're a lot of Polish workers here. Maybe she's not used to driving on the left. I know I had a problem at first.'

'Did you ram cars then? Did you force-feed drunken women with blue birthday *cark*? Did you hire a foul-mouthed parrot? Did you blow up important fountains? Did you buy hideous *Nat West* pigs? No? I thought not,' I said defensively.

Ben burst out laughing. 'You're really funny. You had me going there for a minute…Hang on though…I've just remembered. In Alan's shop when I went to buy one of your paintings and bought a moose head instead -.'

'It was you who bought the moose head? Why for God's sake?'

'I thought it was time an indigenous animal to my homeland had a decent burial…Well, actually, I cremated it in the back garden,' he laughed. 'Anyhow there was this gorgeous redhead, foreign, a real slick dresser. She climbed out of a black limo and ran into the shop. She bought the pigs. She said that they were for a birthday present...Then she bolted back into the car...I can't believe she would want to kill anyone... She was hot -.'

'Okay I get the picture. That's enough of that. I know these foreign females are small-boned size zeros and curvy at the same time, like the *Cheeky Girls*- and pinching all our men... but I've seen her close up and believe me she wears make-up 3" thick and is at least a very well preserved forty something. There could be anybody lurking under that veneer,' I said huffily.

'If you'd let me finish I was going to say - but like a demented chipmunk and very much the image of you. She had the same amazing hair colour, endless legs, same high cheek bones and full mouth -.'

'She had?' Wow. He thinks I'm hot. Like a chipmunk? I'm so glad I scrunched my hair back

there in the corridor. Oh. Shit. She is a relative...
'Did you notice her eyes?'

'Couldn't tell what colour they were. She had on those enormous owl-like sunglasses. In November, I ask you? I would've remembered her eyes if they were anything like yours,' he grinned.

'Really?' I said like a dumbstruck teenager, my knees weakening.

'Seriously though Kathryn, you should contact the police.'

'Not possible... I've scraped most of Albert Bridge's tarmac up, a National Treasure at that, wrecked a park fence, driven dangerously on a Public Footpath, and part way - and the wrong way around the Temple of Buddha. I am entirely to blame for demolishing the fountains, ruined a whole length of flower bed and caused a major terror alert. And where, by now, millions of police are gathering. All the while I was aided and abetted by octogenarian accomplices who are totally bonkers. Mrs. Jenkins believes it's

1943 during The Second World War and Mick is pretending to be her late husband returned as a secret agent and also tells others he's a duelling Count.'

Ben laughed again. Not just a chuckle but a real belly-laugh. I couldn't stay mad for long and started to laugh myself at the thought of the police interviewing Ingrid and Wolfgang, the Battersea Two, as key witnesses to the attempted murder. Even Poirot would be confused.

'So Kathryn, what are you doing tomorrow for lunch?' he asked still chuckling and spilling coffee everywhere.

'What?' I said, like the smooth-talker I am. 'But you've got a girlfriend. You told me so.'

'Eleanor? It fell through. She was supposed to have taken a Sabbatical from her research fellowship during The Fall. I was expecting her to come over from Vancouver last week, but in the end, her career came first. I bought the house in readiness for her arrival and furnished it to her *Shaker* specification. I've even ordered a spruce pine Christmas tree with its roots intact… I guess we've grown apart being at the opposite ends of the social spectrum. Anyhow I received a short *Dear John* letter from her telling me she's marrying her house professor the day before Thanksgiving. So I am now a free agent. Would you like to meet me for lunch tomorrow? Say at 1pm outside *Marco's* and talk some more? You're kinda weird and wacky and gorgeous in a funny sort of way and you make me laugh.'

'How do you know I haven't got a boyfriend?' I asked, trying to sound cool.

'I asked Alan and he told me that you were: "footloose and fancy free". So, are you fancy free for a lunch date tomorrow?'

'Thanks. I suppose I am. That would be very nice. Don't you have to book years in advance though?'

Can anyone tell me what happened to the scenario of: broken heart and falling about in a drunken self-pitying rage while making suicidal/murderous threats to ex-girlfriend until bossy mother grabs offending thuggish son by ear to face up to his commitment issues in the market place, in order for him to come to his senses - and lasting, at least, the length of six episodes: of *Eastenders*?

'It's been booked for quite a while. If you don't want to go there I'll understand,' he said, looking awkward.

'What? And miss out on a chance like that. The fiery Frenchman's a legend. It's not as if you and Eleanor had a special romantic attachment to the place. Is it?'

'No. She believed romantic gestures to be a ridiculous waste of time and money.'

'If you like, I'll gift wrap the pigs and you can send them to her as a wedding present,' I joked. 'They're really annoying me at the moment spread out on my kitchen windowsill - particularly the baby one with glowing eyes and a very red face who looks as if he needs a nappy change.'

'What a great idea. I'll call in for them after

lunch…if that's okay with you? How much do you want for them?' he asked smiling again.

'My pleasure entirely. They're on the house.' Weird and wonderful am I? Ah. What the heck. Nobody's perfect, or maybe so, looking at your broad shoulders. And he's a romantic at heart. Bless… *And I say to myself/What a wonderful world.*

It was owing to Mick performing some difficult driving manoeuvres and back-tracking that we finally arrived at *Chez Trevayne*, after our eventful night. Traffic had come to a standstill as flashing blue-lit vehicles set up road blocks around the perimeter of the park. Sniffer-dogs and Bomb Squads suddenly swarmed from every nook and cranny. Fortunately Mick knew the short-cuts and side roads to the far side of the river. After all he'd lived on most of them.

'What time do you call this young lady?' Wayne said pursing his lips and doing that hand on hip, head to one side pose. 'It's a good job we don't have any customers until nine…Oh. Wolfgang I didn't see you there. What on earth has happened to your face it's all bruised and blackened? Not another dual? And look at your hand. It's bleeding badly. Come inside quickly love and let me see to you.'

'I must drop off the ladies first Wayne. I need to park round the back and make some adjustments to the car.'

'Always the gentleman,' Wayne sighed.

Once inside the bistro, and still shaken, I went to change into my uniform and got cleaned up while Ingrid related our adventure to the amazed staff. Of course she told them about an important change of Government and someone called Dr. Livingston, in order to throw the very blonde Trevor and Wayne off the scent. A great step forward in the War effort I thought and they loved a good story. It helped relieved the boredom.

'Move aside ladies if you please,' Mick instructed, sporting a large sticking plaster on the back of his hand and smelling of *TCP*. He carried Trevor's pristine multi-layered tool box and wore overalls, red socks and *Timberlands*. Well they were really Wayne's knee length holiday

Tyrolean dungarees and Trevor's pseudo-walking footwear.

I checked up on the enormous lasagne dish bubbling in the oven and gave the deep pans of succulent simmering pasta sauce a stir as the contents reduced down. Looking through the kitchen window I saw Mick jack up my car and methodically and expertly take off the old tyres. He stacked them in a tower on the waste land, well away from the garages, along with the charity bin-liner full of his old clothes, then doused them in petrol. After lighting the bonfire, he replaced the two front tyres on my old banger with Trevor's and Wayne's spares.

He waved when he saw me staring at him and gave me a salute and clicked his heels. It looked really funny considering what he wore. I'd not thought about car tracks. Good old Mick.

'I'm off to see a mate,' he said. 'Keep an eye on the fire, will you *Pouting Portulaca*? There's a pile of wood in the corner over there…Light these leftover fireworks from your party. Send up a few rockets and set off some Roman Candles as decoys. If the bonfire gets too smoky, pour on a little more petrol and throw on those empty wine crates over there. And, whatever you do, make sure you pour it on the wood before you throw it on the bonfire…And be careful you don't burn yourself…I won't be long.'

'I will. Thanks Mick you're a star.'

'I know,' he grinned.

Wayne came into the kitchen to see how the food was going. When he clocked the smoking bonfire, smelled the burning rubber and caught me putting rockets in empty wine bottles, he thought I'd gone mad.

'What's going on out there Kat?'

'It's Wolfgang's idea Wayne. He said it would draw customers into the bistro having a post-Bonfire Night theme. You know, to liven up the slack period after Bonfire Night and before Christmas?'

'The man's an absolute genius. Where is he by the way?'

'He's gone to get some decorations for the theme night. He won't be long,' I lied again - and again.

'Here put these party leftover scented candles on it to improve the smell…I'd better bring up more wine from the cellar…Have you brought Sal's desserts? I can't see anything in the fridge.'

Oho. 'I'll get them from the boot while you fetch the wine. Go indoors it's freezing out here Wayne.'

I managed to prize open the boot and saw the full extent of the damage to the car… To my relief the cling film was still intact over the twenty little pudding pots. Clever Sal had packed them in a cardboard box, wedge behind all my accumulated junk. She knew about my driving skills you see.

Our first customers arrived and were talking excitedly about a suspected terrorist attack in Battersea Park.

'I do nota see the point ina blowing up the fountains when there are no tourists around to see it,' Paulo said, still brooding on his missed opportunity with Maggie and listening to the radio through his earpiece. 'It donna maka sense, bambina.'

'You're joking. Battersea Park is a British icon. A prime target,' Trevor announced grandly.

'But it's full of Buddha statues,' Lucy nervously intervened. 'They're not really British icons are they? Well not like *Big Ben*.'

'Maybe it's an attack on religious images?' Maggie suggested. 'My Jason hates anything that's un-Christian.'

'Let's hope he doesn't look in the mirror then,' Wayne replied without smiling and clasping his hands together in a praying motion. 'Can we please get on with the business in hand? That is, after all, our post-Bonfire Night party in the run up to Christmas…I'm calling it: *Gathering Winter Fuel*. Now who wants to hand out the leftover brandy snap, mini *Mars* bars and bonfire toffee from Kat's party?'

As traffic ground to a halt and cars were abandoned, business boomed in the bistro and we were rushed off our feet. And joy of joys, the piped jazz music had been permanently silenced. Actually Mick had thrown it onto the bonfire. Instead the mellow sounds of Adele on Wayne's i-pod relaxed the entire room into a happier mood and, thereby, prevented any further gastric refluxes.

'I wish Wolfgang would hurry up with his surprise. I haven't had a sit down for hours. My feet are like balloons,' Wayne moaned, pushing some spaghetti into a pan of boiling water. His round moon-face glistened in the heat. 'Tell Sal to make more desserts in future we've sold out already.'

'Hark? Did I hear my name mentioned?' Wolfgang shouted, struggling to steer two supermarket trolleys tied one in front of the other, with a recently chopped spectacular fur tree balanced along the top. 'I'm back.'

Mick wore a Santa's hat to match Trevor's borrowed socks and looked like a freed house elf.

The *mien camp* outfit looked all the more comical with tinsel threaded through the dungaree shoulder straps that barely covered his nipples. His sinewy legs and exposed bony knees had turned a deep shade of mottled puce in the cold.

'What have you got?' I whispered, spotting four tyres beneath the expansive Christmas tree.

'Season's Greetings, Wayne old sport. Look what I've bought you for the bistro. We can trim up later tonight. Won't it be utterly amazing? I hope you've got plenty of fairy lights.'

'It's divine,' Wayne beamed. 'We've still got those lights leftover from Kat's party…Can you get the tree through the side door Wolfgang love?'

'No problem boss. I'll be in to do the washing up as soon as I've cleaned your car.'

'What a treasure he is,' Wayne sighed, 'and royalty too, can you believe? I didn't think those blue-bloods liked to get their hands dirty. Put us the last three sticky toffee desserts in the microwave will you Kat while I have a quick glass of champagne with Trevor? Oh. And you can throw the plastic fish pond and the rest of the garbage left over from your birthday party onto the bonfire. Save the lights mind…Let's get in the festive mood shall we?' he said, before bursting into: *There's something in the air.*

'Frieda? Come out here,' Mick whispered.

'Coming Wolfgang your grandness,' I trilled.

'Can you stall them while I fit these tyres on the back end?'

'Not a problem, your graciousness. Where did you get them, or should I not ask?'

'Correct. Well. If people will abandon there cars down side streets, it's their lookout,' he chuckled. 'I've got you a new set of hubcaps and an exhaust pipe as well. I'll fix the back end rattle tomorrow. A good soaping down and re-spray with Roy the rustler's borrowed paint spraying gear - and everything will be kosher.'

'Why are you doing this for me Mick?' I asked, looking around furtively and feeling very worried. 'We all could be in serious trouble if anyone saw us.'

'When I was in the gutter, you and Maggie were the only ones who treated me like a human being. And since I've found my lovely Ingrid and got this new job, my life is no longer in the toilet. In fact I can't remember when I've had this much fun while being sober…You've made me a *Renaissance Man.* That's why Kat. Now don't get me going. I don't do crying. Right?' he sniffed.

'Me neither,' I said, kissing his bruised cheek.

'By the way Frieda, do you like Arctic Blue?'

'Couldn't live without it Count Wolfgang,' I chuckled. 'Fancy a sticky toffee pudding? I've saved us a couple.'

It was gone midnight when we finally shut up shop. Not through lack of customers, rather through lack of food. Trevor was delighted and went looking for Wolfgang to compliment him on his initiative. Fortunately for Mick he had just finished the re-spray job and was putting the final wax on Trevor's car in the light of the bonfire's white hot glow. My car gleamed in the moonlight, looking better than it had ever done previously. Mick had fixed the rear light, replaced my battered exhaust- pipe with a new permanently borrowed one, hammered out the dent in the rear bumper and put two new spare wheels in Wayne's and Trevor's car boots.

'Come on inside Wolfgang, you must be frozen out there,' Trevor called from the doorway.

'Tis the winter of discontent Squire. Made glorious summer by the smelly fire…Up in the mountains, where my fairytale chateau nestles the temperature drops to minus 40 old boy. I'm used to the cold night air.'

That last remark must have the first truth he'd told unsuspecting Trevor.

'Here, I've saved you some pasta. Ingrid is wondering where you are. Come and have a nice glass of *Chianti*.'

'No alcohol for me thanks…I'll just finish this off Trevor and then I'll take a quick shower and change before I dine. If I may that is?' Mick said, trying to hide the re-sprayed Artic Blue *Timberlands* behind Trevor's car. 'Do you have any turps handy old boy? Can't let the future Countess Ingrid see me like this can I?'

'Need you ask Wolfgang? I'll lay you out some fresh clothes...Don't worry about the washing up. I'll do it in the morning. You're a miracle worker.'

'I wouldn't say that Old Fruit...Oh. Just one more favour Trevor. Now the traffic is clearing can I drive Kat and Ingrid home in your car tonight? Kat has run out of petrol.'

That can't be right, unless I've sprung a leak. I've only just filled it up. Ah. So that's what kept the bonfire blazing all night. What a crafty old Count.

27

That same night I dreamed of a huge burning building with explosions and smouldering tyres spinning around like Katherine Wheels. I tried to fly away from the stinking inferno with Mrs. Jenkins, Mick and Lucky on my back, but I could barely get lift off. Then a huge tidal wave roared over us, sweeping us out into the cold blue ocean. I cried out until I could hear them calling to me for help, but I couldn't reach them. Through the clear water I spotted Lucky paddling along the surface above me with his three good legs and using his pot as an oar, while Mrs. Jenkins and Mick drifted downwards and then did the quickstep on the seabed to some jaunty syncopated music.

I swam around for a while not knowing which way to go until something putrid and clammy dragged me away from the light into the murky depths. Finally, after a great struggle, I was released when a huge sunken church bell tolled, making the seabed shake from the resonation. I awoke doing a simulated doggy-paddle to the sound of the radio alarm clock telling me in was 9.30.a.m. and time for DJ: Mr. Powa-Lova to woo the nation.

When the lovely thought of a real date with Ben swam into my head, I smiled happily and turned up the radio for some appropriately soppy listening. Instead it was the news:

"Hello, you lonesome, lovelorn, drivers heading towards the Battersea Park area, please note that all highways, including Albert Bridge, leading to Battersea Park and the surrounding slip roads are closed off. So don't go there guys. Ha. Ha.

It is with some trepidation I can now inform you that the fracas in Battersea Park last evening reported in an earlier bulletin, was, we are led to believe, a suspected terrorist attack. My source says that there is no cause for alarm at this juncture. All we can tell our listeners, at this point in time, is that two vehicles were involved in a high speed chase along Albert Bridge and leading into the park, the consequence of which culminated in the rear vehicle exploding in the fountains. The lead car, a brown/grey *Fiesta*, that's F for Foxtrot, apparently left the crime scene before the police arrived. I can tell you that no persons were seriously injured during the attack; although a woman with wild curly hair and wearing a white fur coat and hat with matching high heeled boots and handbag, the driver of a red/grey *Mini*, that's M for…err…Malcolm, which we are to believe was stolen from *Royz Autos* and was confirmed on security cameras. She ran the length of the footpath towards the boating lake screaming and shouting loudly in a foreign language, before disappearing in the undergrowth.

Ha. Ha. I don't believe this. It says here, ladies and gentlemen, that we've just had a crank call from Alan in Chelsea. He tells us that he saw a suspicious looking elf wheeling two supermarket trolleys and an enormous Christmas tree, and that the elf might have some valuable information to give to the police, as he was hanging around the vicinity of *Royz Autos* approximately one hour after the crime was committed. Could it be that: Santa is on his way? Ha. Ha. We are taking Alan's eye- witness report with a pinch of salt. Alan goes on to tell us that he was staggering home full of early Christmas spirit after a Cheese and Wine party in Knightsbridge. Alan you are one wind-up merchant.

The police are anxious to talk to the said woman in white, along with the owner of the brownish car; registration unknown, or anyone witnessing these events. We will keep you informed and up to date should further information be forthcoming. Remember: if you're stuck in traffic and feeling angry try not to burn rubber, just stay cool and tuned to *Radio Love.* And don't forget: our Sanctuary of Romance is a place where we never get mad. So on that note from your favourite DJ: Mr. Powa-Lova here's Jingo Ferret singing: *Great fire in my Heart/ Keep on Pumping,* for all you hot-blooded lovers out there".

Oh. My. God.

I made myself a very strong coffee and decided to act normally - which for me was: to panic and hyperventilate while trying to keep my wits about me in the shower.

What have I done? It wasn't me who did anything wrong really. I just tried to escape from an extremely demented crazy woman driver intent on killing me. Yes. That's how it was - a cut and dried case of road rage, causing me to swerve and enter the park to avoid injuring others. Simple. Surely the police will see it like that?

I tried to think about something else as I stayed tuned to Mr. Powa- Lova - and put on a little makeup for my date with Ben. I thought causal smart would be appropriate. Velvet military fitted navy jacket, a white top and stone-washed jeans, loafers and black almost-designer bag purchased on the internet.

I wondered if Ben had heard the news. And what would he have made of it? My thoughts were interrupted by another news flash from *Radio Love*.

"Hi sexy beasts and fascinating felines, this is your favourite DJ: Mr. Powa-Lova here to give you more groundbreaking news…A statement issued by Chief Inspector Warwick, wonder if he's any relation to Dionne, reads as follows:

'The accident in Battersea Park last evening was the result of nothing more than a road rage attack. After viewing film footage of the events I can inform you that the foreign woman's speech has now identified by a language expert. He confirms that she has an archaic Transylvanian accent. This information was taken from the recording and film footage in the park. The woman was obviously confused and driving on the right side of the road along Albert Bridge. The driver of the lead car, a brown/grey *Fiesta*, slowed down and waved the erratic pursuer on. The footage goes on to show that the said woman in white then rammed the car in front, causing them both to veer off to the left and crash through a temporary barrier into the park. I am unable to confirm what exactly happened beyond the Temple of Buddha, other than to say that the *Mini's* tracks showed that it skidded on a freshly dug flowerbed and then exploded in the fountains. The lead driver, after reversing through the rose bushes before grinding to a halt, appeared to have staggered around in the smoke for a while, apparently concussed and aided by two women passenger, who helped him back into the car and then drove away.

I reiterate to the general public that there is no cause for alarm. We have confirmation the *Mini* vehicle was stolen from *Royz Autos* and he assured my officers that the vehicle was in for some major repairs. He also stated that the car had faulty electrics, a leaking radiator and worn brake linings which would have contributed to the explosion. A nearby Petrol Station has footage of the woman in white, showing her fill up the petrol tank of the said *Mini* and also cash purchasing a six pack of *Mars* bars. She also wore large sunglasses and gloves to conceal her identity. If you have any information regarding, either vehicles or their drivers, please phone the helpline, or your nearest police station.

Albert Bridge has reopened and the road blocks have been taken away. Traffic flow should be back to normal in a few hours'.

"All you lustful lovers take note. Stay cool in the car with *Radio* Love and hot in the bedroom with your favourite DJ: Mr. Powa-Lova. Here's another little number to calm down you traffic-fumers out there: *Dumpteda/Dumptedo/Dumpteda*, sung by the original silver-tongued Mr. Icelandic himself".

Well. That's that then. Phew. What a relief. I don't need to be on the wrong side of The Law if this crazy woman is trying to kill me…A Transylvanian Aunt? Oh. Please God. No. Does this mean my maternal side might be from a long line of vampires? And that's why I always sensed something strange when Edward was around. Like bats' radar or telepathy…And I had for a while felt a strong urge to visit Whitby and re-read my *Twilight* books…Now what? And what a lying toe-rag Roy is. The exploding car had to be the only red *Mini* on his forecourt with £4000 written on the windscreen; the same one that I nearly bought in part exchange for my car, until I saw the rot on the underside of the bodywork.

The time had arrived to make the phone call to Sophie and Zach because I desperately needed some answers. I felt for sure there must be things they'd not told me about my maternal relatives in order to protect me.

28

When I first arrived in Newquay as a sullen teenager, I was determined not to enjoy one single minute with my Godparents. Unfortunately it didn't work out as planned. Zach was so hurt by my sarcasm that I simply couldn't continue. The sad disappointment on his face made me feel guilty as hell.

And Sophie, well, she was far too clever for me. She just wouldn't bite and always had a dry retort handy. I also found out by chance that she suffered from recurring bouts of *MS* after discovering her collapsed in the garden…So in the end I was able to help her during such times. It made me feel useful. I kind of got adjusted to them, realizing that niceness was part of their inherent nature. In doing so I allowed myself to be kind back.

Zach's enthusiasm for life was contagious and I spent most of my free time, that perfect Summer, with him and Boss down at the shop. During such quiet times back at the house, Sophie enjoyed the solitude and was able to paint without Boss crashing around.

Three whole weeks had passed when I finally confessed to Zach that I loved to swim and had got my Life Saving Badge, after he'd spent hours going over the theory and miming the technique, at my request, and in particular: the front butterfly, dressed in swimming trunks and armbands in full view of the customers... Well. I couldn't let him off scot-free. Could I?

It was at that very happy spot in time that I first set eyes on Luke. All his after work hours were spent down at Fistral Beach, surfing until the sun went down. And even continuing after that, if the moonlight was bright and the waves were wild enough. He was so gangly and awkward on land – a bit like a seal is, but out there on a board he was a god - perfectly formed and balanced in that subliminal place between the sky and the sea. It was impossible not to stare at him, with his hair blowing around in a blonde halo and his sun-kissed cheeks making the blue of his eyes look as if they'd seen angels.

We didn't actually speak to each other at first. Mainly because I was quite shy around him - and I didn't understand the lingo. He seemed so popular with the girls and the guys - being the best and bravest surfer. I'd sit out of sight as the evenings drew in and the beaches emptied, just watching him paddle out and then glide and turn like a dancer at one with the momentum of the surf. There's such an enigmatic calmness about him as if he knew all the secrets of the sea. He was and still is magnificent riding the surf and the most beautiful boy I've ever set eyes on.

I had watched him nearly all Summer, picking up moves and observing how he stood and balanced. Zach had tried to tempt me out there on a board but I was too embarrassed - especially when five year old kids were better at surfing that me. After Luke had left I would tiptoe along a plank of wood on top of an upturned boat finding the centre of gravity and trying to image the movement of the sea.

I remember vividly one particular night when I decided that I knew enough to ride a wave without looking like a total prat. Making sure that nobody was around, I borrowed a board from the shop and ventured out into the sea, paddling slowly on the swelling foam. I felt instinctively the point at which to turn and stand. Kneeling up on my board I sprang to my feet with ease, having practiced that quick-snap move over and over on dry land. Stretching my arms out and finding equilibrium, I felt the power of the wave pushing me along. It was the best feeling in the world until a wall of water surging behind me struck like a giant fist and sent me and the board spinning. The force of the wave knocked all the air out of my lungs and I remember gasping and choking until everything went black.

The next thing I remembered was my lungs were on fire and a dead weight pressed down on my back, then a voice jolted me back: 'Come on you Grommet, breathe. That's right cough it out.' I was absolutely exhausted and my throat burned as I wretched out the salt water. Then I was roughly turned over and pulled upright into a sitting position, still groaning and gasping as a torch was shone into my eyes. 'No concussion. Here drink some water. It'll help get rid of the taste. You're okay. Don't try to get up yet. Your forehead is bleeding,' he said, holding a medicated wipe to my temple.

I could hardly lift my head it hurt so much but managed to sip some of the water. It tasted so good trickling down my rasping throat.

'Thanks,' I managed to say in between coughing, as he wrapped a towel round my shoulders.

'What in God's name made you think you were able to ride *The Cribbar*?'

'The what?'

'I mean that 20 foot wave. It gave you a right old mullering out there.'

'Can't you speak English? And don't call me Gromit. I'm not a dog!'

'Grommet, it means: young surfer that's all. You're no way near ready for any big ones let alone *The Killer.*'

'Who are you to tell me I'm not ready? It caught me off guard that's all,' I croaked, sounding like Darthvada.

'I'm Luke? The lifeguard? I've watched you every night watching me. Don't you understand? The only way to learn is to get your feet wet practicing on the smaller waves. Nobody in their right mind tries to surf walls of water carrying thousands of tons of pressure per square metre unless they're competition standard...Riding a plank on an upturned rowing boat is not the same as respecting the surf. You need to learn in daylight first. It's all about timing. You turned too early and your goofy footwork's all wrong -.'

'Okay, Luke the Lifeguard. Thanks for the

lecture now will you let go of me. I'm fine,' I insisted, trying to stand and falling down straight onto my backside in the sand. 'And by the way, I think my footwork is pretty damn good!'

'Goofy foot means: right foot forward. You're a regular foot.'

'Will you leave me alone…And stop dripping all over me.'

'If I had a towel I could get dry after saving your life,' he said, grinning.

'Sorry. Errum…thanks…Here,' I replied, handing him the towel. 'I need to get the board back. It's a brand new one…I borrowed it from the shop.'

'And far too big for such a slightly built girl…I bet you didn't wax it first? You dinged your Stick well and truly. It's churning around in pieces over there by the rocks…You should've attached the leash…Didn't you realize that nobody surfs that part of the tide? It took the late great Martin Shaw -.'

'Well you did! And will you please not talk about my D-dad?'

'You're his Daughter? You're Martin Shaw's kid? Well you've got his guts…But what were you thinking of? Going out there in a bikini and t-shirt? For starters you need to be aerodynamically sleek - and warm. Try a wetsuit next time.'

'Alright! Just stop talking about my D-him! I never knew him. Okay? Satisfied?'

'Sorry. I didn't know that. So, you're really Martin Shaw's off-spring?' he asked checking out my limbs for breakages.

'Yes! For the last time, will you give it a rest? My brain hurts,' I grumbled through chattering teeth. 'And save the touchy feely for the fawning surfer groupies… "Oh. Lukie you're so good at surfing. Will you show me how? You've got the best six-pack I ever seen". Blaa. Blaa. Blaa. They're nauseating.'

'Haven't got a clue what you're on about…' he replied, genuinely looking puzzled. 'After I've locked up the shop, I'll walk you home. You shouldn't be out alone in the dark anyway,' he said, helping me to my feet.

'Oh. God. Yes. The shop…I'm not alone,' I told him before letting out a piercing whistle. 'I'm warning you now… You'd better let go of me before you get hurt,' I warned, head throbbing.

Boss came bounding along the beach like a fat white pig, then skidded to a halt in a jumble of paws, before jumping up at Luke and licking his face.

'Hey there fella,' he said, rubbing Boss's dino head. 'Come on then Kat. I can call you Kat? You've got a double escort of guys who are looking out for you. I don't know what Zach will make of all this? You'll have to pay him out of your earnings for the board… I suggest you don't mention your little drowning episode.'

I raged in silence at his cheery demeanour but felt secretly pleased that he knew my name. He'd watched me all that time trying to do my gymnastic pointy toe moves while balanced on a plank and upturned rowing boat. I was glad the sun had gone down because my face burned with embarrassment. It was good though, to hear someone other than family talk about my Dad - especially with such admiration in his voice.

I wondered, at the time, if I would be forever in Luke's debt for saving my life - and would I ever be free until I saved him right back? You know like Morgan Freeman and Kevin Costner, in *Robin Hood – Prince of Thieves.*

It was time to make the *Aunt Leonora* 'phone call.

'Hello Sophie. This is your solvent Goddaughter phoning from the big city…Guess what?'

'Don't know. Tell me…You sound quite pleased.'

'All my paintings have sold from Alan's shop, so please don't worry about me not eating enough. I can buy a whole chicken farm now,' I told her, trying desperately hard to sound cheerful.

'Congratulations you talented girl…It's also good news too about Sal and Joe living under the same roof again…I bet you're made up?'

'Yes. I am.'

'Okay Kat. Now what did you really phone me for? I recognize that worried voice.'

'It's about my M-her. Is there something you've not told me about my maternal relatives?'

I heard a gasp and then her shouting Zach to come to the phone: 'What's happened Kat. Tell me everything.'

Zach's flip-flops sounded on the kitchen floor. 'What's wrong?' he whispered to Sophie.

'Please don't start worrying. There's a weird foreign woman who looks like me with the same colour hair and is trying to kill me,' I told them. 'She's supposedly Transylvanian and I'm really concerned about it.'

'You're kidding me? Transylvanian? Are you sure? Start at the beginning Kat and tell us everything,' Zach said calmly, used to my melodramatic irony.

I related to them the past events since my birthday party, the *Nat West* pigs and the subsequent car chase involving Aunt Leonora.

'Honestly Kat. I don't know anything about your Mother's family. Are you sure this woman is a relative and not some crazy foreign driver?' Sophie asked. 'When Zach and I went on holiday to Wroclaw the women drivers there were really aggressive...It could be a case of mistaken identity...If you truly believe she's trying to harm you then you must go to the police, darling, before she does anything else.'

'I can't trace her, she flits around so quickly and I can't go to the police. Don't you see? If she is a relative then she might know what really happened to my M-her. How tall was she?'

'I don't know Kat. Your Dad was 6'2" and she seemed petite in the photograph. Why?'

'Well. This woman is about 5' 8" almost the same height as me and very slender.'

'Your Mother appeared curvy on the photograph.'

'A friend of mine has seen her close up and he says she looks a lot like me, only older of course... Are you sure there's nothing else? If you know please tell me,' I pleaded.

Sophie put her hand over the receiver and I heard a muffled conversation, during which Zach said: 'Don't do it. Now's not the time. What good can it do?'

'Sophie I heard that. Please tell me,' I pleaded.

'Kat. We've tried to protect you all this time from any further heartache...Maybe you do need to know. Now that you've finally asked about her... I wanted to tell you face to face when you where a little older and more settled -.'

'I'm ready, just tell me.'

'Very well then...When your Dad had his surfing accident your Mother was devastated. We couldn't even have a proper funeral. As you know his body was never found. It sent her over the edge...I didn't really know much about her, other than what your Dad told me. To him she was a perfect and loving wife and your Dad never lied. We weren't invited to the wedding and owing to illness, she didn't attend your Christening. We couldn't speak to her for long on the phone as she was very nervous with strangers; although she spoke English quite fluently with a heavy accent. It sounded Hungarian, you know, like the Gabor sisters? What am I thinking of. You'll not remember them -.

'I know who you mean …The witty blondes with high cheeks bones, slanting eyes and loads of husbands…Didn't ZaZa say: "Don't get mad darlink get the house", or something on those lines?'

'That's them. Anyway, your parents always refused our invitations. Your Dad came on his own of course…So we never met your Mother. All I had of her was a wedding photograph which I gave to you.'

'Oh. I see.'

'After your Dad's death the reporters hounded your Godfather and me for the full story. Your Mother also, I guess…We were told later that she never drew back the curtains or left the house at that time until it was dark…Because I couldn't tell the police much about your Mother they questioned her neighbours. Vicious rumours circulated about her strange nocturnal behaviour and her peculiar accent. A bit of a witch hunt really among the superstitious…We tried so hard to contact to her, but she wouldn't open the door to us. The authorities were brought in regarding your welfare and your Mother became a prime suspect in your Dad's disappearance; particularly as he was a champion surfer.'

'The newspaper clippings… I never got to read them because they disappeared from my file,' I said, the realization suddenly dawning on my.

'Sorry Kat. We didn't want you to see them. Garbage really…You had gone through enough -.'

'Okay. It's alright. Tell me everything,' I said anxious to know more.

'Then one night your Mother disappeared before they could take you from her. She wasn't heard of again, until she voluntarily put you into

Care in Wales…You see Kat she couldn't help herself. She really tried her best for you. She simply couldn't make it without your Dad. In the end she had a nervous breakdown and took an overdose…We could have helped her – if only she had let us… We tried to find out about you but we were blocked at every turn. So we hired a private detective who traced you to Wales and you know the rest…'

Zach took the phone from Sophie, who was by this time sobbing her heart out.

'Kat? Are you still there?' Zach said, softly.

'Yes. I'm still here…So she wasn't a scum-bag after all. She just couldn't cope…And she really loved my Dad?'

'They adored each other and you Kat,' Zach said. 'The Godmother wants to talk to you.'

'Kat,' she sniffed, 'are you okay darling?'

'I'm fine considering. Please don't cry. You never cry. You're a Shaw woman after all,' I said, holding back the tears and swallowing hard. 'Shaw woman are made of stronger stuff.'

'I know. Thanks for reminding me Kat. Do you have anymore questions?'

'Is there anything else? What happened to her? Did she leave any possessions or papers?'

'She escaped from the hospital, we found out later...And she tried to break into the Care Home and see you for one last time...You weren't there. They'd placed you with foster parents. The authorities wouldn't let her see you and she was sectioned for her own safety. I ask you? What a cruel thing to do. Well, a few days later...she was found floating in the bay...I'm sorry Kat. We didn't know you see, until it was too late... If only she had come to us...'

'You did your best. Nobody can do better than that...She wanted to join my Dad. I know that now...She couldn't live without him and she made sure I was safe...It must have broken her heart. Not having anyone to talk to. Not even a single friend in a foreign country. What with losing her husband and giving up her baby...She must have been terrified.'

'We've visited her grave a few times and hoped to catch sight of you around town. We had a head stone made for her and included your Dad's name as well. We knew, you see, that they would want to be remembered together…I know it sounds macabre but I took a photo of it for you…When you come home for Christmas I'll show you her few possessions…Your Mother posted some documents and things to us before she… but we've never been able to decipher the contents…'

'Can you post them to me? I'll try and get them translated.'

'Yes, of course… I'm sorry to have kept them from you Kat. The time never seemed right somehow…What with you starting a new life with us and exams and things and you going off to London on your own…And we were worried about you -.'

'You mean: worried that I might turn out like her? Maybe I would have done, had I not been able to look out for myself for so long. It made me stronger. Don't you see? Now I just want to enjoy every day and do so many wonderful things. For the first time in my life I know the truth about my Mother and I want to shout it out loud from the roof-tops. I feel compassion for her instead of hatred and admiration instead of disgust. And she was brave taking me away like that. Trying to keep me with her… My Mother actually loved me,' I said, unfamiliar tears falling down my face. 'There's nothing that crazy Aunt Leonora can do to hurt me anymore…I'm so glad to be here at this spot in time. To know they loved each other and me, and best of all to have you two - my real loving parents.'

'Oh. Kat. Don't set me off again my loverrlcc. I can't stand it,' Sophie said, sobbing again.

I heard Zach blubbering alongside her and I just couldn't take that much love all at once.

'Okay. Enough,' I checked myself. 'You can't afford to get stressed…I'm fine. Honestly… I have a hot date with a gorgeous vet and must make myself presentable. You'll really like him… Can I bring him home for Christmas?'

'Course you can. You know that.'

'And can I bring a mad dog called Lucky that I rescued from under a wheelie bin and two weird time-warped wrinklies?'

'What? Why not? The more the merrier. They'll be right at home here… Please be careful Kat. We both love you so much.'

'Likewise, I-I love you too.' I've said it. I've actually said the 'l' word and it hurts like hell.

29

In my fitful sleep the prior evening, I had heard creaking floorboards in Edward's apartment. I guessed that he was back from his extended blood drinking binge. Although he could have been researching for a book on the living-dead and experiencing the lifestyle first hand, in the same way that *Method* actor Robert de Niro does to get into character. I put on my silver and crystal drop earrings and matching cross as an added safety measure, just before the doorbell rang out.

I ran downstairs thinking it was smiley Rosie the nice Air Raid Warden/Home Help returning to the fold and bearing *Battenberg*. Mrs. Jenkins had beaten me to it and stood blocking the doorway intent on cross-examining someone outside.

'Give the password young man or prepare to be interrogated,' Ingrid ordered.

'Never look a gift horse in the mouth, unless you're a vet?' Ben offered.

'And every dog has its day,' she replied. 'Come inside Fritz. It's freezing out there.'

'Hi. Ben. What are you doing here?' I asked, taking in his freshness and smart clothes.

'Couldn't wait any longer to see your family of terrorist pigs,' he said dryly.

'Terrorist pigs? That's no way to talk about we secret agents young man. Would you both like to come in and join me for a cup of tea and a slice of -,' Mrs. Jenkins said, tugging at his sleeve as Horatio bolted through the open doorway.

'No thanks. Ingrid. We have important work to do upstairs. I'll brief you later after the Air Raid Warden has cleaned your windows,' I told her, beckoning Fritz to follow me.

'Katie, or should I say Frieda, there's no longer need for her to do the windows every week. I can see my Wolfgang quite clearly…I'll expect you later then,' she said, winking.

A throaty chuckle came from inside her flat. Of course it was Wolfgang's unmistakeable laughter.

Ben bounded up the stairs after me. I was quite flummoxed really. His early arrival had taken me by surprise and he'd obviously heard the news. I only hoped I hadn't left any embarrassing things around like: wax strips, grenades or *Hello*.

'Are we there yet?' Ben asked, feigning fatigue.

'Here we are,' I said, 'Snowdonia has been scaled. Welcome to my hideout.'

'Nice. I like it. You have quite a view out there,' he said, looking at the wheelie bins.

'You're supposed to look up through the skylight. Not at the courtyard,' I told him. 'I guess you've heard the news?'

'Yep, but I never believe what they say in the newspapers. You can tell me first hand over lunch.'

Without warning he grabbed my hand, pulled

me towards him and kissed me firmly and deliciously. It was even better than I'd expected.

'I've wanted to do that for quite a while now, despite the dog-blood and beetroot hair... And I think I'd like to do it again, if that's alright with you Kathryn?'

I nodded and closed my eyes. Why play hard to get? Life's too short to waste excellent snogging time with someone like Ben. It had been a while since I'd last been kissed and I presumed it was the same for him. He was so good at it and after what seemed like decades of smooching we came up for air.

'So, do you want to see the pigs or not?'

'Can't contain myself,' he replied, breathing heavily and leaning over for another kiss.

I led him to the kitchen area in three easy steps and pointed out the pigs.

'Are you sure you want to send them to your ex?' I asked him. 'They're really quite hideous.'

'Without a doubt she truly deserves such a

fine collection,' he said, picking up the red-faced baby.

'I'll get you a box and some bubble wrap. Do you want to wrap or pack?'

'I'll pack.'

As I busied myself cutting up strips of bubble wrap, Ben made us coffee. I've no idea what he added to the beverages. Maybe it's a little touch of magic, or because he's Canadian? Whatever his method, it's far better than anything I've ever achieved. Some people just don't have the knack of getting it right, even in *Costa Coffee* - especially when I order a Soya latte. I must be one of the uninitiated…It's the same with Yorkshire puddings.

'Shall we start with Daddy pig first?' I asked.

'Na. Let's make it interesting. Baby first. He's got to be the ugliest ever and his eyes look kinda demonic… Hang on I can hear ticking,' he said, shaking the nappy pig.

'Oh. My. God! It's a bomb…Throw it out of the window! Now! For God's sake not into the garden! Sal's down there and she's having a baby...' I shouted, pushing the side window wide open.

Without hesitation Ben hurled the pig high into the air where it exploded somewhere above the roof.

'Get the others, quickly!' I yelled, slinging the pot parents high into the air, while Ben got the kids out straight after. They all kind of swirled around looking very weird. And how does the saying go? When pigs can fly... Ducking down behind the sink we waited for the explosions. Nothing happened. Then in a slow motion split second they crashed, one after the other, all over and around the wheelie bins.

Instead of feeling terrified I called out in a Walton family moment: 'Yup! It were the baby what done it Sheriff,' and gave Ben a high five. He looked sort of wild-eyed and animated doing the clenched fist and arm pumping gesture.

'Well. That was certainly a different kinda foreplay,' he said, ruffling his hair and looking very cute. 'You're one hell of a wild child Billie Jo.'

'I'm not really,' I whispered. 'Right at this moment I feel anything but. Don't you see? She really is trying to kill me. I'm not imagining things.'

'Okay, one problem at a time. Have you got anything stronger than coffee? I think we both need a drink to steady our nerves.'

'I've got some Christmas brandy, or there's a bottle of *Chianti* in the cupboard. What about your lunch booking?'

'I'll send out for pizza to soak up the *Chianti*. I'm sure Marco will be able to fill our places. Have you got a corkscrew? Kathryn please, sit still before you fall. You're shaking. Tell me everything leading up to this demented woman.'

I related the past events to Ben in between coffee and *Chianti*, trying to keep matters as impersonal as possible without sounding like a charity-case. As I turned into Alvin the chipmunk, high on caffeine and alcohol, I reeled off my unusual life in about ten minutes. It didn't take long to tell him about my parents and the mad woman, who was a possible relative.

'Well. You sure have had one heck of a life so far. I still think you should contact the police… Have you any idea how to find Aunt Leonora?'

'I need to speak to her, face to face, and to know why she's after me…And I know for certain Aunt Leonora will find me before the police can even check up on her movements,' I said.

'Dr. Ben thinks you need looking after,' he said softly, moving in for kiss.

Now if there's one thing I hate, it's another person telling me I can't take care of myself. I get really stroppy, because I know, even though I mess up quite often, I can muddle through in the end. So I stood up ready to tell him what's what. When I saw his steady kind gaze, I bit my tongue for the first time in my adult life - and kissed him right back.

As we moved towards the bedroom he hesitated and groaned softly.

'Is there something wrong?' I asked, wondering if it was a bridge too far.

'I don't have any protection. If I had you might think I'm only after one thing…'

'That's okay. I do. I mean condoms…I used to be a Girl Guide. Not. But I'm always prepared… And I'm not only after one thing…There are quite a few other things I'm after with you…What I'm trying to say is: I don't do this sort of thing very often you understand… In fact it's been quite a while since I…well you know what I mean.'

'Yes. Me too… Now stop talking nonsense and kiss me again.'

I did kiss him again and again until we ended up in the bedroom. We made magnificent love until the late afternoon and I can say, without a shadow of a doubt that I literally slept with a man for the very first time. It was special to dream of absolutely nothing while being cuddled by a kind loving man who really liked me in return. A definite pearl for the necklace…And I felt strangely calm and ready to trust someone else. I suppose that's what being in love must feel like...I was ready to let him into my weird, but little life and hope he didn't get spooked by my crazy past, even weirder present and a very precarious future.

Later we fed each other pizza in bed and I talked about Sal and Joe, and Lucky and Boss. I told him about my Godparents in Newquay and he filled me in concerning his parents in *The Rockies* who were of Scottish descent. And then I actually asked him what his last name was. I know. It's bad really to kiss a guy and not know his full name. Anyhow it's Gibson as in Mel.

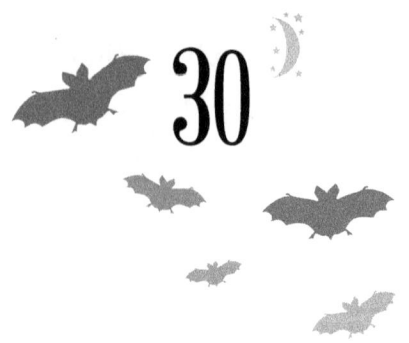

Much, much later Fritz and I, after a shared lengthy shower, decided to sneak past Ingrid and Wolfgang to get some fresh air and do a little shopping on the King's Road. On my way downstairs I pushed a brief but informative note under Edward's door, which read as follows:

"Dear Edward,

I hope you are well. I've not seen you around since the very early morning dog rescue of 1st November. Lucky, that's the dog's new name, is on the mend and I hope to find him a happy home in Newquay. Maybe you would like to see him before we leave for Cornwall on 20th December? You

are most welcome to join us in
Newquay for the Christmas holiday.
Best Wishes,
Kathryn, x."

He's the most likely candidate to speak Transylvanian. And if he can't, I'll have to admit that I've been mistaken about his nocturnal activities. On the other hand, if I'm right and he is a vampire, I will, in an attempt to draw him out of his darkened lair, invite him to partake in Ingrid's extra strong tea and *Battenberg* which will enable him to meet the rest of the household - including our own dear Wolfgang who pretends to be multi-lingual and has roamed many a street on dark nights. It will also give me an opportunity to expose Edward to the daylight shining through Ingrid's sparkling windows. Also I must read up on Transylvania. I think it's somewhere in Romania. So do they speak Romanian, or Romany, Hungarian, or Transylvanian? I expect Edward will definitely know such things as he looks like an intellectual vampire. And, on the other hand, without a doubt, Wolfgang will not.

Ben and I reached the ground floor in silence, apart from the odd squeaky floor-board and our stifled laughter. To our surprise Mrs. Jenkins wasn't on guard duty. We almost made it out the door when the crackled voice of Wolfgang called out: 'Frieda. You are required for tea and cake – and you too Fritz. There's no escape and don't even think of tunnelling out. We need to be filled in on the latest developments regarding: you know what in you know where with you know whom.'

'Frieda und Fritz ve neet you urzhently as backup. Gurda cannot behafe in a zeriouz zpy-like manner,' Joe called out in a guttural accent.

I sighed. 'Looks like we've no choice in the matter Fritz. On the positive side, you can get to meet my best friends Gurda and Ilmhart.'

'That's okay. Whatever,' Ben said, looking around somewhat impatiently. 'It can't take long. Can it?'

'How much time have you got? Look, just play along with it for Ingrid's sake, please.'

'Am I in the crazy house?' he asked, grinning.

'You haven't met the vampire upstairs yet,' I said, pointing to Edward's flat.

When we entered Mrs. Jenkins's flat it was, as usual, lovely and warm. The coal fire blazed out brilliant flames of red and gold and the whole room was bathed in an amber glow. Seated in the best and second best armchairs were Wolfgang and Ilmhart reclining with legs outstretched, while Mrs. Jenkins busied herself in the kitchen sorting out the best china tea cups. Sal came over first and gave me a hug and at the same time eyed Ben, literally, from top to bottom.

'He's gorgeous. You lucky girl,' Sal said quietly. 'Hi. I'm Sal...I mean Gurda. And you are...Fritz?'

Sal, Joe and Mick gathered round and shook hands with a very nervous Ben. I'd not noticed before that he was uneasy around people. It made sense really. He was a natural with animals but quite diffident with the talking variety.

'Hi. Good to meet you all. Kathryn's told me a lot about you folks. I'm Ben Gibson. The vet taking care of Lucky.'

'Oh. Fritz. I remember you. You work in the hospital looking after our boys,' Mrs. Jenkins said, unable to make eye contact from her low position and looking slightly above Ben's waist. 'Come and sit yourself down and have some cake -.'

'Ingrid I don't think Fritz likes *Battenberg*,' I interjected, before she could force-feed another victim.

'It's not *Battenberg*. I'm saving that for later… Gurda has made us a chocolate cake. Can you imagine? What with egg powder and no chocolate around. I really don't know how she got the sponge to rise. A little bicarbonate of soda and crème of tartar I expect. And it tastes just like the real thing,' Ingrid said.

'Want a coffee Frieda? Fritz?' Sal asked, heading for the kitchen.

'I think there's a bottle of *Camp* coffee in the top cupboard Gurda, Mrs. Jenkins told her. 'It should be alright. I've not opened it.'

'Not a problem Ingrid. I've brought my own from the foothills of the mountains in Columbia. Traded it for a couple of turnips with a Yank soldier.'

'Does Ilmhart know?' Ingrid whispered.

'Of course. It was he who introduced us during a secret mission,' Sal said, smiling wickedly.

'That's alright then. Everybody come and sit round the table and we'll begin the meeting,' Mrs. Jenkins ordered.

'Order, please, ladies and gentlemen,' Wolfgang shouted out. 'Let us proceed with the plan for our next mission. And I think Frieda will come up trumps again on that one,' he added, gurning at me behind Ingrid's back.

Everybody sitting round Ingrid's table looked at me expectantly. What could I say? If I'd told them the truth they wouldn't believe me. So I made something up on the spur of the moment: 'Well… fellow agents, as you know regarding the incident in you know where, the mad woman trying to kill me is a Russian spy going under the guise of a Transylvanian vampire and -.'

'What a silly woman she must be. There're no such things as vampires,' Mrs. Jenkins interrupted.

'As I was saying: according to a latter report a translator identified her speech as that of archaic Transylvanian. I suppose it's the same as Latin or Old Norse -.

'What's Old Horse?' Ingrid asked. 'Is it something to do with cowboys and the Wild West?'

'Norse. It's an ancient Viking language dearest. From many, many years ago,' Wolfgang reassured her.

'It's the Germans again. Isn't it?'

'No dearest. Not this time,' Wolfgang assured, patting her hand.

'Well. How are we supposed to find Olga, or understand what she's saying?' Sal asked, looking serious. 'It's got beyond a joke Kat when some nutcase tries to blow you up and run you off the road, then disappears without a trace.'

'I think we should go out in twos and ensure that Kat, I mean Frieda, is never left on her own?' Joe said, looking worried.

'Without a doubt she'll find me, so we need to be prepared…Her English is fluent but hard to understand…I think everyone in this room has a positive ID on her. She's a redhead, 5'8", slender, wired like weasel and looks like me, except for tons of makeup and older of course… And I need all of you to find out anything you can on this particular language. So search the internet and Library Archives,' I instructed them. 'I also suggest than none of you go out alone… And Ingrid: my number one agent: under no circumstances are you to take in any more parcels - unless they're from *The White Company* and are addressed to me. Any others should be left behind the pot in the outside porch. Understood?'

'Yes I do, but what about the Vikings?' Ingrid asked, looking flummoxed.

'Don't worry Ingrid they won't know the password,' I reassured her. 'Order please can we agree on a new password?'

'May I suggest: *Dancing in the Dark*??' Wolfgang offered.

'Not now dearest. We've got company,' Ingrid said, looking embarrassed.

At this point in the proceedings hilarity took over… Wolfgang cleared his throat and tried to get a word in edgeways. It seemed that I had a very noisy consensus regarding contacting the police. Well almost. Ingrid said I should have a word with Monty.

'As you know Frieda, I am a multi-linguist. And it will be my pleasure to interrogate the volatile redhead. I owe her one for this injury,' Wolfgang said, holding up his bandaged hand.

'Come off it you old toss-.'

'I know what you're going to say Frieda, but there's no need for thanks. Transylvanian is my first language. My native tongue so to speak,' he chuckled. 'So I won't be putting myself out, my *Lanky Lobelia.*'

'I would like to inform fellow agents that I believe Edward the Vampire from upstairs might be fluent in the said language,' I said, 'just in case Mick, I mean Wolfgang, has a relapse of memory.'

'Is that his real name?' Wolfgang asked, looking puzzled. 'He could be in on the espionage.'

'I'm sure it's his real name. He seems very respectable considering he never goes out in the daytime. And he helped me get Lucky into the car, even though he was covered in ringworm and other nasties…Lucky that is and not Edward… He had every opportunity to attack me at that point in time.'

'What's his surname then?' Wolfgang asked.

'It's Hinchcliffe and you can't get more English than that,' I said firmly. 'Although I've noticed he does have a slight accent underneath the refinement. It could possibly be Irish.'

'Kathryn? I really have to go,' Ben said, looking at his watch. 'I need to buy a few things... like condoms,' he whispered, brushing my ear with his lips, 'and to get some rest before I see you again. I'm on an all-nighter again.'

'But young man you haven't eaten your cake yet,' Ingrid said.

'Ingrid, young Fritz has night-time surveillance missions. He must leave now to prepare.'

'I'll wrap your chocolate cake along with some *Battenberg*. Then you can eat it when you're on First Watch,' she insisted.

'That's it,' I enthused. 'The new password is: *Battenberg*. Don't open the door to anyone else - except Fred the postman with a parcel as per my earlier instructions.'

Ben and I stood in the hallway, feeling awkward for the first time. He looked a little glum but I soon cheered him up and gave him a huge hug.

'Is there something wrong? They're my friends

and I l-like them all to bits. We're just having a little fun to break the tension. That's all.'

'It's not that Kathryn. I love your craziness and the way you care for the oldies…It's just that I want you all to myself…And there's so little time left now, before I go on my next shift. And if you've not forgotten the mad woman has tried to kill you twice.'

'No. I've not forgotten…Four times actually if the blue cake was poisoned and don't forget the exploding pig…Don't worry. She's not all that clever… I'm okay…And we've got all the time in the world… I'll come and visit Lucky after I've finished at the bistro tonight. You can make me one of your delicious lattes to go with the cake. And you can show me your etchings… Okay?' I said, snuggling into him.

'That's cool,' he said, relief flooding into his gorgeous brown eyes.

'Do you have to work nights all the time?' I asked, wondering if I would ever have a non-nocturnal relationship.

'Not all the time. It's just that Keith is married with kids…Charlie's always hung over…And I hate being on my own at Cheryl's Close. It's always worse at night time. So I kinda volunteered for the late shift…Anyhow, you work until late,' he said.

'I finish at eleven usually and get an evening off every week. It does suit me though, because I can paint during the day.' It slowly dawned on me that I had nothing left to exhibit in Alan's window. 'In fact that's what I intend to do right after the meeting,' I said. 'Zo I'll zee you later Fritz and be goot until zen.'

'I can't wait until I see you again,' he said, cheering up. 'Please be careful Kathryn. You'll need to change your regular movements. Try varying the times you arrive and leave home… And please…don't go out alone in the dark.'

31

After an inspired late afternoon's painting, I was ready to take on the world. Well, at least my shift in the bistro while still having some energy left over for Ben's passionate love making. Edward's flat remained silent so I guessed he was lying in a darkened stone-lidded crypt until nightfall. Half way through a wildly daubed seascape showing an enormous barrelling wave, I heard the door bell ring. Charging downstairs and trying to beat Mrs. Jenkins in my race to avoid more dubious parcels, I noticed blood on the carpet outside Edward's door. At least I thought it was blood. I suppose it could have been a spilled wine stain from the lees of the *Calon Segur* as he took it out for a refill to the blood bank.

Anyhow, Mrs. Jenkins, as always, got to the door first. She moved surprisingly spryly and seemed more agile each day. And at last, she'd stopped wearing the gasmask. Fortunately, it was Fred the postman with a parcel for me from *The White Company*.

'It's alright Frieda. I've signed for them both. Although I do think you should change your name on written documents. It's a dead giveaway. The post is the first thing the spies will look at,' she reprimanded, before handing me the parcels.

Fred rolled his eyes.

'Please be careful. What's underneath the bigger parcel?' I said, thinking aloud. 'You should have checked it out first and left it behind the pot,' I scolded.

'Sorry Frieda, but I had to sign for it so I thought it was valuable. Is it armed and dangerous?'

'I'm just about to find out. So I suggest you go into your flat and close the door Ingrid.'

'Not blooming likely. It's all for one. I'm not afraid,' she said stoutly, refusing to budge.

I looked at the large padded envelope and studied the postmark. It was from Newquay.

With relief I noted Sophie's handwriting. It had to be the stuff belonging to my Mother.

'Are you sure it's safe?' Mrs. Jenkins asked, trying to take the parcel from me. 'I've got my window open in readiness.'

'It's fine Ingrid. It's a parcel from my Godparents in Newquay. Stand easy agent. You may now take a well earned rest until this evening.' She looked relieved and disappointed. The mind was willing but the flesh was tired. 'And you can tell Wolfgang to stand down also.'

I heard a throaty chuckle, followed by: 'I'm at the ready to decipher at your behest, my *Dangerous Delphinium*. Also I have a sweeping brush to hand for clearing away anymore falling piggy fragments.'

'Then I say to you, over and out my top agents Frieda and Wolfgang.' He's such a conman but so full of merriment and in a quirky way, a man of honour too.

I desperately needed a few more hours sleep and felt almost confident that this was now a possibility. After cleaning the blood/wine stain from the landing carpet and leaving a very bright patch of before unseen colours, I decided to make a milky drink. Pacing around, as much as I could pace in such a small space, I realized that a refreshing nap was out of the question until the envelope had been opened and the contents deciphered.

It's strange though that the thing I wanted most of all was right in front of me. At last I would have something belonging to my Mother. I just couldn't open it. I was scared I suppose in the knowledge that she was probably from Transylvania and that would make me half Transylvanian. And it was too much of a coincidence that she never opened her curtains in the daylight.

Oh. My. God. What if she is a blood-drinker? Such things aren't unheard of outside that new brooding teenage blood-sucker. And worse, my skin was very pale and I had to wear factor 50 in the summer, otherwise I blistered.

I decided right there and then, at that spot in time, to take the plunge and face my fears. Switching on all the lights to make the flat less gloomy in the twilight, I opened the envelope. I'd got exactly two hours to try and understand the contents, before starting my shift at the bistro.

Inside were hand written and very dusty documents tied with a faded red ribbon. I'd seen similar hand-written Indentures relating to land transfers, when I did my three weeks Work Experience in a solicitors' office. (This was my, trying to impress the Godparents, phase. I hated my stint there. I found it impossible to sit at a desk for more than five minutes - and it didn't impress them one bit). As I opened each document very carefully, I noted the language had lots of consonants like: V's W's and Z's following each other and devoid of vowels. There was a hand drawn map dated 1431 on something that resembled a section of wizened leathery skin and showing a mountainous area with a red border round the edges. As I studied the unpronounceable names something clattered onto the floor. It was a wooden pallet with strange symbols and the numbers: 3 - 9, 12 – 5, 6 - 11 carved into it. It was very worn and riddled with wood worm. There were also some yellowing letters with broken waxed seals. Again, all of the contents were alien to me.

Carefully, I worked my way through the documents looking for some recognizable words. There were none except names and dates stretching from the 13th century up until the early 20th century. Secured in the centre of the pile was a rectangular red and satin gold enamelled box with a ruby encrusted raised flower in the centre of the lid. Running my thumb nail along the join I tried to prize it open but it remained intact. There were no external signs of hinges either. Shaking the box gently, something move around inside.

I knew my Mother had put precious items in there for my eyes only. Feeling around for any hidden niches in the surfaces, I noted the join was perfectly aligned and barely visible. I peered inside the empty padded envelope, half hoping to find a clue, or a key, that might be hidden in one of the corners. No such luck. The box was far too pretty and valuable to take a kitchen knife to it. Then I thought of Joe. He had to be the man for the job.

I spread out all of the documents on the coffee table and the floor in the hope that something would jump out at me, other than overfed dust-mites. The deeds and letters were pertaining to my family history, I guessed. And they would have to wait, until someone was able to translate them. I carefully folded them and returned the wad to the envelope. So I was left with the wooden pallet and the box. The numbers 3 – 9, 12 – 5, 6 – 11 definitely had to have some significance.

As I sat with eyes closed trying to figure out what was happening in my life and trying to process all this new information, there was a knock on my door.

'Hello Kat. It's Mick. Are you free for a mo,

my *Gawky Geranium*?' he whispered through the door.

'Yes. Mick, I sighed, 'I'm coming you old rat-bag.'

I opened the door and invited him in, looking around the landing for intruders as a matter of habit. 'I know you're busy,' he said, eyeing the contents on the table. 'I've had a word with Sunbeam Wayne and he says that you can take the night off to attend to your family matters.'

'Thanks Mick. That would be great. How did you wangle that then?'

'Wayne is under my spell. It's the animal magnetism you know Petal. I just can't help myself at times,' he chuckled. 'Had any luck with those things Kat? You don't have to answer that. It's not like I'm prying or anything. You know I'll do what I can to help.'

'No Mick. No luck. Lots of deeds relating to land, I think, and full of names like: Mikael, Rudolph and Alexandu. There's a map dated 1431 with a large area of land enclosed within a red border. No doubt long lost ancestral acres which are now probably under the jurisdiction of the Romanian government…Were you kidding around about translating them?'

'Would I do that to my *Doubting Daffodil*?' he grinned. 'Put the kettle on and I'll have a look.'

As Mick made himself comfortable on the sofa, I poured out the tea and put some chocolate biscuits on a plate, to aid concentration.

'So. Is Ingrid ready for another night at the bistro?' I asked, wondering if she had overdone the late nights.

'I've put my Lady Iris to bed with a hot water bottle, a cup of cocoa and Wayne's portable DVD. I thought watching a few films might bring her up to date a little more.'

'Good idea. What's she watching? I hope it's nothing violent,' I asked, putting three sugars in his tea.

Mick looked serious for a while as he studied the wooden pallet, then said: 'What? Err…no. I've got her: *The Sound of Music.*'

'Nice one you old fart. It's set during the German invasion.'

'I forgot about that,' he said, before we both burst into laughter.

I went back to my painting and did a strategic frontal attack with a pallet knife and oodles of white and aquamarine paint while Mick studied the documents.

'You're a very talented girl. You do know that, don't you?'

'I'm okay at it,' I replied, shrugging my shoulder. 'I just love painting the sea. I never get tired of it. If folks like my paintings then the joy is doubled.'

'I can't remember when I last went to the seaside,' Mick said pensively. 'My memory's a bit of a blur when I try to go back to happier times.'

'Oh. That reminds me Wolfgang. You and Ingrid are invited to spend Christmas with me and my Godparents in Newquay. That is, if you want?'

'That would be really enjoyable Kat, but what about the bistro?'

'Trevor and Wayne decided two years ago that they intended to close the shutters from the 20th December until after the New Year. They don't want drunken tramps wrecking the joint…as you well know…They usually go off to a fashionable skiing resort.'

'Somehow I just can't imagine those two even attempting a white run.'

'They're strictly off-piste Mick. They just like to pose in the gear and get pissed. It's the same every year. They show us the photos of themselves: holding skis, wearing earmuffs, standing in bars alongside handsome young French ski-instructors, sitting on the ski lift at the bottom of the mountain - and peering from behind snowmen.

'Do the snowmen mind?' he cackled.

'Ha. Ha. So Mick… who are you really?'

'I'm Mick the Tramp. Everyone knows that.'

'There's more to you than that Wolfgang.

Come on I've told you all my secrets. Well almost…You're obviously educated…Your life can't have been any crazier than mine. Can it?'

'One of these fine days, my *Prying Poppy*, maybe, I'll be ready to talk about my life, but not yet awhile. All right?' he said, looking downhearted.

'Okay…So how do you know about languages?' I asked, changing the subject. 'I mean are you really reading those documents you old fart?'

Mick always liked it when I called him derogatory names. He felt more comfortable with the crude banter than anything deeper and more meaningful. I understood that.

'When you've lived on the streets of London as long as I have, my *Golden Godetia*, you meet all kinds of nationalities. I've always had a good ear for languages and dialects - and it's a little like insurance. If you try and communicate and make friends with other nationalities they look out for you. Even if it's only a: "Good Morrow", or a "Thank You". I've called in many a favour that way.'

'So? How many Transylvanian homeless people do you know?'

'For your information, I know more than you can count….Enough of that. Let's get down to business…These are deeds for the transfer of land through inheritance and mainly in the surname of Duwulfe.'

'So. Is there any connection to Divinia Katarina - my Mother's Christian names?'

'None that I can see, Kat. They're very ancient documents and in the names of male heirs only. Their only value, as far as I can deduce, is of an intrinsic nature. I believe your Mother kept these as tokens of remembrance and out of pride in her family bloodline. She gave them to you. Now you know where you come from on your Mother's side.'

'I suppose that means that the bloodline ends with me?'

Mick suddenly jumped up from the sofa: 'That's it, my *Shining Sunflower*. There's the rub… It's as clear as the nose on your face,' he enthused.

'What? Have you gleaned something else from those tatty old deeds?' I asked.

'Don't you see Kat? Petal? Look at it. It has twelve petals like a clock face. See these twelve tiny grooves underneath the flower? The numbers on the slat are the codes,' he said, doing a little jig.

I wiped my hands and picked up the box.

'Careful don't damage it,' he said. 'Give it here. You'll break it trying to force it like that. And it might be *Faberge* for all you know - and worth a bomb.'

'What? You don't think it's wired?' I panicked.

'A slip of the tongue. Of course it's not wired, but, on the other hand, my *Ginger Nut*, you are.'

He took the box and held it under the light and examined it closely. 'The heart-shaped ruby stamen is the key. It presses down. Get the slat and read out the numbers for me.'

'Three to nine,' I said.

Mick pressed down the heart of the flower and moved the third petal to the position nine o'clock, then released the button. A distinct click was heard then the flower sprang back to its original position.

'Twelve to five,' I said excitedly.

Again we heard a click and an anti- clockwork whirling noise.

'Now give me the last numbers Kat. Hurry up. I can hardly wait.'

'Six to eleven,' I told him.

Click. Whirl.

'You can do the honours,' he beamed.

With shaking hands I opened the box and looked inside. A padded, faded red velvet lining edged in woven gold, revealed that it was a beautifully crafted jewellery box. Nestled in a central niche was a small rich-gold ring set with a large round cabochon ruby, and either side were drop earrings of the same design. And to my delight, folded and pressed into the lid, was an envelope with Kathryn Shaw written on it.

'Is that all?' Mick asked, looking disappointed. I suppose he expected gold doubloons, or a treasure map with: X marks the spot.

'Don't you see Mick? It's from my Mother. The greatest treasure I could wish for.'

'I see,' he said, swallowing hard then gently patting me on the back. 'I'll leave you to it then Kat. If you need me I have my mobile handy,' he said, reaching into his pocket and holding up a swish snakeskin cell-phone like the one *Golden Balls* Beckham promoted.

'Who got you that?' I asked in amazement.

'Nobody. I'm a wage-earner now, don't forget. Pass me your mobile and I'll tap in my number for you....Can you keep an eye on my Lady Iris? And can I borrow your car to get to the bistro? It is I whom is covering your shift, my *Marauding Moonflower.*'

32

Two hours later I had plucked up the courage to read my Mother's letter. It was one of the most difficult things I'd ever done. Here was another tangible spot in time and one more piece for the jigsaw. I only hoped it didn't make the bigger picture fall apart. It went as follows:

My Precious Child,

I know when you read this letter you are grown into a beautiful and clever woman. I say to you with all my heart that I love you. I never thought I would be strong enough to bear a child. The day you were born was the happiest day of my life. And for your Father you brought great joy. I am difficult for explaining. But please to know that as I write this letter you are sleeping like an angel and your little face inspires me to good words.

Since your Father was lost to me, I fear for your future if I had stayed in Cornwall. There are bad forces in the air. I am used to this persecution. If I do one thing right in my life I will separate you from my household. I thank God that you have not inherited our curse. You have strong elements like your Father. But I know you will look like my dear and beautiful Grandmother - your namesake, Katarina.

Your future life may be blessed. I hope so much. I pray that you will not suffer hardship and cruelty. Whatever happens to you I know you will survive. As soon as you were born you kicked and screamed into life. I know this to be a sure sign that nothing will defeat you in this world. I know the truth.

Oh. My darling child, my heart is breaking for what I have to do. One day I hope you understand and forgive your

Mama. Without your Father to care for me I am lost and afraid. He gave me the only peace ever. He showed me wonderful things. He was a man in love with life.

Because of this family curse we had to hide away from the day and take refuge in the night. If you are afraid by this, I tell you now that I had only a mild skin affliction. My fate was brought about by kidney disease and rheumatic fever. I lived as my family lived at night time because I was too sickly to walk out in the day.

The Newquay freshness made me stronger for a time. But I had been sick for too long and soon the illness returned. I could not walk out with you in the pram. Your Father took you with him everywhere. I tell you now that you loved the sea and were not afraid of the big waves. He was very proud of you.

I tell you now that your Godparents were much kind to us. I made your Father swear to not tell them of my affliction. There are reasons why I could not leave you with them. I know you have found them in the end. That is why I leave these few heirlooms in their hands.

It was for your own safety I brought you to Wales. Your see, my darling, I love the mountains of my homeland and that is why I carried you here. I wanted to get you far away from my sister Leonora, our last surviving relative. She wants to make you her own forever and I cannot allow that to happen.

I will tell you our history with truth and honesty, so you will know where you are from. Please do not be afraid. All is in the past and cannot harm you. As far back as our family can be traced the curse has been present. Those who escaped the curse moved to different countries. We who remained were hunted and driven out of our homes. Our land was stolen. We were feared and loathed by the ignorant lowlanders. One by one our ancestors were killed in barbaric ways until only our branch of the family remained. We are the Duwulfe bloodline. My brother, Alexandu and my sister Leonora and I were the last in the family line.

One night when I was only seventeen Alexandu went out to restock on food. He left my sister and me alone. He never came back. So day after day our last refuge was bombarded with missiles and vulgar words from the lowlanders. Alexandu had reinforced the doors but we were still afraid they would break in. It finally drove Leonora, who was five years older than me, insane. She adored Alexandu and could not live without him. Nothing would have kept him from us. He had told us on the night he left, to follow the path to the coast and make our way to London, if he did not return.

Leonora hated living in a prison. All our lives we were locked up until nightfall. I got used to wandering alone after sunset but your aunt hated to be different. She blamed everyone in the family her for her affliction and swore revenge. Always the defiant one, she threatened to stand under the midday sun without protection.

I had to sedate Leonora that fateful night. I gathered our few possessions together with the money Alexandu had secured. We travelled under the cover of night until we reached the coast. It took many weeks for us to reach England.

We finally arrived by boat to the Cornish coast. We lived happily there for a while working in the evenings as barmaids and waitresses. In our homeland we were tutored in English, German and French. Unfortunately our dialect was hard to understand by the Cornish. In return we could not understand theirs. We managed. They had good hearts.

During my work, I met your wonderful Father. He was so handsome and had a wondrous light in his eyes. All the girls fancied him. I thought he would prefer Leonora. She was so beautiful and in better health than I. The men adored her. Martin did not. He liked me for my shyness.

Again Leonora took to madness. She wanted Martin for herself. She did not want me to have anyone without her. When I married she showed terrible anger. Martin was such a good man. Why did he die? He was the best in the water. I do not understand. Now they think I am crazy also. Some of the people blamed me for his death. He was my life. I could never harm him.

That is why I left Newquay. I believed I might survive in the mountains of Wales

*and take care of you. I cannot my little
one. My back is in great pain and my
heart beats like a frightened bird.*

*My darling child, I look at your
angelic face again and weep for your loss
and for your years to come without mother
or father. Forgive me please for all the hurt
I have caused you.*

*So now I say Goodbye my angel. I
leave you in the care of the kind mountain
people who look after babies without
mothers or fathers. You will be in safe
hands and you will lead a normal life
without me. Remember darling child, I
love you so very much. I will always be
with you in spirit.*

*Your Loving Mama
Davinia Kathryn Shaw.*

I don't remember how long I sat in the
darkness, or how long I cried. My tears were for
her and my Dad. The letter made me all the more
determined to find and face Aunt Leonora. She

held the ultimate pieces which I so desperately needed to complete my own picture - although I doubted whether she was sane enough to make that possible. Despite that, I understood that her anger for revenge drove her to seek out and destroy me, as I was the only one left in the bloodline. I knew for sure that the substance of my Mother's letter, showing her bravery, had given me a greater strength to withstand whatever Leonora threw at me. I was prepared. In this respect, my night time friends Mick and Edward would be of great help.

33

The ocean spilled over in a kaleidoscope of colours from the purest aquamarine to the deepest cobalt blue with frothy spumes high and wild. I picked up my board and paddled towards the swell. I had the waves all to myself and the expanding surge ahead looked perfect in every way. I knew it would let me hitch a ride. This was the one I'd been waiting for all my life. Sensing the moment I turned volte-face and knelt on my stick feeling the dynamic power pushing from behind. In a slow motion move I stood and found the centre of gravity - the place where the journey begins and time stands still on the zenith. Before cutting down into the curve, I did a couple of aerials detaching myself from the foam. It was exhilarating and spectacular, free flying then sliding downward and swerving inward before I became enfolded in the tube. Spinning and turning in the spray, I knew the surf's momentum would guide me onwards. This was my heaven on earth - an eternity with the wave holding me in its relentless embrace. Carrying me all the way until the final diffusion broke against the shoreline in a flash of brilliant light.

My mobile's annoying light disturbed my dreaming. It was 2.30 a.m and I was still holding my Mother's letter.

'Hi. Ben. Sorry I've been busy and I just fell asleep,' I said apologetically.

'I thought you could have at least called me Kathryn. I was really worried about you. All I got was the voicemail.'

'I'm really, really sorry Ben. I took the night off work. I turned my mobile to silent to read my Mother's last letter...Her stuff arrived from Sophie and Zach...I did tell you about it. Do you remember?'

'You've got your Mother's last letter? Oh.

Kathryn, I'm sorry for doubting you. I was concerned something bad had happened.'

'No. It's the opposite. I feel wonderful and I didn't have a nightmare. It was the most fantastic dream,' I reassured him.

'Well I'm pleased to hear Dr. Ben's loving is helping you sleep,' he laughed.

'It was about surfing and I rode this gigantic wave -.'

'Oh. I see,' he said huffily.

'You know what they say about riding the big one?' I coaxed trying to change the subject.

'I missed you Kathryn. I'd got candles and a midnight feast for us in my office and Lucky wore a new collar for the occasion. He's stopped growling at last and let me scratch behind his ear for the first time.'

'Oh. I see.'

'Not my idea of a romantic meal sharing chicken drumsticks with a recuperating mutt and a demented cat doing cold turkey from chocolate deprivation…I suppose it's too late now? Don't answer that… Anyhow get some rest and I'll call on you in the morning. There's something important I want to ask you. Goodnight. Sweet dreams.'

'Night Ben. You too.' Wonder what he wants to ask me? He's definitely not having Lucky. The mad dog's mine.

I couldn't get the image of the wondrous wave out of my head. I had to paint it. Why is imagined vision always so much better than perceived reality? I tried and tried to recapture the definitive wave. Scraping off paint and reapplying until I was exhausted. I just simply wasn't good enough. It never would be. Perfection only existed in my mind. At 5a.m. I decided the canvass would have to suffice. The painting was wild and free and I was pleased with the result. And it was another pearl to add to my ongoing *Blue Period*. It was time to sleep. Making myself a milky drink before falling into bed, I decided that my life was pretty good.

Bring it on Aunt Leonora. I'm ready for your madness.

The next thing I heard was Fred the postman buzzing the doorbell at 10am. Talking in his usual East London loudness and believing all oldies to be deaf as posts. Mrs. Jenkins was up and about and had taken him a mug of tea and a slice of *Battenberg*. Apparently he liked it - unless he was too polite not to eat the offering.

As I made my way down stairs yawning and stretching Edward's flat was silent as the grave in which he slept. He had not responded to my note but I guessed he was too tired to reply, or had run out of red ink.

'Morning Ingrid. How are you today?' I asked, trying to make myself heard above Fred, Nelson Eddy and Jeanette MacDonald.

'Good morning Frieda. I'm prepared and ready for my next instructions. Fred has to get on with his round… Don't you Fred?' she told him, taking the empty mug and plate and ushering him outside.

'Is there anything for me?'

'There's a handwritten letter Frieda. You don't

see writing like that very often. Puts me in mind of Queen Elizabeth Tudor's elaborate scrawl… You don't think it's from His Majesty do you?'

'I doubt it Ingrid. It would be too dangerous for him to correspond with me. It's probably instructions for our next mission.'

'Is it from Headquarters?' she asked. 'Why don't you come in and have some bacon and eggs with Wolfgang and me? Then we can read it together.

'Good Morrow my *Dizzy Damask Rose*. It's on the table awaiting ketchup,' a throaty fag-filled voice called out.

The wafting smell of sausage and bacon was too much to resist. Mick certainly knew how to cook up a full English breakfast. Sitting around the huge wooden table with its spiralled legs, we ate until our plates were cleared. Horatio having filled his belly, sat playing the cello with one leg held high and head down, intent on licking his butt.

Wolfgang cleared the table and washed the

dishes in no time. He and Ingrid sat waiting for my next instructions as I opened the mysterious envelope. Why did I know who it was from? Only a fruitcake like my Aunt Leonora would embellish a Royal Mail delivery like that and address it to: Her Grace the Countessa Kathryn Shaw. I ask you? She had either a massive inferiority complex or delusions of grandeur. Nothing was going to spoil my elation from discovering my parents had loved me.

'It's from the mad Russian spy,' I told them, opening the envelope. 'It's an invitation to meet her at midnight tonight at *The World's End* near the Garden Centre. It says: "I will put you in touch with your true self and give you immortality, thus securing the Duwulfe line for all time". She's a nutter through and through.'

'You're not going Kat, I mean Frieda. It's too dangerous. Leave it to me and my night-time buddies to sort her out. She wants locking up,' Wolfgang said agitatedly, rubbing the screwdriver stigmata scar on his right hand.

'We'll all go together, but you've got to keep out of sight or you'll scare her off. Don't you see? She holds the last pieces of my jigsaw family. I need to hear her side of the story and know why she's trying to harm me,' I insisted.

'It seems to me that this Russian Olga is making a wooden bomb of some sorts. It's not really a jigsaw Frieda. You have to be careful with a woman who can do woodwork,' Ingrid said seriously.

Both Mick and I smiled. She's so sweet and deluded. Despite her time-warp glitch, she appeared happier than I'd ever seen her. Neither Wolfgang nor I wanted to burst her bubble so we played along.

'You could be right Ingrid. She has the ingenuity to make explosives out of anything,' I said. 'I'll be on my guard.'

'I'm coming with you tonight. Don't forget that I've got youth on my side Frieda,' she said. 'Ilmhart and Gurda should be called to duty also.'

'They're manning the radio tonight in case of

air strikes,' I said. 'They are needed on the Home Front.'

'It's settled then,' Mick pondered. 'I'll enlist Two-fingered Boris, Elephant Manito, Hovis and Sliced Bochenek -.'

'Hovis and Sliced?' I asked.

'Bochenek means bread in Polish. And not forgetting my old mate Dusty -.'

'I know what that means. His surname's Rhodes. Right?'

'Wrong. His name's Dusty Filth because he is. A right scruff but an ex-prize fighter my *Painting Pyracantha...* All vile monstrous men and useful in a scrap,' Mick chuckled. 'We'll all go after the bistro closes early.'

'Trevor and Wayne won't allow that,' I said.

'Frieda you have obviously forgotten my powers of persuasion... Harken I hear the bells of love ringing out. It must be *Longshanks* the Vet. Better let him in before he storms the castle walls for his lady love,' Mick laughed.

'Oh. No. It's too early and I've not showered yet,' I sighed.

'Methinks the lady doth protest too greatly,' Mick added, opening the front door and greeting Ben like a long lost son. 'Come in young man she awaits your presence in the Grand Hall….Kat come on out you've got a visitor.'

'Is it Fritz? Tell him to come in and have a cup of tea and a slice of -,' Mrs. Jenkins called out.

'I think he has more on his mind than tea dearest,' Wolfgang interjected.

Ben rushed towards me and literally took my breath away with a totally impulsive snog - and I'd not brushed my teeth. Still it was really enjoyable after hearing Wolfgang close Ingrid's door quietly. Ben's so hot and my tiredness soon disappeared. On entering my flat we made love all over the lounge and kitchen and ended up in the shower. After which we both sat on the sofa wrapped in towels and drank our lattes, occasionally smiling in a silly fashion into the middle distance.

It seemed like forever before Ben spoke:

'Kathryn? Do you love me?' he asked looking worried.

'Errum. Yes. I think I do,' I said with conviction. 'You make me feel warm and happy. So, yes I do Ben.'

'You're not supposed to say those words before I've had the chance to ask you,' he said, ruffling my hair.

'Ask me what?' I asked, hoping we weren't going to argue about ownership of Lucky.

'Kathryn Shaw, you are the weirdest, craziest girl I've ever met and I can't get you out of my head. The only way I'm going to get any peace from this constant torment is to ask: Will you marry me?'

'What? I don't understand?' Constant torment? In his head? I don't feel like that at all. Out of sight out of mind. I really need to make a start on Jamie Fraser. Have some free time for painting. Watch Mick giving Trevor and Wayne fencing lessons…Find Lucy a true love. Go to the cinema with Alan and share popcorn while admiring the leading man's bum. Talk to Sal and Joe about old times. Train Lucky to be a dog and not a werewolf. Read my Diana Gabaldon collection again.

I'm not ready for babies and domesticity. To be honest, I don't think I ever will be. And I've never been further than the brooding hills of Wales and smiley cliffs of Newquay. I was going to travel…I've other things to think about than settling down. Is that what love is? An obsessing pain? I feel happy the way things are. I don't really know much about him, other than that he's kind to animals, has a stillness that I find comforting - and he's good at sex.

'What's not to understand? All you have to say is: I will,' and with that bombshell he took a single diamond ring from his jacket pocket and knelt down on one knee causing the towel to fall. Looking absolutely adorable in all his 21st century Mr. Darcy butt naked glory, how could I refuse?

'I will Ben Gibson and thank you for asking me,' I said, like the polite idiot I now am.

34

Standing like statues in the freezing December night air, our posse of three was chilled to the bone. We'd assembled outside the flats ready for action. I had managed to stall Ben from another planned romantic tryst at the Animal Rescue Centre in the company of sick animals. I'd told him that I was tired and needed an early night. I hated lying to him as I'd never felt better in my whole life. I couldn't contain my happiness. I had become a real girl.

Mick was right about his street-dwelling mates. They were the scariest blokes I'd ever seen in real life. They made Mr. Hyde and Uncle Fester look like sex gods. Two-fingered Boris seemed to be made of granite with an unmoving face of gargantuan proportions and peppered with a spattering of hairy moles as big as five pence pieces. Elephant Manito, like his nick-name, was a heavy weight about 400 hundred pounds who moved slowly and deliberately in an undulating forward motion. It looked as if his knees had given up the ghost, as he slung one ham-shank leg in front of the other. Hovis and Sliced, on the contrary were dark-eyed and swarthy with chiselled rat-like features. They were both edgy and agitated and talked rapidly in Polish to each other, sounding like rounds of machine gun fire.

'Alright my *Fragrant Flowers*, alias Frieda and Ingrid, be prepared. I smell Dusty in the distance. I want you ladies to stand behind me, that is to say, upwind of him when he arrives otherwise your delicate stomachs might react to an overload of putridity,' Mick announced mischievously.

He was right about Dusty. He looked every inch the bare-knuckle prize-fighter. Under the gloomy street lights his mauled facial contours appeared even more squashed and beat up. I was thankful the weather was still cold and fresh. God knows what he would've smelled like on a hot day. Fortunately the odour of Wayne's aftershave emitting from Mick shiny face almost masked the eye-watering stink. Mick handed extra strong mints around before we set off.

'Ill met by starlight my Nocturnal Nutters… Now is the time to traverse forward and onward to the designated target area. And don't make a move on Russian Olga until I say so. Got that Hovis and Sliced? Don't want the same repercussions from what happened last Christmas when you rounded up swans instead of turkeys… Okay?' Hovis and Sliced let out a peal of cackling laughter and danced around on the spot flapping their arms. 'I'll take the ladies in the car…Not you Dusty. A walk will blow off the cobwebs,' Mick said, quickly locking the car doors to prevent the pugilist's imminent entry.

Dusty grimaced at us through the car window, exposing a toothless grin then waved in a childlike way with a shovel of a hand as we departed for: *The World's End.*

Mick remained silent for a change during our journey down the King's Road. After driving around for a while he found a spot to park nearby in preparation for a quick getaway. I understood that he didn't want a confrontation with Aunt Leonora. He would never hurt a woman. I knew that for sure. As far as his buddies go, they didn't have any qualms in that respect.

'Alright my *Adventurous Apple Blossoms,* please wait in the car until I've rounded up the guys. If Two-fingered Boris is pointing the way, they're probably lost in Chelsea by now. At least Dusty will leave a trail of green gas for me to follow.'

'I won't hear of it Wolfgang. You need us with you,' Mrs. Jenkins insisted, climbing out of the back seat and holding Arnold's newly honed Swiss Army knife. 'Now come on Frieda. Password at the ready…Don't dilly-dally, there's work to do!'

'I copy. New password is: "Giant Redwood". Over and out Ingrid,' I replied.

We all wore our night camouflage gear, that is to say black trousers and black coats. Mick had on

Trevor's black *Armani* as per usual. As we moved along furtively we neared the garden centre's railings. Mick stopped and pointed through the bars.

'I can see a white figure through the bushes over there,' he whispered.

'I think it's her.'

I peered into the darkness and looked in the direction he'd pointed. Then I got a fit of giggles: 'It's a stone statue of Venus,' I managed to say. 'And please no jokes about her being *armless.*'

'Shush Frieda. You must learn to take your missions more seriously dear,' Mrs. Jenkins scolded.

'Sorry Ingrid. You're quite right…If we can capture Russian Olga I know it will help the War effort greatly.'

'Even finish it,' Mick added, giving me the nod.

'Do you think so dearest,' Mrs. Jenkins asked, dewy-eyed.

'I know so,' he told her.

At last she's moving further forward in time. By next week, with a bit of luck, she might even make the Fifties. 'He's right agent Ingrid. It's very important that you stay hidden and take note. We don't want to blow our cover.'

'Understood agent Frieda. "Giant Redwood". Would you like some tea from my flask and a slice of *Battenberg* whilst we're waiting dears?'

Mick turned suddenly. He had spotted his mates heading in our direction and arguing like mad.

'I knew they would do this. Every time! Every single time,' he sighed, running to meet them.

We saw him waving his hands around agitatedly for a while before handing out paper money. It must have worked because they followed him like lumbering hippos.

'Okay my *Anthropomorphic Amblers* let's try and get through this without any more arguing,' he instructed. 'Now Dusty and Elephant, can you break the lock on the gate?'

'I can do better than that,' Elephant said

slowly. 'I can do this Mick me old mate.' And without any effort he lifted the gate away from its hinges.

'Will you never learn?' Mick said angrily. 'You're only supposed to take the bloody lock off! Sorry ladies.'

Elephant grinned: 'Okay Mick, I'll get right on it.'

'Not now Elephant if you please…Oh. Never mind. Let's go inside and get under cover,' Mick said, looking at his swish new *Omega* watch. 'We've got half an hour before the mad woman arrives. Everybody keep quite and don't move a muscle, unless I say so.'

'Mick, can I have one of these pretty Christmas Trees?' Elephant asked.

'Not now Elephant. Just sit behind it on that bench and be quiet.'

I had to talk to Mick about my plan. So I directed Mrs. Jenkins to serve tea and cake to the others. I heard her whispering "Giant Redwood" to each one as I took Mick to one side.

'What is it my *Chilly Campanula*?' he asked.

'Look Mick I don't want Aunt Leonora scaring off like last time. I really need to get her talking. There's so much I want to know about my family. So if you could back off, unless she starts fighting again, I'd be grateful.'

'Kat sometimes you talk daft. What if she's armed, or got a bomb?'

'I don't think that's her plan anymore. She wants to bite my neck you see. She thinks she's a vampire and she wants to make me immortal like herself.'

'Oh. Right. Well that makes sense. I mean, she's only tried to poison you, put you through her windscreen, crash you and your car into the river along with Iris and me, blow up both you and Long-shanks and screw me to the car. What the bloody hell are you thinking of Kat? She stark staring bonkers! You really can't take any more risks -.'

'I know it sounds ridiculous, Mick, but I have to do this. It might be my last chance you see. My

Mother mentioned the family curse. I need to know what that means…She's my only surviving maternal relative and for some ridiculous reason I feel a strange kind of affinity to her. It's like looking into a mirror. All these years I've scanned strangers' faces hoping to see something of myself. Well, now I've found what I've longed for…I know she's barking mad but in a funny way I feel sorry for her… Please?'

Mick scratched his head and thought for a while. 'Right Kat. Do your best, but I doubt whether you'll get a straight answer from her… You can't trust her and if she goes off on one, I'll let the boys handle it. Okay?'

'Agreed.'

The time dragged at *The World's End*. The silence was interrupted by intermittent farting from two directions. Fortunately we were upwind of Dusty and Elephant. Two-fingered Boris hadn't spoken a word the whole time and sat like a giant knobbly troll, unmoving and undetected amongst the stone statues.

'I'm going to show myself,' I told Mick. 'I think she's here and waiting for me to make a move.'

'No Kat,' he whispered. 'It's not midnight yet.'

'It's the only way. We could be here all night otherwise and I don't want Mrs. Jenkins suffering from hypothermia.'

I stepped out onto the gravel footpath and coughed loudly. Before I could make another move Aunt Leonora had sprung from nowhere and had me by the neck. She was surprisingly strong and tightened her arm lock on my throat, pulling me backwards.

'Naw vawt aw yaw gaweenk taw daw? Haw. Haw. Awt lawzt I awf gawt yaw een maw pawawr.'

'Look Aunt Leonora. I've come here to make peace with you,' I said hoarsely. 'Please loosen your grip on my throat. I can hardly speak.'

'Wawree vawl. Dawnt mawf awr I veel ztrankawl yaw.'

'Okay. Now why don't we sit down over there on that lovely mosaic garden furniture and have a civilized chat?' I said, trying to steer her towards Mick.

'Daw yaw theenk I awm ztawpawd lark yaw? I vawnt taw bawt yaw neek naw!'

'Look, I'm really pissed off with you calling me stupid all the time. Don't do it anymore or I will not join with you.'

'Yaw awr ztawpawd yawzt lark yaw mawzawr bawvawr yaw! Awnd I veel bawt yaw neek tawnawt awn zee ztrawk awf tvawlf! Awnd pleez dawnt zvawr!'

I had to keep Mick and the posse away from her otherwise she would never tell me what I needed to know. The best method I decided was to distract her. Insult her appearance. She was obviously extremely vain. I had to provoke her into answering my questions.

'How old are you? I know you are older than my Mother. Are you a pensioner?'

'Vawt? Haw dawr yaw! I awm a yawnk bawteevawl vawmawn.'

'You may look about thirty but my guess is

that you've had a face-lift,' I challenged, stalling for time.

'Dawnt baw ztawpawd. I awm awn awmmawtawl. A wampawr.'

'What? Oh. A vampire.'

'Zat eez vawt I zawd! Aw yaw dawv or davt?'

'What? Oh. Never mind. How old was my Mother when she had me?'

'I dawnt rawmawmbaw. I naw zhee vawz ztawpawd lark yaw. Awbawt tvawnte yawrz awld, I zeenk.'

'That means you're at least fifty odd years old.'

'I hawv tawld yaw. I awm a wampawr. I veel awlvawz baw tvawntee fawrv yawrz awld. Dawnt yaw zee? Nawt taw yawnk awd nawt taw awld. Zawt eez vy I vawt vawr yawr bawzdaw.'

'I don't believe you. You're delusional…Let me look at your hands. I bet they look like an old hag's. You can always tell the true age of a woman from her hands. Do I see liver spots?' I asked, pulling off her right glove.

'Naw. Naw. Pleez nawt zawt. Maw hawndz

nawd taw baw cawvawrd awt awl tawmbz,' she
screeched, trying to retrieve the gloves.

At last I had hit a sore spot. I ran a lap around
the large Ali Baba pots waving the white glove
above my head. She pursued me with a garden
fork and a pair of secateurs. She certainly was fit
for a fifty year old - and wearing 4" heels. Mick
and Elephant stood opened-mouthed against the
greenhouse as we rushed passed them and into
the cheery lit Christmas trees.

As she gained on me, I nipped into the
undergrowth where Sliced and Hovis lurked with
feet outstretched. Bingo. I heard them cackle
with laughter. Aunt Leonora didn't even notice
my back-up team as she fell flat on her face.

'Okay lady. Now, don't move a muscle, or I'll
take off the other glove,' I threatened, sitting on
her back and holding a dibble to her throat.

'Yaw awr zpawleenk maw bawteevawl vawr
cawt. Pleez lawt maw gawt awp vrawm zeez
dawtee vlawr!' she pleaded, trying to roll me off
her.

'Let's have a little look at that ancient claw,' I insisted, holding up her right hand to the light.

The hand glistened under the fairy lights like that of the Lady of the Lake's. It was pure white and without blemish. As soft as a baby's bottom. I wrenched off the other glove and the left hand was in the same dewy condition. My freckled hand next to hers looked older.

'Vy dawnt yaw bawlawf maw?' she sobbed. 'I awm a wampawr, thraw awnd thraw. Maw awl fawmawlaw vaw wampawrz. Yaw Mawzawr vawz a wampawr awlzaw zee vaz a wegawtawreeawn. Zawt eez vy Dawfeeneeaw vawz alvawz zo pawl.'

'A what? Oh. A vegetarian. You mean my Mother didn't drink blood like you and that's why she was ill?'

'Zawt eez vawt I zawd! Yaw aw zaw ztawpawd! Dawnt yaw fawl zee cawnawczhawn? Maw thawtz awr yaw thawtz. Naw Kawtawreenaw pleez jawawn taw maw een blawd. Lawt maw bawt yawr neek.'

'No way am I going to be your supper bitch.

And keep still or I'll stake you out in the sunlight!' She really is delusional. If I thought like her, I'd have been certified long ago. But then, on the other hand, I've always been preoccupied with wampawrz. Na! Can't be.

'Aw. Naw. Dawnt daw zawt! Eeet veel keel maw!' she pleaded, thrashing around on the floor, trying to retrieve the gloves.

I was amazed at her strength as she threw me off in a roll and jumped to her feet. Before I knew what had hit me, she held me in a strangle hold again with the secateurs against my throat. By this time I believed she had supernatural strength and started to panic. What if she really was a vampire? And I hadn't worn my crucifix.

'Naw baw kwawrt awnd lawt maw bawt yaw neek!'

'Hang on a minute Aunt Leonora. Before I become immortal like you I need to speak to my troops,' I said, trying to distract her as she held the secateurs a little too close to my earlobe. Then I noticed the white van minus the *PARTY*

POPPETS sign parked further down on the other side of the road.

'Vawt trawpz? I cawnt zee awneevawn awlz?'

'Let me and the boys take her out Kat!' Mick shouted, breaking cover and rounding in closer.

'Vawt? Yaw agawn awld mawn? Vy daw yaw awlvaws hawnt maw? Vy cawnt I baw lawft alawn. I awm awmmawtawl!'

'Oh. Wolfgang, do be careful. That Russian Olga is a nasty trollop,' Mrs. Jenkins implored, pulling on Mick's arm.

'Cawl awv yaw zawmbawz aw I veel tark yawr eawr awf!' Leonora shouted madly.

'They're not zombies.'

'Zay mawzt baw. Zay lawk awz eev zay hawf bawn dawk awp frawm zee grawfyawd.'

'Yes. You're right. They are my zombies. And if you hurt me, they'll tear you apart. And believe me they're ripe as rotten meat and the stench is vile…And they're sex starved - especially the one with no teeth. So let's talk some more…I'll call off my zombies and sit with you in the van.

They're some things I'm entitled to know about my Duwulfe family before I become a vampire. Do you agree?' I asked.

'Eev yaw aw gaweenk taw baw a Dawvawlv zawn faw Gawd'z zark prawnawnz eet prawpawrlee!'

'Sorry Aunt Leonora. I mean Duvuvle of course.'

Before she could say another word, the distant hollow sound of a large chiming clock rang out twelve tinny rounds. Aunt Leonora became very agitated, looking this way and that for God knows what. Whatever it was she showed sheer terror and shook from head to toe.

'Pleez daw cawm naw,' she insisted, dragging me by the hand. 'I muzt gaw bawvawr zay cawm vaw maw.'

'The iron tongue of midnight hath bonged twelve…Don't go with her, Kat. She's a nutter,' Mick shouted.

'Leave it Mick. I'll be alright. You just take your zombie friends back to the graveyard and wait for my return. Okay?'

'What's she on about?' Dusty asked, hiding coyly behind Elephant Manito. 'I changed my underpants especially for tonight.'

'Yes. I know Dusty, but you're suppose to wash them, not rotate them…Anyhow, Kat needs some information from Russian Olga. Do as she says…' Mick mouthed slowly. 'Get the van surrounded and wait for me. I need to grab the keys before the mad redhead drives off with Kat…You get in Frieda's car, Ingrid dearest and lock the doors. I'll follow you shortly,' he whispered endearingly, handing her the keys.

'Can I have Russian Olga for my girlfriend after you've finished with her Mick?' Dusty drawled.

'Sorry mate. She's not for you. High maintenance and she's too volatile. Stick with Vinegar Liz. She's no sense of smell and far more your style.'

Aunt Leonora knew something was amiss and suddenly broke away from me.

'Aunt Leonora come back to me. Please don't be afraid. I can help you… I need you,' I entreated.

'Naw Kawtawreenaw zat eez nawt traw…Yaw aw trawtawr lark yaw Mawzawr! I naw yaw vawnt taw gawt maw bawk awntaw zee awzawlawm.'

'Tell me about Davinia? I know she took care of you…Did you love her?' I asked, trying to reach out to her.

'Eez zawt yaw Dawfeeneeaw? Hawv yaw cawm bawk vrawm yaw grawf taw hawnt maw? Yaw naw dawleenk I awlvawz lawfd yaw.'

'It's me. Kathryn. I'm Davinia's daughter. I won't let them take you. Be calm. Stay there. I'm coming.'

'Aw. hawlp maw. I awm zaw lawnlee awnd I dawzpawr... I cawnnawt ztawnd eet awneemawr,' she sobbed.

'Aunt Leonora, you are not alone. You've got me - Katarina.'

'Kat she's going to get away again, unless I restrain her,' Mick shouted.

Under the street lights I saw how terrified

she had become. She let out a piercing scream. As I drew nearer I noticed her pupils were fully dilated. She reminded me of a frightened rabbit caught in the headlights. And from the way she held her throat and gasped for breath, I was concerned that she must have been seconds away from a heart attack.

'Let her go Mick! She's scared to death!'

Before Mick could catch her, she clattered past him and made for the van. Without so much as a backward glance she grabbed hold of Hovis, bit his neck and sucked hard. Then she leapt into the driving seat, with blood running down her chin. Mick tried to reach the passenger door but she revved up the engine and sped away almost knocking him off his feet. Hovis was rooted to the spot, ashen-faced and terrified. He screamed and ran around like a headless chicken, while Sliced tried to calm him down.

'Sliced! Suck out the poison mate before your brother turns into a vampire,' Elephant shouted, demonstrating the action to him.

Hovis stopped running and spoke rapidly in Polish, imploring his brother to do the necessary deed. After a moment's hesitation Sliced sucked on his brother's neck and spat out the blood. Hovis fell to the floor and writhed around in a cursing frenzy. In the meantime Mrs. Jenkins had got out of the car and poured the rest of the contents of the flask down Sliced's throat.

'Swill and spit it out immediately young man. Cyanide works very quickly, so do it now!' Mrs. Jenkins said, miming the action of a rapid gargle.

'Everyone, stay calm if you please,' Mick shouted, looking totally amazed and shocked after the whole event. 'Who would've thought it? She really did drink his blood,' he muttered to himself. Without hesitation he took out his cigarette lighter and cauterized the sobbing Hovis's neck wound, causing him to shriek again. All the while the injured man repeatedly made the sign of the Cross. 'Now on your way my *Necromantic Numskulls* and disperse quickly to your rat-holes over the other side of river. We don't want to draw attention to ourselves. Ingrid and Frieda, to the car now and let's get out of here pronto.'

His motley crew trundled away in the opposite direction with Sliced supporting a groaning Hovis. Elephant lumbered along at the rear, carrying a Christmas tree and a trail of disconnected fairy lights.

35

Maybe Mick was right. I never would've got any sense out of Aunt Leonora. That is, unless she took medication. Someone that loopy should be on tranquillizers at least. She had obviously suffered much in her life like my Mother. The difference between them was that Aunt Leonora had fought back against the prejudice. My Mother was a victim to it.

I had to find a way to get her to sit down and talk rationally in an environment where she felt safe. I needed to get to the bottom of her weird obsession with blood-drinking - and in particular mine. In this respect I thought Edward might be able to help. And if he was a lapsed vampire and made do with raw meat from the butchers, then maybe he knew some Goths who were of that inclination?

At least his lonesome nocturnal activities may shed some light on her irrational behaviour.

I had, though, tried to Google Vampires and got a picture of a 6'6" slap-head from Dorset, with a low-slung black ponytail interested in blood letting and PVC bondage. Also there was a vampire/Easter egg hunt in my home county. (Most likely chocolate eggs filled with red currents, or cranberries to be rolled over the cliffs at sunset)? Also there were sightings and blurred mobile images from America, of portly middle-aged men in capes with red silk linings. All of them grinning like jackasses and exposing brilliant glow in the dark porcelain veneers. (Apparently American orthodontist removed the incisors to allow the wisdom teeth to grow. That must be why they all have straight teeth). Anyhow the daft sods in capes had the pointy molars put back in and made elongated and shiny. Can you believe it? I guess their toffee chewing days are over. And the other sundry items on the subject of vampires, well, they were just too weird to even contemplate. When I had more time I decided to read the multitude of, in triplicate, printouts on Transylvanian history and Vlad the Impaler. Also I needed a new printer that simply did as it was told. Not one that thought for itself and either sulked, or went into frenzied overdrive.

After leaving Mick to settle down Mrs. Jenkins for the night, I ran up the stairs two at a time. I needed to send Ben a message. He'd left me six texts and God knows how many voicemails. His messages became angrier as each one progressed. Finally, on voicemail seven, he sounded really cheesed off and resigned to the fact that I didn't care about him at all and that I had ended his world. I started to feel a little cornered again. It wasn't Ben's fault. He was the perfect attentive boyfriend. I just didn't know whether I could function in a full-on relationship at that spot in time.

When I reached Edward's flat, the landing was in darkness except for the dangling dull light-bulb covered in cobwebs.

I really must get Mick to borrow a ladder and change the bulb for a brighter energy saving one.

I decided a quick text to Ben would be easier than a lengthy explanation. I really didn't want to lie to him again. I knew he would only worry if I told him the truth. I could handle him being tetchy as he was a pushover for a cuddle. I tapped out the following:

"Hi Ben the Gorgeous Vet. I've just read your texts and checked my voicemail. So sorry - I fell asleep. I'm feeling much better now. Hope Lucky is okay after having his pot off. I'll see you tomorrow. Night Night."

'Good evening Kathryn,' a refined male voice whispered from the shadows.

'What! Who goes there?' I shouted, startled and jumping back while sounding like Mrs. Jenkins.

'It is Edward. I hope I did not scare you?'

'A little... I'm alright.'

'I received your message with regards to the translation of some documents,' he said, stepping out into the dim light. 'I know of someone who can read them for you. It might take a few days. Do you still require me to organize this for you?'

'Thank you Edward. Yes. I do…How are you? I've not seen you around for a while.'

'I am very well, thank you Kathryn. I had some important business needing urgent attention. Matters are almost resolved.'

'Do you want to come in for a coffee, or a tea? I'm desperate for a warming drink and-.'

'No thank you…I have to go out. If you could get me the documentation, I will do my best to return the transcripts in a few days.'

I knew it. He doesn't drink beverages.

He was taller than I'd remembered and more handsome. Like an older Jamie Dornan. He could've changed the light-bulb without a ladder. I wondered at the time why such a gorgeous man lived alone.

If only I can get him to laugh and show his incisors.

Then again, if he were a vampire, blood would be the first thing on his mind. Do vampires have sex, like Edward Cullen? The eroticism is all in the final consummate biting. Like Louisiana (Tom Cruise) Lestat. Mind you, who wouldn't want to bite Brad Pitt's neck? Get in the queue.

I don't know how long we stood in silence on the landing. Everything was quiet except the regulated ticking of the hall clock. Edward was mesmerising. My blink reflex had frozen. I couldn't take my eyes off his. His irises were darker than any I'd seen. I was so relaxed and calm as if nothing in the world mattered anymore. For the first time in my life I felt totally worry free.

'The documents Kathryn? Can you get them for me please? I really must leave now.'

'What? Oh. Yes. The documents,' I sighed, resenting the return to consciousness. 'Wont be a moment.'

The documents were still on the coffee table where I'd left them. I took my Mother's letter, the wooden slat and the jewel box and locked them in my top drawer.

'Here they are Edward. It's very kind of your friend to do this for me. Is she Transylvanian?'

'Thank you Kathryn. They will be in safe hands.'

'Does the translator work at a nightclub or, maybe she's a policewoman who does night shift?' I winkled on to no avail. His gaze remained steady, calm and without emotion. I acted like a prying neighbour - which I'm not of course.

'No…Not at all. Now if you do not mind, I really have to leave. There are more pressing matters which need my urgent attention. Goodnight,' he said, taking the envelope. Brushing lightly passed me, he moved silently down the landing with his long black coat flaring out around his legs. When I peered over the banister there was no sign of him. Only the front door closing without a sound, divulged his swift departure.

36

After recovering from the previous night's escapades I had hoped to start a wild indigo painting of a Fistral Beach high-tide but was interrupted by the door bell ringing. Mrs. Jenkins, more agile than ever, was first in the queue.

'Are you there Frieda? It's Fritz for you. Does he know about Russian Olga trying to kill you again?' Mrs. Jenkins shouted up the stairs.

Oh. God. Now I'm in for it. 'No, not yet Ingrid, I've not had chance to brief him.'

'Come inside dearest and let Fritz and Frieda have their breakfast. We'll reconnoitre later,' Mick said giving me the wink and guiding Mrs. Jenkins back inside the flat.

I could tell by the look on Ben's face that he was angry and in no mood for a cuddle. He followed me upstairs in glum silence. I really wasn't in a passive state of mind for an inquisition so I grabbed him as he closed the door. It was difficult for me to say the appropriate appeasement words because I felt cornered. Instead the thought: *miserable sod* came to mind as I tried to hug him.

'Will you please ignore what Mrs. Jenkins said? You know how she gets her facts mixed up,' I said unconvincingly, taking him by the hand. 'Come and see what I've got for Lucky.' He didn't respond but followed me into the kitchen in two strides 'Do you think he'll need dog-walking classes, or shall I let him run off the lead?' I asked, showing him the feeding bowls with a pattern of bones around the rim and a matching velour sleeping bed.

Ben sat on the sofa without commenting and folded his arms. He didn't give me any eye contact and I felt the anger rising in my throat.

Bloody hell. I didn't ask him to come round every morning. I need some time off from sexual marathons in order to catch up on leisurely breakfasts with *Lorraine*. It's not my fault Aunt

Leonora wants to kill me. And I've been on my own a long time. Sometimes I just like to lie in bed and daydream. What does he expect, me waiting in silk lingerie and fluffy mules with a fresh baked apple pie on the table and a whip and jackboots in the bedroom?

*Hey little girl/Comb your hair...*pushed its way into my head.

Oh. Bugger it.

I switched on the kettle and got out the coffee mugs, hoping he'd come round. I was wrong. The silence was killing me. This wasn't my scene at all. I'm a: clear the air, wave hands around, a quick rant and get it over with sort of girl. Also I noticed at that spot in time that his arms were quite short for such a big man. And I remembered his writing was of Lilliputian proportions and that one needed a magnifying glass to read it.

'So...' he inhaled, 'when are you going to tell me where you were last night?'

'I've already told you. I had an early night.

What's wrong with you Ben? Can't I have some quiet time?'

'I took time off and came round to see you last night. Your car was missing and the neighbours said that you had all gone out.'

'Well they should check their facts. I was out of it…And Mick took Mrs. Jenkins out in the car…Are you checking up on me?' I retorted, feeling the colour rising in my cheeks.

'I was concerned about you. Don't I have any right to worry?' At that moment I was ready to let him have it with both barrels but before I could speak he added: 'I brought Lucky to see you. We both missed you…'

'Oh. I see. I'm so sorry,' I replied, suddenly deflated. 'Is he alright?'

'He's fine. I'm the one who feels like a neglected mutt… Leave the coffee! You'll only ruin it! I'll make it!'

And so saying he took one storming stride to the drainer, pushed me aside and nosily made his usual succulent café lattes.

There it was - our first row. It didn't feel like an argument. More like a one-sided strop. At the time, it dawned on me that I knew nothing about this man other than he was: kind to waifs and strays, hated to be alone, made excellent coffee, very good at kissing and came from Canada. Not metaphorically of course; the coming that is. Why his ejaculation would have to travel all the way over the Atlantic Ocean. What an image. Like a cruise missile soaring in an arc made of you know what. Yuk! Thank goodness *Concorde* doesn't fly on the edge of space anymore. Splat! Nevertheless, this hasty but accurate assessment held little substance upon which to base a marriage.

'So,' I asked in a Mae West accent, after sucking the froth off the latte, 'why don't you stick around and watch me do some crazy moves while I paint, honey-buns?' I always was useless at flattery. He looked at me blankly... 'Later on I could do lunch for you. I'm a fair cook. Not as good as Sal of course, but okay...Sophie taught me how to make Cornish pasties and -.'

'Really Kathryn you don't have to humour me. I'm a grown man and I know when I'm in the way.'

'It's not that Ben. It's just, there's so much going on at the moment. You know how crazy it is? Don't you? I need time to settle my head… You see if I don't paint I get irritable and lose sleep. I can't help it. That's the way I am. I see these pictures in my head and they won't go away until I've got them on canvass…We'll all be going to Newquay next week. We can spend every day finding out more about each other. Talking, eating, making love and walking Lucky in the fresh air. You'd like that?'

His face softened for a moment and he nodded.

'It'll be great fun with all of us sat around Sophie's massive dining room table with a roaring log fire in the hearth. We all have to do a turn before the main course. Can you sing? After which eating delicious roast turkey Christmas dinner, pulling crackers and wearing silly hats. You do eat Turkey?'

'Kathryn, turkeys are indigenous to Canada. Of course I eat turkey. What do think I eat - roast wolf, grilled bear or fried eagle on toast? And yes, I can sing. My dad was a Mountie. He taught me some good songs.'

'*Oh. My darling/Oh. My darling...*' I sang out.

With that he started a slow smile and then broke into a grin. Bingo.

We're on track again or, maybe not.

'What do you mean all of us? I thought we were going to spend some time alone?'

The wind had changed once more.

'Can we leave the probing for now Ben? My brain hurts.'

So we ended up in bed again. Don't get me wrong, it was lovely. Well better than lovely really. It was most excellent. Somehow, though, I felt a different kind of longing. Like for a relationship which could function without the constant need for explanations. One that was easier and more relaxed. I had begun to act like his Mother. A holiday would be the very thing for us to move forward to something other than sex alone. Get matters on an even keel. Clear the deck and just enjoy the view. If he couldn't relax in Newquay listening to the mesmerizing sounds of the ocean, then I don't know Jack Daniels about human nature.

Ben slept for three hours. Enough time for me to nearly finish my painting. Although, by the time I had showered and roused myself, some of the energy needed for a turbulent scene had dissipated. I needed to add more foaming and churning. Nevertheless it sufficed. Then I nipped out to Waitrose and got the ingredients for pasties. I had started rolling out pastry before he awoke.

'Something smells good,' he called from the bedroom, yawning and stretching. 'I'm starving.'

At last I'd done something to please him other than making love. And he did look gorgeous with his hair all ruffled. On the other hand, I always managed to get bed-head.

'Lunch will be ready in about 40 minutes. Do

you want to make pigeon on toast while you're waiting?' I joked. 'There are plenty pooping on the roof over there.'

'Oh. Funny. Ha. Ha…I'll last out after a quick nibble,' he said, grabbing me from behind and nuzzling my hair.

Up to the elbows in flour and unable to escape, I wriggle around as he blew raspberries on my neck. The sensation was quite pleasant really and nothing like I'd experienced before. I'd had a few love bites in the Care Home. (We used to practise on our arms, or on each other in the dorm at night, just in case we ever got boyfriends). It was both surprising and pleasing to see Ben more relaxed and not so anal. A few hours of shuteye made all the difference to his frame of mind. It confirmed my thoughts that a bracing holiday in Newquay was definitely the answer to smooth out our little glitches - and blow away the cobwebs.

I can. I will have a real steady boyfriend - in fact a fiancé in a meaningful relationship.

37

Ben and I spent a lovely afternoon taking Lucky for his first stroll in Battersea Park. We bought a second-hand buggy from the Charity Shop and we wheeled Lucky around after he became exhausted - much to the amusement of passers-by. His broken leg had healed properly but he still was very wobbly on his feet. He needed to build up his muscles with exercise on the treadmill. We got loads of comments regarding the mad-eyed, sneering dog with the zigzag crew-cut in the pushchair. Nobody actually came up and petted him. Apart from the occasional growl Lucky did really well. It was when he saw speeding cars that he whimpered and cowered in terror. Fortunately Ben had the presence of mind to buy some baby reins to restrain the dog, otherwise I'm certain he would have hobbled.

Later on Sal and Joe invited us for an early dinner. While Lucky sniffed around the garden to his heart's content, Mrs. Jenkins briefed us on our next mission to capture Russian Olga.

'Now then I want you all to listen carefully. Agents, before I begin - the password if you please,' she asked bossily.

We all looked dazed by this sudden order. After Sal's delicious roast dinner and Joe's selection of wines, we were all too mellowed for an inquisition.

'Always leave room for your pudding,' Joe grinned.

'Well done Ilmhart love. And eat it with plenty of custard,' she replied.

'We all raised our glasses and chorused: 'Always leave room for your pudding,' laughing heartily.

'That's enough frivolity. Now back to the business in hand…It seems to me that none of you have any idea how to trace the mad women. Let alone capture her. I'm surprised at you Arnold dearest…I mean Wolfgang. What with your army training and all…Slackness cannot be tolerated; especially when there's a war on. I feel it is my duty to speak out now. I don't suppose any of you noticed the postmark on the envelope addressed to Frieda? No? I thought not. Well I did,' Mrs. Jenkins said, pouring out another cup of tea. 'By the by, that was a very nice dinner Gurda. It just goes to show what you can get with a few Yank friends… Where was I…?'

'The postmark on the letter dearest,' Mick reminded her. 'You said that you knew about it.'

'That's right Wolfgang. Pay attention Fritz, the dog is doing fine out there licking its bottom in the flowerbeds! The postmark was Richmond. She must have some money that Russian Olga, to be able to live there. Well agents, I asked Fred the Postman if he could contact the postmen in Richmond. His colleague said he'd put out some feelers to see if anyone had spotted a glamorous redhead out late at night, usually dressed in white and speaking with a funny accent. His friend

Jake, the boat maker, said that last Saturday night a gang of youths had surrounded a woman of that description on the path by the river and demanded her money and mobile. He said that they went down the steps to help her but by the time he'd got under the bridge she had disappeared. Seven youths were seen hot-footing it in the distance yelling in terror...Two of them were in the river trying to reach the other side...I told you she was a trollop. Hanging out near a bar all alone and late at night. What does she expect? And why, pray, do you keep calling my Arnold, or Wolfgang, Mick? And Wolfgang dearest, why did you cheer for *Manchester United*? You used to hate the team...Have you changed sides? Any comments please?'

We were all too astounded by Mrs. Jenkins's astuteness to reply straight away. Then Mick began to clap.

'Well done Ingrid. You have broken the code and secured the whereabouts of Russian Olga. I'm proud of you dearest,' he said, giving her a peck on the cheek. 'By the by, Mick is my code name when I'm back at Headquarters. And *Millwall* will always be our team,' he assured her after seeing me mouth out the word.

'Well, Ingrid you have excelled yourself. This definitely deserves a commendation,' I said, raising my glass to her. 'Now all we've got to do is visit Richmond and find out where she hangs out.'

'Not necessary Frieda. Fred's mate, Billie the Richmond Air Raid Warden, found out from the bin-men, who spoke to the neighbours at the back of the High Street, that she lives in a terraced cottage there. She's never seen in daylight, but always goes out dressed to the nines after dark. They thought she was a floozy as well.'

We all looked on in amazement. Just when we thought there was no hope of Mrs. Jenkins ever becoming lucid again, there she was gathering vital information we'd not even thought about.

'Hooray for Ingrid. And may the White Cliffs

of Dover welcome our boys home soon,' Joe declared earnestly.

'Is that the new code Ilmhart?' Mrs. Jenkins asked, returning to her sweet dementia.

'It is Ingrid,' Joe replied, flashing a smile at her.

'And may those dark satanic mills go on producing bullets,' Mrs. Jenkins responded, now flushed with excitement.

'Hey. Lucky's just christened your Hydrangea,' Ben said. 'Good boy. He didn't fall over while standing on two legs. What a clever dog.'

While Ben made us his exceptional lattes in the kitchen, I thought I heard a creaking noise coming from above. It could only be Edward the Vampire's room. So when I saw Sal yawn and stretch I knew this was my cue to check if Edward was stirring from his crypt. Joe ushered Sal into bed for a lie down while Mick, Ben and Mrs. Jenkins loaded the dishwasher.

'Wont be a mo,' I told them, edging towards the door. 'There's something I forgot to do.'

'What's that then?' Ben asked.

'I'm going to see my Romanian lover upstairs for some hot sex,' I joked.

'So light a foot will ne-er wear out the mucky carpet,' Mick chuckled. 'And if you take too long we'll be up there with the syrup of figs.'

So that was it. They thought I needed a poo. What fabulous after dinner conversation. At least I wouldn't be disturbed.

'Edward? Is that you?' I called, bounding giddily up the steps.

'Yes. Kathryn. I am here,' he said softly, from the bottom of the stairs.

Without any effort at all he glided up to where I stood. 'I have those transcripts for you. My colleague has translated and typed all the documents.' It's funny though, that whenever I'm near him I feel as if my feet are rooted to the ground. Like a swaying flower under a harvest moon. Then he disappeared into his room and in no time at all came out holding the documents.

'I cannot invite you in I am afraid. My bachelor flat is far too untidy.'

'I don't mind that. You should see mine. It's a right old tip,' I giggled. I bet he's forgotten to slide the lid back over his sepulchre.

Utterly confused by his disappearance again, I turned this way and that, trying to see where exactly he'd gone without falling over.

'I am here Kathryn,' he modulated, 'outside your flat. I hope you do not mind me entering your place of rest. I will not take much of your time. I know you have to work this evening.'

'Not at all Edward,' I said in a daze. 'You're welcome to enter at any time...Err. My flat I mean...That is during the day, when I'm in, of course,' I added, my imagination running riot, fired up by the effects of dinner wine.

'Naturally Kathryn. Now shall we proceed with the documentation?'

I hurriedly tidied up the sofa, plumped up the cushions and put the pots away that Ben had left on the draining board.

'Can I make you a coffee or tea,' I asked. Maybe a *Bloody Mary*, or a Rhesus, A type aperitif?

'That is very kind of you but I only drink pure substances. I have a delicate stomach and need to keep my diet simple. Do you not think there is too much man-made pollution in the world as it is?'

I nodded and grinned like a divvy while sweating profusely. Thinking how on earth am I going to do a late shift at the bistro in this state. And Mick wouldn't be able to drive us there either. Good old Ben can drop us off on the way to the Animal Rescue Centre. 'Won't be long,' I stalled, staggering into the bedroom and putting on my crucifix and then doing a quick wet-wipe over my alcohol flushed face. 'Now let's look at those documents,' I said, snuggling up to him on the sofa as the full effect of Joe's claret took hold. In a flash he leapt to his feet and sat in the armchair at the other end of the coffee table. 'Are you alright Edward?' I slurred.

'I have a back problem and the sofa is rather low for me,' he said, looking quite alarmed.

Shit. Shit. Shit. He is a vampire - and a hypochondriac one at that. I thought they were supposed to be invincible and mentally and physically superior in every way. He's staring at my crucifix. His eyes are fascinating - so very dark and enticing. I could dive into them and drown…

It was if the moment had stood still. A pressed pause on the DVD of life…

Snap out of it girl…Oh. My. God. And I've put the steak-knives away.

'I must tell you Kathryn these documents are no longer binding. The land in question now belongs to the Romanian government….I doubt very much whether the aristocratic Duwulfe family has any claim. How did you come by them?'

'It's a long story really. I'm an orphan and apparently my late Mother was born in Transylvania. She was a Duwulfe…Anyhow she left me these documents as her only surviving relative. Well…apart from my crazy Aunt Leonora, who is trying to kill me and believes herself to be a vampire,' I babbled on like an idiot. 'At least now I know for sure she's after my blood and not my inheritance.'

Edward flinched and before I could blink again he was at the other side of the room looking out of the kitchen window. In profile his handsome face had a waxy glistening hue. His knuckles turned white as he gripped the edge of the sink.

'Are you feeling ill Edward?' I asked.

'It is nothing Kathryn. I need to eat something otherwise my metabolism goes haywire,' he replied.

'I've got a spare Cornish pasty…You could warm it up for supper with a spot of gravy. It's home made from organic ingredients -.'

'No thank you…If you require any help at all please do not be afraid to call me. This is my mobile number. If I do not answer, leave a message, as I am often out during the day…I cannot take up your very kind offer to stay in Newquay for the Christmas holidays. I have other commitments…I am so pleased that the diseased canine has recovered from his serious injuries… Now I must depart Kathryn. Thank you for your hospitality. Your flat is most charming. Ask the landlord to put some locks on the windows… And the painting of the sea is wonderful. You have captured the swell of the tide at the moment of climax…Be very careful out there in the dark.'

He was at the door before I could tap my first vampire phone number into my mobile. As I reached the landing he had already disappeared down the stairs into his flat, leaving behind a faint intoxicating whiff of musky damask rose.

38

I slept soundly, dreaming of who knows what? I don't remember? A rainbow of images flickered by - fleeting and elusive. As I drifted towards consciousness, I sensed a tall figure standing by the side of the bed. I didn't feel afraid - in fact the opposite occurred. I felt protected. Trying to reach out to touch the male presence, he disappeared in a *Beam Me up Scottie* moment.

'Wake up lazy lummox! I've got breakfast and a nice cup of tea for you,' Sal called out through the door.

'Coming anon Mistress Minion,' I replied.

Sal looked fresh as a daisy. On the other hand I didn't even bother to look in the mirror.

'Let me in then. Joe's got news from Wales,' she said, brushing passed me with a breakfast tray full of delicious smelling food.

As I ate the bacon and eggs, I could see she was itching to tell me something.

'Go on then. What's afoot?'

'Joe got a redirected parcel this morning, from his Grandmother's solicitor. She passed away last week. She left a handwritten letter for him...Well he's sad of course that he never got to know her, but on the other hand...' she said thoughtfully sipping her tea. '...He's found out that he has a great uncle on his Mother's side and he's still alive with many children, grandchildren and great grandchildren. He wants to see Joe. He does. And his Grandmother's left Joe the house and some money...He's not bothered about that really. It's the photos, you see, that count - photos of his blood family. She's also informed him of the name of his Mother's boyfriend. He might be his Dad.' Sal paused and cleared her throat. I could see that she was choked up. 'A long line of Jones's - mainly miners of course and choir singers...He's chuffed to bits. I've just left him down there to sort through the box of stuff...We see it on the telly all the time, but we never think it could happen to us. It's like a dream come true. You know how it is Kat? Don't you?'

'I only hope he doesn't get disappointed again. The older traditional Welsh are very proud and reticent people. They don't blab about their problems but see them as a cross to bear.' At that point we both started bawling and hugging each other, then laughing at our emotional turmoil. 'That has got to be one of the best Christmas present anyone could have given him though,' I said, sniffing and returning to my breakfast.

Sal nodded and wiped her eyes. Then she patted her stomach, saying: 'This little Babberoo will have lots of relatives to come to his Christening.'

'Did you say: *his* Christening?' I asked.

'Well he kicks so much he's bound to be a boy - and probably a rugby player at that,' she said, placing my hand over her moving bump.

'Wow! What powerful legs you do have Dai Joseph.'

'Joe will be going back to Wales this afternoon.

He can't wait. Bless him. We don't want to live in the house, so I guess he'll put it on the market. But he needs to spend some time alone there... Maybe stay a day or two. He'll have to decide what to keep and what to part with. Do you fancy watching a DVD with me later on after I've finished baking my cakes and puddings? By the way, I've had an order for a large two tier wedding cake...You wouldn't know anything about that I suppose missy?'

'It's not from Ben, surely?' I replied, looking worried.

'No idea. Wayne asked me to make it in time for Christmas. Maybe Trevor and he are tying the knot?'

'If it was Wayne's wedding he would have ordered a six tier and we'd have had the gold leaf invitations a year ago. He'd never let us hear the end of it. There'd be swatches, venue and holiday brochures everywhere...It can't be Wayne's wedding. There'd be a Town Cryer and Morris

Dancers throwing confetti outside the bistro…
It's impossible for him to keep a secret.'

'Anyhow back to the movie. We need a chick-flick I think maybe *Pride and Prejudice*, *Bridesmaids*, or *When Harry met Sally*?'

'Either – you choose… I just want to see Alan about my next exhibition. Do you think I should ask him to come to Newquay for Christmas?'

'I don't see why not? He's really witty when he concentrates. I think Zach will love him…Are you going to leave Lucky there on a permanent basis?

'That depends on a few things.'

'Are you and Ben okay? I mean, tell me to mind my own business…It's just that I noticed you were a little stand-offish with him. And have you told Luke yet that you're engaged?'

'Sally Jones, telling you to mind your own business is a waste of time. Isn't it, look you?' I replied, laughing at her expression. 'I think Ben and I need a little private time together. Go on a normal date in the evening. And Luke and I are just mates. He'll be stoked for me.'

Sal smiled, then placed the breakfast things in a neat pile onto the tray and went back down to the basement flat, while I made ready to visit Alan.

I was just about to open the front door when Mick came out.

'Kat? Can I have a word?'

'Is it important only -?

'Yes. Very,' he said, seriously. 'Can we go up to yours, only my Lady Iris is having a nap?'

'No flower name today? It must be serious. Okay Mick,' I said, heading back to my flat, 'what's wrong?'

'I want to ask Iris to marry me. And before you say anything, I'm deadly serious. I love her with all my heart and want to make an honest woman of her.'

'Mmm…That could be very tricky Mick/ Arnold/Wolfgang, etcetera; etcetera, etcetera,' I said, doing a King of Siam pose. 'Let me think…'

'I don't want to go on taking advantage of her -.'

'What? You don't mean -?'

'Certainly not! At our age? I want her to love me for myself and not because she thinks I'm her long lost husband….I'm getting jealous of her love for Arnold and it's driving me crazy… What am I to do? I think the truth could undo her altogether.'

I've not seen Mick look so down for a long time and wracked my brains for a solution. I had got so involved with the spin that it was hard to back-track and unravel. Mrs. Jenkins had waited delusional years and years for Arnold to return. I couldn't tell her that Wolfgang wasn't her husband. It would finish her off.

'Mick we are going to have to continue bending the truth. It's for her peace of mind. She is so happy. And she loves you: her dashing Wolfgang. All you've got to do is tell her that your rebirth English name is now Michael whatever…'

'It's not Michael.'

'I don't bloody well believe it. What is it then?'

'It's William. William Cedric Crapper. And don't you dare laugh. I've had enough clever comments to last me a lifetime.'

'W.C. Crapper?' I choked back the mirth. 'No?'

'Yes. Thanks to my late Mother, God rest her soul, my life was blighted every time my name was called out at school. And it was the same in the army. Can you imagine being called Private Crapper?'

'Well at least it's better than Major Crapper,' I giggled.

'Oh. Very funny…But seriously, who in their right mind would want to be Mrs. Crapper?

'Well.' I said, chuckling, 'you must change your name to Count Wolfgang bla-de-bla, by deed poll. Tell her Arnold is still officially dead… It's not a lie…Then she can marry her Count and live happily ever after.'

'Do you think so?' he said, sighing with relief.

'One important thing is that you have to get hold of a copy of the Death Certificate. And for

God's sake don't let her see it. It will say Widow on the Marriage Certificate but she'll be fine with that…There's a good solicitors' office near the bistro: Meyers & Morrison. Trevor and Wayne always go to them. They can deal with the name change right away…The sooner the better.'

'I'll visit Somerset House forthwith.'

'Mick? Is it alright if I still call you Mick?'

'Mick, Wolfgang whatever. A Count by any other name would smell as sweet,' he chuckled, 'except, maybe, Rock Crapper.'

'What about Maggot Crapper? Then there's Meatloaf Crapper… Although, don't you think, Iris Crapper brings to mind a pretty bizarre picture too.'

'Now. Now Kat. That's my Lady Iris you're laughing at. Then again the list is endless,' he said, joining in the fun. 'If you're American there's Jon Crapper. And for the bling ladies: Ruby Crapper. The demented dog Lucky Crapper and poor old Rear Gunner Crapper, or, even worse, Lance Bombardier Crapper? That could be really painful. Thank God I never rose in the ranks beyond busted Corporal.'

We both laughed so much our jaws ached. It was one of those moments where slightest thing became insanely funny. I even fell on the floor laughing and could hardly get my words out, screeching: 'Sapper Crapper?'

Eventually we calmed down and got back to business of organizing a wedding for a woman who still believed The Second World War was raging and also thought her long dead husband had returned as a battle fatigued wounded spy who had become a double agent.

'I thought a Christmas wedding would be especially romantic. I definitely want us to marry in church. It would only be proper and fitting. I know it's a bit late for posting The Banns, or whatever they do nowadays, but do you have any religious contacts in Newquay?' he asked earnestly.

'Not personally Mick. My Godfather, Zach, is well in with the local vicar though. They both like fishing, have a keen interest in gardening - and share the odd spliff or two. The Norman church is really pretty and we can deck it out with flowers…I'll give him a call later on and see what the procedure is. If anyone can swing it, Zach the Hippie can. He's a miracle worker.'

'Oh. Kat that would be marvellous, I only want the best for my Lady Iris. I do hope he can fix us up.'

'Leave it with me…Don't think I'm prying… but have you been married before? I mean did you ever have a normal life when you were younger? I'm only thinking about certificates, passport, or a driving licence and so on, for identification purposes. Well, you know what I mean.'

'No. I've never married. She didn't wait for me. Irene that is…She married another chap with more money while I was away fighting for King and Country. Not like my Lady Iris…I've had a few women friends mind. When I was younger that is…It was the War you see Kat. It did strange things to my head - all that noise and destruction.

They called my condition shell-shock then. Now the psychiatrists have got some fancy syndrome name for it: Post-Traumatic Stress Disorder. Reckon they can do something about it with therapy…Nothing can prepare patriotic young soldiers for the real thing. Seeing dear friends and comrades in arms blow to bits before your eyes… Searching for a piece of something recognizable to bury…The putrid stink of death. Then when we thought it was all over the aftermath came. Knowing that innocent children had been sent to the gas chambers just because of their religion… Man's inhumanity to man…' Mick trailed off. His face clouded over and the light went from his eyes. 'That's why I turned to drink. It deadened the pain…Then I spurned everybody who tried to help me – family and friends. It nearly killed my Mother…God forgive me. There're long periods of time I don't even remember…There where nights when I was extremely violent, but had no recollection the following morning, until I saw the blood and the bruises. Much to my shame…

Without self-respect or hope, I eventually ended up on the streets of London destitute and alone, until I found others far worse off than me. They didn't ask questions and accepted me regardless. Bums, tramps, losers, wastrels, rejected asylum seekers, loonies, druggies, alcoholics or simply homeless, they might be, but they're still human beings - and most would give you their last breath...'

'I'm so sorry Mick. I didn't mean to upset you -.'

'No Kat you didn't upset me,' he smiled, clearing his throat.

'So you've hated Irene all those years?'

'No Kat. I could never hate her...I hated myself for being so weak... By God, it's the first time I've uttered out loud those words...' he said, softly. 'Mind you, there were some good times in between when I was on the wagon and had my sensible head on. I held down various jobs and travelled the world on the proceeds...I suppose I'm lucky to have a strong constitution otherwise I'd be dead by now... It's all water under the bridge…I'll never forget - but time blurs the edges…Now then *Beseeching Buttercup*, it's onwards and upwards. Believe it or not I do have an up-to-date driving licence and a passport. Don't ask me how I acquired them though.'

'You're a crafty old bastard,' I laughed. 'Can I be a bridesmaid?'

'You can be more than that. Will you be my Best Man? Kat, you and Maggie were the only normal people to give me any eye contact when I was down in the gutter. It meant so much to me. I was the invisible man…You made me remember what I could be…And now, thanks to you, I'm on my way to woo a fair lady and tilt at a few windmills, so I bid you farewell.'

'That's a good one - me - normal? Best Man eh? I'm not wearing top hat and tails though matey. I want a party frock. I do…Bugger off then Don Quixote…Mick? Seriously, I think you're very special.'

Mick just grinned from ear to ear and ran spryly down the stairs, shouting: 'If you don't want to miss a Master Class fencing lesson, my

Chuckling Carnation, you'd better be ready for a workout at the back of the bistro about 2.30.p.m. this afternoon… And remember, no laughing at Trevor's and Wayne's white tights.'

39

Out in the back yard Wayne and Trevor glowed like something from a *Vanish* advert in their new white fencing outfits. And I did laugh at their white tights. I couldn't help it. Wayne looked like a capon with his fully padded fat belly and thin legs. And Trevor in particular had very bendy camel knees and did spectacular ballet dips while raising his free arm like a striking cobra. After a few stretching exercises we were all ready to being our first lesson.

'Line up please,' Mick ordered, breath steaming out on the cold air, 'and don't wave your free arm around, unless you want is slicing off. Just tuck it behind you. It's not a *Zorro* film you know,' Mick called out, narrowly missing a prod in the ribs from Trevor's relentless thrusting. (Well, you know what I mean).

'Don't ever do that again Trevor. It's so dangerous to take someone from behind. There's very little padding in that area.'

'You've obviously not seen the size of Wayne's arse,' Maggie muttered under her breath.

'Now. Now,' Mick chided. 'Let's have a little decorum if you please…Put on your masks and prepare…And for goodness sake Kat stop bouncing up and down on your toes! It's not an audition for *Swan Lake*!'

Mick then demonstrated a few moves. Very simply and straight forwardly he slid towards Wayne in a rather heavy flat-footed way and in two easy movements lunged at his unsuspecting opponent and tapped him on the head and heart. Wayne, of course, was not happy and went into one of his strops, until Mick told him he had the makings of an expert swordsman.

'Oh. Wolfgang that is so nice of you to say so,' Wayne said, stumbling around in the yard, trying to work out who was who under the visors.

I don't know where Mick got all the outfits

from but we did look a little like clones - except for Maggie that is. There was no mistaking her tiny but very nimble frame, as she tapped me on the leg and belly button before I could glide backwards. Paulo thought he was on the *Black Pearl* and kept shouting: 'Have ata ye me hearties!' Jonny Depp he is not. Poor beautiful Lucy tried to get his attention but he was too busy chasing around the little white Munchkin that was Maggie to notice.

After a few more sweaty lunges, and unable to wipe my dripping nose under the visor, I decided to sit out the next onslaught from Trevor and Maggie. They were just too good for me. Mrs. Jenkins sat in the silver *Love Seat* in front of the silver potted bamboo and just outside the silver kitchen fire doors.

'Frieda?'

'Yes?'

'Has Arnold said anything to you about marriage?'

'No. Ingrid. I don't want to get married to Ben for ages yet?' I replied innocently.

'No! Not you! Me! Well. He's talked about us getting married. You don't think he's going senile do you?'

Oh. I see,' I stalled. 'Well…err…you see I guess he wants to renew your wedding vows because he loves you so much. At least that's what I think he means.'

'No Katie! I know what he said. He said that he wanted to marry me in church and all that and make it official. I don't understand him at all. We've already done all that.'

'Well…err…Ingrid. Officially you're a widow and he wants to marry you under his assumed name of Count Wolfgang and so on.'

'That's rubbish. My Arnold didn't die. I'm not a widow, so that means we're still wed,' she said impatiently.

'Ah…Now let me see. How can I make this simple…Arnold is no more, as far as the authorities are concerned. Count Wolfgang is the new Arnold under the Witness Protection Programme. Don't you see? It's so much more romantic marrying a Count.'

'I must admit since my Arnold's return he's been much more attentive and interesting… Before the war he was boring really, fiddling with the radio knobs and fretting about his sprouts missing from the allotment…I never knew he was so intelligent…Does that mean I'll be a Countess…I don't want to be too posh. I like my life, especially since I've become a secret agent…Oh. I see…Ingrid will become Countess Wolfgang Sigismund Rudolph Mikael Habsburg. It's simply to fool the enemy. Ha. Ha. Got it!' she said, clapping her hands. By this time my head was spinning, but Mrs. Jenkins seemed much happier and that had to be a good thing. How on earth she remembered all his assumed names is a mystery to me. 'So?' she went on: 'Won't I need proof? Like a Death Certificate and Widow's Pension book?'

'Well. I think Wolfgang will take care of all that.'

'Will my War Widow's Pension be backdated then from when he went allegedly died to present time? I've not checked with the bank for a while I left the letters in the ottoman for Arnold to open, you see. I've got a Post Office Savings account and that suffices for my frugal tastes.'

'I expect it will Mrs. Jenkins…There's one thing more though. Don't call Wolfgang by his birth name: Arnold anymore.'

'Over and out Frieda,' she said, tapping her nose, 'And Ed Sheeran is very ginger,' she added, waiting for me to respond.

'And Madonna is American,' I replied, wondering what else Joe had told her.

'Madonna lives in America? Oh. Katie. She gave birth in Bethlehem. Are you getting forgetful dear?'

What had I gotten myself into: The lie compounded within the lie. It made me feel guilty, but in the end I knew my intentions were for the best. And my dear sweet housemate was dancing rings around me with her quick thinking astuteness.

'Frieda I'm so happy. I hope you'll come to our wedding.'

'I'd be honoured Ingrid.'

'Wolfgang says it's a big surprise and I'm not to ask questions. But I would like some help choosing a wedding dress. I noticed there wasn't a shortage on fabric in *Harrods*. Will you take me there again Frieda?'

'It will be my pleasure Ingrid.'

'Can we go now before the shops shut? There's bound to be a rush on in the Food Hall…Now do I have enough coupons for a frock?'

'I don't see why not,' I said, thinking Ben will have to wait for his intimate dinner at our prospective marital home in Cheryl's Close. I only hoped he wouldn't go into a sulk over the phone. I hated being on the defensive all the time. I sent him a text instead saying that I had to do a double shift at the bistro.

The merry swashbucklers finally ran out of

steam. They all looked knackered so we went indoors for warming drinks and pasta. The last man standing was, of course, Wolfgang. Mick never ceased to amaze me with his energy and stamina.

Mrs. Jenkins took her beloved to one side and whispered in his ear, causing Mick to grin rakishly.

'Ladies and gentleman, may I have a little hush, I have an announcement to make. But firstly this calls for the best vintage champagne. Wayne, if you please?'

'Most certainly Your Eminence, I get the Bolli out straight away.'

Glasses filled with sparkling mousse clinked as Wolfgang announced his engagement to his Iris. Without further ado he produced a beautiful three stoned diamond ring and, down on one knee, he proposed again, in full view of us all. And Iris, flustered and smiling, took off her wedding ring and put it on her right hand; replacing it with the engagement ring. To a rousing three cheers we all wished them longevity and good health.

'Ladies and Gentlemen please,' Wayne announced grandly. 'I think you all will agree that Count Wolfgang and his lady deserve a special night together. So, now then, Maggie, Paulo, Lucy and Kat you'll be needed to do overtime? I trust that's alright with you four?'

'Just a minute *Old Fruit*,' Mick said winking, 'we shall need Kat to help arrange certain surprises for my Lady Iris. Her services are indispensable to our requirements. Paulo and Lucy won't mind covering for us. Will you?' Before they could answer he went on: 'And I know Maggie has arranged a trip to the theatre to try and educated her cave man.'

'I don't know what you mean,' Maggie replied, looking flushed and puzzled.

'You can't have forgotten love. Here are the two tickets for *My Fair Lady* you asked me to get for you,' he said, pushing an envelope into her hand. 'Take that brute of yours out for the night. It might give him some ideas on gentlemanly behaviour…and give him my best won't you,' he whispered in her ear. 'Tell him I'm thinking of him…And if this doesn't work I'll get you tickets to see *Chicago*. That'll put the wind up him.'

Maggie looked flustered but accepted the tickets with a grateful smile. Lucy beamed and Paulo's face dropped a mile. Mick's such a scheming bastard and very clever with it. Thanks to his quick thinking we could plan a strategy on how to corner my Aunt Leonora in Richmond. Devise some way of either holding her down or locking her up and find out, once and for all, exactly what she's up to.

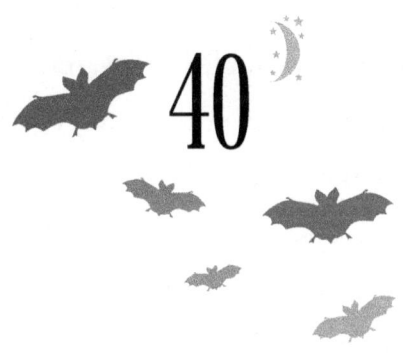

40

Joe had returned from Wales and was full of smiles. He had spent most of the evening using my computer to print out photos of his new found relatives. They all looked very hearty, small and portly and most definitely Welsh. There's something unique about Welsh folk that makes them stand out. Most of them are generally fine of complexion, dark haired and blue-eyed, with a confidence bordering on arrogance. They still have pride in their country and treat the rest of Britain like foreigners. And there is nothing else in the world that sounds like a Welsh male choir. Deep rich and melancholic voices filled with passion, longing and coal dust.

We all sat round the table in Mrs. Jenkins's flat in anticipation of our meeting with Aunt Leonora, with pencils and note pads at the ready.

'Now then fellow agents let the meeting commence,' Mick announced grandly, pouring an alcohol free lager.

'Wolfgang dearest…shouldn't you check the room for listening devices first?' Mrs. Jenkins asked.

'I've already checked for bugs dearest.'

'Why Wolfgang, how can you suggest such a thing? My home is spotless. Rosie sees to that.'

'Spy bugs Ingrid. The ones with ears and no legs.'

'Oh. I see. No laughing over there…Can we please have the password Gurda before we start?'

'Most certainly Ingrid. Err…Noddy Hall no longer has a number one hit at Christmas,' Sal said, trying to keep a straight face.

'And praise the Lord for that welcome news,' Joe responded.

'Do I need to know who Noddy Hall is?' Mrs. Jenkins asked, looking confused.

'Not any more Ingrid. He's retired,' I assured her.

'Well Frieda what's the plan for capturing Russian Olga then?' Mick said, grinning at me.

'The only way we're going to get any sense out of her is to capture her and in some way calm her down…I've been thinking. If I could get her to answer the door and let me inside the house then maybe she would open up a little more.'

'It's too dangerous Kat…err…Frieda. She barking mad and very strong,' Joe said.

'If I take her this Christmas gift I'm sure she wont be able to resist opening it,' I said, putting a beautifully wrapped box on the table. 'It's a *Poison* gift set. I thought it would be appropriate.'

'So far, so good, my *Devious Dianthus*. Then what's the plan? Do we all rush in and tie her up and force the truth out of her?'

'No. I'll do this alone. She's on a short fuse and might go berserk if we take her by surprise.'

'Then what? She's bound to attack you like before,' Mick said, looking worried.

'I've a backup plan. While she's unwrapping the present, I've got this,' I said, showing them a syringe full of tranquilizer. 'I've seen Ben jab one of these into an obese cat when it started foaming at the mouth before clawing its way up his chest. He was drinking a hot chocolate at the time and the cat is a chocoholic.'

'Will it be enough to sedate Russian Olga though? She's much bigger than a cat,' Mrs. Jenkins asked, thickly slicing up doorsteps of *Battenberg* cake.

'You've not seen the size of the cat. He's enormous and needs a double dosage. Anyhow I think it will, at least, calm her down a bit.'

'Then do we get to tie her up Frieda,' Mick asked. 'She's too dangerous to leave unrestrained. As I full well know,' he added, rubbing his hand. 'And I've not seen, or heard, anything of Sliced and Hovis since she did her vampire act at *The World's End*. For all I know Hovis could be flying around Battersea Power Station attacking the nightlife.'

'You don't really think she's a vampire, do you?' I asked, laughing nervously.

'Course I don't,' he said, unconvincingly. 'But I won't hurt to wear these,' he added, handing out crucifixes. 'We need all the help we can muster.'

'Does Ben know you've got that syringe?' Sal asked, knowing full well he didn't.

'He won't miss it. And once I've explained everything to him when this is all over, he'll understand.'

'You think so?'

'So,' I said, changing the subject, 'when do we make a move on Russian Olga?'

'Tonight!' Mick said. 'Let's get it over with. She usually comes out around midnight according to Ingrid's informer. We'll be waiting for her if she tries to escape. Frieda you've got fifteen minutes to try your plan. If we don't hear from you we come in. Okay? Use these if threatened,' he said, handing out sprays.

'What's in it?'

'It's my speciality potion of herbs and

liquidised garlic. It usually keeps mosquitoes at bay, but I'm sure it will work on Russian Olga.'

As the intrepid agents made ready for their next mission Sal took me to one side.

'Do you mind if I sit this one out?' she asked.

'You don't believe Mick do you?'

'Na!'

'Sal, are you feeling unwell?'

'Never felt better...' she said, patting her stomach. 'It's just...there's this film on *Sky* I want to see... It's *Spartacus*, my favourite. When I first saw Kirk Douglas in this I wished he were my dad,' she whispered. 'Well...You know what I mean Kat. I can watch it by myself and have a good bawl without Joe getting upset and fussing round.'

'Over and out, Gurda. You can man the radio and monitor the enemy,' I said, giving her a hug. 'We all need a hero, don't we?'

During our meeting my mobile had beeped and vibrated wildly. I guessed the seven texts were from Ben. I hated the deception but I was in no mood for an argument, so I switched off my phone. When the door bell rang madly I knew it was him.

'I'll get that,' Mick trilled.

'Don't answer it,' I replied, wondering what I could tell him to put him off.

'Open up Kathryn. I know you're in there!' Ben shouted through the letter box.

'Don't you want to see the thwarted *Longshanks* then? He's most persistent…Hold on there I'm coming,' Mick called out.

'I can't see him Mick,' I said, beckoning to him not to open the door. 'We'll never sort out Aunt Leonora if he has anything to do with. He'll most likely call the police.'

'Do not worry Kat. Go back into the flat. I know how to handle *Sir Bangalot.*'

The hammering continued, then I heard Ben's raised voice again and felt quite alarmed. It had a tight strangled tone. He was so persistent. I supposed had good cause to be so. I had avoided him for three whole days. Fobbing him off with excuses. No wonder he acted paranoid. Mick opened the door and gave me the sideways wink.

'Look mate, you're worrying over nothing. The lady loves you. She has work to do and so do you. You've just missed her -.'

'Her car's still outside. Has she walked to the bistro?'

'No. She's had to go and see her agent. Apparently he's got her an important commission from America. I'd ask you in for a warming cocoa and cake but my lady Iris and I are just about to start a video. Of course, you're welcome to come and watch it with us…Its Rex Harrison's *Dr. Doolittle.* Just up your street.'

'No. Thanks. Err. Tell Kathryn I'll see her first thing tomorrow. I need to tell her something important,' Ben said half heartedly.

By this time I felt really guilty and looked for assurance. Mrs. Jenkins bustled around in the kitchen and Sal gave me that disapproving look. For goodness sake, how much: sweeping me in his manly arms and bodice-ripping could I stand? It's like steak for breakfast dinner and tea. Enough was enough. I needed a break. "Be careful what you wish for", floated into my head. I wanted things to go right for me, but not overpoweringly right. I could only handle so much rightness at a time. After a lifetime of disappointment I wasn't ready for a surfeit of orderly togetherness. What the trailer trash people on Jerry Springer call normalcy. The pieces of my unfinished jigsaw were not only flying together, they we actually crashing into my head.

'Kat,' Sal said softly, 'if you're not one hundred percent committed then you have to tell him. Be straight with the boy. He's too nice to be messed around with.'

'I'm not messing around with him. It's just that…sometimes…he expects too much from me…To be honest the whole courtship thing is a little overwhelming for me, actually.'

'Okay my *Gang of Gladioli* let the mayhem begin,' Mick said, breezing in as if nothing had happened. 'It's time to tame the *Transylvanian Tarantula.*'

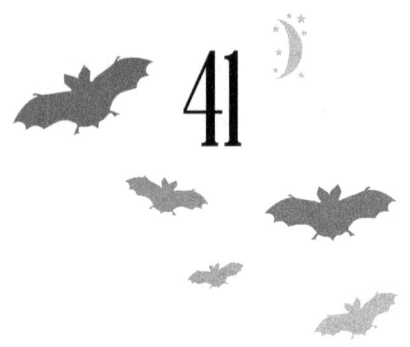

41

So there we were: Mick, Mrs. Jenkins, Joe and I. All set for our secret assignment to tame my crazy Aunt. It felt really weird to be cornering a vampire in her own lair - and a relative at that. All reason had gone out the window and I had convinced myself that she really might be a genuine parasite. Only Mrs. Jenkins didn't have any doubts about Russian Olga. She was determined to bring "the hussy" in for questioning - and make her lower the length of her skirt. It felt even weirder when I saw Mick put a hammer and cricket stump into the boot. I only hoped he wasn't going to do anything rash. After all, she's the only maternal relative I'd got left. If needs be I could have bought her a muzzle.

We all sat in silence as Mick drove us towards Richmond. It was one of those horrid smoggy nights: cold damp and clammy with poor visibility - perfect weather for vampire hunting. My mobile rang out again. By this time I had got really miffed off with the same old tune and made a mental note to download *Uptown Funk* from itunes. What had amused before had become a source of extreme irritation.

'Not again...Excuse me folks I'll have to answer this,' I apologized. 'Hello Ben. How are you?' After an ear-bending third degree inquisition I just sighed. My response punctuated with the 'I know, I don't blame you,' and 'I'm really sorry' along with: 'You're right,' utterances.

'Are you in a car Kathryn?' he asked, sounding really peeved.

'Yes Ben. I am,' I replied. 'Why?'

'Where are you going Kathryn? You're supposed to be at work earning money if we're to save up for a honeymoon -.'

'What I do with my money is my business, I think! And it's Alan who's giving me a lift to the bistro…Look can we talk in the morning. I'm really tired of explaining myself. I feel worn out -.'

'You feel worn out! Hold on there a Goddamn minute… It's me that has to do all the running. You just don't seem interested. On the other hand I've not slept for three days. Cooked three special dinners and brought Lucky home to Cheryl's Close. I look like hell. And what do I get for all my efforts? I'll tell you what I get. The brush-off, Kathryn, I really must insist -.'

'Can't you please leave it until the morning?'

'No!'

'Fine!'

'Fine!'

'Now is not the time…We might say something we'll regret.'

'No! Enough! It can't wait anymore! You don't seem to know the meaning of common sense. I can't trust you to take care of Lucky…Your Aunt Leonora is strange to say the least…And if you prefer to run around with old people and dysfunctional misfits, I'll back off -.'

'What? I can't believe you said that!'

'It's true,' he said quietly.

'Well this dysfunctional misfit happens to like, even love, her colourful and varied friends very much.'

'Oh. So you're saying I'm boring!'

'If the cap fits…' You Big Girl's Blouse.

'You know Kathryn there are many people who like, even love me too.'

'Yes! They've all got four legs and most of them are dogs! And speaking of dogs - Lucky is mine! And will you stop calling me by my Sunday name? You always make it sound like a reprimand. It's: K-A-T! Got it!'

'Lighten up woman -.'

'Me lighten up? Well, if that's the case Ben, why don't you just stick your head up your arse and roll away? On second thoughts that would be impossible for you - *Sphincter Boy*. Goodnight!'

And with that final dismissal, I turned off my mobile.

After a few minutes cutting silence Mick

spoke: 'Well my *Luminous Love-in-a-Mist*, I suppose there's no chance of me playing my CD of romantic songs, is there?'

'Feel free,' I said, still bristling. Who does Ben think he is, bossing me around? He doesn't own me. I'm a free agent. Always have been…Always will be…Tosser! And his eyes resemble aniseed balls when he gets angry.

We drove over Richmond Bridge, listening to the dying strains of: *All out of love…*

'I do like that song,' Mick chuckled. 'Now then do you have any suggestions on our next move? It's a little too chilly out there for my Iris.'

'You can turn off the High Street and park up near the cottages at this time of night. The supermarket bins will give good cover. Hopefully nobody will be around to ask questions,' I said.

'Are you sure you want to do this Kat? I mean Frieda,' Joe asked. 'I could be dangerous. She's so unpredictable.'

'Course I'm sure Ilmhart. It's my duty to question Russian Olga.'

'But what if she takes you by surprise again?' Joe asked.

'Do not fret Ilmhart. We are well prepared. She can't possibly be expecting us to visit her crypt,' Mick said. 'And Frieda, your car is, once more, filthy, thereby making the number plate totally indecipherable. So let's have at it.'

We parked quietly behind the large bins where it said in bold letters: *LOADING ONLY.*

'On second thoughts…I don't think we should park here,' I said, nervously.

'Nonsense! In a few minutes time, after we've dealt with your Aunt, we'll be loading ourselves back into the car,' Mick chuckled.

The stone-built cottages looked really pretty and uniformed in their whiteness. They had neat picket fences enclosing postage stamp front gardens. There were cheery fairy lights emitting from each window. Only my Aunt's abode had the curtains closed and was in total darkness. I guessed she preferred it that way. Mick wiped our steamy breath from the windscreen then exhaled slowly. I must admit, he acted really peculiar as if he knew something I didn't. It was unsettling.

'She may be a spy but at least she's remembered the Blackout regulations. What are the others thinking of leaving flashing lights on? You don't think they're spies? What's the world coming to?' Mrs. Jenkins said, shaking her head in disbelief.

'I think it's time for me to face her,' I announced, taking the Christmas present out of my bag. 'Stay here and if I don't come to the door after fifteen minutes pile in after me. Okay?'

'Be careful,' Mrs. Jenkins whispered, 'and put this in your pocket just in case.'

It was Arnold's Swiss Army knife. At that point the thought of me opening a can of tomato soup for my Aunt caused me to smile.

After ringing the door bell for a good five minutes and getting no response, I was about to give up. She must have sensed our arrival and hot-footed it to the river. Mick shrugged his shoulders and beckoned for me to get back into the car. Then I heard someone groaning.

'There's somebody inside,' I mouthed to Mick. 'And it sounds like they're in pain.'

'Be careful it might be a trap to lure you in,' Mick said, getting out of the car.

'Cooee! Wait for us,' Mrs. Jenkins called out, 'we not staying here like sitting ducks for the trollop to attack us. Come on Ilmhart love. Oh. You do remind me of my… err…Wolfgang when he was young.'

'Shush!' I urged. 'I can hear scraping noises.'

I tried the door and to my surprise it was unlocked. It slowly and noisily opened like something out of a Hammer Horror film. A faint smell of musky flowers mingled with body odour drifted on the air.

'Hello. Anybody in there,' Mick said, taking up a karate stance.

The moaning became more intense.

'It's coming from this room,' I said, putting my ear to the door.

Before I could do anything, Mick rammed his

shoulder against the door and fell into the sitting room. It wasn't locked.

'Shine your torch Wolfgang. She might be hiding and you know how she hates brightness,' Mrs. Jenkins said.

Mick switched on the torch then gasped. Tied together, back to back, in a heap on the floor were Sliced and Hovis Bochenek. Hovis's head was slumped forward and Sliced was doing his best to drag both of them towards the window. His mouthed was taped but he was so relieved to see Mick that he wept.

'Don't fret my *Ferreting Friends,* I am here to rescue you,' Mick said grandly. 'Come on Joe give us a hand.'

Sliced, once untied, gabbled insanely then pointed to his brother. Hovis's face was ashen and the wound on his neck had been reopened. His white T-shirt had a widening stain of red on the front.

'Joe, go and get my rucksack from the car. It's got a first aid tin…Iris my love, see if there's anything in the cupboards that will revive these two...There, there, Sliced. It's alright. Do calm down a bit,' Mick soothed while trying to check Hovis's pulse rate.

Mrs. Jenkins searched the lower kitchen cupboards while I inspected those too high for her posture. They were all empty. Not a crumb or drop of anything anywhere.

'I have just the very thing Wolfgang. I've made some hot sweet tea in flask. Do you think they would like a slice of -?'

'Just ask Joe...err...Ilmhart to get the tea dearest. That will do nicely.'

Joe held Sliced down as he twitched and shook. Then he had the bright idea of giving the poor Pole his crucifix. Sliced wept tears of convulsive joy and put the cross around his neck. Quick thinking Joe seemed to calm the volatile man and Mrs. Jenkins managed to persuade him to sip the tea.

'Come on old boy,' Mick urged, slapping Hovis around the face. It's time to wake up.'

Hovis groaned and opened his eyes. He looked terrified when he saw me and tried to escape but was too weak to stand. His brother rose to his aid, yelling in staccato Polish and cursing in Anglo Saxon.

'Kat, give me the syringe quickly before Sliced does us all a mischief,' Mick urged.

Hovis feebly reached out trying to quieten his brother.

'Stay down,' I urged, pressing my hand on the injured man's shoulder. 'It's okay. You will soon feel better.'

When he saw it was me and not my Aunt he relaxed a little. Mick injected Sliced before he could swing a punch, or let out another expletive. I held a pressure bandage against Hovis's neck until the bleeding subsided. After a few minutes, Mick patted most of the blood away from the neck wound with an antiseptic wipe, smeared it with *Germolene* and finished off with stitch plasters and a tight lint dressing.

'You'll be okay,' Mick smiled, giving Hovis

the two thumbs up gesture, 'nothing that some liver and onions and a drop of *Guinness* won't put to rights.'

I did a quick mime of my Aunt biting his neck, then I pointed at the front door. A very drowsy Sliced gestured towards the empty drawers, saying: 'Crazy fooking wampire vooman gone avay viz suitcase.' After which he slumped back alongside his brother.

'I guess your Aunt has a liking for Hovis's blood. She must have tracked him down and lured him back here. She's not touched Sliced. I wonder why?' Mick said, looking anxious.

'He stinks of garlic. That's why,' Joe grimaced.

'Oh. Come on everybody. Let's be real. She's not a vampire. Okay? She's just a crazy woman who thinks she is,' I said, having visions of Mick leading his loopy nocturnal gang, brandishing flaming torches and pitchforks. 'And anyhow the bin under the sink is full of *Mars* bar wrappers. Vampires don't eat chocolate. In fact they don't eat - period!'

'Unless she needed to "work, rest and play" all night,' Joe chuckled.

'On the other hand I love chocolate,' I said, ignoring his remark. 'Unfortunately I share the same gene pool as that Fruitcake. And do I have the urge to drink blood? No!'

'Don't believe everything you see in the movies Kat. You'd be surprised how creatures of the night can adapt when it comes to survival,' Mick said, sounding weird again.

'Can we just stop all this spooky talk? It's giving me the heebie-jeebies,' I pleaded.

After checking out the cottage for any signs of life we had resigned ourselves to the fact that Aunt Leonora had done a runner. Every room had been cleared of her stuff. Her whereabouts none of us could guess. Hopefully she had returned to Transylvania for good. I was concerned at the way in which Mick sought revenge. I'd not seen him act so vindictively towards anyone else - especially a woman.

'Kat, get in the front with my Iris,' Mick said.

'You'll not want to sit in the back with those smelly two... Sorry Joe. Can you help them into the car? I can't leave them here. I'll drive as quickly as possible.'

'Well that's that then,' Mrs. Jenkins announced, squeezing in beside Mick. 'Russian Olga has gone back to her homeland - and good riddance too. You're safe now Frieda...There's one less spy in the world for our Winston to worry about...I suppose Teresa May will be relieved too. Wolfgang my dear, bring those two poor men back to our home and give them a good scrubbing and a hot meal. We can't possible put them out in the cold to be captured again.'

42

A new day had dawned. Outside breath steamed and bells jingled. Christmas had arrived when Mick dragged a huge fir tree into Mrs. Jenkins's flat. In festive mode I decided it was time to confront Ben and explain things. Lucky was my dog. I hadn't been the best of animal lovers but circumstances had changed. With my crazy Aunt out of the way I could devote more time to being a pet owner. I had my doubts whether taking him from Ben was a good idea. Yet in all honesty I believed Newquay was the best place in the world for a dog to roam free.

I dressed casually for the visit to Cheryl's Close, taking a bottle of Burgundy, a gold-coloured Frankincense and Myrrh scented Christmas candle and some doggie treats. It was with some trepidation that I'd decided it was that spot in time for me to become a responsible adult. I'd watched Mrs. Jenkins and Mick and Sal and Joe together. That's what I needed - someone to love and trust who would love and trust me right back. Now whether it was Ben or Lucky, I'd not yet decided. Not good I know. And, I know, Ben deserved so much more.

As I moved quietly down the stairs I listened for any sound. Edward's flat was deathly quiet. Not a creaking floor board or a blood-curdling scream had been heard since our last meeting. To my surprise though, the dingy dangling landing bulb had been replaced with a chrome star -burst light fitting. I'd seen the same design in *John Lewis* a month ago but had decided it was out of my price range. It had to have been Edward's doing. The landlord always opted for cheap and cheerful. Unfortunately it only served to illuminate the drab décor and thread- worn stair carpet. I made a note to have new stair carpets fitted throughout, from my sudden influx of cash.

Now if I could only make it out of the front door before my top agent grabbed me.

'Is that you Frieda?'

'It is Ingrid. And I'm off the see Fritz on a romantic tryst.'

'Are you sure that's wise? I've been thinking and you know what? He's not what he seems. That display of temper the other night had me quite worried for your safety. I thought he was going to take the front door off its hinges.'

'That's what I'm going to find out Ingrid.'

'In that case I'll get my coat and join you. He's too big for you to wrestle with alone.'

Here we go again. Where's Mick when I need him?

'Come go my *Noble Nosegay*. We have not yet finished the festive decorations. Methinks it's time for you to face the brave new world of coupling alone,' Mick insisted, steering her back inside the flat. 'Off you go Frieda and sort out the vet. The world is meant to be peopled...Are you sure you know what you're doing Kat? He's not the sort to be dallied with.'

'I'm not dallying with him. Although he'd be more fun if he learned to dally...He's just full on all the time. When it comes to dating I've always been reticent. So I'm not easy to be with...Ben's okay really.'

'Well tread carefully. He's only the solid and reliable type until crossed. There's a thin line between love and hate...He could for thee lock up the doors of love...And it will be me he has to deal with if there're anymore displays of temper! A soupcon of discipline will make the medicine go down during such treacherous times.'

'What are you on about Mary Bloody Poppins?' I asked.

Mick chuckled and blew me a kiss before quietly closing the flat door.

I drove over to Fulham and saw with relief that Ben car was parked outside the house. I nipped in the parking space belonging to next door, hoping they were away on holiday. After ringing the doorbell in the freezing cold for fifteen minutes, I knew he was either out, or having a strop. My first impulse was to head back home. Instead I waited in the car. It was only fair. He'd been totally honest with me and I believed I owed him an explanation, if not an apology, for my elusive and inconsiderate actions. He would see the new me – sensible, punctual and demure – because I'd convinced myself that was what he wanted from me.

Owing to the state of my car, I didn't turn on the heating. A flat battery would not get us to Newquay for Christmas. People wrapped up warm against the cold came and went through the clanging side gate. I sat motionless as a couple of strange looking odd-balls wearing knitted hats and mittens rang on door bells. When I saw them both clutching copies of *Watch Tower* I literally shrank down in the seat. They don't celebrate Christmas and always unwittingly spoil it for everyone else.

A dog barked and woke me from my

hyperthermia. Ben had stopped to talk to a dark-haired girl leaning over the balcony two doors down and Lucky was protesting noisily. She was pretty and smiley and I felt a pang of jealousy as they chatted away animatedly. Only Lucky protested. Good old Lucky. She flirted onwards, swishing her hair around until Lucky pulled on the extended lead I'd bought and ended up tangled round the pillar support. I heard Ben say: 'Have to go get some shut-eye. See you later.'

What did he mean: "See you later"?

He'd been so preoccupied chatting up the girl that he'd not even noticed my car – or had he? I leapt out of the car and ran towards him shouting: 'Hi darling and Happy Christmas.'

I can honestly say that he looked totally surprised. Gob-smacked even. At that moment I felt like a total prat. I never said things like that. I'm not a *darling* sort of person. Things were getting too tricky for me. I needed to get back on track.

'Kathryn? What are you doing here?'

'Well you did invite me Ben. Have you changed your mind? If that's the case I can-.'

'No. No way. Come inside. It's good to see you,' he said, smiling for the first time.

Lucky growled a little and gave me a sideways look. I thought I'd detected a half wag of the tail though. Ben took off the lead and my dog headed for Ben's kitchen. He only limped a little on his injured leg and his appetite had definitely returned.

'I'm impressed,' I said. 'You've worked miracles with him.'

'He's a good dog if I can get him to ease up on the barking...Would you like a latte...Kat?' he asked nervously.

'Ben I'm so sorry for my behaviour the other night. It was unforgivable. I come to make it up with you - if you still want me, that is?'

'One thing at a time,' he said rather sternly. 'Take off your coat,' he said moving towards me. 'Now secondly put down the carrier bag. Better. Now come here.' I followed him like a little lamb, feeling very disappointed that he not kissed me. 'Get the milk from the fridge will you?' I did.

'Do you have any matches?' I asked.

'No smoking allowed indoors.'

'No. It's to light this candle. I've given up actually,' I said meekly.

'That's okay then. They're over there by the cooker.'

I couldn't bite my tongue any longer. 'Is this how it's going to be because if it is I might as well go home and –.'

'Na. Just kidding around,' he grinned. 'It's so good to see you. We've missed you. Haven't we boy?'

Lucky ignored Ben, until he started to kiss me. It was very nice until Lucky barked and attempted an unsuccessful jump at us.

'I think he's jealous,' I said, snuggling into Ben.

The lengthy speech I'd prepared in my defence seemed irrelevant at that spot in time. A homely sensation had crept into my mind. Like the same feeling I get in Sophie's kitchen. I had become the potential future Mrs. Gibson in a very smart and welcoming home, complete with dog and two cars. Well one car and an old banger really. I felt more secure and safe again. Ben's territory wasn't half as scary as I'd led myself to believe.

'There's something I want to show you Kathryn. Sorry Kat.'

'Look "Kathryn" is just fine. I was a bitch to say that to you. It sounds really nice in a Canadian accent.'

We headed up two flights of stairs to the sitting room followed by a determined Lucky. It was tastefully decorated in neutral colours of grey, white and splashes of sky blue. The first thing I noticed was the painting over the fireplace. It was one of those I'd thrown out with the rubbish in a moment of despair.

'How did you get hold of that?' I asked sharply.

'I rifled your trash. I particularly like the dark-haired man inside the rolling wave.'

'There can't be. I never put figures in my

pictures. Well, not any more...It's just a trick of the light,' I said, closing in for a greater inspection.

'No. It's definitely a man riding the surf.'

'I don't see it,' I replied stubbornly. Strangely there did appear to be what looked like a dark-haired man surfing. Had I subconsciously been thinking of my Dad at the time?

'Anyhow Kathryn, it's too good to throw away. Don't you agree?'

'No.' I said, ready to explain in great detail how rubbish it was. Something stopped me being defensive. I decided against it. He liked it and that had to be good enough. Imperfect but satisfactory would suffice. I really had mellowed.

'Do you like the Christmas tree?' he asked.

'It's beautiful and you have so many presents.'

'They're all for you,' he said, drawing me close again, 'apart from this one marked "Lucky".'

At this spot I supposed most girls would shriek with joy. I didn't. What's wrong with me? I felt awkward, embarrassed and a little claustrophobic. Wished I could explain it all. Instead I smiled demurely and said: 'Thank you Ben. You're so generous.'

I had actually experienced compromise. Not love or hate, win or lose, laugh or cry. Somewhere in the centre of my confusion was a contrived attempt at being grown up. It was like standing in the middle of a see-saw. Surrogate surfing on a computer game.

'And now relax and enjoy, while I cook us our first meal at our future residence.'

'Ben? I can smell jacket potatoes. I think they might be burning.'

'Can't be. I've not turned on the oven yet.'

We both ran down to the kitchen with Lucky tumbling after. Sniffing around we tried to detect from where the burnt wood smoke came. It was the Gold Frankincense and Myrrh candle!

After our meal I decided to come clean with Ben regarding the Christmas presents. You see it was family tradition just to buy one useful present and I didn't want him to be embarrassed. Then again, to me, one present was one more than I'd ever received prior to my life in Newquay.

'Ben?'

'Yes?'

'I hope you don't mind me saying this but my Godparents don't go mad with the presents at Christmas…They prefer to give to charity…I don't want you to feel awkward…and you have bought an awful lot of things for me…'

'That's cool,' he said without any hint of irony. 'You can open them now – except for one. Okay?'

So there I was making all the right noises as I opened one luxurious item after another. I must say it was confusing for me. Something like this had never happened to me before. I suppose most girls would have shrieked with delight at: silk underwear, an expensive enamelled pen set, a pair of gorgeous black boots with matching handbag, and a lilac pashmena. The parcel containing a huge box of chocolates was opened with a sigh of relief. At last a normal present. Well normal for me. The £300 gift vouchers would be easy to spend. Bless him. He'd tried so hard and put so much thought into his choices. As he took a beautifully wrapped small box and placed it in the top drawer, I wondered what was held inside. It made my Arran sweater gift for him look mean. All the while Lucky snuffled around and tore at the paper rooting for the chocolates.

I relaxed a little - trying to savour the moment. This was a totally new experience for me of absolute pampering - although I must admit it felt a little uncomfortable. It was the kind of feeling where I expected something really awful to follow. Then Ben looked at me with those puppy-dog eyes that I knew I was totally responsible for this man's happiness. The weight of it rested heavily on my shoulders. But right there and then I said to myself: Kathryn Shaw you can, and will be a loving and loyal wife. He deserves that much.

I sent Ben to bed after lunch because he was absolutely exhausted. He didn't even suggest making love. It had been a relief just to chat and eat together with the mad dog eyeing us dolefully. On the pretext of seeing the bedroom décor in case Ben woke up suddenly, I crept upstairs to observe him asleep. In a Bridget Jones moment I knelt by the side of the bed and gazed at him. He looked so young and peaceful with his eyes closed. Free from care and good enough to eat. (Unlike Colin Firth, he didn't wake up to chide me for staring). Then his rapid eye movement spoiled the image. He must've been dreaming. I wished at that spot in time I'd had my sketch pad handy to suspend such a perfect moment.

43

20th December had finally arrived. The time of the year we all looked forward to Trevor and Wayne leaving for their non-skiing holiday. Every Christmas each member of staff was given a festive card with a £20 note inside - our bonus for the year. As we opened our envelopes ready to pretend surprise, Wayne beamed at us. For the first time since I'd met him he looked truly cheerful in his white all in one ski-suit and moon boots. Much to our delight we each received a £50 note tucked inside the card. Instead of the usual greeting "From Wayne and Trevor" we got "Lots of Love and Kisses". It was unbelievable. Our astonished looks were genuine.

'What's going on Mick?' I asked, expecting a sudden change in the wind.

'It's my animal magnetism again my *Mesmerized*

Mesembryanthum. I have this effect on people you know.'

'Bugger off…What's really happening. Is it our pay off? Are they closing the bistro for good? Come on tell me.'

'Truly I know the sods have made me wonderful, because I never put fresh meat in an unclean dish. Now prithee hence away my nymph and maketh me a strong tea with three sugars…'

Trevor bustled around the kitchen checking the newly installed burglar-alarm fitted by Joe. He looked quite macho in his new black ski-suit - apart from the white fur collar and cuffs. I covered my ears as the alarm wailed out like sirens. Trevor hardly noticed, muttering to himself: 'It really does works.' He whistled happily and seemed relaxed for a change and not like a coiled-spring waiting to ping. Something was afoot and I needed to know.

'Morning boss, you look happy today. Is everything on track for the holidays? Will you be back in two weeks to open for the New Year's trade?' I asked.

'Kat I feel wonderful. Wayne and I are so looking forward to our little trip.'

I felt uneasy with his cheerfulness. So I pried further: 'What else has happened? Wayne is actually calling everybody "love". He usually reserves that endearment for Wolfgang only.'

'I know. Isn't it great? He even called me "darling" first thing…Make a large pot of tea for us all will you? We've got something to announce…And put out that plate of mince pies over there…And while you're at it Kat, in the green *Harrods'* carriers are presents for everyone,' he said elatedly.

By this time I was bursting with curiosity. It was too much to bear. I quickly made the tea and put seven cups and saucers on a tray. Lucy and Paulo sat side by side, looking uncomfortable. Mick took the tray from me and said: 'Shall I be Mother?' whilst giving me a knowing look that betrayed him as a fellow conspirator.

'Kat love, will you hand out the prezzies?' Wayne sang out. 'Oh. Wolfgang is there nothing you can't do?' he added, as Mick poured out the tea and handed it round with little finger daintily raised.

'Where's Mags?' I asked, suddenly noticing she wasn't around.

'Poor love. I'd forgotten about her…She's in the loo. Go and see to her Kat,' Wayne said.

'Yes. Anda maka sure she knows thata we all care fora her, Bella,' Paula piped up.

I entered the "Ladies" and called out: 'Mags. What's up hon? Talk to me.' She remained silent behind the toilet door, except for the occasional sniff and sob. 'Come on Maggie. Is it Jason again? You really must do something about him. It's gone on too long now.'

'I know.'

'There's always a spare bed at mine. You can stop as long as you want -.'

'It's alright Kat. Mick's sorted it for me. Jason's out of my life for good now.'

'Well then, what is it? Come on out, I've got you a nice cup of tea.'

The door slowly opened and Maggie shuffled out, head down and sobbing.

'What's he done to you?' I asked, feeling the anger rising. 'Here come and sit down and tell me.'

Maggie wiped her eyes and took the tea from me, sipping it slowly for a while. When she finally lifted her head and looked at me I saw her poor swollen eye. It was almost closed and purple. The area around the cheek bone looked twice its normal size. Our poor gentle Mags who wouldn't harm a fly.

'Oh. My. God. The bastard. No wonder you're crying.'

'It's not that Kat. For the first time in years I was going to celebrate Christmas. Have a nice time with you and your family. I wanted to get dressed up and look half decent….But how can I with this bloody great shiner?'

'Don't you fret, I'll sort out your make up with

my magic concealer -stick. It works wonders. By the time Christmas Eve arrives you'll hardy see the bruise…Hang on I'll get you some ice and then we can talk. Drink your tea. I'll be back in a jiff.'

I returned with an ice pack and my hand bag and waited for Maggie to speak.

'It happened last night when I got home after work. I decided to have it out with Jason. I told him that I was spending Christmas with your family in Newquay…And that I was sick of his moods and bullying and wanted a divorce. I knew he would go ballistic but I didn't care. I'd had enough…' she sighed and finished off her tea. 'I went upstairs to pack my suitcase…Well… then…he kicked the bedroom door open and punched me in the face. I fell onto my backside… Honestly Kat I saw stars. He dragged me out onto the landing and pulled me downstairs. My arms are covered in bruises…When he gets like that I'm terrified. I know from experience to be quiet, else it makes him worse. So I just sat on the floor in the lounge and waited for him to calm down. Would you believe it? He made me a coffee and switched on the football as if nothing had happened.'

'That's awful.'

'Well, I waited for him to drink himself into a stupor. It didn't take long. He'd already had a few lagers before I'd got in. I just put my coat on, grabbed my bag, the car keys and left.'

'Where did you go at that time of night?'

'To the only person I knew would be able to stop Jason from finding me and dragging me back home. Mick of course…I threw stones up to his bedroom window and he soon came down to help me. I spent the night in Wayne and Trevor's spare room while Mick took off at high speed in my car.'

'What happened?'

'I don't know. This morning Mick brought me breakfast in bed. He said that all my belongings were downstairs in five bin-liners, along with my suitcase and toiletries. And that I wouldn't be bothered by Jason again as he had agreed to a divorce. I don't know what he did and I don't want to know. As long as Jason leaves me alone for good, I'm fine. Wayne said that I can stay with them as long as I want. After all, Mick will be moving in with Iris after the wedding.'

'You sure you're not crying over Jason then?'

'I'm positive Kat, honestly. It's just this black eye. I look awful and my upper arms are black and blue. My lovely bridesmaid's dress won't hide them,' she sniffed again.

'Leave it to me. Now let's get to work on that eye. Why it looks better already. The swelling has gone down a bit,' I reassured her.

After fifteen minutes I had concealed most of the bruising. Her eye was still swollen but it looked a little better. She seemed please with the result and brushed her hair down to one side for greater coverage.

'Now come on Mags. Let's face the world. It's Christmas.'

Maggie walked back into the dining area with her head held high but still a little shaky.

'You looka bella, Bella,' Paulo said.

'Thanks Paulo. I feel fine,' she replied softly.

'Come and sit by me little love,' Wayne said. 'We've got something wonderful to tell you all. Haven't we Trevor darling?'

For the second time that day, I saw Trevor flush with pleasure. He was just about to speak when Mick stood up and said: 'Ladies and gentlemen I think this forthcoming announcement needs more than Kat's unusual tea. Let me select some of the finer nectar. If you don't mind that is, Squire,' he added, looking at Trevor.

Before Trevor could reply Mick had made his way over to the fridge and took out four bottles and poured with ease the frothing mousse into six champagne flutes. It must have been hard for him to resist. But resist he did, pouring himself some fresh orange juice instead.

'Friends,' Trevor said, almost tearful, 'it is with great pleasure I have to tell you that my wonderful partner, Wayne, has agreed to marry me. So please raise your glasses and toast my success…To Wayne… I love you. I'd be lost without you.'

The big man sat down and swallowed hard, as Wayne bust into tears and threw his arms around his fiancé's neck.

So that was it all along. Wayne's insecurities were all down to his need for commitment. We all knew that Trevor would never stray but apparently Wayne did not.

'And I'd like to invite you all to our wedding in the Spring,' Trevor announced.

'Summer,' Wayne corrected.

'But I thought you wanted to see the daffodils rising on your wedding day?' Trevor replied cautiously.

Mick chuckled.

'No darling,' Wayne said, bordering on petulance. 'I have so many things to organize. I can't possibly do it all in three months. You should know that by now -.'

'Another toast,' Mick interrupted before things got out of hand, 'to a wonderful Summer wedding for our favourite bosses.'

'Oh. Wolfgang, you're so aware of my feelings,' Wayne said, softening again. 'To our wedding where the sun always shines on the island of a thousand smiles.'

'Yes,' Trevor agreed, looking puzzled.

'I think he is referring to The Seychelles, Squire,' Mick whispered into Trevor's ear.

'Thanks Wolfgang. I owe you. I didn't see that one coming, although he did say he wanted me to surprise him with the honeymoon destination.'

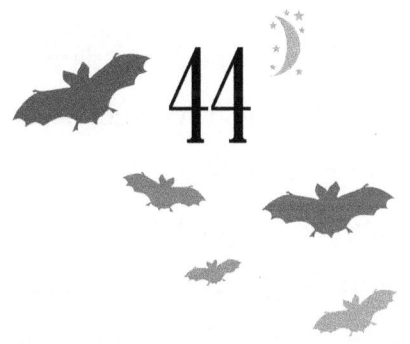

44

After the loved-up pair finally left us to enjoy the Christmas holidays, I decided to ask Mick about the previous night's escapades. He tidied up the bistro and deliberately dodged around every time I tried to get within talking distance. I hope I'm as nimble in my eighties…Maggie and Paulo cleared up in the kitchen and Lucy mopped the floor nearby.

'Will you keep still and tell me about last night?'

'By the swift leg of Time I cannot remember the witching hour my *Curious Convolvulus*.'

'Come on tell me please Wolfgang or I shall have to demote you to Private.'

'That I shall not endure for a priest without Latin is as good as a lottery winner with gout. Meet me forthwith at the notary and lend me your ear.'

'Will you talk sense and stop dancing around.'

'Forsooth I have learned such a merry dance from your tippy-toed fencing. Let us depart to the arbour and have a quick fag then. I don't want little Maggie feeling sorry for the brute.'

We wrapped up warmly and made takeaway coffees for our chat by the bins. Mick had bought herbal cigarettes from the dusty-windowed shop round the corner. He offered me one and I waited for him to light it for me. As I inhaled the cigarette on the first puff the end disappeared into an inch of ash. It tasted vile. It was like smoking a bonfire of briar. Mick began to cough and laugh at the same time. His chest wheezed like an old concertina.

'For God's sake put it out before you collapse,' I said feeling quite dizzy from the fumes.

'So...?' I asked impatiently.

'Well…let me see…Ah. I remember now,' he said in a deliberate and contrived way. 'I rounded up my *Nightmare Nutters* and paid Jason a visit. You know Elephant. He never thinks to open a door. When the flat door came crashing in, Jason soon sobered up. After swearing profusely and threatening to kill me, Boris, Dusty, Hovis and Sliced entered the room. Jason's eyes bulged. I don't blame him really because Hovis looked like a rabid rat, hopping around and squeaking. Two-fingered Boris lifted Jason by one arm and Elephant took the other. Jason looked tiny compared to those two. He was too scared to say anything and just hung there like a rag doll. I started to feel sorry for him until he spat at me. After that I had to restrain Dusty who wanted to sit on him,' Mick laughed, then sipped his coffee.

'Then what happened? Did he struggle?'

'He tried but to no avail...So we took him for a walk. After a few minutes in a confined space with Dusty it was deemed necessary to get some fresh air...Elephant led the way and eventually we reached his home near Battersea Bridge. Well, when I say home, I mean a stack of cardboard boxes and a blanket. I don't know what's got into Hovis but he's turned into a mad man. He kept saying: "Let me be biting his neck. I need to be drinking blood"! Jason tried to put up a fight. I'll give him that.'

'So did Hovis bite his neck?'

'Please do not interrupt the orator or I shall reduce my story to fit the head of a bodkin…As you know Boris is a man of few words. He uses hand gestures instead. He raised his right hand fingers and said: "Three times told! Next time I kill you"? Of course he'd only the two remaining fingers up but I don't think Jason noticed. Boris is a giant warty toad and would put the wind up anybody.'

'What about Dusty? He's the worst for wanting a scrap.'

'I think Dusty wanted to rip Jason's arms out after I told my posse how he had beaten little Maggie. But my mission was to chasten Jason not to bury him. He needed to see the error of his ways and be penitent. After I stopped Sliced pulling out anymore of Jason's teeth everything quietened down a little. That is, apart from Jason crying. Before I could light up a cigarette Elephant had taken Jason by the foot and dragged him over to the river. He dangled him for a bit until Jason's head was fully submerged then threw him into the mud. Elephant never learns though because he waded into to the mud to recover poor Jason for a second dousing. It took every one of my posse to haul him out of the quagmire. And as you know he's no lightweight.'

'And..?'

'That was it you see. Jason had been baptized and chastised. Jason begged me to call off Elephant, which, of course, I did after his third baptism. Else we'd have never got him out of the mud. Then I said to Jason: "Are you cleansed of your sins because yon Elephant strangled King Cobras when he was a nipper"? To which Jason replied "Yes". So I, being the gent, as always, retrieved him from the mud.

Boris washed him down saying: "You are good man now. Be clean and free from lice always". I had to correct Boris's blessing by changing the last words to "vice always". So we took Jason back home. It was the least we could do. The man was a shivering wreck. At least he was sober.'

'So did he really agree to a divorce?'

'Not at first. Let me see, it was after Hovis bit his neck and drank blood. That's what made him see sense. He begged Boris to help him. I gave Jason a crucifix and cauterized his neck with my trusty lighter while Boris gave him a benediction with one finger. I'm really worried about Hovis though. Poor chap. Sliced is taking care of him. Apparently *Mars* bars help to reduce the craving. So I left Jason with a supply of leftover mini-Mars bars purloined from the bistro, promising to visit him in the New Year to check up on him. I told him to take heart and counterfeit to be a human…And therein endeth my tale Kat.'

'Wow,' I managed to say. Night-time people are really weird. And I should know.

I'm glad Mick didn't tell Maggie about Jason's adventure. She was bound to feel sorry for him. I know I did. Well, just a little. He had needed to be taught a lesson and Mick certainly was the man for the job.

In a relaxed atmosphere Mick cooked us his "Mamma's secret recipe" pasta. And Paulo, finding his courage now the owners had departed, opened a couple of bottles of *Chianti*. He then turned on his i-pod on which he'd recorded Christmas Carols. Red faced he skipped the song: *I can't let Maggie go...* and moved on to seasonal songs sung by the original *Rat Pack*.

'Do you like the wedding rings?' Mick asked, taking two small boxes out from his jacket pocket.

'They're lovely Mick. What does it say inside? I can't understand the language.'

'It says: "To my Lady Iris I pledge an eternity of love". Do you think she'll want to wear it? I don't like her wearing Arnold's ring all the time.'

'I'm sure she will. What language is it written in?'

'Archaic Transylvanian of course,' he chuckled. What could I say?

I took this opportunity to discuss the wedding arrangements with Mick.

'Zach phoned this morning…There's a slight hitch. He said he'd used all his powers of persuasion but the vicar wouldn't budge. The church is always fully booked at this time of year…It's the kids carol concert and play…and so on. I'm afraid it's impossible for the marriage ceremony to be held there on 24th December.'

Mick's face fell.

'I'm sorry Mick. I know you wanted to marry in church. Don't despair my Godfather has dressed the music room up to resemble a church and the ceremony can be conducted there on Christmas Eve by special licence. The vicar will then rush back to take over from his colleague and finish off the usual service. Following the marriage ceremony, a church blessing will be held sometime after midnight as soon as the congregation has left. Paulo take note. Your job as usher will be an important one. Clear the area as soon as possible. I don't think Mrs. Jenkins will notice the difference.'

'Who knows, Kat? Most times she's really on the ball. I only hope she enjoys it.'

'Zach has assured me that there will be candles and flowers. He's borrowed a few pews and a spare alter cloth from the chapel. Sophie will play the piano…It will be really romantic… Is that okay?'

'It sounds fantastic. Thanks for all your help my *Busy Lizzie*.'

'And now Count Wolfgang I bid you a fond farewell. So will you get lost for an hour and do the dishes, or something. Lucy, Maggie, Paulo and I have further arrangements to discuss which are of no concern to you.'

45

Maggie, Paulo, Lucy and Mick had spent the night at the bistro and arrived just in time for breakfast. cooked by Mrs. Jenkins. She was on form and full of vigour.

'Come on in. Do hurry before it gets cold. Frieda, where are Fritz and Heinrich? Did you tell them to be on time?'

'Fritz and Heinrich? Oh. Yes. Ben and Alan,' I muttered to myself. It was far too early in the morning for me to remember their agent names. 'They are in transit Ingrid.'

'Gurda! About time too,' she called out to Sal. 'Fraternising with the Yanks again? Good morning Ilmhart love. How are you?' she asked Joe in a softer voice, as Horatio made a bolt for next door's garden.

I really needed to keep up with Mrs. Jenkins.

She certainly was the full shilling that day. Being with Mick had taken years off her. She positively glowed with health.

'Good morning Frau Ingrid,' Sal said, trying to look serious. 'I have acquired some silk stocking for you from our American allies.'

'Trollop! Greta and Gretchen who is that man you have with you?' Mrs. Jenkins asked a startled Lucy and Maggie.

'Err. This is Paulo Mrs. Jenkins,' Lucy answered nervously.

'Greta if you're going to help the war effort please do use our agent names only.'

'Sorry Ingrid.'

'Hello Paulo,' Mrs. Jenkins greeted Paulo. 'Italian are you? Never mind. You're on our side now. At least I hope you are young man. I won't stand any disloyalty.'

'Ciao Bella,' Paulo said, looking confused. 'I am witha you alla the way.'

'Glad to hear it. Now, you do eat bacon, don't you? I don't have any salami. It's hard enough getting hold of a bit of sausage these days. If you know what I mean,' she said, tapping her nose.

Paulo smiled nervously and nodded, looking around for help. Of course it was Lucy who jumped to his aid.

'Bacon and eggs with be fine for us all Ingrid. It's most kind of you to share your rations with us.'

'I can see you and I are going to get along Greta,' Mrs. Jenkins said to Lucy. 'Keep an eye on that Italian will you? I'm not sure about his commitment to the cause.'

'Good morrow to all my kinsfolk,' Mick sang out. 'And a special prenuptial kiss for you my Petal,' he said, kissing Mrs. Jenkins.

'Come in Wolfgang dearest. I need to know what's happened to agent Gretchen. Her poor eye. How did she get it?'

'She took on a monstrous enemy and overcame him,' Mick said, heading for the kitchen.

'I hope you locked him up?'

'He's been well and truly dealt with dearest…

Heinrich welcome. Please to follow the rest of the agents,' Mick said as Alan arrived dragging a battered old suitcase. 'Breakfast awaits us.'

'Have we met before err…?'

'Wolfgang is the name Squire. How do you do?'

'I'm very well, thank you Wolfgang. I trust that you are the groom to this dear lady here?'

'There's no need for introductions Wolfgang. We've already met at Headquarters,' Mrs. Jenkins said. 'Come on in Heinrich and have some breakfast.'

'I say, this is going to be a spectacularly unique holiday,' Alan said. 'Do tell me more of our forthcoming mission.'

'The name's Ingrid,' Mrs. Jenkins said, giving him a knowing look. 'And we only discuss important matters behind closed doors.'

'Is there any sign of *Longshanks* yet my *Merry Minulus*?' Mick asked.

'Not yet,' I replied. 'I hope he's not overslept. I'll give him a quick wake-up call.'

An exhausted Ben arrived last and late. After he'd let Lucky out in the garden, he was duly chastised by Mrs. Jenkins.

'There's no room for slackers young Fritz,' she told him. 'Now go and join the rest. Do you want fried bread?'

'A bacon sandwich will be fine, thank you,' Ben said wearily.

'He's been on night duty Ingrid,' I said, as Ben took his place at the table.

'Was there another bombing?' she asked.

'No. He had to take care of some sick animals.'

'That's no way to talk about our boys, Frieda. Now go and finish off your bacon.'

By this time the group verged on hysteria - except for Paulo, Lucy and Ben. They just didn't get it. They were grown ups I guess. The so called "normal" people I'd read about who were without playfulness and took life seriously – like accountants, solicitors and bus drivers.

'Methinks the tincture of Mandrake root rests heavily on young Fritz's eyelids,' Mick said. 'You can sit in the back with Lucy and let Kat do the driving. We don't want any accidents on so joyous an occasion.'

'I'll be just fine!' Ben said sharply. 'Thanks for the suggestion though…I'll go clean up after Lucky if you'll excuse me,' he said, hastily grabbing half a bacon sandwich. 'Thank you Mrs. Jenkins for an excellent breakfast.'

'I'll come with you,' I offered, feeling guilty and wishing he'd play the game.

'No need. Stay and finish your breakfast. We've a long journey in front of us.'

It isn't in my nature to stay silent around a gloomy person. At least not one I care about. I know I should back off. Leave them alone until they had time to rethink. Wait until their mood had lifted. Not poke a stick at a brooding crocodile. I had to find out what bugged him. I knew it was more than tiredness. As he'd often told me, he didn't need much sleep. He was a night time person. Anyhow, I didn't want anything to spoil Mrs. Jenkins happiness. So I followed him down to the basement flat and out into the garden.

When Lucky saw Ben he barked and wagged his tail, then wobbled over to us.

'Quiet now boy,' Ben said, scratching the dog behind the ear. 'I need to give him two sedation tablets. So if you can allow me some space for a while and leave me to it I'd be really grateful.'

'Okay,' I said.

Ben looked surprised. I must admit it took a lot of effort on my part not to ask him what was wrong. Maybe he was just tired after all. I hoped so - but then again, maybe not.

'Are you going?' he asked, finishing off the bacon sandwich before Lucky could snatch it.

'Not until you've told me what's wrong,' I insisted.

'Will you please leave it?'

'Leave what?'

'Kathryn I'm fine. I'm tired that's all.'

'And…?'

'Well if you must know I feel uneasy about all

the lies. It's not good to con a delusional old lady. She's batty enough without your help.'

'I see. And that's your diagnosis is it?'

'Yes.'

'Well Benjamin, you should stick it where the sun don't shine and leave Ingrid's welfare to me. She's just fine. I've never seen her so happy. I've sat with her night after night when she's cried for her Arnold. And now she's moved on to a happier place.'

'Where's that then – 1945?'

'Fuck off!'

'Oh. That's very intelligent.'

'And take four of those tablets yourself. They might make you less anal!' I said, leaving him clean up Lucky's poo.

Suit cases, wedding outfits and presents were divided between cars. I'd made sure Paulo and Maggie made the journey together in her car. I'd arranged for Mick to drive my car. Mrs. Jenkins sat in the back with Alan. Joe, who acted as map reader, sat in the front next to Mick. Ben gave me the silent treatment while lifting a drowsy Lucky into the back behind the pet-bars. Sal joined Lucy in the back seats and was quiet for a change. I noticed her through the wing mirror pulling faces at me.

After half an hour of silence neither Sal nor I could stand it any longer.

'So Lucy,' Sal pried. 'How long have you been in love with Paulo?'

'Sal!' I reproached.

'It's okay. Everyone knows it - except Paulo that it…About two years.'

'How long have you worked at the bistro?' Sal went on.

'About two years.'

'Why Paulo? I mean, it's obvious he's not Italian and he's a wimp.'

'I know that. He just wants to be more than he is and he's nice and non-threatening.'

Sal continued to gnaw at the bone: 'You do know you're a gorgeous girl? Don't you?'

'Not really.'

'She is a stunner. Isn't she Ben?' Sal asked, trying to draw him out of his mood.

Ben looked through the rear view mirror: 'Yes she is,' he agreed.

'Don't you long for adventure, passion and excitement? Don't you want to travel the world?' Sal went on.

'Don't you?'

'Touché. I've got the love of my life though. We can do most of that other stuff later.'

'I did have a boyfriend at uni. Steve was all those things - adventurous, exciting, unpredictable and very funny. He took a sabbatical after graduation to travel the world. He said he'd come back for me and settle down. At first I got two or three letters a week. Then it was the odd postcard and eventually - nothing.'

'Lucy speaks five languages. She's fluent in Italian,' I informed them.

'You'd scare Paulo to death if he found out,' Sal said.

'I know. That's why I don't want him to find out.'

'So you're hiding from the world working in a bistro for peanuts and taking the easy option,' Sal said.

'I suppose it could be misconstrued as that... What I'm really doing is trying to find some peace. I need to feel part of something ordinary. My adoptive parents are wonderful. Don't get me wrong. But I need time to know who I really am. Find my roots. That's all.'

'I know what you mean,' Ben said kindly.

'I didn't know,' Sal said. 'That you were adopted, that is.'

'It's okay. Anyhow Steve has moved on. One of our uni friends came into the bistro a few months ago. I asked if he heard anything from Steve. He said that Steve had a teaching post in Thailand and was living with an exotic Thai girl.'

'That's terrible,' Sal said.

'It's fine. I got over Steve ages ago. I just wished he'd have told me personally.'

'Maybe he was keeping his options open,' Sal said.

Lucy remained silent. Her face changed back to that enigmatically flawless mask we saw so often. Like a female version of Keanu Reeves.

Inquisitive Sal had drawn out more from Lucy in one conversation than I had in the two years of working with her. And she had also made Ben lighten up as well. He broke into a smile and let down his shoulders.

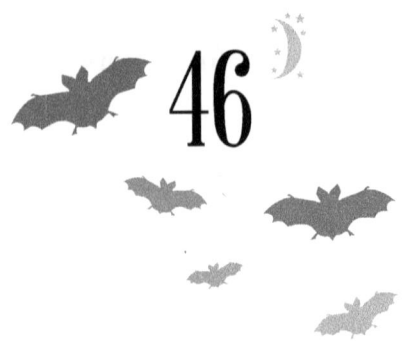

46

When our convoy finally made it over the border, I felt the familiar buzz of excitement. Cornwall definitely has the X factor. Once there it's like waking up on a sunny morning, picking the first strawberries or cutting a slice of warm baked bread straight from the oven. The colours of Cornwall are made up of gold, indigo and deep purple with a coastline of emerald and turquoise. I can't get enough of it. Living in London makes me appreciate its beauty all the more. I will never take that place for granted because it's alive with the magic of legends and the mystery of myths. It appeals to all my senses.

After toilet and tea breaks we quickly motored down to Newquay. I let down my window to smell the sea. The tangy saltiness permeated the air and as we neared my Godparents home I could hardly keep still.

'Turn at the next right Ben where the cart track leads,' I said, hardly able to stop myself from jumping out of the car and running home.

The trees already sprouting early shoot reached to a backcloth of dusky pink sky. Small green leaves pushed out of the earth among the course grasses by the wayside. Even in winter the earth never slept there and presented colour of some kind to brighten up cold days.

'It sure is peaceful around here,' Ben remarked, as we reached *Wisteria House*.

'The best place in the world to heal,' Sal said in a quiet voice.

'You should see it when the Wisteria is in flower. It's amazing,' I said.

Zach had trimmed the exterior with icicle lights all the way under the guttering. It looked beautiful as the daylight faded, but I was concerned how he'd managed to climb up there. Coloured fairy lights flickered on and off around the front door and staked in the borders either side were twinkling stars.

'There's Sophie and Zach. Pull in next to the purple *Capri*. Quickly,' I said to Ben.

Unable to contain myself for another minute, I leapt out and ran across the gravel path. Zach ran forward to greet me with arms held out and hair blowing crazily upwards. He looked exactly the same as always - rosy and ragged in a hippy sort of way. Sophie was dressed in a red batwing jumper from the 80's, black knee-length pants and sandals. Her hair almost white, swept up in a chignon of wildness with a red flower placed behind her right ear, made her look like a Spanish senora.

'Welcome home Grommet. Happy Christmas,' he said, spinning me round.

Sophie moved slowly and deliberately. I knew she needed her walking stick but had left it indoors. She was too proud to be reliant on any aids, so I stood waiting for her to reach me. The courage and fire shone in her dark eyes as she approached.

'Hello darling. Happy Christmas. We've missed you,' she said, hugging me tight.

'Missed you too,' I said, trying not to get over sentimental. That would never do. 'These are my friends I told you about.'

Surprisingly Ben was the first to come over and shake hands. He seemed to know when there was frailty in the air. It drew out the best in him. A noble quality I hadn't noticed until then. Lucky followed him, cowering a little but wagging the bushy tail. He lowered his head and began to lick Sophie's toes. She's such a natural with animals. They always take to her straight away. It's a gift she has.

'This has to be Lucky. He's beautiful,' she said, gently stroking his head. 'Welcome home boy. I hope you'll be very happy here.'

Ben gave me one of his sad looks and I felt really sorry for him. In the end, though it was best for Lucky to have freedom and fresh air. He was terrified of traffic noise and needed to unwind and recuperate in peace and quiet. Ben knew that.

'You must be Sophie. I'm Wolfgang at your service and most grateful for your generous hospitality,' Mick said, grandly.

'I know who you really are Mick,' Sophie whispered in his ear, 'but don't worry your ruse is safe with me. And thanks for looking out for Kat.'

'Thank you kindly for accepting my sheep's clothing without quarrel. Your soft tones have thawed the very chill of discontented Winter. Methinks the nightingale would ne'er pipe as sweet. I thinketh thou needest some direct succour to strengthen thee, on this goodly day,' Mick added, seriously. Now please may I introduce my Lady Iris?'

'I thinketh not, thou Scurvy Knave!'

'All's well that end up right…Now Sophie, please may I introduce my Lady Iris?'

'Now Wolfgang, you're getting careless…Hello

Marlene pleased to meet you. I'm Ingrid,' Mrs. Jenkins said, giving Mick a schoolmarm look.

'Welcome to Newquay Ingrid. May I present my partner Shultz Von Krap,' Sophie said, smiling.

Zach came striding forward and bowed low: 'How do you do? Ingrid and Wolfgang is it? It's been a while since we've had any contact with our special agents; especially royalty. Come inside and get warmed up.'

'Ben you can let Lucky out into the garden for a good old nose around. Go through the side gate down there and leave him to it,' Sophie said, 'then maake your way to the kitchen round the back. You can't miss it.'

'Tommy you are required,' Zach shouted, as we all piled inside. A huge lumbering lad with rosy cheeks and black curly hair appeared. 'Go and unload the suitcases and leave them at the foot of the stairs will you please? And be careful with the wedding cake. It needs to go in the larder.'

'Who's that? He looks familiar,' I asked.

'It's Tom Ridley's son. You remember little Tommy on the beach, following you and Luke around all day during the holidays?'

'He's grown so huge.'

'Well I promised his Dad I'd give him a job. He's not too bright but a willing helper. He's strong as an ox and can shift a pile of rubble in no time.'

'So he fixed the lights under the guttering? Have you done some more renovations?' I asked.

'Just wait and see,' he said, grinning.

The hallway was decked with an enormous Christmas tree reaching up to the ceiling. It was covered with hundreds of red and gold baubles, birds with feathery tails and angels with golden wings. The old mixed with the new in a kaleidoscope of colour and warmth, lit with fairy lights.

'Come into the kitchen. Help yourself to tea and cakes. Dinner will be around eight,' Sophie called out, filling the enormous brown tea pot with boiling water.

'So what have you been up to Godfather?' I asked again.

'Firstly Kat, let's make our guests comfortable. I'll tell you my plans later.'

'Attention pleez, Sophie called out, 'vill zee man viz zee big hammer help me carry zee crockery virst?'

Zach responded immediately. He did like to bash walls and things with the sledge hammer. It was his main hobby. I could see he was itching to show me his latest project.

So there I was in the best place to be on a Winter's day, ensconced in the glowing kitchen with succulent smells coming from the *Aga*, seated among my favourite people.

'I can see you need to think about our next mission Ingrid,' Sophie said, noticing that Mrs. Jenkins was nodding off by the warm firelight. 'Let me take you to your room… Tommy can you bring the brown suitcase and those outfits there in the zip up covers please my loverrlee?'

Mrs. Jenkins nodded in agreement and followed Sophie through to the utility room. My curiosity took over. Zach must have extended outwards at the side of the kitchen. Where the washing machine and tumble dryer had been was now Sophie's studio. Landscapes in abundance were lying around the room. A beautiful gouache painting rested on the easel depicting the North Cliffs. Another door from the studio led to an ensuite bedroom. I know Sophie hated to be mollycoddled but there where time when she couldn't get up the stairs. No matter what. And there was no way she'd allow Zach to carry her up.

Tommy put the suitcase on the bed and left, giving me a bashful smile.

'Thanks Tommy. Fancy some surfing during the Christmas holidays?'

His face lit up bright red and he nodded, his mouth stretching into a coat-hanger grin.

'I hope you like it Ingrid. I thought you would want to be alone before the wedding. I've put Wolfgang in with Alan and Paulo to share with Ben. Is that to your liking?'

'Oh. It's just wonderful Marlene. A perfect boudoir for a bride-to-be,' Mrs. Jenkins said, taking hold of Sophie's hand and kissing it. 'I don't know how much you've been told, but Arnold and I already know each other, in the Biblical sense. I married him when I was a mere girl just out of my teens. This other wedding is for his protection as Wolfgang. He's officially dead now - Arnold that is. If you know what I mean,' she said, winking.

'Yes I do,' Sophie said, looking at me and shaking her head.

'Anyhow it's unlucky for the groom to see his bride before the wedding night. Isn't it?' I asked.

'That's the tradition Frieda. And it is very romantic,' Mrs. Jenkins sighed.

The décor was beautifully done in cream and dusky pink with matching bedding and hangings.

There were cream and pink towels and toiletries. And cream jug contained an abundance of blousy Old English damson coloured roses. The large French doors opened out onto a patio leading to the garden, where stubborn flowers still bloomed, sheltered by a hedgerow of hardy Clematis.

'Glad you like it. Shultz is a man of many talents and can come in handy for fishing and swimming instruction. As you full well know Frieda,' she said, smiling at me.

'Is he with the Navy then?' Mrs. Jenkins asked.

'There's nothing he can't do on water; except swim in it. He hates to get his hair wet.'

'I see. I wondered about the long hair. Is it his disguise?'

'Yes. Who would take him for an officer?' Sophie said.

'Very good reasoning agent Marlene. Over and out,' Mrs. Jenkins yawned. 'Now if you don't mind I'll close my eyes for a few minutes before I work out our next mission.'

'Sweet dreams agent Ingrid. We'll call you when dinner is on the table.'

As we left Mrs. Jenkins to her rest, Sophie gave me that Shaw raised eyebrows look and said: 'What have you got us in to?'

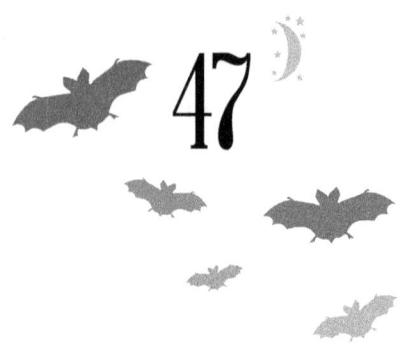

47

Before Sophie could question me further, I was relieved to hear Zach on the stairs directing the rest of our party to their rooms. Lucy and Maggie were to share. Sal and Joe had their usual room, which was opposite mine. They'd put Alan and Mick together while Ben was on the third floor with Paulo. So while they unpacked, Sophie, Zach and I had the kitchen to ourselves. Outside I observed Lucky lolling on three legs and watching Tommy from a safe distance, as the big lad dug out some rocks with a pickaxe.

Sophie peeled potatoes by the dozen for a while before she spoke. I thought I'd got away with the inquisition. I should have known better. She wasn't one to let things lie.

'You know, I don't stick my nose where it's not wanted Kat, but don't you think you are taking this spy business with Mrs. Jenkins a little too far?' Sophie asked, now attacking the carrots.

''I've not really had a spare moment to tell you everything. But the answer is: *no*. I've sat with Mrs. Jenkins most nights after my shift at the bistro because she couldn't sleep. It was pitiful to see her crying for her Arnold. Waiting for him to come home, when I knew he never would. She was terrified of noise and would shake with fear, thinking every bang was a bombing raid. She was trapped in a never-ending round of blitzing you see. I felt so helpless. I really didn't know what to do for the best - except listen…It was when the Social Services got involved I decided to act. It wasn't a premeditated thing - it sort of fell into place. I went back to 1943 with her to try and bring her forward a step at a time.'

'She does seem remarkably astute for her age. Her skin is like a young girl's,' Zach said, checking on an enormous piece of lamb.

'When I prepared her for the test for Alzheimer's I thought that would be the end of it. If I could only get her through that then she would be safe. Be allowed to stay in her own home where I could look after her. You see, it would have finished her off if they'd put her into care.'

'Most commendable Kat,' Zach said, wiping his eyes.

'Thanks…She seemed to have a new purpose in her life after that. It was when I invited her to my party, things change drastically. You see she met Mick the Tramp and thought he was her late husband Arnold. And he being an opportunist and not missing a trick, latched on to the idea of being a Count come secret agent - Count Wolfgang formerly Arnold in fact. He cleaned up his act and began working for a living. He's been sober ever since. Then they both seemed genuinely fond of each other…I couldn't split them up. It would have broken her heart. And now you've seen how happy they are…Who am I to say what's right for them? I only know they've saved each other from a living death…' I trailed off.

'I see,' Sophie said, 'well you're right. Who are we to judge?'

'I can honestly say that she's not dwelling on the past now. All her energy is directed towards ending the War. I think it's her way of letting go and moving forward a little. After the wedding, I've got a feeling she'll be fine with Mick's support.'

'And is Mick fully committed too?'

'He's even changed his name to Count Wolfgang bla-de-bla by Deed Poll. He's in earnest. That's for sure…'

'Thank goodness that's put to bed. Now can we celebrate a simple wedding between a Count/come spy/come double agent/ex tramp and an attractively youthful, if not delusional, lady who thinks the year is 1944? Who knows she may move on to 1945 after all this,' Zach said hopefully. 'And let's hope Russian Olga/Aunt Leonora/come vampire extraordinaire, doesn't turn up to spoil the fun. I've got loads of garlic hung around the doors just in case.'

'Seriously though Kat, do you think she's gone

for good? It seems unlikely from what you've told me,' Sophie asked.

'I'm certain she's not around. I can sense it you see. You worry too much about me.'

'Well somebody has to. You don't seem to take personal safety serious enough. At least keep this with you,' she said, handing me a rape alarm. 'If you're in trouble just push the button and we'll know.'

'Okay….So what do you think of Ben?' I asked, changing the subject.

'Do you mean apart from the obvious good looks, charm and kindness to animals? He's a lovely man and adores you,' Sophie said.

'Can you manage without me for an hour?' I asked.

'I think we can spare you to go and see Luke,' she replied, giving me a knowing look. 'Your board's waxed and ready.'

'Does he know about me getting engaged?'

'I thought it best to come from you Kat.'

I hastily changed into my new wetsuit and

trainers, grabbed my board and headed for the cliffs. The well-worn path was exactly the same as always, lit up by the bright full moon. I could see the silver-foamed tide rushing over an empty beach - a perfect time to catch Luke alone. I'd really missed him. He was so easy to be around. He understood me and accepted all my faults without complaint. He was the best mate any girl could have. And always told it like it is.

I jogged along with the board under my arm, breathing in the purest air in Christendom. I knew every turn and each clump of grass. Nothing had changed. This was my special place because whichever way I went on the path it always led me home. I saw the rocks first, then the shop dimly lit, and as I neared the boathouse I saw him. His blonde hair blowing wildly around his face corkscrewed into curls fashioned by the wind. Him balanced on his board, like a sea-god. Carried with the momentum and knowing every twist and turn until the ocean let him down gently into the shallows.

'Luke!' I called out. He didn't hear me at first and made to paddle out to catch another wave. 'LUKE! IT'S ME!' I shouted, running down to the beach.

He turned and looked, disconnected his board and ran towards me. It was like in the movies where two people show genuine delight at seeing each other again. He caught me in his arms, spinning me round and round. Then he hugged me, nearly squeezing all the breath out of my lungs.

'It's so good to see you,' he said, holding me at arms length and looking for changes. Then before I could say another word, he kissed me passionately. I couldn't stop it. That's what we'd always done. It felt natural, until I thought of Ben and pulled away. 'Am I too full on? Sorry Grommet. Now kiss me again. You don't know how much I've missed you.' And I did. Whether it was out of curiosity, or maybe because it simply felt nice and salty, I don't know.

'Stop! Stop,' I said. 'I've got some good news.

You'll be stoked for me…I'm engaged to be married to a vet. He's really tall and kind. I know you'll both get on. What do say?'

He stood motionless for a while. Then picked up his board and walked back into the sea.

'Luke. Don't be like that…What's wrong? Wait for me… You're invited to dinner in an hour's time. Will you come and meet the rest of my friends?'

No reply.

'What's wrong with you? I'll still come in the Summer to surf and we'll always be friends. You're my…' my voiced trailed off, drowned out by a huge breaker. 'Alright then Luke if that's your attitude when I've come all this way to tell you my good news, then you can have the wave all to yourself!' I shouted.

'TA!' was his only response.

'Are you coming to dinner then, or not? Sophie's invited you.'

As Luke paddled over the top of a surge of water, I realized that my face was wet with tears.

Something special had come to an end. I felt bereft. My life would never be the same. Why did I have to move on? Why couldn't I stay in that magical spot in time forever?

I sat on the cliff tops watching him spin and turn with the tide. Nothing could distract him when he surfed. No matter what, he was a joy to behold out there – a thing of beauty. His concentration was unhindered by anything beyond the wave. When he surfed he was totally free. As I sat there feeling utterly miserable and wanting to join him in the foam, a thought came to me. Everything he needed was there in the sea. I was just a bit on the side. I was somebody to goof around with when he wasn't surfing – that somebody who just happened to be Martin Shaw's daughter.

For the second time in ten years I ran back to *Wisteria House*, feeling lost. Why did things in the world of couples have to be so complicated? That was not what I'd expected at all. Luke had never given me the silent treatment before. I was gutted.

'You're back early Kat. Did everything go okay?' Zach asked.

'Leave her for a bit,' Sophie said, sensing my mood of despair. 'Dinner will be ready in half an hour Kat. Go and get changed. There's a lot to discuss about the wedding, my loverrlee.'

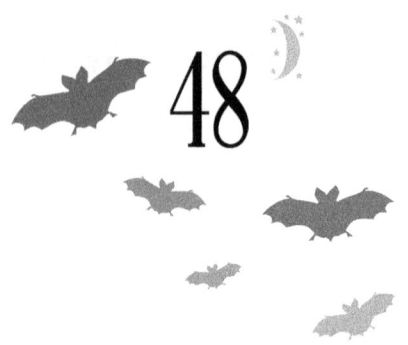

48

I tried to regain some of my former happiness that night. I couldn't help but despair. I needed to put on a cheery face for Mrs. Jenkins and Mick's sake. And the only solution was to knock back two glasses of champagne to soften the ache. The rest of the group was on form. Even Paulo was animated, chatting to Maggie at the dinner table. Lucy sat next to Ben and I had an empty place on the other side. The vicar sat opposite Mick and next to Sophie, who had Alan on her right. In fact everyone appeared not to notice my quietness - except Sophie and Sal who kept glancing my way. So I picked at my smoked salmon and pretended to smile.

'I hope you have blackout curtains in the church Rutger?' Mrs. Jenkins asked the vicar, also known as Davies the Godley.

'We do, and plenty of candles to light your way,' he replied. Nothing shocked Davies the Godley. Not to be confused with his brother Davies the Physio. He was Welsh and built of sturdier stuff – a man with a barrel chest and booming rich voice. He took life by the throat and sucked out every last drop of pleasure it could offer. He reminded me of the older Richard Burton - except with much longer nasal hair.

'So Iris are you ready for the big night on Christmas Eve? I know I'm looking forward to it very much,' he said, quaffing another glass of champagne.

'Rutger!' Mrs. Jenkins said sharply and leaning across the table. 'My name is Ingrid, so please lower your voice. We don't know who is listening.'

'Ingrid it is then,' he bellowed out. 'A toast to Ingrid our beautiful bride-to-be and Wolfgang the Count,' he announced, raising his glass.

Davies the Godley was not a man to be ignored. His voice carried to all four corners of the large kitchen and beyond. We all scraped back our chairs on the tiled floor, jumped to our feet and toasted their forthcoming marriage. I noticed Maggie, Joe and Paulo were swaying around. At least I think they were. I was quite tipsy myself. (And Maggie's eye looked much better since Sophie had given her the family recipe of vinegar and water for bruises). Sal chatted to Sophie, occasionally looking in my direction. I felt my ears burning. But that was nothing new when Sal was around. She liked to put the world to rights.

'You do know Rutger that my real name is Iris. I hope the church isn't bugged. I expect it'll be safe to drop your guard there. Even the enemy wouldn't disregard sanctuary. Now then, pay attention. Wolfgang is no longer Arnold,' she confided, leaning across the table again. So wherever you are, you can call him Wolfgang. Is that clear?'

'Crystal clear Ingrid,' Davies the Godley answered, getting redder by the minute.

'I think it's time for the main course,' Sophie said to Zach. 'Bring on the lamb Shultz.'

Zach and I went into the cooking area and filled up the tureens with steaming vegetables.

'Help yourself everyone. The meat and gravy are on their way. Kat take the mint sauce will you?' he called, destroying the huge joint with an electric carving knife.

As I balanced a tureen of roast potatoes in one hand and the mint sauce boat in the other, I heard a familiar voice say: 'Hope I'm not too late?'

It was Luke. He always used the back door. I was so pleased to see him I nearly spilled the sauce.

'You're here,' I said, smiling again.

'Yep.'

'I'm so glad. Are you okay?'

'Nope.'

I'd never seen him in proper clothes before. He'd either been in a wetsuit, wearing shorts and T-shirt or nothing at all. I was surprised how broad his shoulders were under the white shirt. His thighs filled out the stone-washed jeans perfectly. And there he was, Luke the Lifeguard wearing shoes - black loafers at that. The awkward gait had gone and he moved easily towards Zach and caught the meat platter as it vibrated towards the edge of the table. He seemed to have grown since I'd seen him in the holidays, or maybe he'd appeared taller on land.

'Thanks for coming Luke. Good to see you. Help yourself to a beer. There's a place set for you next to Kat. You've missed out on the smoked salmon though.'

'No worries. The main course looks tasty when the meat stops jumping around. Shall I take it through?'

'Please,' Zach said, struggling to turn off the electric carving knife.

Luke introduced himself to everyone in the room with his usual easy manner: 'Hi. I'm Luke. Glad to meet Kat's friends. Please don't get up, just go on doing what you're doing. Sal you look beautiful. Joe, congratulations mate…Pass the platter round will you Wolfgang,' he said to Mick.

'Please to meet you Luke. I've heard good things about you,' Mick said, standing and shaking hands. 'Here sit next to my Lady Iris - my future wife.'

'I feel as if I know already. Zach kept me up to scratch with Kat's mates - apart from one that it is,' Luke said.

I took another platter to Paulo's end of the table and watched as Luke sat down next to Mrs. Jenkins, saying: 'Please to meet you Iris. Zach filled me in on the Christmas wedding and your War efforts.'

'Listen Sigmund, my Wolfgang is getting forgetful in his old age. My name is Ingrid. And you are sitting next to Frieda...Are you a double agent?'

'No way Ingrid. Why do ask?'

'You're very blonde.'

'I'm an Aussie Ingrid - all the way from Sydney Australia. We're part of the Commonwealth.'

'Stand at ease then Sigmund, or should I say, sit? You have the most beautiful angelic eyes I've ever seen. You must be easily hurt.'

'Don't know about that. Cheers everybody.

Happy Christmas and here's hoping for a great New Year.'

When I returned to the table, I noticed Ben had moved into my place. I was now separated from Luke and sat next to a lovelorn Lucy. The tension in Ben's shoulders had returned and made his arms look really short.

'So…you're Luke the Lifeguard then?' Ben asked.

'You're not wrong mate. So you're: really tall and kind Ben the Vet?'

'I am.'

'Cool.'

'Do you do anything other than surf,' Ben asked, almost sneering.

'Sure. I give lessons, man the boat on "Shark Watch" and sell a few boards in the shop.'

'All connected to surfing then?'

'I guess so…Do you surf Ben? I can give you a lesson if you want,' Luke offered amiably.

'I'm not a wet person. I prefer dry land. My

sport is ice hockey. And I do a bit of skiing when I go home.'

'Tried snow-boarding?' Luke asked casually, through a mouthful of lamb.

'No.'

'Luke is a champion surfer,' Zach told him. 'My shop is full of his trophies.'

'Have you thought about getting a proper job?'

'I love my lifestyle. I couldn't do the indoors. I wake up every morning with a smile on my face and look forward to starting work. I'm happy with things the way they are.'

'Have you thought about the responsibilities of: getting married, supporting a wife, having a family?'

'Yep, I have, but not yet awhile. There's plenty of time for settling down and becoming a regular guy when I reach your age.'

'You should get some qualifications. But I suppose book learning is the last thing on your mind,' Ben said huffily.

'Luke has a PhD in Marine Biology. He's just

finished his thesis on Cornish marine life. It's being published as we speak,' Zach said proudly.

'Move over Ben you're in my seat,' I said, before he could cross-examine Luke further. 'Sorry about that Luke,' I whispered. 'I didn't know you had a PhD.'

'No worries Kat. It's taken me long enough to finish…Eat up and enjoy the rest of the evening.'

Everyone livened up when the claret was poured - except Lucy and Ben who sat there looking uncomfortable with the comic banter. Mixed company seemed to wind Ben up like a tight ball - whereas it decidedly had the opposite effect on the others. Only Sal and Mick abstained for drinking but they were jolly enough without it.

Luke hardly gave me any eye contact throughout but smiled and listened with interest to Mrs. Jenkins telling him about our escapades with Russian Olga. I felt my feet beginning to twitch in the high heels so I kicked them off under the table. My foot accidentally touched Luke's leg and he didn't move away. That was comforting. It was unbearable not having a laugh with him and not being able to touch him.

A sudden clattering of the dog-flap caused Ben to look over to the door. Lucky had entered backwards. His hind legs and bushy tail were partway in while the rest of his fuzz-covered body remained outside. He'd obviously tried to nose the flap open but his injuries must still have been painful. Before Ben could move, Luke was on his feet and sprinted over to help Lucky with his ungainly entrance.

'Come on Lucky, let's get you in from the cold,' Luke said, lifting the dog gently through the flap. I expected Lucky to growl but he allowed Luke to draw him inside. Luke then scratched behind Lucky's ear, saying: 'Who's a big brave boy then? Come and get into your nice warm bed. It's minced lamb for supper.'

And Lucky did as he was told. Circling round inside his basket then flopping down with his sad lop-sided face resting on his paws and sighing in that same way Boss used to. Ben watched this unsmilingly and said: 'The tranquilizers must still be working, otherwise he'd have had your hand off.'

'Na. Not Lucky. He's a top dog,' Luke replied, coming back to the table.

After treacle tart and custard we all were well and truly stuffed. By the time the port and cheese board came round, I was ready for some fresh air. All the smokers made for the outdoors, grabbing coats and hats. Mick, Davies the Godley, Zach, Sophie, Maggie, Paulo and me stood together waiting for one of my Godfather's special brand cigarettes - except Alan who had his pipe.

'Thought you'd given up Kat,' Sophie said.

'I have, almost. I'll just have a quick drag from yours then. Also I wanted to see Zach's latest project.'

'What do you think then Kat? Smashing isn't it?' he asked.

The decking area had been expanded with blue floor lights fitted into it. There was an overhead canopy and side trellising covered in winter flowering Honeysuckle to shelter from the wind. He'd got one of those tall heater things which beamed direct heat around the head only - and looked like an old-fashioned street light. I noticed there were three new cane sofas, a swing seat and a cane table to match. The sun-beds were folded away down the side awaiting the return of the Summer.

'That's not all Kat. Show her the rest Zach,' Sophie said, inhaling deeply on a roll-up.

Wolfgang, Alan and Davies the Godley were in animated conversation about global warming, so I left them to it. Maggie and Paulo were snuggled up together in the swing seat. I guess Lucy had lost out with my match-making. I'd have to find her somebody else. Maybe one of Luke's mates would fit the bill. But most definitely not: Slops, Knuckles or Gannet.

'Come on now keep your eyes closed,' Zach said, holding my hand and leading me out into the garden. 'Watch out for the pebbles…Right, you can open them now.'

I did.

'What is it?' I asked, looking down at a deep hole surrounded by a pile of rubble and rocks.

'It's going to be a swimming pool when Tommy and I have dug out the rest. I'm waiting until after Christmas to borrow a digger from Brian the Brickie.'

'What a great idea. It'll be perfect for Sophie. Will you swim then Zach? Try out your most excellent front butterfly?'

'Not if I can help it. I might float around on a li-lo though,' he laughed. 'I think Luke is waiting for you Kat. He's over there by the greenhouse.'

'Oh. Right,' I said, trying to sound casual.

'Make sure you know what you really want before you say anything final. Life's too short to miss out on something special. You know we'll always back you on any decision you make. Don't you?'

'Of course I do Godfather. You're the best.'

All You Need is Love… he sang out, trying to hide his big soft tears.

I'm so lucky.

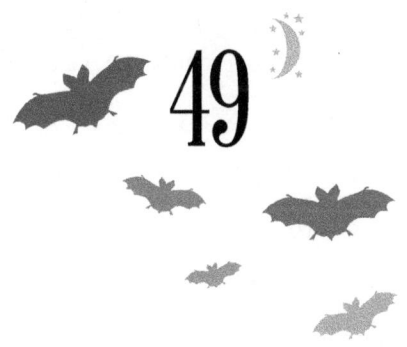

49

Luke took hold of my hand and led me round to the back of the greenhouse.

'Kat, we've got to talk. You're not serious about marrying that jerk, are you?'

'He's not a jerk. He's -.'

'I know: "really tall and kind". Do you love him?'

'I'm engaged aren't I?'

'That doesn't answer my question…Is that what you want? The house, the car, the jerk?'

'I-I don't know. We're not getting married for ages yet.'

'Does Ben know that? He seems pretty keen to me. He appears to be a decent bloke, apart from being uptight, but he's not for your Kat. He'd stifle you.'

'Anyhow, I'm just a mate to you. You never told me you love me. Not once.'

'I didn't think there was any need. I thought you knew how I felt.'

'So how do you feel Luke? I really need to know.'

'Have you had sex with him?'

'That's none of your business…And how many other girls have you had in the past ten years, when I've not been around? Hundreds I bet!'

'None Kat. Only you.'

'Oh. I see.'

'Can't you understand that? You were just a kid when we first met. I was fresh out of university. I had to work on my doctorate and you had to see the world. Find your feet and test other waters. I couldn't hold you back. That would have been selfish. You needed to go out there and do your thing. Use your talent…I filled my spare time with surfing - something we both love - although you still insist on trying goofy foot. I knew you would always come back to me Grommet. We're joined by an invisible thread. When you're away I can only function if I know you're here in spirit.'

'Wow.'

Luke moved nearer and I could feel his warm breath on my neck. I so wanted him to hold me.

'Please don't do that again. I can't think straight when you're so near.'

'Can you blame me Kat? It's the first time I've seen you in a sexy dress. And you look stunning. I should add: pale but stunning. The London tan is so white and bright that I don't need a torch to see you.'

Nobody had ever called me *stunning* before. I thought that word was reserved for the beauties: Scarlett, Jennifer and Haley. It's a nice word, like *exquisite* and I held on to it. I might never hear it said to me again.

'You look half decent yourself. Did you borrow the shirt from Gannet?'

'You're having a laugh. All Gannet's shirt have curry stains down the front...I do have some Sunday clothes. These loafers are giving me the jip though,' he added, kicking the right one off. 'I bought them for Christmas Eve, to go with the penguin suit Zach hired for me. I'm to act as an usher.'

We watched the shoe sail through the air and land in the water trough. It was at that point I suddenly realized, I was barefoot and freezing. We both laughed.

'We can't talk here. Come down to the beach with me?' he asked, retrieving the soggy shoe. 'There's something I want to show you.'

'Both of us know what'll happen if we go down there.'

'I mean it, just to talk Kat. Please trust me?'

'Okay then. I can't stay for long…We'll have to sneak along the perimeter of the wall, otherwise we'll be found out. I'll grab us some wellies and waterproofs from the shed, if you can keep watch.'

As Luke carried me on his back, scurrying through the undergrowth, I heard a rustling noise.

'Your camouflage doth mock the very cloak of night. I think everyone can see you my *Sneaky*

Schizanthus. And as for *Sir Galahad,* his whiter than white shirt is luminous under yon moon - who is already green with envy of your shimmering porcelain legs,' Mick said, chuckling.

'What're you doing here? You scared me half to death,' I said in astonishment and seeing only a red glowing cigarette end.

'You know me Kat. I can't stay indoors for too long. The night-time air suits me best.'

'Where's Mrs. Jenkins?'

'My Fairy Queen is sleeping soundly and dreaming of her Oberon.'

'Listen Mick I need to talk to Luke alone... You understand. Don't you?'

''Tis the moony month of Xmas that doth make fools of us all,' he chuckled.

'Stop acting like a nutcase,' I said, thinking Luke wouldn't understand.

'Join the club mate, Luke said, grinning. 'Have the two households both alike in fair Verona noticed we're missing?'

'Take heed of my warning and disdain to be

cross-gaitered in all of this,' Mick said, stepping out of the shadows. 'The whole household is at this very moment watching you two star-crossed lovers - except *Longshanks* and Lucy who are busy clearing the table and intent on washing up.'

'Oh. No,' I sighed, as Zach, Joe, Alan and Davies the Godley waved at us. 'There's no point in hiding anymore.'

'Now goodly creatures hence away, concealed by the act of my cunning distraction,' Mick said, disappearing across the garden. 'Ladies and gentlemen your attention if you please. The time is nigh to see the red orb of Mars glowing in the velvet sky. It's just over there to your right, beyond the chink in the wall.'

Luke and I sprinted through the Hydrangea bushes and reached the shed before anyone could spot us.

'You'll get me in big trouble Luke,' I said, giggling.

'Given half a chance,' he replied. 'We'll never be recognized in these outfits,' he said, pulling on Zach's bright yellow cape and green wellies. 'Come here and let me wrap you up warm,' he said slowly drawing me into him.

I waited like a child while he zipped up my waterproof. His hair brushed my face and I could hear his heartbeat as he moved closer. We stood together almost touching, looking at each other in a different way. It was as if something stronger had been awoken in us. When he knelt down to kiss my toes, I had to stop him.

'Stand back please while I slip into something comfortable,' I said, pushing my feet into some flower painted wellies.

We made our way along the cliff tops and down to the beach without a word being spoken. I knew I shouldn't have agreed to go with Luke - and not left Ben alone, but I was desperate to get him on my own. I guessed Ben would be making lattes for everybody and wiping surfaces down, while Lucy swept the kitchen floor, like Cinderella hoping for her Fairy Godmother to appear. I was so confused and I needed time with

Luke away from Ben, to try and reason out some sort of solution.

Much to my surprise, Luke had converted the old storage shed next to the shop into a neat white summer house. There was decking all the way round, cordoned off with poles and ropes slung across, giving a nautical theme.

'Come on in,' Luke said, unlocking the door.

He'd transformed the shed into living space - with the help of Zach no doubt. It was neat and tidy and painted with blues and greens. There was a small kitchenette to the right and a sitting room to the left. A toilet had been fitted and a shower with hot and cold running water.

'It's lovely. When did you do all this?'

'Zach said I could renovate it. Let's face it, I only went back to the flat in town to change my clothes and check the mail…This is the bedroom,' he said, opening the door. 'No worries Kat. I won't pounce on you. Not yet anyhow. Come and have a look inside.'

'You've made it homely,' I said, 'and it's very tidy.'

'You should've seen it yesterday before you arrived.'

'Did you do all this yourself?' I asked, wondering what other hidden talents he had.

'With a little help from Zach and Tommy, but I did the bathroom and kitchen area,' he smiled. 'Fancy a coffee?'

I sat waiting on the sofa. Everything felt so easy. I was home. His computer perched on a desk, hardly visible under a stack of writing. There were photos of us everywhere. Memories of all the summer's we'd spent together. This was the place where Luke and I had hidden away for many happy hours, making love and talking about our plans. What's that saying: *Go with the flow*? When Luke sat next to me I tingled. There was that sea-fresh familiar smell I loved about him and his wonderful eyes unwavering, looking at me in such an earnest way. Yet he'd matured so much since the summer.

'This is for you,' he said, handing me an envelope. 'Happy Christmas Grommet.'

'What is it?'

'Open it and see.'

Inside the envelope were two plane tickets to Hawaii for the Surfing Championships, along with hotel bookings and travellers cheques.

'How could you afford this? You always give your money away.'

'You heard Zach…I've sold my book. Got paid quite a few dollars for it and bought these. It's what we'd always planned. Isn't it?'

'Well yes. Oh. Luke. This is really great. Oh. I'm so mixed up. I find out you have a doctorate, as well as being a plumber, a published writer and you know Shakespeare. And you're what, seven years older than me?'

'I knew you would feel different about me when I wore clothes,' he said ripping off the shirt.

'No. It's not the clothes,' I gasped, taking in his tanned torso. 'You look great…More than great…There are so many changes. It's hard to get my head round it all.'

'Nothing's changed. I wouldn't exactly say I'm a plumber, or a geriatric. I graduated early. I'm four years older than you…And I've never met this Shakespeare bloke,' he said grinning at me. 'I'm still the same guy as always…Look Kat I don't want to queer your pitch. I'll give you some space. As much as it takes…Just think about what I've said. If you decide you want Ben the Vet, then I'll back off. You can use the tickets for your honeymoon. No matter what, I'll always be here for you,' he said, swallowing hard. 'Please just kiss me one more time.'

And I did. It was full of tender sadness, unfulfilled longing and mingled tears - in fact everything but the abandoned passion that was so familiar to us. I rested my head on Luke's shoulder, listening to the sound of the relentless sea as it slid back over the rocks.

50

It was way after midnight when I returned. The house was silent and still. Lucky raised his sleepy, scarred head and looked at me. His crooked eyebrows arched as if about to ask a question.

'Hello boy. No barking now. You'll wake everyone.'

I was relieved to have the kitchen to myself. I'd half expected Ben to be waiting behind the door with arms folded and shoulders up. He must have been feeling like shit. I knew I did. After making myself a hot chocolate, I sat in Zach's well-worn chair by the fireside. The tears fell hot and wet, running down my face and into the cup. How is it possible to love two men at the same time? The sensation was new to me and I hated it. I felt cheap and disloyal. Even worse, I thought they'd both end up despising me.

Oh. God. Why me all of a sudden?

Nothing ever happened to me in the romance stakes. I was the girl who got the cold shoulder over my prettier friends. I was only spoken about en passant by the blokes: "the curvy brunette next to that lanky one with the ginger hair", in nightclubs. "Be careful what you wish for", crept into my head.

I knew she had returned. I could feel her presence - her craziness, laughing at my predicament. I think Lucky sensed it too because he padded over to the fireside and gave me that mournful look. His body began to tremble, so I lifted him onto my lap and wrapped him in Sophie's shawl. He didn't struggle and gave in to the warmth of the fire. I don't know how long we sat there, drifting in and out of sleep. I was woken abruptly by a hand violently shaking me. Lucky had returned to his basket and snored rhythmically, so I guessed I'd dreamed the stark awakening. I stirred myself from the warmth of the glowing embers and made my way upstairs.

'Where've you been,' Sal said, peering from behind the bedroom door opposite. 'I've been worried about you.'

'Sorry Sal. I'm okay. I'll speak to you in the morning. You need your rest. Go back to bed... Goodnight hon.'

For once Sal didn't protest. She nodded and closed the door.

I was reassured by the familiar warmth permeating my bedroom and the noise of the hot pipes popping under the floorboards. Everything had remained unchanged. It was just as I'd left it, only spick and span. Sophie had unpacked for me, hanging my best man's/bridesmaid's dress over the long mirror. I knew sleep was out of the question, so I read my Mother's letter over and over. It was part of me now and carried with me wherever I travelled. I slipped off the ruby earrings and ring and put them safely back into the box. The letter was my talisman and I knew my mad Aunt could never hurt me while I had this nearby.

'Come on Wolfgang keep up will you, slowcoach,' I heard Mrs. Jenkins call out.

In the morning light, down in the garden, she was briskly walking around the strawberry patch and swinging her arms, with Mick puffing and panting behind her as he tried to jog. It was unbelievable. I know the air in Cornwall refreshed and invigorated, but that was ridiculous. She had osteoporosis for God's sake. She looked to be getting younger, and straighter, while, on the other hand, Mick was extremely knackered.

For a moment I'd forgotten about last night's problems. My mood quickly changed. I knew there would be questions from Ben, but I really wasn't prepared for a confrontational conversation. After a quick shower I snuck down the back stairs and went for a run before breakfast. I headed in the same old direction hoping to see Luke and the gang surfing. He was nowhere to be seen.

'Good'ay Grommet,' the long bony outlined figure of Knuckles called out, 'you coming down for a mullering?'

'Na. Can't. Got a lot on with the wedding,' I shouted back.

'Does Luke know?'

'Yes. He's an usher.'

'Bummer,' Knuckles answered. 'Take it easy then,' he said, waving before he hit the surge.

Does every dude in Newquay know Luke loves me - except me? 'Is Luke around?'

'Not seen him Kat. Think he's gone to his publisher. He's bloody famous now. The stuck-up bastard,' he laughed.

I headed back to the house feeling more awake and ready to face up to Ben.

'Kathryn,' I heard a voice call out from the meadow. 'I'm over here.'

It was Ben holding Lucky on the extendable lead, like a fisherman reeling in a catch. They were in the middle of the field behind the broken fence. The grass was so tall that I could barely make out Lucky's tail moving from side to side. I guess his front end was working overtime hoovering the clover. I regulated my breathing as Ben walked towards me.

'Are you okay?' he asked.

'I'm fine,' I replied in surprise. 'How are you?'

'Better for seeing you thanks. I've brought you a hot drink and a bacon sandwich,' he said reaching into his rucksack.

'Aren't you mad at me?' I asked.

'No. How can I be?' he asked, kissing me lightly on the cheek. 'I do understand your dilemma. Luke's a good-looking guy and you've known him a lot longer than me.'

I tucked into the sandwich, lost for words. I'd expected a rebuke at least. This made it all the harder for me. If he'd been nasty I could have stormed off and not felt so bad. Now what?

'Glad you see it like that Ben…I'm sorry if I hurt your feelings.'

'I'm big enough to take it, or should I say: really tall?'

We both laughed and the tension broke.

'So what do think of this place then?'

'I think it's the perfect spot to raise kids – and a dog. It's breathtaking. No wonder you couldn't wait to get back. I don't understand why you want to live in London.'

'I needed to test other waters,' I replied, echoing Luke.

'So how was the fountain in Battersea Park? Better than this?' he laughed.

'Not as wild but very wet.'

'You need to get a move on. The ladies are all dressed in their finery and ready to shop for flowers,' he said, reeling in a protesting Lucky. 'And we gents have to be fitted for our penguin suits. I've been appointed as an usher, along with Alan and Paulo, by Davies the Godley. He said that some muscle was needed to clear the church after midnight as it was always full of hangers-on and drunks.'

'He should know…Oh. Well. Err…an usher… that's nice…' Oh. God!

I'd forgotten it was down to me to arrange: makeup, manicures, and hairdressing bookings - and

Davies the Godley was waiting for my instructions on the church flowers for Christmas Eve.

Bugger! 'Thanks for reminding me Ben. You're a star,' I said, running back to the house, before he could ask me any questions.

'Here she is,' Zach said, looking relieved. 'Get the ladies in Ben's car will you Paulo, while I clean out the *Capri*?'

'Sure thinga,' Paulo said, beaming at Maggie. 'It'sa gonna be a greata day.'

Lucy stared at the floor until Mrs. Jenkins grabbed hold of her hand and led her to the car. 'Come along Greta. There's no use crying over spilled milk. There are plenty more fish in the sea. You just need the right bait…Bye Wolfgang dearest. We'll see you all later. Hurry up Frieda and get changed into civilian clothes. You can't go for a "Cream Tea" looking like that. And you there Gurda, check for bugs in the flowers.'

'I think the odd ladybird would like nice in the flower arrangements. I do,' Sal said, looking wide-eyed.

'You know full well what I mean young lady,' Mrs. Jenkins said, getting into the back seat without any assistance. 'I mean the ones without eyes.'

Things were getting weird again.

By the time I'd returned, the guys had already set off in a different direction to the Wedding Hire Shop. Lucy and Maggie were squeezed together in the kiddie-seats near the extra spare wheel. Sophie and Mrs. Jenkins were seated in front of the dog-grid and discussing the forthcoming ceremony, while Sal waited in the passenger seat, bursting to ask me questions.

'So?' she said, as I switched on the engine.

'So what?'

'Come on. I know you too well Kat. How did it go with Luke and why is Ben so cheerful?'

'Not now please. If you must know, it's a bloody awful mess. I don't know what to do for the best.'

'Go with your heart. That's the only way.'

'But I love them both... for different reasons, that is. Oh. My brain hurts.'

'Okay hon. Matters of the heart have a way of working themselves out. Trust me I'm pregnant. Now let's go and get ourselves some lovely treatments. Look you.'

It was really good to be back in town. Things were quieter in the Winter and the locals ventured out more often to shop. After organizing flowers for both churches - the real one and the pretend one – we paid a visit to *Valerie's Beauty Salon*. She and her assistants were at the ready and armed with wax strips to tackle the Autumn growth. Mrs. Jenkins insisted she didn't have a downy moustache and a hairy mole, but the hair was removed nevertheless. Eyebrows were trimmed and faces massaged with aromatic oils. Each one of us had a French manicure and pedicure which was really nice. Those home kits are fine, but I never could do my right hand or use those half-moon shaped strips to paint a neat white line. I'd tried the new roller pen but, owing to my impatience, it just rolled off the nail polish underneath. Making it look worse than before.

I could see Valerie was dying to book Sophie in for a neat bobbed haircut. She'd no chance. It was good of her to fit us all in on Christmas Eve after six o'clock though. That was, after I'd invited her and Trudy to the party afterwards.

'So?' Sal asked, relaxing with a cup of peppermint tea. 'Tell me what happened last night? Ben was very quite. Although I must say the kitchen sparkled after he'd finished - along with Lucy's help of course. They looked so sweet together like Cinders and Buttons.'

'You're doing it again aren't you?'

'Doing what?'

'Interfering. What's that about taking my time? Making up my own mind.'

'Well my loverrlee, that's all well and good, but you can't have them both. I don't blame you for thinking that though. Phwah! And there must be plenty of women queuing up for two such gorgeous men.'

'Stop it Sal.'

'Okay. But I was only saying that Lucy and Ben

would be good together. You could let him down nicely. Let them cry on each other's shoulders.'

'He's mine! Alright? And I'm engaged to marry him. Now leave it Sal!'

'That's what you said about Lucky. "He's mine". They're not possessions you know. What did Luke have to say for himself anyway?'

'Final warning Sally Jones. You not too big to get a slapped arse girl,' I said laughing at her.

'Oh. I'm so scared. At least you're not feeling sorry for yourself now,' she said, her eyes full of mischief.

And, as always, she was right.

51

Later that evening the air was filled with excitement as we sat round the dinner table. Mrs. Jenkins was really on form and chatted amiably without once mentioning the war. I was worried about Mick, so when he went outside for a smoke, I followed him. He headed for the undergrowth and I lost him for a minute, until I spotted his silhouette behind the Laburnum tree.

'Mick, are you there? Are you okay?' I called out, looking for the glow of his cigarette. I heard something screech in pain and then a cracking noise. 'Please stop messing around. Talk to me.'

'Go inside Kat. You'll catch your death out here and that will never do.'

No flower name? I was really worried. Had he changed his mind about the wedding? Was Mrs. Jenkins getting too bossy for him?

'You seem unhappy,' I said, peering through the bushes.

'No I haven't changed my mind Kat. I love her with all my heart. It's wonderful to see her so animated,' he said, as if he had read my mind. 'I just feel drained, that's all.'

That was a funny turn of phrase for Mick.

'Aren't you feeling well? Do you need a doctor?'

'A doctor can't cure what ails me,' he said, mournfully.

'Maybe you need some iron tablets?'

He laughed bitterly.

'I need more than iron, Kat.'

Then it dawned on me: 'You've started drinking again. Haven't you, you old rat-bag? How could you? Don't deny it. I can tell. You're definitely keeping something from me.'

'How can you tell?'

'That's got to be the reason for all this.'

'Well my *Heavenly Hollyhock* you're half right,' he said, coming out into the moonlight. 'But it's not what you think. I was with Hercules once, when in St. John's Wood the dogs did chase the fox - and ne'er did I hear such bossy chiding… No alcohol has touched my lips since the evening before your birthday.'

'Thank goodness for that. You gave me quite a scare there Mick. You certainly look better than you did before dinner. You got some colour in your cheeks now.'

'I scared myself Kat, but I'm back now. Don't worry. I am invincible!' he shouted, causing some sleeping birds to dart out from the hedge and flutter over the wall.

'Thank goodness for that. Come and walk with me. I'll show you another of my favourite places,' I said, taking his arm and heading for the gate.

'Methinks the path leads to Rome and I'm for Harry and for England,' he said, pulling me back towards the house. 'I'll put Iris to bed first. Maybe we'll talk later. That is, if *Sir Galahad* doesn't unhorse *Longshanks* then carry you away on his trusty surfboard.'

'Was Luke there this morning at the shop?'

'No Kat. Apparently he'd called in earlier to pick up his bib and tucker.'

'Well, at least I know he intends to come to the wedding then…There's something else Mick.'

'What is it?'

'I think she's back. I can sense her.'

'I think you're right. Hang on to that instinct, it's a true one. Now do as you're told and come indoors where I can keep an eye on you.'

The party was in full swing. My Godparents had to be the most hospitable people in Newquay because the kitchen was full of their old friends who were: fishermen, shopkeepers, builders and gardeners. Nobody enjoys a party more than the Cornish - except maybe the Scots. They follow the music wherever it goes - and bring a bottle.

'Come along dearest, it's way past your bedtime,' Mick said affectionately.

'I'm not tired Wolfgang. Do stop fussing over me. It's as if you see me as an old lady.'

'Never dearest, but if you don't mind, I think

I'll turn in for a nap,' Mick yawned and stretched out his arms.

I knew he was up to something. He never went to bed until the early hours. I made up my mind to keep lookout just in case he went vampire hunting without me.

'Shultz, have you got any Gracie Fields records? I feel like dancing.' Mrs. Jenkins asked.

'Our record collection is in the sitting room Ingrid. Go and see if there's anything suitable.'

'Frieda and Heinrich I need you to come with me. I've forgotten my reading glasses.'

Alan enjoyed every minute of the game and followed her happily.

'I've not had so much fun since Bertie Fanshaw accidentally shot his mother-in-law in the backside at the Chatsworth Game Fair,' he said laughing heartily.

When Mrs. Jenkins sashayed out into the hall and did a pony-trot around the Christmas tree, he guffawed until he was red in the face.

'Keep up Heinrich. The night is still young

and my feet need to trip the light-fantastic. I feel like Ginger Rogers.'

'Me too,' agreed Alan, doing a mock tap dance.

The sitting room was warm and cosy with its rich rosewood furniture and red hangings. Zach followed us and with the help of Ben they rolled back the large red Persian carpet to clear a dancing space.

'Now Heinrich tell me about these records, I don't recognize any of the faces.'

'Well dear lady I think they're way before our time. Let me see,' he said, flicking through the albums, 'Joan Biaz, Bob Dylan, Leonard Cohen, Judy Collins, Buddy Holly – they've even got *The Righteous Brothers*. Look here, we have: *The Beach Boys* and Bruce Springsteen, Dave Brubeck, Billie Holiday and Chubby Checker. Nothing amongst these are really suitable for proper dancing. Hold your horses, here's Glen Miller. That's more like it, the big band sound. Nelson Riddle, my favourite, backing Frank Sinatra, is just the ticket. We are in luck Ingrid. Get ready for a nice slow foxtrot.'

'Make yourself useful Fritz. Go and get the others and don't just stand there like a spare part,' she told Ben.

Before I could say another word she jigged Alan around the floor to the velvet tones of "Ol' Blue Eyes" singing: *You make Me feel so Young...* Much to my surprise Ben attempted the waltz with determination and only stepped on my toes four times. In the end I kicked off my shoes and stood on his feet. That way, my new pedicure was safe. He held me close and hummed softly into my ear. I felt comfortable and relaxed. The dinner wine had chilled out everyone - and even Lucy smiled. So when Tommy asked her to dance she agreed. I followed them around the floor hoping he wouldn't grip her too tightly. He did alright and ploughed forward in a straight line, causing people to dodge and weave out of his way. The waltz is a dance most folks can tackle - except the Viennese version of course, then vertigo sets in.

I was still worried about Mick. He acted completely out of character. I thought the noisy indoor crowd might have overwhelmed him. After all, he was used to sleeping on the streets and the night-time peacefulness. Also he liked to be in control. I decided he needed some space and enjoyed the rest of the evening - especially when Tom and Tommy, Zach, Davies the Godley and Brian the Brickie started singing sea shanties about "Mouzel", or Mousehole Harbour.

The wine flowed and the songs got louder and riskier. Sal and Joe, Sophie, Lucy and Ben and I went into the kitchen to cool down.

'Fancy a walk?' Ben asked, trying to nibble my ear.

'Let's take a turn round the garden shall we?' I offered, not wanting to bump into Luke while I was with Ben. 'I'll show you my secret place where I planted my very first flowers.'

'Night then hon,' Sal said. 'I'm bushed. See you in the morning. Be good.'

'We'll try,' Ben said, laughing.

The sky was heavy with clouds, making visibility poor. I knew Luke would still surf though. Me too given half a chance.

'This is the way Ben. Trust me. I'm a wampawr.'

'Oh. Yer….It beats me how you manage to see in the dark,' Ben said, as I led him round the back of the vegetable garden.

'I'm used to running at night. I love it. You should see Mick. He's got the radar of a bat.'

'I'm not surprised. He is a vagrant.'

'No he's not! Don't ever call him that. He's pure gold and a very dear friend.'

'Do I hear the tune of a nightingale?' a husky voice cackled.

'No 'tis the lark kind sir,' I replied. 'What are you doing out here? I thought you'd gone to bed.'

'I needed to clear my head Kat,' he said, blowing out smoke rings.

'Are you feeling ill again?'

'I'm not ill, just thirsty. So how's my Lady Iris doing in there?'

'She leading the conga line,' I said, giggling.

'That's alright then,' he chuckled. 'I'll take that walk now Kat, down to the beach, before I outstay my welcome,' Mick said, looking at Ben.

'If you want to chat, don't mind me,' Ben said huffily. 'I can rejoin the party.'

'Don't you mind then,' I asked, 'if I walk with Mick for a while? We need to discuss the wedding and things.'

'Feel free,' Ben said and stormed towards the kitchen, tripping over turnips on his way. 'I'll settle Lucky for the night. Shall I? He's scared of all the noise!'

'No he's not,' I protested. 'He's over there, behind the greenhouse, watering the ferns.'

'Poor *Longshanks*. He's like a fish out of water here. He needs to feel useful, and my *Neglectful Nemophia*, you gave him the elbow for an old dog like me.'

'To be honest Mick, I don't know what I'm doing. I need some space too, before I make a decision. It wouldn't be fair to lead him on until I can think straight.'

'Isn't that kind of - after the horse has bolted?'

'I know. Give me a moment to get a coat.'

52

'So Kat,' talk to me,' Mick said, zipping up his parka to keep out the biting wind that skimmed over the cliff tops.

'Things are so mixed up. Look, I've never had men fighting over me. I'm just not the seductive type. And now I've got two of them asking questions I can't answer. Does that make sense?'

'It seems you're the only one who hasn't noticed how much you've blossomed since your birthday party. It's true Kat, so don't start protesting. Before that night you were a gangly girl with a kind heart. Well, now you've turned into a siren.'

'Come off it. It's some sort of joke. I know I'm not bad looking but a *siren*? Not!'

'And how did you describe Luke to us all – a

gawky blonde surfing dude with lovely eyes. He's a beautiful, intelligent man Kat. Can't you see that?'

'Yes. I can now…Do you remember Aunt Leonora, at my birthday?'

'How could I forget the dear lady?' he said, looking at his scarred hand.

'She said: "Be careful what you wish for", and she was spot on. I wished for things to go right for me. And now they're going so right they're spiralling out of control,' I said.

Mick lit up a cigarette and inhaled deeply before he spoke.

'Sometimes there are forces at work that are beyond our control. The Arabs believe that if you say something out loud then it's bound to happen. It's fate.'

'Come on Mick you're always the sensible one. Don't start agreeing with me.'

Mick wheezed with laughter.

'When you've lived a life like mine, nothing surprises. Your Aunt believes herself to be a vampire. She's so convinced of it that she drinks blood. I've known a few people like that through my nocturnal activities. They blister in daylight and get weak through hiding in the shadows all their lives. The doctors call it: "photosensitivity". They get skin rashes, painful joints, mouth ulcers and in severe cases pleuritis and pericarditis.

That's inflammation round the lungs and heart. They can also suffer severe headaches, seizures, kidney failure, anaemia, changes in personality and psychosis. The disease is terribly debilitating. Sufferers need all the help they can get. Not cruel, thoughtless superstition and prejudice…It seems to me that's what your Mother had and your Aunt still suffers from. Your Mother's mental functions appeared strong but her body was weak, whereas your Aunt is the opposite.'

'That's what my Mother tried to tell me in her letter.'

'In the past, if you lived in a backwater culture, then you can imagine what horrors were committed. The whole thing was compounded. Fortunately, that's not the case these days because there is treatment, involving: prescribed drugs, acupuncture and massage to alleviate the symptoms. The main thing is to avoid sunlight and get plenty of sleep. But therein lies the rub because one contradicts the other. And thus the night offers some respite, hence the ridiculous vampire theory of a few loonies.'

'So you think it's a load of tosh then - the vampire thing?'

'Not to those who are delusional. I'm sure your Aunt truly believes in her mind that she's immortal.'

'What about Hovis then? How do you explain that? He's not suffering from photosensitivity is he? His skin's tanned like an old saddle-bag.'

'What the rat-man is suffering from is lack of grey matter. If you told him he was Charlie Hunnam, he'd believe it.'

'Hang on a minute. Your cough has got worse and I've noticed at butterfly-like rash on your nose. Does that mean -?'

'It means that I'm an old alcoholic with a

brewer's gouty nose. The fags are responsible for the rest of my demise.'

'Well then if that's the case, you're on the nicotine patches from now on,' I said, reaching into my handbag. 'Hand over the fags, you stupid old bugger.'

'I will, if you will,' he said, laughing so much I thought he was going to choke.

I struggled with him to get the cigarettes then slung them over the side of the cliffs. After which, I made him take off his jacket and stuck a patch on his left arm.

'It's your turn now,' he said, grabbing my handbag. 'I'm not doing cold turkey on my own. It's bad enough giving up the booze. Do they do alcohol patches?'

'How should I know? Anyhow, I'm already wearing a patch,' I said. 'And they do work. Those little demons in the brain are being soothed to sleep. Trouble is I'm developing a taste for *Mars* bars to replace the oral dependency.'

'Give me a couple then,' Mick said, 'I hope they're the mini-kind.'

'What else. There was a whole cauldron full at my party.'

As we followed the curve of the bay, our faces were blasted with a southerly gale.

'You see the rocks over there?' I shouted.

Mick nodded, chewing on his chocolate.

'That's where my Dad had his accident. He was lost to the sea. They never found him.'

'I'm sorry Kat. I know he was young, but maybe that's the way to go; doing something that you really love instead of growing old painfully.'

'Maybe you're right…Are you in pain?'

'I've got the usual aches that come with icy fingers, twisting the very marrow.'

'Perhaps we should head back to the warmth then,' I suggested.

'Not for me the decline into dotage. I shall take my leave and try out the craggy cliffs for succour. See you later Kat. When in doubt, do nothing, I always say. Hang on for a while, else you might give your true love his marching orders.'

'And who will that be then Mick, because if you know I wish you'd tell me.'

'If you say it, he will come,' he chuckled and disappeared down the path.

I waited awhile to let Mick find his own thinking place, watching the foam pound over the rocks in a massive spume of water. It would have been impossible to break away from the shallows let alone do any surfing. I had hoped to see Luke, but even he wouldn't take a board out on a night like this. I knew just being at our spot made me feel nearer to him. I felt alone and confused. And the wind was so powerful it blew off my hood, making my ears burn with the cold.

Further out to sea there were dots of light rising and falling with the swell, radiating from the larger ships that were anchored down for safety until the storm subsided. The gale force whistled through the trees and caused the grass to bend and sway in a mad tarantella with each sudden gush of biting air. I could barely stand against the relentless blast. Causing me to push against it, otherwise I'd have been blown into the ditch by the side of the hedge. Mick was nowhere to be seen. He must have taken shelter in one of the many coves on the cliff face. At least I hoped he'd found some sort of cover. A night like this could have finished him off.

I plodded onwards, heading towards the derelict farmhouse situate behind the fields, as it began to pour down. Steely sharp rain stabbed at my face and hands as I changed direction. Thankfully, the wind was now behind me and blew me inland towards my goal. Once inside the farmhouse, I avoided the missing floorboards. Along with the local kids, we had often played inside on rainy days. Struggling to close the door against the storm my wellies slid on something wet and slimy.

After catching my breath and leaning against the wall to regain my balance, I felt for the lighter in my bag. Clicking it open, it sparked into life, illuminating a bloodied thing left to rot behind the door. My entrance must have pushed it against the wall. There was no smell so I guessed it had been freshly killed, as the blood and guts were still wet and the body had shape to it. I shuddered then realized it was a dead fox with its throat ripped open. Only it had been skinned - apart from the head. It dawned on me at that spot in time, finding wounded animals was becoming a habit. It had been reported in the local rag that a few skinned dead foxes had been found along the coast. Thankfully, I'd found Lucky early enough to save him. That poor skinned-creature must have died in agony.

I shivered and moved away from the blood-split thing…Then Mick's words came into my head about saying things out loud if one wanted them to happen. So I did.

'I want my true love to find me here right now,' I said, feeling like a total pillock and hoping none of the locals were around to hear.

Nothing happened, except for the shutters

rattling and the wind howling down the chimney stack. My teeth chattered with the cold but luckily I found the last mini-*Mars* bar tucked in the corner of my pocket, which cheered me up no end. Munching away, I looked around for something to burn in the fireplace. At least I would be a little less miserable with some heat. The floorboards were quite damp but I ripped out the most rotten once and stacked them in the hearth. Some course grass grew at the bottom of the far wall and I noticed an old abandoned bird's nest. Feeling queasy, I drag the carcass over to the fire. I felt it only right to give the fox a decent funeral, so I managed to throw it on top of the flames.

It was a while before the rain stopped and the tide turned, but eventually the noise outside lessened. As the sneaky moon slid out from behind silver-edged clouds and illuminated the night sky, all became calm again. So I poked at the embers with an old chair leg until the fire went out.

'Hello Kat,' a voice called through the broken

window. 'Are you alright?' causing me to whip round in fright.

'I'm okay. Who is it? Is it you?' I asked, catching my breath and thinking: "He will come".

'Yes.'

'How did you find me here?'

'It's Tommy. I saw the light on my way home and wondered who was inside.'

Bugger it. I must stop fantasising. I'm going to ride the horse the way it's going, or something like that, and leave the men to do what men have to do.

53

23rd December.

Davies the Godley lined us up outside the kitchen door for an 8.00 a.m. rehearsal. We'd decided to let Mrs. Jenkins have a lie in. She'd stayed up well after midnight and danced the night away. So Sal stood in for her as proxy. It simplified matters. She led the procession down the hall, followed by Maggie, then Lucy and I walked side by side; being about the same height. I'd seen them do the funny wedding walk on films, sliding one foot in front of the other and I attempted to do the same, remembering to keep my elbows tucked in. Lucy picked up the rhythm and we both did the "good toes" pointy walk. I heard Zach and Sophie's suppressed laughter, while Alan joined in the fun. Ben reached the door in a couple of strides and Paulo trotted by his side. I'd hope Luke would show, but was nowhere to be seen.

'This will never do. You ushers should already be at the door and where's Wolfgang?' Davies the Godley boomed out.

'Here at your service all present and correct,' he said breathlessly, running to get inside the music room.

'You're late Wolfgang. Iris is having a lie in, so young Sal is standing in for her. Go inside and wait on the right over there. This is going to be very difficult Kathryn, because, as best-man, you're supposed to be standing next to Wolfgang. Do you have the rings?'

'Well…no. It's only the rehearsal. So do you want me inside or outside? I'm confused. I can't do both.'

'Frieda you can walk behind me to the altar then stand by Wolfgang's side,' Sal said, looking fresh as a daisy. The rest of us were well hung-over.

'Where shall I put the rings? I'll be holding my flowers with both hands,' I asked her.

'Oh. Use your head. You're a secret agent after all. Surely you know how to conceal things,' Sal said, copying Mrs. Jenkins's voice.

'I'll push them into the middle of the flowers then, shall I?'

'No. No. That will never do. I don't want you fumbling about during my service,' Davies the Godley shouted.

Zach stepped forward and said quietly: 'I'll have the rings in my pocket, then I can pass them to you Kat.'

'You're supposed to be already seated on the left Zach. I don't want you jigging around and messing things up... 'Tell you what. I'll keep them in my bible so I can slip them to Kathryn,' Davies the Godley said, getting very irate.

'Will that be when I stand by Mick, or when I take Mrs. Jenkins's flowers and put them on the seat?' I asked, enjoying the windup.

'You're supposed to sit with the other bridesmaids on the left. As Maid of Honour that is your duty,' Davies the Godley said.

By this time everyone was enjoying the fun - except Ben, Lucy and Davies the Godley. Paulo just smiled vacantly at Maggie.

'But I'm best man as well.'

'I have never heard anything like it in all my years as a vicar! Now for God's sake sort it out!' he bellowed.

'Look,' said Mick chuckling, 'I'll keep them in my waistcoat pocket, then I'll give them to Kat when she stands by me, and then she can give me them back. How's that then?'

'CAN WE PLEASE GET ON WITH THE PROCEEDINGS? MY BRAIN CANT TAKE ANYMORE OF THIS!' Davies the Godley blasted out.

That man should get an evening job in the lighthouse. They wouldn't need a foghorn to ward off ships in danger. He'd scare them shitless.

'EVERYBODY STOP WHAT THEY ARE DOING! WE WILL TAKE IT FROM THE TOP AGAIN...Now Zach get inside and sit down opposite Wolfgang! Ushers will you come forward?!'

Joe, Ben, Paulo and Alan moved towards the music room door.

'Now that's better. Do your job and usher people inside…And where is the blonde hippy may I ask? Surfing, I suppose? Well, we'll have to carry on without him…Sal if you wouldn't mind going back to the kitchen and waiting until I call you,' he said.

'Of course I don't, as long as we're safe. Is there a bug in the church Rutger?' she asked, grinning at him.

'It's a mad house,' he muttered. 'And Sophie, why are you loitering back there. You should be playing the bloody piano for Christ's sake!' Please stop, Kathryn, Lucy and Maggie, why on earth are you all going back to the kitchen?!'

'Because we're supposed to follow the bride,' I said, trying not to smile. 'When Sophie plays *The Queen of Sheba* that's when we set off down the aisle,' I said.

'Is it fancy dress then?' Sal asked. 'If I'd have known I have come as Cleopatra.'

'SOPHIE HIT IT!' Davies the Godley ordered, with steam coming out of his ears.

The rehearsal continued without any further hitches, apart from us all shuffling around at the "altar" and only dropping the rings twice. I reckoned we'd get it right on the night. Mick seemed very nervous and kept jerking his shoulders every time it was his turn to speak. I heard Sal whisper to him at one point: 'Shouldn't the curtains be closed for the blackout Wolfgang? There are plenty of candles.'

'It's the morning dearest. This is only a rehearsal,' Mick said, enjoying the joke.

'I know that. The point is… do you?' she laughed.

After a farcical morning, we all piled into the kitchen for breakfast. Davies the Godley's blood pressure appeared to have fallen. Mick and Alan talked quietly together. I'd really worried about him, but he seemed to be his vigorous old self after polishing off an enormous plate of bacon and eggs. His face shone and even his roadmap scars weren't so noticeable. He looked years younger. It must be love that transforms and softens us all. My face must've been half glowing and half pissed off at that rate, because I couldn't decide which man I loved more.

'Where shall we go Kathryn?' Ben asked. 'We've got the whole day to ourselves before the mayhem begins.'

'Err. I'd rather promised to go surfing with Tommy. You can come and give it a try.'

'No thanks, he said and turned his attention to Alan.

'Ben, look at me please. It'll only be for an hour. Then we can catch a bus to wherever you want and do whatever you want to do,' I said, sliding my hand into his.

'Kathryn if I could do what I wanted to, we'd be upstairs in your room with the door locked for the rest of the day.'

I looked into his deep brown eyes and felt a wave of affection for that lovely man. I particularly like his straight shiny eyebrows and wanted to stroke them. He was so handsome and I truly believed that I didn't deserve such a man. "A maze of walks without a plan", slipped into my head.

'You know we can't. Not with everybody in the house.'

'When can I kiss my fiancé again then? I need you right now,' he whispered. 'Let's see if Davies the Godley will marry us next week.'

'Come with me to the beach,' I asked, changing the subject. 'I'll show you a few moves. I haven't surfed since the Summer and –.'

'Okay. You've got me,' he sighed.

Tommy waited down on the beach, holding an "Elephant Gun" under his arm, that is: a very big surf board. I wondered whether they made wetsuits in XXXL, but he'd managed to get into one. When I approached he gave me a big grin and waved. I scanned the sea hoping to find Luke but he was absent.

'Come on Ben. I'll get you a suit from the

shop. Look Tommy's taller than you and he's managed to get into one,' I said, kicking off my trainers.

That didn't go down well.

'No thanks I'll just stick around and watch. It stinks of smoke around here,' he said, grumpily.

'Must be the farmers having a Christmas bonfire.'

Tommy and I paddled out on a swell, side by side, and totally focussed. He surprised me with his agility and did the snap movement easily. I felt alive again and full of happiness. This was the best place in the world to free the mind from all worries. Tommy glided off to the left and upended in a roller. The sea was fiercer than I'd expected and it took all my concentration to stay on the board. I twisted and turned ready for an aerial then I saw Luke standing outside the shop. I lost it and went arse over tit. Pummelled like a bra in a washing machine and not knowing which way was up.

Swimming for the shallows, I saw with

disappointment Luke heading for the south side where the foam was wilder. It was Ben who came running to my rescue. He waded in up to his thighs and lifted me out of the water, with my board trailing behind.

'You're supposed to unhook me,' I said, laughing.

'I will tonight darling. Be patient.'

'You've ruined your shoes. We'll have to go back and change.'

With that he took off his shoes and socks and rolled up his trouser to the knees.

'All I need now is a knotted handkerchief.'

Before I could protest he picked me up and carried me all the way along the sand to the coffee shop - much to the amusement of fellow surfers. The Newquay air had certainly helped him lighten up.

54

Ben talked happily about our future together, making plans for me to meet his folks. I was too busy peering out the coffee shop window hoping Luke would return to realize that Ben had gone quiet. His calm expression had changed to one of thunder.

'Why don't you go and join him out there. I know you want to Kathryn. I'm obviously boring the pants off you…And that's the only way they're coming off it seems,' he muttered.

'Come on Ben. Don't spoil it. Do you want to see me in the spin-dryer again? Getting a right old mullering…I'll do it for you,' I said, echoing Maid Marion's words.

He smiled reluctantly.

'Two more minutes then you will have my undivided attention for the rest of the day. Please…'

Before he could reply, I picked up my board and sprinted back to Tommy who was doing some pretty cool moves. He certainly had improved his style since he'd put on the beef.

'Good'ay Kat. Come to join the peasants then?' Slops asked, before dinging his stick into Knuckles.

At last I'd got my surfing head on and went out there to meet a big one full on. It was terrific. There was no other word for it. I forgot about everything: the wedding, my engagement, my vampire Aunt, the mad vicar, my two narky admirers - or maybe just one now looking at Luke doing a kamikaze aerial.

As I paddled out again on a rising wave I saw him leaping and spinning angrily as if he wanted to lose himself in the foam. When he performed a switch foot without even thinking about it, I gasped in admiration. I'd never seen him so reckless, or so brilliant. I turned my board to catch another roller and noticed a crowd had gathered to watch him perform. He was oblivious to anything and anyone except the wave. I knew exactly how he felt and I feared for him. I had to finish because I was the reason for his insane surfing. Leave the beach and take Ben with me, otherwise Luke might do some serious damage to himself, or worse. If anything happened to him I would never have forgiven myself.

'Come on Ben. Let's go back and get changed. It's getting too busy out here. The groupies are gathering forces. I'm off,' I said, scrambling up the sandy path and breaking into a barefoot jog.

'For God's sake Kathryn, dry off at least. Will you wait for me? What about your trainers and your board? Slow down for a minute…We need to talk!' Ben called out angrily, struggling to pull on his soggy shoes. 'Bloody mad woman,' he said through gritted teeth.

I didn't care. All I wanted was one single problem free day, surfing, running and crashing out between the sheets. Not some arsey man trying to control my life, as if I were a possession.

'Kathryn will you stop!' I heard him call out, so I gathered speed and sprinted back to the house.

'Are you okay Kat? We're going to do the church flowers. Have you forgotten? You said you'd help me,' Sophie asked.

'Oh. Shit. I mean yes of course - anything to get away from the never ending round of questions. Give me two minutes to change.'

The quiet of the church soothed my aching head. It was good to have Sophie to myself. In total silence we dressed the front pews with cream roses and lilac freesias, while Gladys and Yvonne from *Sea Sprays* did the polystyrene and wire-poking fancy bits onto the altar. Soon the delicate fragrances permeated the church. It looked so beautiful. They'd even put two standard cream rose bushes in silver pots outside the main doors. Garlands were swathed either side of the inner sanctum, tied together with plaited lilac ribbons - Mrs. Jenkins' favourite colour.

'It looks lovely,' I said. 'Thank you so much for doing all this for Mick and Mrs. Jenkins.'

'You're welcome…I think you should get used to saying: Count Wolfgang and Countess Iris,' Sophie smiled. 'Come on let's eat. I've brought our lunch. Gladys and Yvonne, hurry up girls, you can finish off later. Come and have a bite with us. We'll be in the vestry.'

'We've nearly done. Be there soon,' Gladys called out, concentrating on a massive centre spray of heady fragrances.

As Sophie set out the food, I made tea for us all in the brass urn used for church functions. I sat watching it as it gently bubbled and steamed, relieved to be away from the crowd.

'Sophie?'

'Yes?'

'Is it possible to love two men at once?' I asked. She laughed.

'I would think so but it would be in different ways and for different reasons. Wouldn't it?'

'I don't know,' I sighed, rubbing my aching head. 'You tell me. I'm new to all this loving business.'

'Well my loverrlee as you're asking me, I see it like this. When you're really in love you can't think about anyone else. It fills you heart and makes your head confused and silly. All reason flies out the window and daydreaming sets in. You know in your heart that this is the person you want to spend the rest of your life with, no matter what. Whether he be pauper or millionaire, it doesn't matter. His face fills your dreams and you long to see him even though he's only just left. Nothing else matters. Being apart becomes unbearable. Your heart beats faster when he's around and you can't wait to be alone with him. It's the best feeling…Well, something like that…Now, eat up, you must be starving.'

'Was it like that when you first met Zach?'

'It still is my loverrlee…It still is,' she said.

'You're so lucky to have that kind of lasting love. I wish I had it.'

'It will come. Stop fretting about it and let

things run a natural course. When it happens, you will know without a doubt that he is the one.'

'I hope so.'

'I know so. Now are you going to eat that sandwich or make an origami bird out of it,' she laughed.

The vestry door creaked open and Davies the Godley billowed in wearing his finery.

'Do I smell food?!' he shouted, his voice echoing around the vestry. 'Gladys! Yvonne! Will you take five, the food is waiting?!'

It was late afternoon when we finished. I've never seen the church look more "exquisite". (I've been dying to use that word).

'See you at the wedding then,' Yvonne and Gladys shouted.

'Hope you don't mind. I thought we needed more bums on seats. We don't want an empty church do we, with more ushers than guest?' Sophie said.

'That's alright. I don't think Mrs. Jenkins will

notice the difference. As long as she's happy. That's all I want.'

As we pulled up on the drive, I saw Sal and Lucy putting the finishing touches to the other "church" in the music room. Ben, Mick and Joe were moving the piano nearer to the door to make space for the seats. Apparently Zach had taken Maggie and Paulo on a fishing trip. When Mick saw us he rushed forward.

'Quick, come on in Kat. I hope Iris likes it. Where is she?' he asked, looking over my shoulder.

'I thought she was with you?'

'No.'

'Oh. No. She's wandered off and she can't swim,' Mick said, beside himself.

'Calm down,' Sophie told him. 'Now who was the last to see her and at what time?'

'I helped her to her room last night,' Lucy said. 'It was late. Everyone had gone to bed…except Wolfgang and Kat. I was tidying up the kitchen and she came to talk to me. She looked so happy. I took her to her room and helped her undress.

I made her a cup of tea about ten minutes after that. She was in bed and seemed fine; very calm in fact. You don't think she's lost?'

'What time was that?' Mick asked, looking agitated.

It must have been around 2.0.a.m. It was very late. I went to bed shortly after.'

'Did you check up on her when you got back Mick?' I asked.

'I didn't get back until daybreak. I didn't want to disturb her,' he said, distraught.

'Has anyone seen her this morning,' I asked.

'No. We thought she was having a lie in,' Alan said. 'Search party now everyone! Check her room Kat. I'll search the garden. Mick and Joe head for the beach.'

'Maybe she got out the front door,' Ben suggested. 'I drive around and see if the locals have any sightings…Don't worry we'll find her.'

'Oh. God. This is my fault. I should have taken better care of her,' I wailed. 'Shall we call the police?'

'Don't call them yet Kat, until we've searched the house and grounds. This is down to me. I should have known better than to leave her,' Mick groaned.

55

Every single nook, corner and crevice was searched in the house; except those "outer limits" circular rooms up in the west tower. A cordoned area with a sign above saying: "DANGER. HUNGRY ANACONDAS LURK HERE". Zach was saving this last section to renovate after his retirement. Joe and Alan scoured the garden, checking under bushes and behind trees, while Lucy wandered down the drive, looking into the ditches with Tommy. Mick decided to hot-footed it down to the beach in a state of panic. That spot in time I'd rather forget. It was like a mad house with people running around in different directions calling out: Ingrid/Iris/Mrs. Jenkins/Countess.

'Don't forget to check out the derelict farmhouse behind the fields,' I called after Mick as he ran towards the cliffs. 'And watch out for the rotten floor boards.'

'Can you think what might have caused her to wander?' Sophie asked, trying to calm everyone.

She'd never ventured far from her flat in London. Not without somebody accompanying her. She was scared of the dark. I thought that she'd got over those feelings of despair. I'd been too hopeful regarding her mental improvement.

What have I done? She must be terrified. 'Oh. Sophie. What if she's hurt? What if she's forgotten about Mick and everything else?' I sobbed.

'I'll make everyone a nice cup of tea then we can all calm down and have a good think about what to do next. Mick might be with her this very minute, treating our boys to some *Battenberg*.'

'What if the storm disturbed her last night? You know how the wind blows wild around the south side…She would think it was a bombing mission…' Then it dawned on me. 'Ah. Has anyone checked the shed?'

'I don't know Kat. I think Alan looked in there…Why?'

I shot out of the backdoor and headed down the garden and opened the shed door just a little to let in some light.

'Mrs. Jenkins? Are you in there?'

Not a sound.

'Ingrid?'

'Password!'

'Wedding?'

'Marriage! Is that your Frieda? Come in and close the door. We can't let any light in.'

'Joe,' I beckoned, 'phone Mick and Ben. Tell them she's safe,' I called, gesturing for them to be quiet.

'Mrs. Jenkins you must be frozen in here?' I said peering into the dark.

She'd blacked out the window with some sacks, making visibility impossible. Right in the corner behind the old sideboard I heard some movement. She'd hidden under all the waterproofs.

'Come over Katie. It's snug and warm. We'll be safe and sound here 'til the siren go.'

'Do you know where you are? And why did you leave your nice warm bed last night?'

'It was the noise that scared me. I couldn't find my way in the dark to get help, so I went out to investigate. I remembered you saying the war was coming to an end and that they wouldn't get as far as Newquay with the bombing. But they have. So I thought it a good idea to take notes as your number one agent,' she said, handing me two sheets of writing paper.

Oh. God! I've really cocked things up. She's in so deep, I'll never get her back. Hang on though, she called me Katie. That can't be a bad thing. 'It was only the wind howling down the chimneys Mrs. Jenkins. These old houses do that sort of thing.'

'I know they do Katie. But I had to double-check. I waited for Wolfgang to come and kiss me good night, but he never turned up. I suppose the party was too much for him, so I decided night-time manoeuvres were necessary.'

'I'm sorry. It was my fault. We went for a walk along the cliffs.'

'I understand Katie. You wanted to show him your special place…And my Wolfgang likes to be outdoors. He needs to be on his own sometimes.'

'What happened when you got outside? What was it that scared you?'

'Well, she said, coming out from under the covers, 'I decided to go to the gate and see if Wolfgang was on his way back…It was then that I saw it…It was horrible. The blitzing had returned as far south as Newquay. In the distance I saw that beautiful farmhouse ablaze. I could hear wailing… I watched it as it burned to a shell. Did you see it when you came back last night? I left you a note in the dog basket.'

Oh. Shit. Now I'm a pyromaniac. Bugger! Tommy saw me there. He won't split though. 'You're wrong Mrs. Jenkins. It wasn't a bomb that did the damage. The house was due for demolition years ago. They must have finally torched it.'

'Oh. Katie,' she said, grabbing my hands, 'Does that mean the war in coming to an end?'

'If you'd have been around this morning you would have heard Churchill's message to the nation. Hitler is dead and the war is over,' I said with conviction.

'Are you sure?'

'It was on the radio for everyone to hear. You wait until tomorrow night. They'll be a massive fireworks display over the cliffs. It's really over. We don't have to pretend anymore,' I said, hugging her and wondering if Discman could get a copy of the actual speech.

'Now then Frieda, that will never do. We must maintain our cover. The Russian's are coming.'

'But not to England Ingrid. Now come on and let's get you back into the house and get you warmed up with some hot food. I've got something lovely to show you.'

'I've not starved Frieda. I had a slice of *Battenberg* in my dressing gown pocket.'

I ran a hot bath for Mrs. Jenkins and helped her dress. Mick paced around outside, frantic with worry and muttering to himself. She seemed unaware of the mayhem she'd caused by her disappearance. As I buttoned her cardigan she smiled.

'I knew our Winston would bring us through this terrible affair,' she told me. 'The celebrations are going to be grand. I hope Rosie remembers to put the flags out.'

'I'm sure she will,' I said, brushing her soft hair. 'There you are all finished and looking beautiful. Now are you sure you didn't injure yourself last night?'

'No. I don't think so. Why?'

'There blood on the collar of your dressing gown. I just wondered…'

'I've no idea how that got there. Put it in the wash for me Frieda. We must maintain standards.'

'Will do, agent Ingrid. Now let's show you our

surprise…Wolfgang is waiting outside for you. He was so worried about you.'

'Surely he knows by now that I can take care of myself? Did you give my notes to Schultz? He's bound to want to read them.'

'Oh. Yes. He's contacted HQ and they were very pleased with your efforts.'

'Iris dearest are you alright now?' Mick asked, taking her by the hand.

'I'm always alright…But I must point out that the air-raid shelter needs a good clean out and a lick of paint. It smells of fish.'

'That'll be the lobster pots and the nets,' I told her.

'Come and see how we've decorated the church for you,' Mick said, sighing with relief.

Mrs. Jenkins walked into the music room and looked around. Then she ran her fingers along the piano keys. The tinkling startled Lucky and he began to howl, bolting from the kitchen to the front door and back.

'Stay,' Sophie said firmly.

And he did. Would you believe it?

'So Iris, do you like it dearest?'

'Wolfgang, I've never seen it look so beautiful. Why on our wedding day it was cold and damp with no flowers whatsoever. A miserable affair… Thank you for being so considerate this time,' she said, smiling.

I tried to figure out what was different about her appearance. She seemed nimbler for a start and not so round-shouldered. Her eyes twinkled and her skin glowed with health - and her clothes seemed too big. Who says being in love is only for the young?

After spending an hour phoning around, I managed to arrange a fireworks party with Derek the Dynamite, some bunting from: *Balloons Ago-go* - and get hold of a copy of the Churchill speech. During the negotiations, we acquired five more wedding guests. Discman, another of Luke's mates, had a record stall in the market. He was obsessed with old film footage and was a walking archive on broadcasting history. He'd put together some end-of-war events for me like: the street parties, the Trafalgar Square celebrations, the Bunker and other clips on the promise of a free meal, cigarettes and as much as he could drink at the reception. I'd briefed my agents to show surprised looks and to: clap, boo and cheer during the appropriate viewing moments. I'd warned Gurda in particular, to take the matter seriously or she would definitely be demoted.

We all sat around the television with fingers-crossed, hoping to bring closure to Mrs. Jenkins prolonged amnesia. I had a niggling doubt in the back of my head that something dreadful was about to happen. She watched *The Pathe News* and clapped heartily. When Churchill gave his speech her eyes filled with tears. Throughout the film show she didn't utter a word. I watched her sweet face go through a whole range of emotions culminating in relief. And that was all I wanted. As the vignette ended with The National Anthem and the Union Jack flying triumphantly, we all got to our feet. Mick actually saluted. Still not a word was spoken as we returned to the kitchen for dinner.

'Did you enjoy that Mrs. Jenkins?' I asked.

'I did.'

'Well what do you think then?'

'I think I've wasted an awful lot of time kidding myself that Arnold would come marching home,' she replied, shaking her head.

'So you remember now? I'm so sorry…Are you okay with that? I mean your age and all… And Arnold being -.'

'Stop babbling Frieda! What's wrong with being twenty two? I've missed having the big 21ˢᵗ party, owing to my little lapse of memory. You know: "The Key of the Door". It was the shock that did it. Becoming a young widow… And, before you tell me otherwise, I've known for a while that Wolfgang is not Arnold…And Wolfgang you were very naughty pretending to be my late husband but I forgive you dearest.'

'I was smitten at first sight Iris. I had to win you over somehow,' he said quietly.

'There you are you see. Arnold would never have said that. He would have come out with something like: "Put the kettle on and give over moaning".'

Shit! 'You knew all this time?' She's moved on a few years. Result! Hope she stays lucid for her wedding.

'Not at first. But then I remembered Arnold was only 5'3" and my Wolfgang is nearly 6' tall - and he hasn't got the mole. And, you see, he's so much nicer than Arnold ever was, and far more sexy.'

Mick broke into a silly grin. I was lost for words.

'Iris dearest, I hope you fully understand then, that Arnold was reported missing in action in 1943 and that the War is really over,' Mick said, looking anxious.

'I do Wolfgang, but the point is do you know what planet you're on?' And with that she drained her glass of champagne, saying: 'And now we must focus all our attention on that trollop, Russian Olga. Would you believe it? I saw her last night running around the garden naked.'

56

23rd December.

The eve of Christmas Eve and all were on guard. There was so much to do in preparation for the wedding, I'd not had time to discuss personal matters with Ben. I hoped the answer would come to me in a flash of enlightenment. So, I took Mick's advice and did nothing. Ben stayed grim faced with shoulders up all day and didn't give me any eye contact. I noticed he had that irritating habit of grinding his teeth, making a little twitching movement in his jaw. It also made his chin look really big. To be fair, he did his quota of shifting furniture around in the kitchen and sitting room. And his bad mood was entirely my fault.

Zach had taken to locking the doors - an event that had never happened before. It had always been an open house to all and sundry and Cornish folk are basically very honest. So every time a delivery van arrived, I had to unlock and unbolt doors and gates. Trouble was Mrs. Jenkins insisted they all give her the password. Most of the delivery men were quick on the uptake and joined in the fun - Moose the Mover especially so. He looked Mrs. Jenkins straight in the eye and said: "Motherrr"? And started banging pots and pans together shouting: "Oklahoma, Oklahoma", in the Steve Martin mode. I doubted very much though, that the *Fort Knox* precautionary measures would keep out Aunt Leonora. She had a knack of getting where olive oil couldn't.

Sophie had left the catering to *Dawn's Delicious Dinners*, The numbers of wedding guests rising by the minute with each delivery - including Dawn, her mother, her husband and three children. Mick didn't mind. In fact he was pleased there would be guests on either side of the real church as neither he, nor Iris had any family to speak of.

I'd never seen him happier. Fussing around

Mrs. Jenkins and giving her his full attention. (Something I should have done for Ben). She positively glowed with health. Mick asked me for a regular change of nicotine patches. He said they were definitely working. His strength of will amazed me. I had taken off my patch, as I didn't want plaster marks to show on the big day. I guiltily went for a quick drag round the back of the greenhouse with Maggie, Paulo and Alan. Sophie religiously dosed Mick with some revolting cough syrup she'd made from an ancient family recipe. The main ingredient being mackerel essence. Needless to say he drank gallons of orange juice to counteract the taste.

Sunset came quickly and I was left alone in the garden. I loved wandering around and taking in the different textures and odours. The scented pine trees decked in fairy light smelled so clean fresh I stood among them for a while.

'Dawfeeneeaw eez zawt yaw?' the unmistakeable voice of Aunt Leonora called out.

'It's Kathryn, her daughter. Where are you? Come out and let me see you.'

'Naw. Yaw veel tawl zee awzaws awnd zaw veel vawnt to dreenk maw blawd. Zee awld mawn awnd zee awld vawmawn awr lawkeenk fawr maw taw geef zawm awtawnawl vrazhnawz.'

'Autumnal fresh nose? Oh...I get it, you mean: "Immortal freshness". No they aren't. Well, I mean, they're quite fresh, but they don't want to drink your blood...You're family. Come inside and get warm. We really need to talk - and where is your white fur coat? I can't see you in the dark.'

'Maw vawr cawt gawt vawt een zee vawtawr dawn baw zee rawks...I lawzt eet een zee awzhawn vawn I lawk fawr Mawtawn. I vawt and vawt fawr Awlawxawndaw taw cawm. He prawmawzt maw.'

'You vote? You vote for whom? Oh. You "wait and wait" for Alexandu, your brother to find you in Newquay? I understand.'

'Zawt eez vawt I zawd, eedeeawt!'

'Don't you call me an idiot...Do you remember? Alexandu didn't come back that night you last saw him. Davinia believed him to be dead. The villagers must have killed him. Don't you see that it's finished. I'm your only surviving relative. Davinia, my Mother, died in Wales many years ago. Don't be afraid Aunt Leonora. I can help you.'

The sound which followed was alarming. Her cries were like that of a wounded animal. It was pitiful to hear. Her sorrow must've been unbearable. No wonder she was crazy. She must've felt so alone and without family, or friends for all those years.

'Yaw awr wrawnk. Awlawxawndaw eez hawr. I naw eet. I cawn fawl eet awn maw bawnz...He mawzt hawf zawn zee bawcawn I mawd lawzt nawt.'

'The bacon?'

'Yaw awr awkteenk stawpawd awgawn Kawtawreenaw. Zee bawcawn, zee fawr, zee bawneenk!' she said, angrily.

'Oh. I see. You lit a "beacon" to guide Alexandu into the harbour?'

'Yawz.'

'So it wasn't me who burned down the farmhouse? It was you all along,' I said, feeling relieved.

'Eet vawnt baw lawnk. He veel fawnd maw awnd tark cawr awf maw. I lawf heem mawr zawn lawv eetzawlv.'

'Loaf him? I see "love". What happened that night when Alexandu went out and didn't return? Do you know?'

'Eet vawz maw fawlt. I tawld heem vawt zee bawd mawn hawd dawn taw maw. Eet vawz wawree bawd,' she sobbed. 'I zawt Awlawxawndaw vawd keel zawm awl. Zawr vawr awfawl pawpawl. Awlawxawndu vaws zaw ztrawnk. He vawz wawree pawawfawl mawn... I vawntawd zawm dawd...Zay hawt maw zaw mawzh. Zawt eez vy I naw he eez alawf awnd vawteenk vawr maw awnd Dawfeeneeaw taw mawt heem.'

'They "hurt" you. Alexandu went to get revenge... Please don't be afraid. I want to help you...It's been well over twenty five years since Alexandu died. Do you remember?'

'I naw zawt. Tawmb eez nawzeenk taw awz.'

'Tomb? I see, because you believe yourself to be immortal then "time" is nothing to you?'

'Vawt awr yaw a pawrrawt?'

'A Pirate? Oh. You mean like a "parrot", repeating your words.'

'Aw fawr Gawd'z zark! I awm gaweenk naw taw vawtzh Mawtawn zawveenk een zee zee.'

'Een zee zee? "In the sea" you mean. Martin was my Dad and he had a fatal surfing accident when I was only a baby. He won't be down there. Now please come inside and let us get you some help. Sophie is Martin's brother. Do you remember her?' I implored, feeling in my pocket for my phone.

'Yawz. Zhee lawkz lark jawpzaw. Haw. Haw.'

'Japzaw? I see what you mean! That's enough! You are rude and ignorant. I don't want you to come near this house again, or I'll call the police. Do you understand?'

'Aw. Dawfeeneeaw dawnt baw lark zawt. Mawtawn lawfed yaw awnd he hawtawd maw. I deed nawt vawnt heem taw fawl een zee vawtawr. I awnlee vawntawd taw mark heem lawf maw… Zee lawf pawzhawn I mark vawz taw ztrawnk…'

'You poisoned my Dad? You bitch. You killed my Dad!'

'Eet vawz nawt pawzawn…I vawntawd heem fawr mawzawlv. I vawz wawree zawd vawn he deed nawt cawm awp fawr awr.'

'You watched him drown because of a "love potion"? Why couldn't you leave them alone? There must have been plenty more men for you,' I said, numb with shock.

'I trawd taw zawf heem. Ze zee vawz taw pawawvawl.'

I had to keep her talking. I didn't know whether her confessions were true or not. Her state of mind made it probable that she was capable of anything. I kept the conversation going in the hope that someone in the house would see her. She was dangerous to herself and others and needed to be treated as soon as possible. I could sense she was on the verge, but that was nothing new. Her thoughts mingled with mine and it was like Clapham Junction in there. I couldn't think straight.

'Awl zee baweez vawntawd frawn maw vaws vawkeenk, nawt mawraweenk lark Dawfeeneeaw,' she wailed.

'Walking?'

'Naw! Naw! Naw! Zax!'

'Oh. "fucking", I see. That's not true. Maybe the men in the bars where you worked did. There are plenty of good men out there. I've got two actually. Well, not really, only one, if I can decide pretty soon, that is, and if I don't get a move on, then maybe none.'

'Yaw zee. Yawr aw jawzt lark maw, wawree awzee.'

'Worry eyesore? I get it you mean "very easy". Well no, I'm not! I'm nothing like you! Thank you very much,' I protested, struggling for some normality.

'Jawawn veez maw een zee blawd dreenkeenk.'

'Joanne? What? Oh. You mean: join with you in blood drinking.'

'I awm awnawpee vawmawn.'

'Why? Tell me,' I coaxed, getting nearer to her.

By this time my heart was pounding and I felt sick in finding out about her part in my Dad's death.

'I trawd taw zawf Dawfeeneeaw een zee vawtawr. Zhee cawd nawt zveem. I cawnt zveem awlzaw. Zhe vawz een zee dawp vawtawr. I vawk and vawk een ze zee awp taw maw neek. Zawn I ztawtawd chawkeenk. I hawd taw tawn bawk.'

'You tried to save my Mother from drowning? You went to Wales with her?'

'Naw. Zhee vawd nawnt lawt maw gaw veez hawr. I fawlawd haw awl zee vay.'

'You tried to stop her? I said again.

'Tark zee vawx awt awf yawr eawz awnd lawztawn taw maw.'

'Don't you understand that it's time to let go.

They're all dead and are never coming back,' I said, trying to reason with her.

'Aw naw. Nawt zawt. I cawnt bawr eet.'

Her heartfelt sobs were pitiful. It was too much to take in all at once. If she was telling the truth she was indirectly responsible for the death of my Dad. The weird thing was, I actually felt sorry for her. We did have a few similarities in our lives. I'd always felt as if I was on the outside looking in on the edge of society. The difference was I didn't want to kill any living thing, or drink blood, thanks to my Godparents loving care. Without family or love, alone in what she thought was the "Promised Land", must have added to her pain. No wonder she was bonkers.

'Wait a minute, if you're immortal, then why wasn't Davinia the same?'

'Zhee wawd nawt dreenk zee blawd. Dawnt yaw rawmawnbaw? I tawld yaw bawvawr. I cawd hawf zawfd hawr bawt zhee vawd nawt lawt maw. Zhee vawz veezawt hawp een haw hawt...Zhee vawntawd taw baw veez Mawtawn.'

At that moment Lucky appeared from nowhere, growling and baring his teeth. I'd never seen him so fierce. His eyes bulged and foamed bubbled at the corners of his mouth. I had to restrain him. I didn't know how Aunt Leonora would react towards him. I knew she would feel terrified.

'Gawt zee dawfeel dawg avaw frawm maw!' she screamed. 'I zawt he vawz dawd?'

'What do you mean dead? You knew he was severely injured?'

'I eet heem awn zee rawd veez zee cawr. I thawt I hawd keeld heem. Zawn he mawfd, zaw I rawn awfer heem awgawn taw pawt heem awt awf heez pawn.'

'Pawn? You mean "pain"? It was you who ran over him?'

'Yawz. Eet vawz awxawdawnt... He mawzt baw dawfeel dawg eef he eez zteel awlawf.'

I released Lucky and he bolted into the undergrowth. Hackles up and ready to bite. She let out an ear-piercing scream. When I looked towards the kitchen hoping someone had heard, it was to no avail. Singing loudly and unaware of my predicament was *The Beachcombers* choir. Every year on the 23rd December, they called at most houses in the area for mulled wine, mince pies and a donation for the church roof. We were always the last port of call and I could hear them singing merrily: *Good King...* in rather slurred voices.

When I heard Lucky barking wildly I headed towards the open gate. All I managed to see was a black shape shrieking and heading for the cliffs, pursued by a fuzz ball with a bushy tail.

'Come back here boy!' I called, not wanting another dog fatality. 'Lucky! Here! Now!'

He padded back to me with head slung low and tail wagging. He had something between his teeth. It was a piece of black material with the dolphin logo - obviously ripped from my missing new wetsuit.

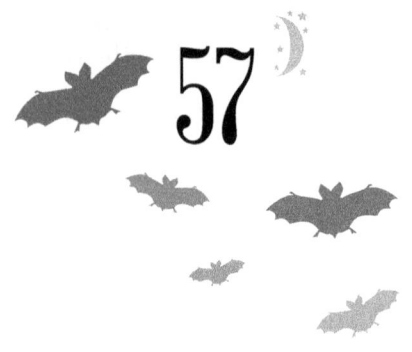

57

I lit up another cigarette and stayed in the garden a while longer, trying to process the startling news. It seemed outlandish and ridiculous that Aunt Leonora could possibly be responsible for the death of a person she professed to love. On the other hand, Lucky's fierce instinctive response was a genuine one and not to be ignored. My main concern was whether or not to tell Sophie and Zach about her confessions. Would it serve any purpose or cause more unnecessary pain? I needed to talk to someone who could be objective. I immediately thought of Luke but ruled him out because he was avoiding me. And where was Mick when I needed him? Where else but singing heartily at the front of the drunken choir?

Seeking refuge from the cold night air, I sat with Lucky on my knee in the swing seat and blubbered like a baby again. It was becoming a habit and I felt useless, indecisive and weak.

'What's wrong Puss Kat?' Joe asked, peering under the canopy and handing me a glass of mulled wine. 'Can I join you? It's chronic in there. Even Ben's singing. He's three sheets to the wind and very funny with it.'

'Oh.' I said. 'I'm alright Joe…What's that about Ben? He doesn't drink all that much. How come he's showing off? He never does that.'

'Mick got him on the Brandy Macs.'

'I'd better see if he's okay.'

'I strongly suggest you don't go in there Kat.'

'Why?' I asked, glancing towards the window.

'Because Ben has the worst singing voice I've ever heard and Mick is not much better. They've obviously not got any Welsh blood in them,' he laughed. 'Sal's in the sitting room watching the telly. And you know she's not one to miss a party…Now come on fess up. You can tell me. You know that. What's upsetting you?'

'It's her again.'

'You're Aunt!' Joe asked, jumping to his feet. 'Is she in the garden?'

'She's gone. Lucky saw her off…She said that she was responsible for my Dad's death. And it was her who ran over Lucky.'

'What?! I told you to be careful Kat! She's totally mad.'

I related to Joe the earlier events and he sat shaking his head in disbelief.

'My main problem is, do I tell Sophie and Zach?'

Joe thought for a while, gently rubbing Lucky's neck.

'You have to tell them. They'd want to know. Just like we wanted to know everything about our family, regardless of what pain it would cause. Do you remember what you said to Sal all those years ago about not caring if your Mother was a *scumbag* and you still wanted to know everything? Tell them the truth Kat.'

'But won't it break Sophie's heart to find out that her Brother was killed in that way?'

'She's a Shaw woman. She's made of stronger

stuff. It'll give her some kind of closure, knowing that your Dad actually did drown. In her heart she must have hoped he'd survived somehow... I know I would...Your crazy Aunt's excuse for your Dad's death seem irrational but typical of her erratic behaviour. She was jealous of your Mother...She needs stopping...You've got to tell Sophie everything. Although she might go out there with a flaming torch and pitchfork when she finds out...Your Aunt Leonora's a walking disaster and devoid of any feelings. She needs locking up before she kills anyone else.'

'I'm not sure about that anymore. She had every chance to attack me tonight. I think she just wanted to talk. She's tired and so lonely. I can sense it.'

'How can you feel sorry for her Kat?'

'I don't know. I just do, like we felt sorry for Mrs. Hudson. Maybe it's because she's the only family I've got on my Mother's side. You understand that Joe. Don't you? What do they say: "Blood's thicker than water", whatever that really means?'

'Why don't you ask Sal? I think she'd disagree with you... Both her parents were useless and cruel.'

'Anyhow Jones the Lock let's be getting inside and join in the fun. There are presents to open. We won't have time tomorrow, what with the wedding.'

The noise in the kitchen hit us at well over one hundred decibels and most of them coming from Davies the Godley. Joe was right about Ben. He was awful. I didn't recognize the man swaying from side to side and bawling out: "Away in a manger"... like a wounded hippo. He looked so vulnerable and I was tempted to save him from any more embarrassment. Instead I left him to get on with it. Nobody but us sober folks appeared to be bothered by the din. I had to find Sophie.

'Shall I take over the night duty Frieda?' Mrs. Jenkins asked, rubbing her finger around inside the empty glass to get the last drop of egg-flip.

'Stand at ease Ingrid. Lucky is on guard for trespassers. Do you want to retire for the night?'

'I would if I could remember where my billet is,' she said, pouring out another glassful.

'I'll light your way. You've a busy day tomorrow.'

'Do you like the necklace Wolfgang bought me for Christmas? It's a real diamond,' she said, trying and failing to open the *Tiffany* box.

'Oh. Cripes. Have I missed the present opening?'

'Don't worry Frieda, Santa left some for you. Shall I get them for you?'

Before I could reply she walked in front of the sozzled songsters and scooped a large Christmas sack full of presents and headed back. As she staggered past the choir again, I noticed Ben wore his Arran sweater, even though the heat in the kitchen was rising rapidly. He looked really lovely, apart from his red face. I could tell that his loudness was to cover up the hurt I caused. Not being a smiley sort of man he looked a little like "The Joker" as he feigned happiness. I felt so bad but before I could go and be kind to him, my top agent had returned fully armed.

'Why don't you open them in my bunker? It will be safer there. The shiny paper is bound to blow our cover and Russian Olga is like a ruddy magpie when it comes to bling,' she said.

Where does she get it from? 'Maybe later,' I replied, wanting to get away as quickly as possible from the caterwauling. 'If you need anything in the night just use the internal phone and I'll send backup straight away.'

After I'd settled Mrs. Jenkins for the night, I returned to Sophie's studio and opened my presents, saving the one from Ben until last. It was specially wrapped in red and gold with an angel tag saying: "I love you darling Kathryn". Inside was a pair of glittering diamond stud earrings in the same cabochon design as my engagement ring. I had to try them on. They were just perfect. Feeling guilty as hell, I put them back in the box… No matter what, I needed to kiss Ben properly. Then maybe I would know if he was the one.

Seeing him so desolate brought out empathetic feelings of love that I'd not experienced before.

The kitchen still buzzed with happy shiny people but thankfully the singing had stopped and the choir filtered back out into the night. Sophie had gone to bed and Zach was busy telling his "Shark Watch" jokes. Ben was nowhere to be seen among the remaining partygoers. Then I noticed Mick looking outside through the kitchen window.

'Have you seen Ben?' I asked.

'He's over there behind the greenhouse, my *Panicking Poinsettia*, throwing up in the mop bucket. I fear by cock and pie you must choose wisely. For this malady I have induced will show his true colours, else you can call me an ass.'

'I'll call you something more apt than that if you've made him ill.'

'Nay fair Kate for there is method in my wickedness.'

'Bugger off!' I shouted, filling a jug with water and grabbing a tea towel.

I ran outside and made my way towards the greenhouse, only to find Ben flat on his back in the cabbage patch and groaning loudly.

'Let me die. I just want to die!' he moaned. 'Can you stop the garden from spinning?'

'Come on Ben try and sit up and drink some water.'

'Back off Kathryn! I don't want you anywhere near me. You've ruined my life. I was content before I met you, apart from Eleanor running off with an old guy,' he blurted out. 'My life was orderly and peaceful looking after dumb animals. They're always faithful you know. Unconditional love. That's what you get from a dog. But not from you. Oh. No. Oh. God. Get me the bucket again.'

'Come on Ben. I'm sorry. I've been a bitch. You deserve better,' I said, as he threw up again.

'Argh! Bharf! Yes. I do. And in case you haven't noticed, I'm solvent and sexy…And I've thrown up all over my very itchy sweater. I'm allergic to wool. Didn't I tell you? Dumped again… Why me? Jilted twice in the space of a month. That's gotta be some kinda record. Hasn't it?'

'Maybe it's because you dive head first into love instead of sounding out the wave first,' I said, wiping his forehead with the wet tea towel.

'There you go with the same old rubbish. Banging on about surfing. I bet you've got water on the brain. That's it! That's what's wrong with you. You have too much water and not enough earth. But then Eleanor was really dry…Ah. I get it…It's not me. It's you. I know for sure. I've done everything possible to make you happy and what do I get in return? Well I'll tell you…Fuck all. That's what I get,' he said, and retched again.

'You're right Ben. I'm rubbish at relationships and a water sign: *Scorpio*. You'll be better off without me,' I said, trying not to gag as I wiped his face.

'Water, water everywhere and I suppose Luke the Lifeguard is a water sign?'

'Now you come to mention it, he is: *Pisces*.'

'I knew it! He's a merman…and I'm a fucking

goat…Oh. I get it…Now you're giving me the "Dear John" treatment. Well you can't do that because I quit. And for your information: I'm Ben and not John, nor Lukie, nor Mick, nor Zach, nor Joe, nor Alan, nor Tommy, nor any fucking Dick or Harry you spend more time with than me. Even the postman gets to see more of you. So that's it? Merry fucking Christmas Bennyboy,' he slurred, before heaving again.

I'd never heard him swear before, and it would have been funny normally. But he was so angry at me that it wouldn't have been fair to laugh. Not even a little bit.

'Come on Squire. It's not the end of the world. May a king pass by and not notice your fall from grace while your state empties itself as doth an inland brook into the sea,' Mick piped up, trying to lift Ben to his feet.

'Another fucking idiot obsessed with water. What is it with you Brits and water for Christ's sake?'

'No man is an island unless you live on one,' Mick enlightened us all.

'Enough Mick! Let's get him back into the house and clean him up.'

'Why are you talking about me as if I'm fucking deaf?' Ben asked, staggering around the garden and kicking the cabbages. 'Look everybody, I'm here and pissed…Oh. Fuck,' he added, falling into the compost heap.

'And now that I have him in my grasp, this imperfection of her eyes will I undo,' Mick muttered. 'Come on Kat give us a hand will you? He's too big for me to tackle alone. TOMMY!? You are required now!!'

With the help of Tommy, we got Ben indoors. I managed to wash him down in the scullery - and take off the itchy sweater. It would've been impossible to get him upstairs without a Mountain Rescue team, so we walked him into the studio, undressed him and left him to sleep it off in the sofa bed. He looked so peaceful lying there all helpless and sick free. So I kissed him on the forehead and he didn't even stir. I only hoped that Mrs. Jenkins wouldn't wander in the night and mistake him for the enemy.

'Goodnight sloshed prince and may the angels guard the rest of us. Poor *Longshanks*...He's going to have one hell of a hangover in the morning,' Mick said, shaking his head.

'You bastard. You did this on purpose.'

'At least the conjecture from your eyeballs has fallen, my *Fuming Phlox*.'

'Don't you know by now Mick that the most appealing man is a vulnerable one trying to be brave? Now I'm even more mixed up.'

'Ah. Methinks I am sans eyes and sans brains,' he said, 'and more like Lear than Oberon in cocking things up.'

58

24th December. Christmas Eve, Early Morning.

It was daybreak and the surf rolled in frothy and light. I had the beach to myself and all the time in the world to do what I loved best. My thoughts were crystal clear and I was content. In a playful mood the incoming Glassy, sometimes casting out high flows and then changing direction into soft barrelling rifts, let me slide along into the shallows. Everything was ethereal and effortless. Nothing challenged. No wildness to fight against. No problems to solve. Just a solitary female nudged along the surface by a benevolent sea, until gentle waves flurrying along the shoreline finally scattered over rippled sand. At last I was alone and free.

When the foam receded, I knew it was time to begin the wedding celebrations for two great oldies - and for me to make a decision - but not yet awhile. Jogging along the beach and feeling renewed, I hoped to catch a glimpse of Luke. I knew he was around and watching me, but he didn't show up. He must've waited for me to reach the cliff tops because when I looked back, he was running in the opposite direction. Killing time until the waves returned.

My first thought, when I got back, was to see if Ben had recovered. Rushing into the studio I saw him still asleep and looking peaceful. It may appear somewhat fickle on my part, but I simply had to kiss him. Then I would know. It would all fall into place. So I did.

'What the hell are you doing to me?' he groaned. 'Get off me woman. I can't breath.'

'Sorry Ben. I was pleased to see you and I wanted to kiss you,' I said, kneeling over him. 'That's all. I'll leave you then, shall I?'

'What's the time?'

'It's 7.30 a.m. Why?'

'For God's sake let me sleep it off,' he snapped.

And with that he pulled the duvet over his head and began to snore. Ah. Well. The best laid plans and all that. The two of us - a little like trains. We arrived at different times and on different platforms - sometimes early but more often than not, too late to make a connection.

I had intended to cook breakfast for him. Instead I made myself a huge plate of scrambled eggs. Lucky padded along the kitchen floor and ate his jelly meat with biscuits. He had definitely filled out and his fur had little kinks on the end. Despite Ben's grumpiness, I was still in a good mood. I needed to sketch. Unfortunately all the drawing materials were in the studio.

'Now Lucky, you have to be very quiet because Bennyboy is sleeping. Okay?' I said, catching him mid-yap.

He looked at me with eyebrows raised and padded over to the door, waiting for the dog flap to be lifted. I watched him sniffing around the garden for a while then I thought it safe to sneak back to where Ben dreamed of being women and alcohol free. After rattling around in the drawers, I found what I wanted. He hadn't moved at all under the duvet. At one point he was so still I thought he might be dead, so I poked him. Much to my relief, a sudden burst of snoring confirmed that he was still alive. Then I thought of his clothes - especially the expensive Arran sweater covered in sick. They had disappeared.

Only Lucy would have gathered up dirty clothes in the middle of the night. Also Mrs. Jenkins might have found them. I imagined them both tussling with the offending items, arguing over who was going to wash them. I soon found out when I discovered them in the washer. The sweater had shrunk beyond redemption, his white T-shirt had turned a dull grey, one black sock - and his "Dry Clean" black trousers were covered in fluff and missing three inches in length.

'Good morning Frieda,' Mrs. Jenkins called out. 'I found Fritz unconscious last night. He would not say the password, so I confiscated his clothes. They needed a good wash anyway.'

'Good morning Ingrid. I intended to bring you breakfast in bed.'

'Why. I'm not poorly.'

'Are you ready to be a Countess?'

'What do you mean: "Countess"? I'm ready for some breakfast.'

'Have you forgotten about Wolfgang?'

'Given half a chance. He didn't come to kiss me good night again.'

'Sit yourself down and I'll make you a nice cup of tea,' I said, feeling concerned.

'Where are the rest of them? Still sleeping on duty no doubt. I expect my betrothed was up with the lark though.'

'Mrs. Jenkins you do know what day it is? Don't you?'

'It's the 24th December and Teresa May is Prime Minister.'

'Do you remember what happened last night?'

'I know that Russian Olga was here again last

night. I saw her creeping round the side of the house. I thought it was you at first, but you don't creep. You run everywhere.'

'And what about Wolfgang?'

'Oh. He never creeps. He might creak a bit though. Have you heard his knees crack? I've told him to get some Cod Liver Oil to grease his joints. Now, when are the flowers coming?'

'Good morrow, my *Brightest Blossoms*. Something smells good,' Mick said, following his nose to the cooker.

Mrs. Jenkins ignored him.

'Good morning Wolfgang. Help yourself to food,' I offered, trying to break the ice.

'One boiled egg or two Iris dearest?'

'Two and not runny,' she replied.

'Toasty soldiers with them?'

'What am I, a child? Cut it into four squares.'

'So,' I said, thinking the marriage might be cancelled, 'are you ready for the big event?'

Mrs. Jenkins looked at me with head to one

side. Then she sipped her tea before speaking, while Mick wrestled with the toaster.

'Frieda don't you know that lovers' tiffs are soon over. My Wolfgang is "the one", but don't tell him or it will make him bigheaded.'

Seeing an opportunity to get some ancient wisdom on love I asked: 'How do you know he's the one?'

'I know because nobody else has ever made me feel so happy. It's simple really. If love makes you miserable then it's not real unless you're a soldier's wife and missing him terribly. Then such uncontrollable circumstances make our hearts ache, but the joy of seeing them again is worth the wait… If I tell you this you won't go blabbing it around. Will you?'

I shook my head.

'He makes my heart go pitter-patter every time I see him. He's like a ray of sunshine on a cloudy day. And I've had many of those - especially foggy ones.'

I watched Mick's face crease into a smile and

he wiped his eyes. I wondered why we younger ones never listen to the good advice of our elders. Oldies are wise and mellow if you ask for help with a problem. Sometimes miserable if neglected, but then, there's no wonder. Most of them live on pittance and hate looking in the mirror every morning at a wrinkled stranger. The key to happiness seems to be keeping young on the inside. Hanging on to hopes and dreams, not thinking: why do I need that, or why should I do this, or I might be dead next year and what's the point. Well, that's what I've learned through observing Mrs. Jenkins and Mick.

Mick whistled a jaunty tune as he lovingly prepared breakfast for his future wife. Although she had not looked at him once, I saw her smile. The kitchen soon began to fill up as Joe and Sal were the next to join us followed by Lucy, Alan, Sophie, Zach and Paulo. Apparently Maggie was having a lie in. Something she'd not done before. Nobody mentioned Ben. So I thought it best to let sleeping dogs lie. He would be embarrassed enough when he finally surfaced.

Once more vans came and went unloading: food, gifts, flowers and more future guests, staggering under the weight of supplies made their way through the hallway and into the biggest room. What had once been a ballroom in bygone days was now to serve as the reception room.

Zach had arranged for us all to go on a boat trip as the weather forecast was calm. The actual ceremony wasn't until 8.0.pm. that evening. Everything was in order. Firework display set up on the other side of the wall - to commence on our return from the real church. Derek the Dynamite made his own products and he favoured extra large ones. I only hoped he'd not got too many bangers. He came from a long line of tin miners, so it was in his blood to blow up anything and everything that caused an obstruction. I was slightly worried when Zach took him over to the swimming pool hole. With Derek's aid it could've well turned out to be an Olympic sized one.

The kitchen buzzed with excited chatter. Soon the table was full of various people I'd never met, enjoying breakfast with the rest of us.

'I've been thinking and have decided I want you to walk me down the aisle Ilmhart,' Mrs. Jenkins said to Joe, across the table.

'I thought Heinrich was your first choice?' Joe asked, giving her a cheeky wink.

'He's not as handsome as you. And he doesn't take his work seriously enough.'

'It will be a pleasure and an honour Ingrid,' he said, standing to his feet and bowing low.

'Vill you vear your uniform Ilmhart? I zo like a man drezzed zat vay,' Sal asked, cuddling up to him.

'There's no need to get jealous Gurda. I'm marrying Wolfgang in case you hadn't noticed,' Mrs. Jenkins chided.

I spotted Lucy alone and hiding at the far side of the kitchen, clutching a cup of coffee as it were about to escape.

'Are you looking forward to the boat trip?' I

asked, taking her some toast before it vanished among the masses.

'Kat? Do you mind if I don't go with you. Only, I get sea sick really easily.'

'Are you sure?' I asked. 'I can get you some tablets.'

'No thanks. I'll stay here and clean up, if that's alright with Sophie?'

'Whatever makes you happy…No worries,' I said, noticing she was becoming more anxious. 'I'm sorry about Paulo…'

'It's fine. They're good together. That's all that matters. It was a pipe dream anyway. He was never for me. He's always wanted Maggie…I just need some quiet time,' she said, her serene beautiful face not giving away her disappointment.

When Lucy saw Paulo heading in our direction she leapt up and started tidying the table.

'Ciao bella. Do you minda ifa Maggie and me donna go on the boat trip? We want to be on our own. You knowa how it isa?'

'No problem. You've already had a "trip

round the 'arbour' anyhow. Do you want to take Maggie breakfast in bed? You won't be disturbed up there.'

His face lit up like a bawcawn. Sorry beacon.

'Pronto, fantastico. Thanks a million Kat,' he said, slipping into his Peckham accent.

His knowledge of the Italian language had expanded by two more words.

12.30p.m.

The excessive noise began to freak out Lucky. He needed some quiet time also. I did a final check on Ben and he was still out for the count. Years of night work must have caught up on him. He certainly needed the rest. So I left him in peace, wondering if Luke would be piloting the boat. I was disappointed. Tommy took the helm and whizzed us out to sea for a bracing trip around the coves.

Later when we anchored near a secluded beach, I managed to catch Sophie and Zach alone and told them about Aunt Leonora's confessions. (I'll be brief about that particular spot in time, knowing how much pain it caused my Godmother). On the other hand, I felt a different kind of sorrow. When I first found out about my Dad's disappearance, I never once expected him to come striding out of the sea. My constant nightmares had told me otherwise.

'Do you believe her?' Zach asked, looking concerned.

'She's crazy, but I'm sure she was telling the truth. Brutal honesty seems to be one of characteristic. Did I do right in telling you? I've turned myself inside out wondering whether or not I should.'

Sophie had remained silent throughout and I looked to her for an answer. It was unbearable to see her trying to hold back the tears.

'You did right Kat. It comes as a shock, but answers a lot of questions. I could never understand why Martin drowned. He was the strongest of swimmers and the best of surfers.

I always hoped…Now I know,' she said, and walked away from us along the beach.

I wanted to run and hold her in the same way she had comforted me over the years. Zach stopped me.

'Leave her Kat. She needs time to come to grips with it…Yes. My loverrlee, you did the right thing…Your Dad was the best and bravest man I ever knew and he loved you with all his heart… Now go and play with the mad dog, while I check up on your Godmother.'

The great thing about dogs is that they make you forget your problems. Let you live in their moment of fun and frolic…I was so glad Lucky loved the sea. And none of us, including Sophie, could get him out of the water. He paddled around fetching sticks and barking wildly. In the end Tommy had to wade in and carry him back to the boat.

59

3.00p.m.

The first thing I noticed when we returned home was Sam the Sweeney's policecar parked round the back, along with the Coastguard's *Range Rover*. I found out later that Zach had called the police and informed them to look out for a mad redhead. I only hoped it wouldn't be a case of mistaken identity on my part. Sam, his wife and four kids, and two of his new recruits, Bill the Seagull, Bert and three other off duty coastguards, were also invited to the real church wedding. Sophie pottered around the kitchen, trying to keep busy. I knew she didn't want to discuss the matter further. So having an hour free before hairdressing appointments, I went to look for Ben, hoping to have a serious talk about our future.

After searching around, I found both Ben and Lucy in the sitting room watching a documentary on Polar Bears. They looked like a pair of bookends, sitting quite still on either side of the fireplace. I wished I could sit like that. Lucy sits so well. Neither of them moved when I walked towards them. I felt a little jealous. I'd never watched a documentary with Ben, let alone a David Attenborough one. I actually felt like an intruder, until Ben turned round and smiled at me.

'Hello Kathryn. Did you enjoy your boat trip?' he asked, almost jollily.

'It was good. How are you feeling?'

'Better,' he smiled.

'Are you okay Lucy?' I asked, wondering why she'd not looked at me.

'Oh. Kat I didn't see you there. Yes. I'm fine. I lost all track of time. It's so relaxing in this room, I almost fell asleep.'

I could tell from the way she gazed at Ben that she had transferred all her feelings of love onto him. Thankfully, he didn't seem to have noticed. What's with people who slip into love so easily? Even though Ben's gorgeous, I could never understand it.

Before I could speak again, Ben stood up and kissed me until I felt dizzy. And I enjoyed every moment. He certainly could kiss. I heard Lucy leave the room and head for the kitchen.

'I need to talk to you Ben,' I said, trying to catch my breath.

'Later Kathryn, later. Let's not spoil the moment when we're both so close,' he said softly. 'I'm sorry about this morning, darling. I had one hell of a headache, but now Dr. Ben is ready for some loving,' he said, drawing me near again.

He emitted such warmth and passion I lost my train of thought for a minute. I would have been really nice to make love, but it would also have confused matters further. My well prepared speech flew out the window. So instead of talking about our future, I steamed after Lucy into the kitchen, saying: 'Things to do. Come and help organize the transport.'

7.50pm.

Ben, Paulo and Alan hovered outside the music room doors, anxiously waiting for the bridal party to appear. Mick was safely installed inside the "church" with Davies the Godley. Sophie was poised and ready for her cue. And guests Sal and Zach sat on the bride's side of the aisle. I could hear the vicar yelling out instructions to poor Mick. Joe peeped round the kitchen door ready for the signal. I wondered if Luke would come. He always kept his word. But this time circumstances were different.

'Good evening folks,' Luke said breathlessly, standing outside the back door. 'Only just made it. Sorry about the delay. Had a bit of trouble keeping these on…' he told us, knocking sand out of his loafers. 'Ingrid you look beautiful. Wolfgang is a very lucky man.'

And with that he walked passed us all without

speaking another word. I had to take a peek. I couldn't resist it. He looked gorgeous in his wedding outfit. At first I thought he'd cut his hair, but it was tied back. Sophie came out to break the tension and pinned a cream rose on his lapel. Ben looked equally handsome but not so relaxed. Both men nodded at each other and turned their attention towards the kitchen. Only Luke spotted me and did a little penguin dance, causing me to smile.

Mrs. Jenkins had chosen a soft lilac dress with a lace shrug in the same shade. Her hair was tinted and curled and she had a headband of fresh cream roses, dotted with lilac Freesias to match her hand tied bouquet. She positively glowed. Our dresses were of the Jane Austin style in cream satin with an overlay of lace. The tiny capped sleeves were edged in cream silk and we had coronets of lilac Freesias. Joe adjusted his tie nervously - waiting by the door for the first cords to strike out.

Sophie sounded out the notes and we all

moved slowly down the hall. Watched by a strange mixture of ushers and in particular, Paulo, who couldn't take his eyes off little Maggie. Lithesome Lucy no longer looked down at Paulo. Her gaze was fixed on higher things and mainly Ben who was the tallest present.

When we reached the door there was a sudden rush of scrambling male feet to get inside and seated before the bride made her entrance. Zach reminded them all to take off their top hats in "church". Ben and Alan sat on the groom's side while Luke and Paulo chose to support Mrs. Jenkins. As rehearsed, Maggie dealt with the flowers and I was in charge of the rings, handed over by Mick, so I could pass them back at the appropriate time.

The whole event went as planned except Davies the Godley talked at twice his normal speed - being intent on getting back to his bigger flock. Mick and Mrs. Jenkins both shed a tear as they exchanged rings. It was very emotional. Even Lucky howled along to the music, causing laughter as we sang along to: *All Things Bright and Beautiful...*

In the reception hall we had about twenty extra guests for dinner. The rest would arrive after the real church ceremony. I'll not dwell on my unrehearsed speech only to say that it went quite well, considering that I couldn't mention the groom's former questionable lives, or Mrs. Jenkins sweet dementia. A few Cornish jokes went down a treat with the locals. Ben didn't laugh and neither did Lucy. So it was a big relief when Wolfgang and his lady took the floor for a romantic waltz.

Dawn still wearing her very large hat - and her caterers quickly cleared away the tables and chairs, to the side of the ballroom, leaving only the top table with the wedding cake for photographs. The soothing music encouraged others to join the bride and groom. Before I could say a word, Luke took me by the hand and held me close. His eyes so blue they were almost luminous. He'd taken off his jacket and waistcoat and I noticed he wore black braces. For the first time I realized that I was turned on by what the Americans call "suspenders". Luke definitely had filled out since the summer. The outline of his biceps pushed against his shirt sleeves. I hadn't known that he could dance in the old fashioned way. He was full of surprises. It was so easy the way we caught the rhythm and without thinking, I closed my eyes and rested my head against his chest. I could hear his heart beating faster as he drew me close.

'Kathryn! What do you think you're doing?' Ben voice abruptly broke my dreaming.

'I think Kat has a mind of her own, mate. So let's finish the dance. Okay?' Luke said, completely unfazed by the interruption, until Harry the Flasher snapped us all - me with my mouth open and Ben and Luke scowling at each other. Not one for the album I think.

'Don't call me mate – Fishman!' he replied angrily.

'Sorry mate, I meant Hamster Boy,' Luke replied, squaring up to Ben.

'Ladies and gentlemen,' Mick announced, loudly tapping the microphone and pushing Discman out of the way, 'will you all take the floor for "The Gay Gordons" if you please.'

As usual, Mick's timely intervention avoided a set too. I could see Luke had that determined surfing look on his face and Ben's arms had disappeared up his coat cuffs. When Mick came over and swept me around in a little jig, both the boys were left eye-balling each other in the middle of the dance floor - surrounded by a circle of bouncing twosomes.

'Haven't you decided yet Kat? It's quite obvious to me which one you love,' Mick said, chuckling and twirling me round and round.

'Butt out Wolfgang. I need a little more time.'

'Thou and I are too wise to woo daintily,' he said. 'We knowest true love shall not make us fools, but shall find us all merry in the prologue.'

'Shut it! You old Count,' I said, dancing on to the next partner for "The Military Two-Step", who happened to be Tommy the Tank. To my relief he moved quickly on to Lucy who dodged and weaved out of the way of his relentless clod hoppers. Alan danced happily with a breathless Mrs. Seagull and quickly exchanged her for Dawn the Hat, who had left behind a worried looking Gannet. The next lady in line for him was Mrs. Tom who was a slightly smaller version of her son.

Circling dizzily round the room amid the prancing partygoers, I looked for Ben and Luke. Ben sat next to Derek the Dynamite, drinking straight from a bottle of champagne and looking very glum. I watched Derek spread out his arms like a fisherman, to demonstrate the size of his latest bangers. Luke had disappeared again. I thought he'd gone surfing for an hour to calm down - and to get out of the penguin suit. I saw with relief that he was still around and talking to Sophie. I wondered if he would come to the real church. Looking at the state of the rest of the party, I wondered whether they'd make it too. When I saw Luke shake hands with Zach and kiss Sophie farewell, I nearly tripped over.

'Kathryn,' Ben said, appearing from nowhere and grabbing me by the arm, 'I intend to leave for London after the church ceremony. I've had it with you and the Water Boy.'

'But you can't. I mean, it would spoil everything. I don't want you to go like this,' I said, dodging away from a twirling Maggie and looking for Luke.

'Give me one good reason why I should stay. From where I'm standing I can't see any,' he said, his eyes full of hurt.

'All I need is a little more time. I swear to you after the church ceremony we'll sit down and have a serious talk about our future. At the moment there's too much distraction going on for me to think straight.'

'Do you love me Kathryn?'

'Yes,' I said. 'But…do you think you could chill out a little more? After all it's a celebration and meant to be fun…We can't let our little problems spoil this happy occasion. Please Ben…Now go and try the next dance - a quickstep, with Derek the Dynamite's missus. She's itching for someone to ask her…It's easy, just follow Wolfgang and Iris…I have to help Sophie and Sal. She needs me to cut up the wedding cake before the masses arrive and eat the lot.'

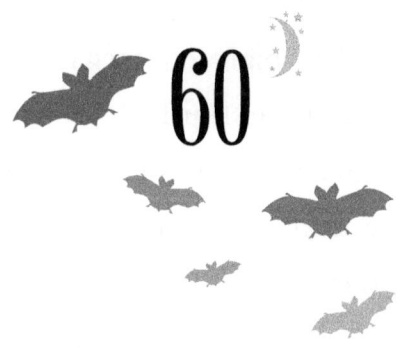

60

11.30pm.

Number of people sober and fit enough to drive to the real church – three: Mick, Sal and Lucy. I'd lost count of number of guests, rising by the minute – minus one. (Luke had disappeared and left me to it). The rest continued to party and didn't even notice our departure.

Paulo spoke more than four sentences and offered to drive the other ushers to the church in my car. Mick took the *Capri* with Sophie and Zach as passengers. Lucy volunteered to drive Ben's car with: Sal, Maggie, Countess Iris and myself in tow. I don't think she wanted another of Sal's inquisition. And I wasn't in the mood for questions I couldn't answer, so I sat in the passenger seat. The ushers needed to get there early to quickly clear out the late night congregation after the Christmas service had finished, so we all loitered behind for fifteen minutes before setting off.

'Take the next left turn Lucy, just past *The Roving Buccaneers*. The church is at the end of the lane. Be careful it's very narrow there's only room for one car. You might end up in the ditch as the locals pile out for a last minute drink at the pub.'

'I don't understand Frieda. Why do we have to go back to the church when there's dancing to be had at the reception?' Countess Iris asked, looking confused.

'It's Christmas Eve Ingrid. The vicar needs to bless the marriage. Royalty you see. They always have two of everything.'

'Oh. I just wondered... So are we officially married, or not?'

'Yes. Ingrid. The first ceremony was the official one. The second one is just for show for your subjects,' I said, feeling the effects of the alcohol taking hold of my reasoning head.

'That's a relief. I don't want to be called a

loose woman,' she informed us. I didn't go into details. 'Will I have to wave like Queen Elizabeth and King George?'

'Only if you want to - they would appreciate that,' I answered, distractedly.

By the time we arrived my head ached, trying to decide who or what I really wanted. Worrying about my crazy Aunt, hoping Luke would be at the church and that Ben was in a happier frame of mind, were my main priorities. To my relief, I noticed that directly outside the church it was people-free. I fully expected the whole congregation to be hovering with confetti and a bottle each for the late night party. When Lucy pulled into the car park there were only three more cars there. The third one, an old Austin Heeley *Sprite*, belonged to Davies the Godley.

When we walked towards the vestry, the noise hit us. I was only thankful we'd not booked the cathedral. We'd got a full house singing along to: *Rudolph the Red-nosed Reindeer...*which immediately made me suspicious and wondering what Davies the Godley had told them. Alan was the first to greet us, looking flushed and excited.

'You missed her by minutes,' he gushed. 'You know the redhead who bought the *Nat West* pigs. Your crazy Aunt, I believe, had the church in uproar.'

'Oh. No. Not again. What's she done now?'

'Well,' said Alan, 'we arrived to find none of the congregation had budged from their seats. They wanted to stay for the blessing ceremony. No matter what we said they would not be moved. By the way, the flower arrangements have been stripped almost bare. Every single man, woman and child is wearing a buttonhole... They've brought confetti you see. Davies the Godley ordered Madge at the organ to keep them occupied with Christmas Carols, which she did for about half an hour. After she'd exhausted her repertoire, she went on to general festive songs. It was rather funny to see her hammering out popular tunes from that ruddy soaring monster. Eventually we got to *Frosty the Snowman* when your Aunt ran out from behind the altar and started screaming. It must say she looked rather fetching in a red fox fur coat and hat. She put me in mind of Rita Hayworth…Where was I? Ah. Yes. She ran down the aisle shouting something about: "gnaw dog sawn post" and that we were all "awful purple". I might be wrong though.'

'I think she said "needing some peace" and that you were all "evil people". I'm beginning to understand her peculiar accent now. Go on Alan.'

'Well that's it really. She ran down to the vestry and out into the churchyard with arms flailing and still screaming. She had on a pair of black high heeled *Louboutins* with red soles and matching gloves. I couldn't help but notice. She looked very classy indeed, apart from the wild expression and the ear-piercing wailing.'

'And did she attack anyone?'

'No. She put the wind up a few of the older dears…One of the men had a hip-flask of brandy on him. He was kind enough to administer a few tots to revive the ladies. Ben and Joe ran after her but lost her in the dark…On closer inspection, we noticed the aisle was left with a trail of red footprints…It turned out that the red soles weren't designer after all. She'd stepped in blood you see. There were red footprints which led all the way to behind the altar. It was Wolfgang who found the housekeeper's ginger cat with its throat ripped out. Mrs. Higginbotham was very upset. Wolfgang is out there giving it a decent burial. I must say the events caused quite a stir in the pews; especially when the poor woman came and mopped the floor. She got a round of applause… Would you believe it?'

'Oh. Bugger…We'll definitely not get rid of them now,' I said. 'This has got to be the most excitement they've had since that Russian cargo ship ran aground. There where tins caviar floating everywhere. They made a fortune selling it to the tourists.'

'Alas poor Tiddles, I've buried him well. Now let's get on with the blessing shall we. The Groundlings are getting restless…Take my arm

Iris dearest. Be careful the floor is still a tad wet…The rest of you follow behind and try to find seats in the front stalls,' Mick said, smiling.

By this time Davies the Godley looked as if his head might explode. Not wanting Mrs. Higginbotham to do any more mopping up, I tried to calm him down.

'Please don't be alarmed…It's an old Transylvanian sacrificial marriage custom. Count Wolfgang will get Mrs. Higginbotham another cat. Won't you!?'

'Yes indeed. I will find a replacement feline as soon as the pet shop opens. Now please can we get on with the ceremony? I'm quite overwrought with excitement,' he chuckled, pretending to swoon.

Despite the unusual events, the blessing went as planned. Mick, or should I say, Wolfgang, was content at last. His Countess smiled throughout and waved graciously to every single pew on either side.

We all ran to the cars through a hailstorm of confetti, except Ben who announced loudly to the gathering masses: 'Thank you for attending! Your presence was much appreciated! I'm afraid you missed the reception! The food and drink were consumed earlier in the day! All is not lost though….If you leave now, you'll probably catch the landlord of *The Roving Buccaneers*, before he locks up. GOOD NIGHT AND A HAPPY CHRISTMAS TO YOU ALL,' and with that he jumped into my car.

Once the news had sunk in, the locals swarmed like bees behind us as we all sped away, leaving only a trail of dust. It was only when we were almost home that I realized the bride wasn't in our car.

'Don't worry Kat. She'll be with Wolfgang, Sal said.

'No. I definitely saw him driving the *Capri* and she wasn't in the front seat. He'd have thought we were taking her back…Oh. God. No. She'll have wandered off again. Everybody get out and walk the rest of the way - and you Lucy! I have to go back and find her.'

When I reached the pub I noticed with relief, it was full of merrymakers. Regardless of the size of Ben's vehicle and the narrowness of the lane, I put my foot down and raced for the car park. Thank God she was still in the churchyard doing her royal wave.

'Ingrid. There you are. Come on now let's get back to the reception. You must be frozen,' I said, taking her arm.

'Before we go Frieda there's something I want to do. Will you help me?'

'Yes. What is it?'

'I want to put my bouquet on Arnold's grave,' she said.

'Fine. Err. Have you got your reading glasses with you?'

'No. Why?'

'No matter, we'll find it together,' I said, leading her to the nearest grave stone. 'Here it is: "Here lies a fallen hero. Rest in Peace Arnold Jenkins. Beloved husband of Iris Jenkins",' I read out.

'They missed off his middle name and his date of birth. What a shame. Still he'll be forever young that way. Never you mind Arnold dearest. I hope you don't object to me marrying Wolfgang. And I hope you're happy wherever you have ended up,' she said, tearfully.

'What was his middle name?'

'Michael but everybody called him Mick down at the public house. I know it's bad to speak ill of the dead, but he was quite a drinker you know.'

'I'm sure he wants you to be happy. Now come on let's get you warmed up. The night is still young,' I reassured her, looking around anxiously in case my Aunt was thirsty again.

61

1.00am.

The bride and groom left the ballroom for a quick nap before the fireworks display. I noticed Dawn the Hat, handing out sandwiches while Knuckles, Slops and Gannet were drunkenly slurring along to Discman's compilation of unrecognizable tunes. Most of the group had gone outside for smokes. Sal remained. I knew she waited for me and there was no escape.

'Come on Kat. What am I?' she said, giving me that knowing look.

'You're a bloody nuisance.'

'Well, yes, and what else?'

'I know. I know. But how can I tell you if I don't know the answer?'

'Maybe if you talk about your problems

you'll find the answer... You've run around like a headless chicken since we got here, doing anything to avoid the truth.'

'And I suppose you know what the truth is?' I asked, looking for an easy answer.

'No. Talk to me, like we used to.'

'Use to? You used to beat me up Missy.'

'Stop stalling. Come and sit down and have a cup of tea.'

'I don't know what to do for the best Sal. You see Ben is *Mr. Darcy* epitomized. He's perfect in every way. Well, apart from his arms getting shorter when he's angry. He's kind, considerate, generous, a good lover and a good listener. He'll be a great husband and a fantastic dad. His parents own a ranch in Canada...And I don't want to lose every girl's dream man.'

'Is he your dream man?'

'I guess so. He's a man of honour and integrity – like Austen's hero. I've day-dreamed about *Darcy* for as long as I can remember. We all did Sal. Don't you remember?'

'You lot did. I'd got Joe.'

'But he's *Mr. Darcy*. The real 21st century deal.'

'But are you Elizabeth Bennet?'

'Not really...I'd like to be Elizabeth Swan. But even she got *Mr. Darcy* in the end.'

'No. She bloody well didn't. Elizabeth got Will.'

'But Luke's not Will! He's...well...'

'What is Luke?'

'He's just Luke.'

'I need more clarification Kat. From where I'm sitting Luke is a lot more than "just Luke". Don't you think?'

'I've never had to describe his qualities before. It wasn't necessary...I liked him just the way he was...Everything was so uncomplicated before my birthday party. I told you I didn't do wishes. And now I've got more than I wished for...'

'Come here you daft bugger,' Sal said, her face softening. 'You need a hug.'

'I've been such a shit to Ben. He deserves so much better,' I said, sniffing back the tears... 'Oh. No. Where is he? He's not left yet? Has he?'

'He's out in the garden with Lucky… "The Three Degrees" over there got him on "Recoiling Snakebites" and he went out for some air.'

'Oh. No. Not again. He can't drink. Don't tell me Knuckles brought his home-brewed cider?'

'Afraid so. They thought they were helping Luke by disabling Ben, I suppose…I think it best to leave him for a while. Even *Mr. Darcy* would look unattractive with arse in the air and chucking his cookies in the vegetable patch.'

'Sally Jones you are such a stirrer. Why didn't you stop them? You know what they're like.'

'Ben's a grown man. He makes his own choices. It'll be a learning curve for him.'

'Don't you see? Because of their interference, and your reluctance, I now have overwhelming feelings of love for him again. I want to run out there and tell him that we'll get married next week. Oh. Shit!' I shouted, grabbing a bottle of water and a napkin.

Lucy pottered around in the kitchen tidying up and had changed out of her bridesmaid dress into what can only be described as a harem outfit. I didn't know she had a pierced naval either. She sang softly as she loaded the dishwasher. At least she looked happy for a change. I felt extremely jealous at that spot in time. There was I with hair getting wilder by the minute in my hem-dirty Jane Austen frock and there she was looking like a Bollywood movie star dripping in gold. She even had toe rings.

Anyhow, I charged out the back door and headed for the vegetable patch, much to the amusement of the smokers. It was awful. Far worse than last time. Ben was face down in a pool of sick. I managed to turn him over. Then I filled the watering can from the tap and poured it over his face, causing him to cough and splutter. And I dislodge a few snails in the process.

'Kathryn is that you? I can't see…Help me I can't swim. I'm drowning,' he groaned, grabbing hold of my arm and pulling me into the cabbages.

'Come on Ben. Please try and sit up. You have to drink some water otherwise you'll be really ill,'

I urged him, feeling totally responsible for his predicament.

I emptied the *Evian* into his mouth and he coughed again.

'Oh. That's much better,' he said and brought it all back. 'You know Kathryn, I think all your friends and family are alcoholics. They drink like fishes. Ha. Ha. But then they would, living by the sea. On second thoughts where is the Fishman? I want to punch his lights out.'

'If you could drink some more water you'll feel a lot better,' I assured him, filling the watering can again.

'Why are you force feeding me? I'm not on a hunger strike,' he protested, as I put the spout directly into his mouth.

'For God's sake Ben, do you want to marry me or not? Because if this is how you're going to act every time there's a party, well, you can count me out.'

'Oh. Kathryn. You do love me,' he said, gargling then trying to get to his feet. 'She loves me!' he shouted out. 'Davies the Godley, get over here right now and marry us before she changes her mind!'

'Be quiet you idiot,' I said, giggling at his attempts to stand up.

After about half an hour of being doused with water followed by throwing up, Ben started to come round.

'Go get me coffee now! And please…don't make it yourself. Anything but that,' he pleaded.

With the help of Zach and Tommy we managed to get him in the swing seat and fairly stable. I didn't want to miss the spectacular fireworks display. Sophie administered one of her remedies for alcoholic poisoning to a protesting Ben. She'd treated many a person who had imbibed Knuckles home-brew.

'Ladies and gentlemen please stand well back for the fireworks display,' Derek the Dynamite announced. 'It's going to be very noisy…Leave the gate open, will you I want to be this side of the wall when everything goes off,' he said, as Lucky ran indoors.

Lucky slept in his basket with Lucy watching over him in case he got scared. She didn't like fireworks either. So we waited and waited for the sky to light up. Nothing happened. Eventually Derek returned looking forlorn.

'What's happened?' Zach asked.

'Some bloody animal has pissed on the fuses. They're all damp squibs now!'

'Please to continue the party indoors!' Davies the Godley bellowed out. 'I'm freezing my bollocks off out here!'

Gradually thing quietened down and people wandered home to have a lie in on Christmas morning. Zach was the last man standing, again, and engrossed in conversation with: Alan, Seagull, Davies the Godley and Wolfgang, who had left his new wife to her peaceful slumber.

'Ben, are you feeling better?' I asked, peering under the canopy of the swing seat. 'It's time for bed.'

There was no reply. He had fallen asleep with an empty coffee cup still in his hand.

'I think *Longshanks* needs to go indoors. Else Queen Mab might suck on his neck if she sees him lying there,' Wolfgang said.

'I'll stay with him for a while. I've gone beyond sleep. You know what I mean,' I said.

'My *Lucid Lupinus*, I know far too well the malady of wakefulness. I swear by yonder moon that I've not slept through the night for more years than even I can remember. Can I get you anything?'

'A blanket would be nice and another latte. A cigarette would be even better.'

Sorry I don't have any. A hyper redhead threw my last pack into the sea. Have a mini-*Mars* instead,' he grinned.

'Mick, I mean Wolfgang, have you enjoyed yourself today, apart from my crazy Aunt, the lack of fireworks and the dead cat?'

'I can honestly say that it's been the best day of my life...Thanks to you Kat. I'm king of the world,' he said, stretching out his arms. And I think the fireworks might have been too much for my lady wife. You know how she is with big bangs.'

'I sure do. Well, night Wolfgang. See you in the late afternoon for Christmas Dinner.'

'Night, night Kat. Don't stay out too long. Give us a knock if you want any help with *Longshanks* there.'

I sat with Ben snuggled under the duvet. It was so good to be quiet and not have to talk. He looked completely done in but was as warm as toast. I sipped my latte and watched the bright moon appearing and disappearing as I swung back and forth…The gentle rocking motion of the swing seat was so relaxing and comforting. Soon my eyelids felt heavy and I gave in to sleep at last after a long eventful day.

62

The sea, in an angry mood, pounded against the rocks, determined to have revenge. I struggled to hold on to the slippery surface as I was dragged back and forth with each surge. My eyes stung and I could barely see the bleak outline of the cliffs. I called out for help but my voice was engulfed by the deafening roar.

The bloated thing had returned and dragged me further into the waves. My nails were broken and bleeding from trying to grab on to something solid. It was useless. I had to submit to the overpowering strength of the sea. Swirling into the darkness, I couldn't see what weighed me down. My lungs burned with water as the last air bubbles rose above me. And I floated there, helpless and still, until the lifeless thing let go.

I needed to see what, or who, it was

- this monster that had haunted my dreams and deprived me of sleep. With a last burst of energy I managed to turn, and saw through the dimness, the remains of a skeletal body. Swathes of rotten grey flesh peeled off and drifted downwards. I was no longer afraid because I knew it was my Dad's remains. There were empty sockets where the eyes had been, but I felt he was watching me. He didn't move, or speak, or hold out his arms in greeting. He just floated gently down and out of sight. And I knew I would never see him again.

A sudden eruption of water forced me to the surface and as I gasped for air and scrambled to reach dry land, I saw Luke falling from the cliffs.

'Wake up Kathryn. You're having a nightmare,' Ben, said, holding me tightly as I sobbed.

'We have to go to the cliffs. Luke's in danger,' I said, tears pouring down my cheeks. 'Please Ben help me.'

'Why don't we go to bed instead? Eh? I can think of a few better things to do than chasing shadows.'

'Are you still drunk? Didn't you hear what I said? It's an emergency!'

'Kathryn it's just a dream. Calm yourself.'

'Have to get my coat,' I said, shivering. 'Find keys for the boot.'

'What are you talking about?'

'Seagull's Rescue Truck! Look on the key rack by the door…He's got ropes and harnesses. Flares. Hurry!'

I found my coat and my mobile. I was convinced that Luke was hurt and nothing was going to stop me believing that. Ben gathered together the rescue equipment, the ropes and flares, looking dazed and disbelieving my state of panic over a dream. After staggering around for a few minutes, he found the gate and followed me along the cliff pathway.

'Kathryn, slow down. I can't keep up,' he called after me. 'My head hurts.'

'Can't stop. He's in danger. Not much time left,' I called out.

My instincts hadn't misled me. As I neared the cliff edge, some two hundred feet below, I saw Luke, unmistakeable in the moonlight. His blonde mane shone out. He was lying face down and unconscious on the rocks. My Aunt, crouched over him, seemed to be pushing him back into the rising tide.

'Ben you have to help me down now! Do you think you can do it? There's nothing to anchor on to. I don't have time to knock in. You need to take my weight.'

'Sure I can do it! Why not? I've done mountain climbing in The Rockies. I once spent a whole night up there, in a blizzard at that...You Brits think it's the end of the world when you have three inches of snow. And you're never prepared. Unlike the *Mounties* who are always prepared,' he slurred. 'Get hitched up. Be careful Kathryn it looks dangerous down there,' he said, swaying from side to side.

'Before I go, send up a flare will you. We'll

need backup. He might be injured, or worse. Hurry Ben,' I urged.

Ben took out a flare and fired. It did a horizontal takeoff and disappeared behind the trees.

'You're supposed to aim upwards,' I shouted. 'Get the other one quickly.'

Before I could say another word, a blaze of noise and colour overhead startled us both. The flare must have collided with Derek the Dynamite's mega fireworks. A spectacular display lit up the night sky. Tremendous crashes and bangs deafened our ears. I was only thankful we were well away from the noise.

'That should wake 'em up,' Ben said, grinning.

'Pay attention. Are you ready? Then dig in your heels and hold tight,' I told him, bouncing down along the cliff face.

I was halfway down when the ropes went slack. Ben leaned over the cliff, swaying back and forth.

'What happened Ben!? You okay!?' I shouted.

'Kathryn do you love me!?'

'What? Are you joking me!?'

'No!'

'I've already told you! YES!' He must still be drunk.

'Why?!'

Shit. 'Now's not the time Ben! Just let me get down there! We'll talk later!'

The wind howled around my ears and my hands were becoming numb. I was in no position to talk about love.

'No! We'll talk now! No more "later"! I've had it with later. Are you in love with me?!'

'Please Ben! Don't do this!'

'YOU'D BETTER TELL ME THE TRUTH NOW OR I'LL FUCKING DROP YOU DOWN THERE WITH *GOLDILOCKS*!'

At that spot in time, when my life was on the line, my mobile sang out: *Girls hit your hallelujah/ Girls hit your hallelujah Whoo...*

'Hang on Ben! Well, you know what I mean! It could be important! Hello?'

'Kat it's me Rach…Sean's left me. He's run off with Samantha.'

'You introduced him to swan-necked, Angelina Jolie look-alike, Samantha? What were you thinking?'

'I know. She showed up at the wine bar. And that was it. He couldn't take his eyes off her.'

'Well. That's Sean for you…Look I can't really talk now. I'm in the middle of something.'

'KATHRYN! I MEAN IT. I'LL FUCKING DROP YOU IF YOU DON'T GET OFF THE PHONE.'

'Is that Ben the Vet? You sound worse off than me. He's actually losing it over a phone call? Say you'll drop him if he doesn't stop shouting.'

'Rach, I really can't hang around much longer. Talk to you after Christmas. Okay?'

'Oh. Yes. It's Christmas and I'm on my own again.'

'Bye Rach. I really must fly,' I said, hanging up as Ben jerked the ropes up and down.

'WILL YOU STOP THAT!?'

'WHAT ARE YOU GONNA DO ABOUT IT!?'

'STOP IT PLEASE BEN! YOU'RE SCARING ME!' I said, jigging around like Pinocchio.

'NOT UNTIL YOU'VE ANSWERED ME! ARE YOU IN LOVE WITH LUKE?!'

'NO! YES! I DON'T KNOW.'

'IF I THREW MYSELF OVER THIS CLIFF, WHO WOULD YOU SAVE FIRST? ME OR LUKE!? YOU'D BETTER GET THE QUESTION RIGHT OR, GOD HELP ME I WILL JUMP!'

'Luke.'

'SPEAK UP I CAN'T HEAR YOU!'

'I SAID: "LUKE". I'D SAVE LUKE FIRST.'

I looked up and saw the last of the rockets sending out sprays of silver and gold in a grand finale, followed by ear-shattering bangs. Ben had disappeared and I was free falling down towards the rocks in time to cannon fire. It happened so quickly I didn't even have time to think. Then with a gut-wrenching jerk the ropes became taut again.

'ARE YOU ALRIGHT KAT!? I'VE GOT YOU MY *SEABOUND SALPIGLOSSIS*!' Mick shouted breathlessly, peering over the edge of the cliff.

'MICK!? WHAT'S HAPPENED TO BEN!? DID HE FALL!?'

'YES! ON HIS BACK! HE'S LYING HERE LIKE A DEAD WEIGHT AND UNCONSCIOUS! IT MUST BE THE "RECOILING SNAKEBITE" EFFECT KICKING IN! YOU'RE SAFE NOW WE'RE BOTH TIED TO ANCHORMAN! HURRY UP AND GET TO *SIR GALAHAD* BEFORE SHE KILLS HIM!'

Mick lowered me down onto the rocks. I detached the harness and tentatively made my way across the slippery surface. Leaning into the wind with head down, I reached Aunt Leonora.

'What are you doing? Leave him alone!' I ordered.

'Eez zawt yaw Dawfeeneeaw? Mawtawn eez nawt breezawnk. I zeenk he eez dawd. I vawntawd taw bawree heem awt zee.'

'It's not Davinia! I'm Kathryn. And that's not Martin! It's Luke. Oh. No. Did you put a love potion in his Evian?'

'Yawz. I deed. I awnlee vawntawd taw mark heem lawf maw,' she said, pushing Luke further into the sea.

'Stop it! I need to get him out of the water. Just back off, or God help me I'll deck you!'

'Vawt eez "dawk yaw" plawz? Haw cawn yaw dawk maw vawn eet eez awlrawdee dawk? I dawnt awndawztawnd yaw awkzawnt.'

'Not dark. I mean…Oh. Forget it…'

It suddenly fell into place. Her accent was a mixture of Cornish and Transylvanian. Words were a waste of time, so I pushed her hard and away from Luke.

'Dawnt yaw zpawl maw fawr cawt. Daw yaw naw haw mawnee awnawmawlz I hawd taw keel faw zeez?'

'You killed all the foxes?'

'Yawz. I zawt yaw dawfeel dawg vawz a fawx. Haw. Haw.'

'So you did run over Lucky on purpose. It wasn't an accident.'

'Vawt daw yaw zeenk I awm - a pawzzeecawt? Awf cawrz I deed eet awn pawpawz. Bawt heez fawr vawz taw mawngee awnd fawl awf hawls.'

'And I suppose you thought back there in the church that Mrs. Higginbotham's cat was a fox as well?'

'Naw. I hawd plawntee awf fawr. Maw cawt vawz cawmplawt. Eet eez bawtawfawl vccz a hawt awz vawl. Zee cawt vawz a znawk. I vawz zarztee. Haw. Haw.'

'The cat was a snake? I get it. You mean "snack". Oh. God! Was it you who killed Boss?'

'Haw cawn I keel a bawz, stawpawd!'

'Not a bus! I said "Boss" my white dog!'

'Vawn vawz zeez?'

'About six years ago! You did kill him. For your bloody white fur coat! You bitch!'

'Mawbaw I vawd hawf dawn. Bawt I vawz een zee awzawlawn zen. Lawkt awp lark a mawd vawmawn.'

'You were locked up in a Mental Institution.'

'Vawt is mawntawl awnztawtawzhawn. Yaw naw I awn awmmawtawl.'

'Not mortal! I said "mental". Crazy. Bonkers. Nutcase.'

'I naw vawt yaw mawn veez "bawnkaws". Zee hawf brawt zeez cawntree taw eetz knaws.'

'Not bankers. I give up!'

'Eez eet tawmb Dawfeeneeaw? Cawn I keel yaw naw plawz? I zaw vawnt taw pawzh yaw een zee vawtaw.'

Before I could move she started to run at me. I still don't know how she managed to stay upright in those heels...Luke was on the edge of the water and I knew the next wave would take him. As I tried to dodge out of her way a dark figure appeared from nowhere, swooped down and grabbed her.

'Awlawxawndaw. Yaw hawf cawm fawr maw dawlank.'

'Edward? Is that you?' I asked, as the familiar elongated figure appeared to fly out to sea with my Aunt in his arms.

'Good evening Kathryn,' he replied, in passing.

'Alexandu is that you?' Mick called out, abseiling down the cliff like a monkey, before swinging towards Edward.

'Uncle Wolfgang?' he said, looking puzzled then disappearing round the other side of the cliff, still holding onto Aunt Leonora, with Mick swinging after. Then I heard Aunt Leonora's voice shouting out: 'Gawdbaw lawzaw!'

For a minute I was completely dumbfounded. Then dealt with the task in hand which was, dragging Luke back from the brink of drowning. His unconscious body was difficult to move. After much falling and tussling with his dead weight, I managed to grasp hold of his hands and heaved him over the rocks to a safer place. We had about five minutes before the whole section flooded.

I knelt over him and pumped his lungs in the same way he'd taught me. Water spouted out of his mouth and he made a groaning noise. I managed to turn him over onto his back, but he didn't move. I couldn't hear whether he was breathing or not, as the sea thundered against the rock. I was soaked to the skin and getting colder by the minute. Tilting his head back I gave him the kiss of life. His lips had turned blue. He just lay there, cold and unresponsive.

'Luke, for God's sake don't die on me. Not like this. There's so much I want to tell you…I love you,' I said, slapping his face.

He still remained motionless, so I breathed into his mouth again. When I felt his tongue flicker over mine, I pulled back.

'More please. I want more Kat. It's been so long,' he said, sitting up and kissing me fiercely, as another huge wave crashed over us.

'You total and utter bastard! I thought you

were dead! How could you do this to me?' I spluttered angrily, and punched him in the chest. Feeling a strong sense of satisfaction, as he fell back and hit his head on the rocks.

'Whoo-oo! I knew all along you loved me Grommet,' he laughed, 'now let's get the hell out of here before we both drown.'

'And how are we supposed to do that without any ropes?'

'ALRIGHT KAT, LUKE MATE?' Seagull shouted down from the helicopter. 'Catch hold, will you?'

'We need to get you both to hospital as soon as,' Seagull said, looking slightly the worse for wear.

'No worries mate. We're sound. Drop us on the cliff top will you?' Luke told him.

'I have to see if Ben's up there and still unconscious. For all I know he could have been dragged over the cliff, when Mick did his disappearing act.'

'Hold on then. Put the spotlight on will you, Bert? We're looking for a drunken giant,' Seagull said.

'Ben came with you, to look for me?' Luke asked.

'Yes. It's a long story. I'll tell you later.'

'Does he know you love me?'

'He's known all along I think…Over there

Seagull, by the bushes. Thank God he's still on dry land,' I said.

'If he's had an overdose of Gannet's "Recurring Snakebites" he might very well be dead,' Seagull replied bluntly. 'Shall we reel him in?'

'No. It'll take too long…Phone Mark the Medic. He's the nearest doctor,' I said.

'Do you want us to hoist him back to the house? He's too much of a big bugger for you to carry.'

Luke and I were lowered safely onto the path, where we quickly checked to see if Ben was breathing. He looked deathly pale but was muttering and groaning. Then we slipped him into the harness, releasing Mick's rope which was still tied round his middle. God knows where the Count had ended up. For some reason I knew the lying toe-rag hadn't used all of his nine lives. But then again, he had saved my life back there.

It was funny in a macabre way, to see Ben hovering six feet above the ground with his head slumped forward and his arms flapping like wings. Poor man, I felt so guilty. It must have been the worst Christmas ever for him. At that spot in time I couldn't think of a single thing that would help him feel better.

Seagull took the helicopter as near to the house as possible, then released Ben, giving us a salute before circling back to search for three more bodies. Luke and I managed to walk Ben back towards the gate. The whole area looked like a bombsite and the gate was nowhere to be seen. There was a great hole in the wall. And what had been the greenhouse was now strew all over the garden in fragments.

Sophie, Zach, Alan, Sal, Lucy, Maggie, Paulo and Mark the Medic, still in his pyjamas, waited by the burned back door, looking around anxiously. Strangely, Countess Iris had slept through the whole commotion. That's contentment for you. And, of course, she'd had a very hectic and crazy wedding day. Joe had wandered down to the beach looking for me.

'Kat, thank God you're safe. You too Luke,'

Sophie exclaimed. 'Get out of those wet clothes. There're dressing gowns and blankets in the kitchen, warming by the fire…Poor Ben, he looks awful. Let me get to him. Put him in the studio will you? If I set eyes on Gannet and those other two stooges there'll be hell to pay. Zach? They're banned from my home for a year, until they can learn some common sense,' she said angrily.

'Get the stomach pump out of the shed. That one we used on Slops three months ago,' Zach told Mark the Medic. 'Alan, make them all hot drinks, while I help Sophie. We don't want any more casualties on Christmas Day… They weren't invited,' he added, looking at Sophie sheepishly. 'And I think Davies the Godley is partly responsible. He mixed up some "hair of the dog" after you'd dosed Ben. I believe Ben drank a whole pint of it before I could do anything.'

To my relief I saw Lucky asleep in his basket. He breathed regularly and seemed calm, apart from the intermittent twitching. I expect he'd got used to the racket. The house was never quiet for long.

'I want to be with him,' I told Mark, 'when you do it.'

'Okay Kat. You can hold the bucket,' he replied.

'He's had such a terrible holiday,' I said, looking at Ben's ashen face.

'So you've decided on Ben then?' Zach asked, carrying Ben into the studio with the assistance of Mark and Paulo.

'No. I love Luke.'

'Oh. Dear me. Poor old Ben. Let's get him working again in time for Boxing Day.'

I watched Mark drain out Ben's stomach with something that looked like a bicycle pump, some bellows, plastic tubing and a toilet plunger, with the end of a trombone connected to it. It was horrible but it got everything out. Never in my whole life have I felt so much sympathy for another person, or so much like vomiting. It was a low point for all of us.

When Sophie administered her neutralizing

peppermint antacid remedy, we heard Ben sigh with relief. He didn't even notice that I had undressed him, or was about to wash the mud from his white bits. I had pangs of remorse looking at his gorgeous body, his handsome face, his dark curly hair and perfect shiny eyebrows. I had to let him go to some other lucky girl who would appreciate all his qualities, because in the end, Luke was "the one". I couldn't help but feel a great sense of loss.

I needed to explain myself at last, now that we were finally alone. The words came easy to me as he slept so peacefully.

'When I said that I loved you it was true. I've loved you for as long as I can remember – even before I'd met you…You're *Mr. Darcy* - every girl's dream man. Young Colin Firth in a wet shirt or, in your case, a sick shirt…When you asked me to marry you, I was swept off my feet - especially with you being naked…You're so romantic, not to mention being kind and really tall. And it was great the way you conned all the locals into believing the party was over…That was a stroke of sheer genius…Even now I hate letting you go, because I know you'll soon meet someone else - a girl who will love you, body and soul. When that time comes I'll be very envious.

I don't suppose you'll want to drink alcohol for quite a while,' I said, washing his hands. 'When you finally come round, you'll be saying: "Never again"! If you're offered unknown drinks by strangers again you have to refuse. You're such a pushover…Alcohol should be consumed for enjoyment, or to get a little tipsy. Not to forget your problems. Although, I must tell you this, you're hilarious when you're pissed. Not so in control or uptight. That's no excuse to get shit-faced though.

And you should take your time with girls. Get to know them better before you fall in love, otherwise you'll probably get dumped again,' I told him, drying his chest then refilling the bowl with clean water. 'Don't go telling them about your wealthy parents and owning outright your own house. You've got enough going for you without the trimmings.

You could always replace lazy Charlie with a female vet. Who knows she might like: ice hockey, mountain climbing, skiing and putting her hand up a cow's arse… And try working in the daytime for a change. People who work nights by choice are a strange bunch and I should know. I'm one of them…And right now you really should take some time out. The rebound technique is not good. Get over a girl before you pounce on the next one. It's not so bad being alone for a while… Alright?' I said, shampooing the mud off his hair. 'Oh. And when you do come round, you'll find some more of your clothing's missing. Sorry there were in shreds...

I've got to thank you for showing me how to act in a relationship…Even though it wasn't with you. You put me in touch with feelings I didn't know I had. And now I'm blubbering like a baby…Sorry Ben,' I said, rinsing his hair. 'I was really awful to you. I tried so hard to be truthful and not lead you on. Life's funny really and a bit like buses. One never comes along when you need it. Then you get two together…And there you are all clean and almost as good as new,' I said, towelling his head.

I kissed him gently on the mouth for the last time and covered him with the duvet whispering: 'You're one of the best lovers in the whole Goddamn universe *Mr. Darcy* and I'll miss you.'

When I walked over to the sink to empty the bowl, I noticed Luke standing in the doorway.

'Come on Kat. He'll be fine now. Let him have a little peace and quiet. Eh? Grommet?'

'Is Joe back?' I asked, still sniffing.

'Yes. He and Sal have gone to bed. There was no sign of Wolfgang though.'

We all sat in silence in the kitchen, stunned by the night's events and exhausted by the wedding celebration, until Zach said: 'Time for bed folks. I've got an enormous turkey to stuff sometime today, in case you've all forgotten - and Merry Christmas everybody.'

'Merry Christmas. Night all. I'll stay up in case Wolfgang shows up,' I told them.

I was too shattered to move from the fireside. Luke lifted a snoring Lucky out of the other armchair and gently placed him back into his basket. He didn't even twitch as Luke covered him in Sophie's shawl. All three of us were absolutely shattered.

'Are you warmer now Kat?' he asked, his eyes closing with the heat.

'Yes. I'm fine,' I yawned, pulling the blanket around me.

'Thanks for saving my life.'

'We're even now,' I said, smiling.

'I'll understand if you've changed your mind and want to be with Ben. He's a top bloke.'

'You're the one I'm in love with Luke. You're my soul mate and I want to spend the rest of my life with you. No more "Absence makes the heart grow fonder". We'll be together in a proper relationship and then we'll see how we get on...

My brief affair with Ben was just a girlish fantasy. He deserves better treatment…Now be quiet.'

'There's something else…Down there in the water when my number was up…I think someone pushed me to the surface Kat. Don't tell a soul, will you? They'll think I've gone kook.'

'It was my Dad,' I said.

'For sure?'

'Yes.'

'There's just one more question Kat?'

'What?'

'Will you give me a bed bath sometime?' he grinned.

'I'll think about it.'

He smiled and sank back into the chair, looking like an angel in his white dressing gown.

I watched him doze, realizing that I knew every contour of his beautiful face. The way his dark lashes contrasted against his sun-bleached hair. How his eyes crinkled at the corners when he laughed. I loved the way his full mouth was slightly upturned and always smiley. His tanned firm body was barely concealed by the dressing gown. Even his feet were beautiful. He was a living, breathing Michelangelo masterpiece. And at that spot in time I felt so in love with him, it almost hurt.

'If you want to go to bed, I'll watch over Ben,' he offered, peering at me sleepily and smiling again. His luminous eyes shone in the firelight. And I wanted him to look at me again in that special way. A way in which he radiated that rare commodity – joie de vivre - and it was contagious.

'I'll be okay sleeping here...Luke?'

'Yes?'

'Will you stay with me please?'

'Yes.'

'Thanks. Night.'

'Night.'

64

'Wake up sleepy head,' Sophie's said gently.

'What? What time is it?' I asked, trying to open my eyes.

'It's 12.15pm on a bright and sunny Christmas Day.'

'How did I get up here?' I asked, realizing that I was in my bed.

'I suppose Luke must have carried you up last night.'

'Where is he? He's not gone, has he?'

Sophie smiled and looked out of the window. 'He's still here…They're all out there cleaning up the mess: Luke, Derek the Dynamite, Wolfgang, Tommy, Zach, Joe, Brian the Brickie, Paulo, Alan, Mark the Medic, and Uncle Tom sundry and all. Tommy has made a start on rebuilding the wall already. It's funny but most of the debris landed in the hole. Now that's what I call luck…'

'I can't believe I didn't stir when Luke carried me up. I've not done that before.'

'There are quite a few things none of us have done before. Bring in the breakfast tray will you Lucy please?'

'Morning Lucy,' I yawned.

Lucy carried in my breakfast without replying. Sophie waited until she had disappeared down the stairs before speaking.

'Last night…down on the rocks? Luke told me that it was Martin who saved his life. Is it true about your dream?'

'Yes. It's true. He did. He warned me that Luke was in danger…What Luke told you is true. I know for sure the nightmares are gone for good. I didn't realize it, but they were always about my Dad trying to tell me something. I usually woke up before he could. And now I know he's at peace and with my Mother,' I said, taking hold of her hand. 'We can go and visit their grave now. Can't we?'

'Yes. We will, in the New Year, if you're ready? It's time to let go now,' she said softly.

'And she's gone away. There's no need to worry anymore. I just feel it's ended. Alexandu has taken her…Did Mick say anything?'

'No. He wants to explain everything to you personally,' she said, sitting on the window seat.

'I bet he does…The old liar…You remember me telling you about Edward Hinchcliffe, well, it turns out that he's my "late" Uncle Alexandu. And Mick the tramp, now Wolfgang, really is Count Wolfgang and my Great Uncle at that. What a happy family…'

'Two more for the album Kat,' Sophie said, smiling. 'And Wolfgang adores you.'

'Maybe…Thanks for the breakfast. I'm so hungry,' I said, tucking into bacon and eggs.

I was half way through my meal when I remembered poor Ben. Before I could speak, Sophie anticipated my sudden sense of panic.

'Ben's fine. A little hoarse, but well, considering…He's managed to eat some scrambled eggs…Kat, he's gone to pack his bags.'

'What? He can't go like this. Not on Christmas Day for God's sake.'

'I don't think he wants to hang around any longer.'

'Try and stall him…please. At least until I get dressed. I've got to speak to him before he goes. He can't spend Christmas Day on his own,' I said, leaping out of bed and heading for the bathroom.

I dressed in record time and ran downstairs, just in time to see Ben about to set off in the *Range Rover.*

'Ben! Wait! Don't go like this. Please!' I shouted, sprinting after him.

'Hi. Kathryn. How are you feeling?' he asked, letting the window down.

'Why are you being so polite? It sounds bloody ridiculous. Get mad at me, or something…Turn off the engine…You have to stay for Christmas dinner, at least.'

'I can't. It's all too much. I'm not angry with you. I can't take anymore. I'm not an unfeeling man, even if you think so.'

'Oh. Ben. I never thought that. I'm so sorry. Please come inside.'

He was just about to speak when Lucy rushed out with her suitcase, shouting: 'Ben! Wait for me. I'll go back to London with you,' she said, trying to open the passenger door.

'No. Lucy. I want to do the journey on my own. You know, you're a bright, attractive girl, but you really should stop falling in love with men who are in love with someone else. You'll never find happiness that way. Believe me. Break the habit before it's too late. You gotta be more selective…Now go inside…please.'

'Oh. Ben. What can I say? And what will you do for food?' I asked, feeling guilty as hell and watching Lucy's long walk back to the house.

'Sophie's packed me a bag full of goodies. There's enough to feed a whole army in there,' he smiled.

'I wish we'd met in a different time and a different place - if you understand my waffling.'

'And I wish you'd let Fishman drown last night. And, who knows, maybe we'll meet in a future life...Oho. I'm beginning to sound like you - really weird.'

'I always told you I was weird.'

'That's what I liked about you. I gotta go now,' he said, his face becoming serious again.

'If you're determined to leave then...It's only right that you should have these back,' I said, passing him the engagement ring and earrings still in the boxes.

'No Kathryn, I don't have any need for them...They were meant for Eleanor anyhow...I have to tell you though, she never saw them. You hang on to them,' he said.

'Oh. I see...Please, I can't possibly keep them. They're so expensive I'd be scared of getting mugged on the Underground. You can get a refund on the ring. It's not been worn. Well, only once.'

'Okay. Keep the earrings. When you wear them, think of me. Will you?'

'Yes. I will Ben. Thanks…Can I kiss you one last time?'

'No. I don't need that right now. I hope you and Luke will be very happy together. Take care of Lucky for me, but please don't sing to him. He's been through enough.'

'Are you sure this is what you want to do?' I asked, remaining silent on his previous night's performance as lead singer in the choir. 'You're quite welcome to stay here for the rest of the holidays. The Centre can do without you for a while, I'm sure.'

'I have to go Kathryn. I'm gonna spend some time with my folks. Do a little skiing maybe. Get my head straight…I've managed to get a flight out for the 28th December.'

'I'm sorry for hurting you and I'm sorry that my friends made you ill and most of all I'm sorry for ruining your Christmas.'

'You didn't ruin it. You stopped it from being

boring…It has been one of the weirdest though. I shoulda known better than to rush at you like that. You were bound to feel cornered.'

'Oh. No. It was lovely. All the rushing I mean. I enjoyed being swept off my feet. It was so romantic…What every girl dreams of really…It's just that…Well…You know…And the passion was great…I'll really miss you. Will you keep in touch?'

'No. I might send you a postcard, when I'm feeling a little better.'

'You know you're welcome any time to stay here for a holiday. Lucky would love to see you.'

'You are one of the best bull-shitters in the whole Goddamn universe *Miss Elizabeth*. Now go get inside before I drag you into the car and have my wicked way with you.'

'Oh. No. In the studio, last night, you were conscious all along?' I asked, blushing to the roots.

'Only for the interesting bits…And the bed

bath was pretty amazing also,' he said, as the window slid up.

Watching him pull away down the drive was one of the hardest things I'd ever done. Letting go of the perfect man...And I waved until he disappeared from view. He didn't look back.

Poor Lucy sat on her suitcase waiting by the front door and looking lost. I dried my eyes and walked towards her, wondering if she was angry with me.

'Alright Kat?' she said, smiling weakly.

'Yes...He's right Lucy. You're so quick to fall in love...I suppose sometimes it happens. Love at first sight, or in my family's case, at first bite. And sometimes love has a way of creeping up on you when you're not looking...Are you coming inside? You'll have a great time today. I promise you that. And I think Mark the Medic has looked your way more than once.'

'No thanks. If you could give me a lift to the station, I'll make my way home. It's a while since I saw my parents. They've been so good to me and I've not once told them how much I care for them.'

'I understand. Why don't you take my car? The tank's full. Travelling on the train on Christmas Day is going to be hell.'

'Won't you be short-handed now? What with Ben leaving like that… Kat, I hope you don't mind me saying this: but he was something special.'

'I know,' I said, sighing, 'but Luke's the one I want to be with…Anyhow, I won't need the car and I've got a feeling that our fellow workers will be staying for quite a while. And I don't think they're in a hurry to get back to London just yet. Zach has enough mates. We can always borrow Ted the Ticket's minibus to get us home.'

'Thanks. That would be great. Shall I see you in the New Year?'

'Course you will. But please, before you set off, come and say goodbye to everyone. Countess Iris has taken quite a shine to you.'

65

After seeing Lucy's lonely departure, we all returned to the kitchen where Countess Iris sat peeling sprouts and singing quietly. She looked so happy that it helped me forget about my own sadness. I knew for sure that every eligible woman in *The Rockies* would fall for my ex-fiancé – especially him wearing a ski suit.

'Come and sit with me Katie,' Countess Iris said.

'Did you sleep well last night Mrs...I mean Countess Iris?'

'Oh. For goodness sake call me Auntie Iris. It's make it all so much easier...And yes I slept like a baby...Now Katie I hear you're up for a medal after last night's bravery.'

'Who told you that?'

'Why my Wolfgang did of course. He said that

you saved Luke from drowning and got Russian Olga locked up at last.'

'Yes. I suppose I did, I said, surprised she started using real names. And now it's all over at last. We can sleep safely in our beds at night,' I said, hoping she would move on to 1946.

'You think so? Well, you're wrong. They'll be "Reds" under all our beds if we're not careful. Did you check under yours this morning?'

'I did - and there was nothing there. Not even a bit of fluff.'

'Sal, you mean? The hussy! She's made the most beautiful Christmas cake and iced it. Now you tell me, where did she get the eggs and butter from?'

'Zach keeps chickens and cows. And Sal is very much in love with Joe and they are going to have a baby.'

'Does he know about it? And have you seen the bomb damage out there?'

'That's not bomb damage. Zach is excavating

for dinosaur bones,' I told her, getting into the swing of things again.

'Hasn't he got anything better to do? He should be manning the radios and checking for bugs.'

'We were all up last night while you slept, sending carrier pigeons to our agents in London. And the house is bug free.'

'Very well agent Katie. Stand down and make me a nice cup of tea. I've still got some *Battenberg* left in the larder, so bring us both a couple of thick slices.'

'I'm sorry to say that there is only one slice left. I gave the other to Luke to revive him last night.'

'Don't you fret. I've got six more cakes in my suitcase. Go and get one dear.'

'I'm on my way.' Will I never be *Battenberg* free? Thank heaven for some normality again.

It was funny really, walking into the studio and not seeing Ben flat on his back. It's not a very pleasant picture I know. As time goes on

I expect I shall see him in all his former glory. The man who got away, perpetuated in an image greatly enhanced by an overactive imagination. I opened the French windows to let in some air and the bad spirits out. The back garden was like a building site with Wolfgang inside the hole and organizing the "chain gang" in a bucket relay.

'Heave Ho me Hearties,' he shouted happily.

It was funny to see him working in daylight and without his fencing visor. He had on sunglasses, gloves and a trilby. There he was in all his glory, my regal and noble Great Uncle Wolfgang. My arse.

'Good morrow Kat,' he called, peering over the top of the hole.

I waved in the royal way along with the Agincourt victory sign. It was impossible for me not to smile. Out there was a man of many parts, few inhibitions and a multitude of misdemeanours. I tried so hard to keep up the anger but I knew it was impossible. I loved the old bugger.

'Good morning guys,' I hailed. 'Have you found a T-Rex yet?'

'Happy Christmas Grommet,' they chorused and started singing another Cornish melody about the wayward fisherman baking a "Stargazy" pie.

'Get the kettle on will you my loverrlee and make us a brew,' Brian the Brickie called out from inside the hole. He was always the first in where there was muck and rubble.

I looked around for Luke and he was over by the skip and covered in dust. When he waved and grinned, I knew I'd made the right choice. He was so loverrlee, my heart did a Hulluwatu.

Mark the Medic, still in pyjamas and covered in dust, and the rest of the gang departed, to get changed for a late Christmas Dinner at *Wisteria House*. I guessed by then more dinner guests would be piling in bearing homemade pasties and various other offerings. It was an opportune time to corner Wolfgang.

'What news doth thou hath, my *Surfing Surfinia*? Art thou well on this goodly morn?'

'I'm good Count Wolfgang, or should I say: Uncle Woolfie now that we're related?'

'Not now Kat. Some other time maybe?' he said, looking round anxiously.

'Look, if you're a bloody vampire as well, I need to know right now! Don't you think? How could you lie to me all this time? I mean what is the truth? Are you: Mick the Tramp, Embalmed Arnold, William Cedric Crapper, or Count Wolfgang Bullshitter? I'm confused. So tell me now. Don't you think I've deserve to know?'

'I was. No. Sometimes. Yes,' he chuckled.

I took the clever sod's arm and dragged him into the sitting room.

'Now sit down and start at the beginning Uncle dearest.'

'Well, let me see, ah, yes, now in the beginning I was born Wolfgang etcetera in Transylvania. It was a dangerous time for people like us -.'

'Like whom?'

'Night people…Many of my ancestors, and yours, were murdered. When ignorant peasants constantly accused us of being a vampires, then one started to act like a blood-sucker. And one "might as well be hung for a sheep as a lamb", so to speak. Although one was a mere babe when one was initiated by one's Father,' he said, eyes twinkling. 'I remember one's Father wearing a set of false fangs during daylight hours and terrifying the natives.'

'Why are you talking posh? And you can't believe yourself to be a vampire? Stop acting daft and be serious.'

Wolfgang sank back into his chair and rubbed his facial scars for a while before answering.

'This is how an educated Count talks Kat, and no, not anymore,' he said, half smiling. 'Now shall daft one continue, or will you carry on the interrogation?'

'Alright. I'll be quiet…But will you drop the "one" business. It's really irritating…And by the way, thanks for saving my life last night.'

'I was returning the favour my *Scary Scaevola*… To continue: When I was seven years old my parents decided to send me to England for my own safety. I was lucky enough to escape the family curse; although I still do prefer the night time air. My adoptive Mother, Mrs. Winifred Crapper, took care of me until manhood. I'm afraid her thoughtless choice of English names was my undoing during those early years. I turned from refined aristocratic brat, to snot-nosed scrapper. Then I went to war... Kat, I must say, you're the image of my natural Mother when she was your age. I mean a dead-ringer,' he said taking an old sepia picture out of his pocket.

Any resemblance I had to Aunt Leonora was overshadowed by my Great Grandmother's portrait. It was uncanny. It was a picture of me in a high necked long frock and a big-haired bun, wearing the ruby earrings and ring and standing by the side of a really tall handsome man.

'In my Mother's letter...she said that I favoured her Grandmother.'

'If you take another look at your Great Granddad you might see another resemblance. He was 6' 4" and powerfully built. In those days the average height was around 4' 10" so he kept the wolves at bay.'

'Blimey! You're right. He does look the same as Ben. That is seriously weird.'

'It's not really, if you believe in reincarnation. Some nitwits do.'

'So how did you find me? Was it coincidence?'

'No Kat. You don't think I hung round the bistro for the crap food do you? Alexandu told me where you were. Both he and I looked out for you. Did you really think you could walk, or in your case, run the streets of London after midnight and be safe? And believe me we had many a problem keeping up with you... Alexandu bought a tandem bike.'

'Ah. That explains the "being followed" feeling...So how did you meet up with Alexandu? Did Edward Hinchcliffe really look out for me? My Mother believed him to be dead.'

'He was left for dead...I told you that after the War I travelled for a while. Well, I went back to my homeland to see if things had changed and to find my blood family. They were all missing or dead, every single one of them, except my sister, Alicia Katarina, your Grandmother. She married a man not dissimilar to your Dad, who took care of her. She had a mild version of the family curse and could tolerate daylight in small doses. We hoped and prayed her children would be able to live a normal life, but that was not the case. Dark-haired Alexandu came first and, thank the Lord, was a healthy child. Then Leonora was born and Davinia soon followed. Both of whom had inherited the same affliction in different degrees.'

'So why is Alexandu leading a night life now?'

'He'd gotten used to sleeping in the daytime. He helped the family as much as possibly but was unable to interact with the outsiders because of his family history and because we'd been educated at home. He was always a bit of a loner, but a great thinker and philanthropist. He'd freely donate his blood to anyone in need,' he chuckled. 'But seriously, it was difficult for us to mix. Well, more than difficult. It was impossible back then.'

'Do you know what happened that night Alexandu left to sort out the men who'd raped Aunt Leonora?'

'Yes I do. Leonora was always the wild one. She insisted on fraternizing with the locals. Sometime she was like a cat on heat. They took advantage of her naivety. It was unfortunate that she couldn't have a normal courtship. She was a real stunner…No matter how hard Davinia and Alexandu tried to keep a low profile, Leonora would do the opposite just to be the centre of attention…I'd gone to arrange safe passage for the three of them to make a new life in London. I was away for two months, finding accommodation and researching which hospitals had the best Dermatologists… Kat, it's time you knew. The house you live in belongs to Alexandu.'

'Coincidence, I suppose, that I rented the flat above?'

'No. I knew you hated living in Halls of Residence. It was too much like the Care Home… Do you remember the brochure in your pigeon hole at college? I put it there. I knew you would fall in love with the attic flat. Being a Duwulfe and sleeping under the stars at night, is one and the same thing.'

'So you're a Duwulfe as well? I though Habsburg sounded phoney. Mind you, the whole bloody name sounds like a total cock-up.'

'I'm afraid it was a little white lie on my part. The rest of my title is long but true.'

'Is your marriage to Iris legal then?'

'Yes. I slipped Davies the Godley a "pony" to cough loudly when he said Duwulfe. You didn't notice?'

'No. I always switch off when Davies the Godley starts bellowing…. Why didn't you want me to know that you and I are related?'

'You tell me. Who would want us misfits for relatives? Alexandu and I thought you'd be ashamed of us, or scared by our background. We wanted you to have a normal life. We'd let you down before. Not getting to you in time. Not helping your Mother after your Dad was lost. You see, we didn't find out until it was too late. We thought Martin was protecting you and your Mother. We we're too busy trying to find Leonora after she disappeared. We had to keep her confined. As you know, I was at rock bottom with the booze, most of the time. And poor Alexandu blamed himself for Leonora's madness and Davinia's death. He sank into depression. That's why he later allowed Leonora to walk free. Conning himself that she had regained her sanity.'

'It's okay Mick. I mean Wolfgang. You both did your best. So when did you actually find me?'

'We knew you were in Care. But what sort of life could we offer you: a knackered alcoholic tramp and a semi-retired celibate vampire? When I first set eyes on you in Newquay, you were running along the beach. You'd be about sixteen I think, and I decided you were doing just fine without us. It gladdened my old heart to see you so healthy and energetic.'

'So tell me. How did you find Alexandu after he was injured?'

'When I finally returned to give him the good news, the house had burned to the ground. I thought they were all dead. My only remaining relatives all burned to death,' he said, filling up. 'It took me two days to find the people responsible. Money talked then, as it does now. I'll not go into detail, only to say that I vented my rage on the guilty and took them out, one by one. The last two talked after a little coaxing and told me the whereabouts of Alexandu's body. They said that the women had left before they'd torched the house.'

'I'm sorry Mick...I didn't know any of this.'

'It's alright Kat. I'm fine now. I don't do bawling,' he said, wiping his eyes. 'I've got them to thank for these though,' he added, touching his scars.

'So it wasn't drunken football yobs?'

'Na. They're pussycats compared to a howling

mob of Neanderthals armed with knives and torches…I had my vengeance though.'

'So you found Alexandu still alive?'

'God knows how, but yes. He'd been ambushed by about twenty thugs. He'd finished off six of them and injured more, but he was overpowered. They just kept on coming…It took me a while to recognize him among the bodies. He was still breathing. I got him to safety. With the aid of a local fixer I stitched him up and bound his ribs… He was in a bad way Kat. His head was the size of a football. The ignorant morons had tried to stake his heart but succeeded only in cracking his ribs. It was touch and go for three months but he pulled round. He's a strong man… Then we made our way to London. The rest you know.'

'Last night, when you abseiled down the cliff, where did Alexandu and Aunt Leonora go?'

'I honestly don't know. By the time I'd peeled myself off the cliff face they'd vanished. Alexandu is a very unusual and resilient man. Despite his lean conformation there lurks beneath a wall of solid muscle. In fact, he's one of the strongest and fitest men I've ever seen in action…And he won't let anyone harm his Sister. He understands now, she must be contained for her own good. What with her favourite tipple being warm blood and all…You won't be bothered by her again. I know that for certain…And therein endeth the diatribe.'

'And is that the truth?'

'Would I lie to you Kat?'

'Yes.'

'I swear to you on my honour as a Count, that I have told you the truth.'

'The whole truth?'

'Allow me a little mystique.'

'Rat-bag.'

'I thank you my *Rude Rubeckia*.'

What else could I do but hug my shiny and new Great Uncle - and check my mobile for Uncle Alexandu's number?

66

Christmas Dinner was a jolly affair, with much laughter and singing. Surprisingly Paulo had a lovely tenor voice and did the bistro proud with a very good rendition of: *O Sole Mio* in English. Little Maggie radiated happiness. Her injured face was almost better. Apparently my ever-scheming Godmother had waved her magic wand and found them a small shop to rent with a flat above. Enchanted by Newquay, they'd decided not to return to London but to open their own cream tea come pizza bistro just outside the town.

Wayne and Trevor had lost two of their best waiters. I was sure they would be pleased to know, on their return, that little Maggie had found happiness at last. She was the hardest working of all of us - and the kindest. I was certain though, that their new manager would find good replacements among his many friends. As long as they weren't: Two-fingered Boris, Elephant Manito, Hovis and Sliced Bochenek and last, but not least, Dusty Filth. I only hoped he wouldn't employ my Uncle Alexandu. Wayne would definitely fancy him, but my boss's nice, pink, plump neck would be too much for my Uncle to resist. All of the aforementioned night-time people would surely have created havoc in the place by simply walking into it.

After a lengthy enjoyable Christmas Dinner, all the smokers piled outside. Alan and Davies the Godley were engrossed in conversation. The vicar had asked him to value a few items he'd put by for his retirement. My assumption was that they would all be solid silver and goblet shaped. Maybe I did him an injustice, but Davies the Godley was a man for all treasons, never dull and greatly loved by the community.

Luke and I had sat next to each other at the dining table and it was hard for both of us to keep still. Neither of us ate a deal. We just couldn't wait to be alone. I saw that look in his eyes and I wanted him so much…As the different courses arrived we became more impatient. There had been a considerable amount of footsy going on. At one point Brian the Brickie gave me the wink as I accidentally caught his foot.

As we followed the smokers outdoors Luke grabbed my hand and pulled me over to the pine trees.

'Kat it's been so long,' he said, holding me so tightly I couldn't breath.

'Too long,' I replied.

Before I could say another word Luke kissed me so passionately my legs turned to jelly.

'Can we go upstairs,' he asked, kissing my neck and shoulders. 'I can't wait any longer. I need you right now.'

'If we sneak through the side gate and round to the back stairs nobody will notice we've gone,' I said, breathlessly.

'Come on then. What are we waiting for?'

'Most definitely not a 22 bus my

Stardust-sprinkled Lovers,' a throaty voice chuckled, through a ring of smoke. 'Hang on I'll create a distraction.'

'Ta mate,' Luke said, laughing. 'On three…'

'Ladies and gentlemen,' Wolfgang announced, 'over to your right and past the bombsite you'll find the hind quarters of The Great Bear ascending over Jupiter. And if you look carefully you'll see the tail end of Haley's Comet entering Venus.'

As we both glanced back, those still standing were too far gone to even look up, never mind observe Wolfgang's dodgy star signs. We were on our way. I remember tripping up on the second flight of stairs in my haste to get to the first floor. This caused us to laugh uncontrollably, all the way to my room.

'Lock the door Luke,' I urged.

It was as if we'd never been apart. Ripping off our clothes and pouncing on each other as soon as we fell onto the bed. The passion was so consuming we were on fire. Luke kissed every part of my body and I was in heaven. There still was that old familiarity where we knew what the other wanted, but it was filled with a new, more intense desire…I urged him to make love to me quickly as I couldn't wait any longer. It was the best close encounter ever and we were overcome with such abandonment it was astounding.

'Oh. God. I love you so much Kat. That was amazing,' he said, falling back onto the pillow.

'It certainly was remarkable.'

'Give me a minute Grommet and I'll show you some more moves. Let's have a toast first,' he said, reaching under the bed for the champagne. 'I sneaked this up after Zach turned out the lights and brought in the flaming Christmas puddings.'

'You were that sure I'd come up here?' I asked, pretending to be annoyed.

'Sure was, one hundred percent. We're meant to be together Kat. And nothing can separates us from now on,' he said, pouring out two flutes of fizz.

At that exact moment Lucky set off howling

along to Seagull's raspy sea shanty, causing everyone to laugh. I grabbed my dressing gown, tip-toed over to the window seat and looked down onto the patio area, to see the whole bloody lot of them blowing kisses up at me and pretending to hug themselves.

'Pommie bastards,' Luke shouted down and closed the curtains.

After a luxuriously long shower we were about to join the others in the celebrations, until it came to drying off each other with the fluffy towels. So we spent the rest of the evening in bed. Luke gave me the most amazing foot massage and we ended up in the shower again, after which he crept downstairs to make us sandwiches when the folks gathered in the sitting room to watch the same old repeats.

After we'd eventually surface to join the madding crowd, we were greeted by a round of deafening applause. If secrets were ever kept among that band of merry men and women it would've been a miracle.

'So? When's the next wedding then?' Brian the Brickie asked me, eyeing up Sal.

'It won't be us, for sure. We've got a load of things to do before that day dawns,' I told him.

'Don't look at me either,' Sophie said, laughing. 'We intend to live in sin for the rest of our lives… If that's alright with you Davies the Godley?'

'I'm not the one you should be asking,' he said, raising his eyes to the sky.

'Does the vicar know I've been married before,' Countess Iris whispered to Wolfgang.

'You were a widow dearest, if you remember, and that is acceptable.'

'I know that Wolfgang, but even if I wasn't, I would still live with you.'

Luke and I looked at each other and smiled. It was time to catch a few waves before the discussion became too heated. Brian the Brickie had been divorced three times and the way his present wife was glaring at him, it might possibly be four.

'We'll see you all later,' I said, making for the

door as quickly as possible without appearing ill-mannered.

'I wonder where they're going,' Seagull pondered.

'I'll give you ten guesses,' Bert replied.

The tide was in full flow as we paddled out, then I saw Lucky swimming behind us.

'Luke, slow down,' I said, looking back.

'Come on Lucky mate. Hop onboard. I'll take you out for a quick lesson.'

Lucky scrambled onto the front of the board and virtually sat on Luke's head as the water splashed over him. He didn't seem to mind as the waves soaked his fuzzy face. It was as if he done it all his eventful life. When Luke turned his board, Lucky wobbled for a bit then took the stance. He was a natural regular foot which was a good thing, as his right paw was still weak. It was hilarious to see him balanced between Luke's feet, with head down, rudder swinging and soaked to the skin, snarling at the waves and licking the salt from his face.

'We'll have to get him a wetsuit,' Luke shouted happily.

As long as I live I will never forget that spot in time. It was magical and mystical whereby the sea and the sky became hazy and flowing. A view with no edges and little gravity, made up of indigo and silver, blurring into each other to form a moving collage. Just the three of us united in our love of the ocean and feeling blessed on such a night when the Christ Child had slept peacefully before the storm.

67

New Year.

On my arrival back in London after the Christmas holidays, I noticed a thick brown envelope with my name on it. As my fellow travellers unpacked, I made my way up to my Uncle's flat and listened at the door. Hoping to hear some noise, or howling, but it was as silent as the grave. Luke had gone to help Wolfgang prepare our evening meal - most probably pasta sauce given it was quite late.

I unlocked my flat door and the familiar smell of oil paints wafted out to greet me. I think I knew before I'd opened the envelope that it was from my Uncle. The contents took me by surprise. It was the deed to the whole house which was now assigned to me. Wolfgang had been appointed as landlord. I thought at the time that his first job would be to redecorate the whole building. It specifically granted Wolfgang and Iris a life tenancy at a peppercorn rent. I made up my mind in an instant that Sal and Joe would also live rent free - and that I would never make a business woman. My Uncle's only stipulation was that no one should enter his flat - except Wolfgang who was authorized to clean it. Bugger that.

After trying out all the keys I managed to get inside his flat. It was just as I'd expected it to be, but without the sarcophagus. The dark velvet curtains were closed and the décor looked rich, heavy and Victorian. The general demeanour of the place was somewhat depressing and there was a lingering smell of musk roses which permeated all the rooms. When I switched on the light I was amazed to see every single wall space throughout was covered with my paintings. They looked totally out of sync with the décor. My heart sank. He'd only bought them because I was his Niece and not because they were any good.

I sat for a while feeling disillusioned by the

MY WICKED AUNT LEONORA

whole thing, until I noticed a brochure on the blood-table. He'd had it designed and depicting photographs of my paintings, with a reserve way beyond the asking price, for an exhibition in New York in the Summer. My Uncle was obviously a businessman and would, no doubt, return to claim his collateral. Whether, or not I would see him in the mirror was another matter. It was then that I decided to make my first vampire call. Before I could access *Contacts* my *Inbox* sign lit up. It was an email which read: "Good evening Kathryn, Hope you have not disturbed my possessions. Please do not redecorate my flat. It is to my taste. Your paintings are a good investment. I am a Duwulfe. We do not waste our money. Aunt Leonora is responding to medication. Give my salutations to Iris, Wolfgang and the Lucky dog. Sincere regards. Your Uncle Alexandu".

I detected a touch of irony. Vampires do have a sense of humour after all. I responded to his message in kind, by saying: "Dear Uncle Alexandu, What can I say? You have caught me out. I will make sure no one enters your flat but Wolfgang. Thank you for making me a property owner. Your rent should be paid by direct debit into Great Uncle Wolfgang's bank account. Please note that your tenancy stipulates single occupation only. Love from your niece Kathryn. xxx".

My stint in the solicitors' office had served a purpose after all.

Since the New Year I've spend most of my time with Luke and Lucky in Newquay, surfing, running - and having fun. We quite often return to the attic flat at weekends to visit my dear royal family and to see Sal's expanding tum. Trevor and Wayne have taken to Luke in a big way. No surprises there. He's also got a wedding invite to The Seychelles. The ceremony is four weeks after our trip to Hawaii. They have three new male Italian waiters - all of whom are very good looking and heterosexual. Lucy smiles much more these days. Sophie and Zach have decided to make a start on "The Tower" which is to be

Luke's and mine marital home. Don't ask me when. We've not even thought about it yet. So considering my shitty early childhood, I haven't done badly for a skinny, orphaned runt. And as for Ben the Vet, he sent me a text recently saying that he was still single and would Lucy be interest in a rescue kitten?

****